IN TOO DEEP

For more information see www.jackreacher.com

IN TOO DEEP

Lee Child
and
Andrew Child

bantam

TRANSWORLD PUBLISHERS
Penguin Random House, One Embassy Gardens,
8 Viaduct Gardens, London SW11 7BW
www.penguin.co.uk

Transworld is part of the Penguin Random House group of companies
whose addresses can be found at global.penguinrandomhouse.com

Penguin
Random House
UK

First published in Great Britain in 2024 by Bantam
an imprint of Transworld Publishers

A CIP catalogue record for this book
is available from the British Library.

ISBNs
9780857505590 (cased)
9780857505606 (tpb)

Typeset in 11.75/16.25pt Century Old Style Std by Jouve (UK), Milton Keynes.
Printed and bound in Great Britain by Clays Ltd, Elcograf S.p.A.

The authorized representative in the EEA is Penguin Random House Ireland,
Morrison Chambers, 32 Nassau Street, Dublin D02 YH68.

Penguin Random House is committed to a sustainable future
for our business, our readers and our planet. This book is made
from Forest Stewardship Council® certified paper.

For Richard Pine – ten years and counting . . .

ONE

The pain hit first, then the sound followed, the way lightning beats thunder in a storm.

The pain was in Jack Reacher's right wrist. It was sharp and sudden and hot, and it was more than strong enough to eclipse the dull throbbing ache that filled his head. The sound was a single, round, lingering note. Metal on metal. Distinct, but inconsequential next to the ringing in his ears.

The pain and the sound came after he tried to move his arm. That was all Reacher knew. He had been asleep – no, somewhere deeper and darker than sleep – and when he floated to the surface he was rocked by waves of dizziness. He was lying on his back. Not in a bed. Not on the ground. On something smooth and artificial. And cold. The chill was seeping through his shirt and into his shoulder blades and down his spine. A sharp ridge was cutting into his calves. His head felt like it was being crushed against the hard surface.

So he had drawn his right elbow back, ready to lever himself up. Or he had tried to. And it wasn't just the discomfort that had stopped him. Something was fastened around his wrist, preventing it from moving more than a couple of inches. Something cinched in tight. It bit into his skin, but that wasn't what hurt the most. It was one of the bones in his forearm. Maybe more than one. Some kind of major damage had been done beneath the skin. That was clear.

Reacher tried to move his left arm. There was no pain, but that wrist was also restrained by something sharp. So was his left ankle. So was his right. He couldn't see what he was attached to, or what he was bound with, because there was no light. Not the slightest glimmer. The space he was in was completely dark. There was no noise, now that the metallic *clink* had died away. And no movement of the air. Reacher had no idea where he was. No idea how he had gotten there. But someone must have brought him. And shackled him. And whoever had done those things was going to rue the day. That was for damn sure.

The same time Reacher was slipping back into oblivion a man was standing at the side of the road, five miles away to the north, watching for smoke or flames. He had used plenty of names over the years but at that moment he was calling himself *Ivan Vidic*. He was heavyset and a little stooped, which made him look shorter than the six feet two he claimed on his driver's licence, and his bald head was all sharp angles and ridges, like it had been carved from stone by someone without much skill. His car was parked by the second of a set of three switchbacks. It was a notorious spot for accidents. The turns were sharp and close together and poorly lit. The road was separated from a steep drop by a wide shoulder and

2

a rusty safety rail and the camber coming off the apex of the first bend was way out of whack. Something to do with ancient geological deposits deteriorating and undermining the layers of bedrock deep down, way below the surface. Nothing that couldn't be fixed, given the right amount of money. But money was scarce in those parts so the local Department of Roads and Bridges had just thrown up a couple of warning signs. They didn't help to keep vehicles from crashing, but the county lawyers said they might keep the department from getting sued in the aftermath.

An SUV had crashed there, a little earlier that day. A Lincoln Navigator. It had left the road, clipped a tree, rolled three times, and come to rest back on its wheels. Its roof was caved in. Its bonnet was dented. Its doors were bent and twisted and all its windows were starred and opaque. Vidic had watched the accident unfold. He'd had no alternative because he had been following, driving fast and sticking close behind. He had mashed his brakes the moment the Lincoln lost control and had skidded to a stop while the other vehicle was still moving. Then he had jumped out and crept closer to the wreck, sniffing the air for gasoline fumes and straining his ears for any hint of fuel dripping from a fractured line or cracked tank.

The Lincoln had wound up in bad shape, but its driver had come out even worse. He was dead. His neck was broken. There was no doubt about that. Vidic had smiled when he saw what had happened. It wasn't the outcome he'd expected. But it was one he could use. More than that, it was like the answer to a prayer. An echo from his childhood floated into his head: *God helps those who help themselves.* His grin grew wider, then he turned his attention to the passenger. At first Vidic thought the guy was bound for the morgue, too, but

3

when he checked he felt a pulse. So he adjusted his diagnosis: the guy just had a concussion and a broken wrist, judging by the sharp edge of the bone he could see jutting out beneath his skin. The guy's size had saved him. He looked huge. Comfortably six feet five, even slumped against the door. Easily 250 pounds. And all bone and muscle. No fat.

Vidic had called a couple of guys for help and while he waited for them to arrive he had hauled the driver and the passenger out of the wreckage. That wasn't easy. The driver's head was flopping around all over the place and his body was slack and soft and difficult to grip. The passenger was worse because of his size and shape. His arms were bigger than the driver's legs. His wrists were too broad for Vidic to wrap his fingers around. Vidic was out of breath and sweating despite the cool air when he heard wheels on the asphalt behind him, and he only just had time to finish rifling through the passenger's pockets and transferring the few possessions he found there to his own.

The new guys had shown up in a Ford pickup truck, which turned out to be a practical choice. There was no way they'd have been able to manhandle the passenger's unconscious body onto the back seat of a regular car. He was too big. Too awkward. They wouldn't have had enough room to manoeuvre. So the three of them heaved him up onto the load bed and tossed the driver's corpse in next to him.

The guy who had been driving the pickup was called *Darren Fletcher.* He was a couple of inches taller than Vidic but slimmer and maybe twenty pounds lighter. He slammed the tailgate into place then turned to Vidic and said, 'You saw it happen?'

Vidic nodded.

'When you called and said it was Gibson's Lincoln I was hoping you were wrong.'

'Have you ever known me to be wrong?'

Fletcher grunted and said, 'Walk me through it.'

Vidic shrugged. 'Gibson was driving pretty slow. Pretty careful. I caught up to him by chance. I was heading back to base. Guess he was, too. He kept going the same speed for maybe a mile. His usual Steady Eddy self. Then he must have seen my car. Seen it, but not realized it was mine because all of a sudden he tried to lose me. He hit the gas, but at exactly the wrong time.' Vidic nodded at the wrecked vehicle. 'As you can see. Exhibit A.'

'Did you flash your lights? Honk your horn? Make it look like you were up for a race?'

'No. Why would I? I'm not sixteen.'

'So why did he try to lose you? Or whoever he thought you were?'

Vidic shrugged again. 'Paranoia is my guess. It's in the air. It started when O'Connell died and it's been worse since Bowery disappeared.'

Fletcher was silent for a moment, then he said, 'The big guy who was riding with Gibson. Who is he?'

'No idea.'

'He doesn't have ID?'

'No.'

'Any luggage? A backpack, at least?'

'Just this.' Vidic took a pistol from his waistband and handed it to Fletcher. 'A Glock 17. The FBI's weapon of choice. Make of that what you will.'

TWO

Fletcher and the other guy had taken off in the Ford and left Vidic to deal with the Lincoln. He had checked the glove box and the trunk for anything containing personal information then turned his attention to the driver's seat. He had been ready to clean up any blood that had been spilled, but there wasn't any. Gibson's skin must not have been pierced in the accident. Or at least not while his heart was still beating. Vidic had smiled. That made his next task easier. He glanced across to the passenger side and noted the position on the doorframe where the impact with the big guy's head had left a bloodstain. He took a knife from his pocket, made a nick on the pad of his left thumb and squeezed a few drops of blood onto the frame of the driver's door in a corresponding spot, only around three inches lower. He grabbed the steering wheel. The gearshift. He adjusted the rearview mirror. Prodded a bunch of climate control and entertainment system buttons. He took a cellphone from his pocket, double-checked that it was the right one, and jammed it down the side of the seat. Then he put his foot on the brake and turned the key. Nothing happened. Some kind of safety system must have shut off the ignition when the vehicle hit the tree. And isolated the fuel supply, with any luck, Vidic thought. He used his knife to pry off the cover from the gear-shift release, selected Neutral, then opened the door and jumped down. He climbed into his own car, fired it up, pulled in behind the Lincoln and gave it a gentle nudge. It rolled a couple of yards and ground to a halt. Vidic leaned a little harder on the gas. The Lincoln rolled faster. It kept going this time and picked up more speed. Enough to help it bust through the safety rail and disappear into the darkness on the other side.

Vidic had stopped his car and hurried to the gap the Lincoln had made in the rail. He could see the vehicle fifty feet below, on its roof, three wheels still turning. He had stood and watched. There was no explosion. No sign of fire. He waited twenty minutes, to be sure. Then his remaining cellphone began to ring. The call was from a number he recognized. He hit the answer button and said, 'Hey, Paris. What's up?'

A woman's voice came on the line. It was low and curt and a little shaky around the edges. She said, 'Is it true? Gibson's dead?'

'He is. Yes. Another one bit the dust.'

'It was an accident?'

Vidic didn't answer.

Paris said, 'I heard he crashed his car. Broke his neck.'

'You heard right.'

'You saw it happen?'

'The whole thing.'

'Someone was with him?'

'A stranger.'

'What kind of stranger?'

'Just some nobody hitching a ride. Nothing to worry about.'

'You sure?'

'Absolutely.'

'Because I can't help thinking – Bowery disappears then a mystery guy shows up and just happens to hitch a ride with one of our crew?'

'Sometimes coincidences happen.'

'Maybe. Or maybe Bowery grew a conscience. Ratted us out.'

'He didn't rat us out. That's not his style.'

'Then where is he?'

'He stiffed us, is my guess. Made the exchange and ran off with the cash.'

'Why would he do that? It's pocket change next to what we've got coming. He knows what's at stake. He'd be nuts to run now. Unless he knows there won't be another payday. And how would he know that? Unless he made sure of it?'

'Even if he wanted to, he couldn't have ratted us out. He doesn't have anything on us.'

'He knows about the report.'

'He doesn't have a copy.'

'He doesn't need a copy. He knows what it's about. Broadly speaking. He knows where I got it. Either one of those things would be enough to get every agent in the lower forty-eight crawling up our asses before we could blink.'

'All right. Take a breath. Trust me. What happened to Gibson had nothing to do with Bowery. And nothing to do with the stranger.'

'What *happened to* Gibson? So it wasn't an accident.'

Vidic didn't respond.

'Gibson was a good driver. He knew that road. He wouldn't just crash his car for no reason. So the crash wasn't an accident, was it? Tell me straight.'

'It was. And it wasn't.'

'That's your idea of *straight*?'

'Listen. I found something out about Gibson. Earlier today.'

'Found out what?'

'I can't say. Not on the phone. But it has implications.'

'What kind of implications?'

'First and foremost, we need to shift up our timetable.'

'By how much?'

'We have forty-eight hours, maximum. Then we need to be gone. Like we never existed.'

'That's not possible.'

'It is. Grab what you need from the house. Just the essentials. Not so much as to be suspicious. We have the one physical job to take care of. Then we can cash in on the report later.'

'The job's not happening for five days. It can't. We have to wait for the final delivery.'

'No. We have to take what's there now. Eighty per cent of something is better than a hundred per cent of nothing. I'll talk to Fletcher. Get him to move up the schedule.'

'And if he won't?'

'We'll walk.'

'I don't want to walk. I set the job up. Found the opportunity. I'm invested.'

'I get that. But, end of the day, that job's a luxury. It's not make or break. We have to stay focused. Think about the future. Our new lives. Not what we're leaving behind.'

Paris didn't reply.

'That just leaves one loose end.' Vidic glanced down at the wrecked Lincoln. He thought about the two men he'd dragged out of it. Gibson. And the giant stranger. One dead. One alive. For now, anyway. He raised the phone back to his ear and said, 'I'm going to need a bunch of phosphorus. Can you bring some to the house?'

'I can try. How much?'

'Enough to burn a body. Completely. Prints. Teeth. DNA. The full nine yards.'

THREE

Reacher was again woken by a sound. A door opening, this time. His eyes were closed but he could sense light. Fairly dim. Then much brighter. He heard footsteps approaching. One set. They came close, then stopped. Reacher opened his eyes, slowly, against the glare. The dizziness had receded a little but everything looked pale and washed-out, like a watercolour made by a beginner who didn't throw enough paint into the mix. A man was standing by Reacher's side. He was wearing jeans and a grey T-shirt. He was slim, like a runner, and maybe six feet four. His fists were clenched and Reacher thought he looked angry, maybe even scared, but was trying to hide it.

The man said, 'I'm Darren Fletcher. Who are you?'

Reacher ignored him. If they'd searched him, Fletcher would already know his name. And if Fletcher hadn't searched him, he wasn't worth wasting breath on. Reacher concentrated on his surroundings instead. He saw that the

11

restraints on his wrists and ankles were handcuffs, and that he was secured to a rectangular steel table. The floor was covered with white tiles and the walls were lined with steel shelves. The place was some kind of food storage or preparation area, Reacher figured. Then he turned back to Fletcher because the thought of food was making him feel sick.

'This silent act? It isn't helping you,' Fletcher said. 'You need to understand how serious this situation is. A man is dead. He was my friend. So you need to tell me who you are. You need to explain why you were in his car. And what made him go crazy and smash into a tree.'

Reacher couldn't remember anything about a car or a crash or a dead man but he figured that wouldn't make for a strong negotiating position, so he said, 'Release these cuffs. Then I'll tell you.'

Fletcher shook his head. 'Convince me you had nothing to do with my friend's death. Then I'll unlock the cuffs.'

Reacher said nothing.

'Not smart. I can make you tell me, if you don't start talking.'

Reacher said, 'Can you? Because I can only see one of you.'

'You don't want to test me. Believe me. So be sensible. Convince me.'

'Then you'll release me?'

Fletcher nodded.

'You have the key?'

'Of course.'

'Show it to me.'

'No.' Fletcher paused for a moment. 'Why?'

'To demonstrate good faith. Prove you can keep your word.'

Fletcher sighed and pulled a small silver key out of his pocket. 'Satisfied?'

12

'One more thing. Release my left hand.'

'Talk first.'

'Here's the problem. My left wrist is broken. I can feel it swelling. It's getting constricted by the cuff. That can be serious. The damage could be done by the time we've talked. I could lose my hand.'

Fletcher didn't respond, but he didn't put the key away.

'Come on. Release one broken limb. What am I going to do with it? My three good ones will still be secure and you have the only key. Release it, and I'll talk.'

Fletcher hesitated for another moment. A broken wrist had been mentioned at the scene of the accident. He remembered that. But he was a cautious man. He switched the key to his left hand, took the Glock that Vidic had given him from his waistband and stepped forward, gun raised, finger on the trigger.

Fletcher said, 'Try anything and I'll shoot you with your own gun.'

Reacher had no idea why Fletcher thought the gun was his but he had no time to waste on questions. So he just said, 'I get the picture.'

Fletcher kept the gun lined up on Reacher's face. He leaned down. Inserted the key into the cuff around Reacher's left wrist. Worked the lock. The cuff sprang open. It swung down, empty, and clanged against the table leg. Fletcher straightened up. The gun was still in his right hand. The key was still in his left. Reacher struggled to focus on either. The dizziness was building again and the images were threatening to split into two. Reacher willed his vision to stay clear then whipped up his hand and caught the Glock by its barrel. He forced it up and to the side. Then he jammed it back. The move was sharp and vicious and Reacher kept it going until the gun was horizontal and the muzzle was pointing at Fletcher's chest. Fletcher's finger was trapped by the trigger guard. It was bent backwards, all the way to its limit. Reacher pushed harder. Fletcher's knuckle joint gave way. Cartilage tore. Tendons ripped. Fletcher screamed and let go of the grip. Reacher let the gun fall and dragged his hand across Fletcher's body. He caught Fletcher's left wrist. Pulled until Fletcher's hand was above his chest, then started to squeeze. Hard. Fletcher screamed again. Reacher increased the pressure. He could feel bones and ligaments begin to twist and crack. Fletcher screamed louder. And dropped the key.

The key hit Reacher's chest and bounced straight back up. It was spinning and sparkling and arcing away to the side. Reacher couldn't follow its flight. His vision was too blurred. He pictured it skittling off the shiny surface of the table and rattling down onto the floor tiles. In which case it might as well land in Australia for all the good it would do him. But then he felt something. It was like a butterfly landing on his right bicep. He still couldn't see what it was, but Fletcher stretched for it with his damaged hand. Reacher twitched his arm and felt something hard and cold slide down against his side. Fletcher tried to pull away. He scrabbled at the back of his waistband. A second gun was tucked in there. A Sig Sauer. He got it free, but he couldn't hold on to it. His broken finger wouldn't bend. Reacher heard the gun rattle onto the floor. He let go of Fletcher's hand and grabbed his neck instead. He found his Adam's apple. Shifted his thumb down and to the side. Did the same with his middle finger. Then jammed both into the flesh of Fletcher's neck and pinched them together, crushing his carotid arteries. Fletcher howled and grabbed Reacher's wrist with his good hand. He pulled and heaved and scratched and gouged with his nails, but Reacher just increased the pressure. He held it for five seconds. Six. Fletcher kept on struggling. Seven seconds passed and Fletcher's energy started to fade. Eight seconds, and that was all Fletcher could take. His brain was out of oxygen. He slumped forward. Reacher pulled his arm aside and Fletcher collapsed face-first onto Reacher's chest.

Reacher gave himself a moment for his heart rate to subside, hoping the hammering in his head would die down with it, then he slammed his fist into Fletcher's temple and let his unconscious body slide onto the floor. He retrieved the key from where it was wedged against his side. Eased himself into a semi-sitting position. Paused to fight a sudden wave of nausea and dizziness, then got to work on the cuff on his right wrist. He moved slowly to avoid jarring the damaged bones. He released his right ankle. His left. Then he swung his legs around to the side and stood uncertainly on the floor.

Reacher was wearing his only pair of shoes. He had bought them years earlier, in England. They were quality items. Expensive. Solid and sturdy right out of the box, and the leather had only gotten harder with time and weather and uncompromising use. Now the toe caps were like steel. Reacher turned and kicked Fletcher in the head. Partly to make sure Fletcher wouldn't regain consciousness any time soon. And partly because he was pissed about his wrist. And being dragged to this place against his will. And the whole business with the handcuffs.

Reacher searched Fletcher's pockets using just his left hand. He came across a set of keys, which he took in case they would aid his escape. And to cause Fletcher extra inconvenience down the line. Next he found a wallet, which he

15

also took. He figured he would check it for ID or credit cards later, when he could see better. Then he retrieved the two fallen guns, crept to the doorway, and peered out. It led to a kitchen. It was large and was kitted out with all kinds of appliances and machines Reacher didn't recognize. He was no expert but he figured it was the kind of place that would belong to a big private house rather than a restaurant or a hotel. Either way, there were no people around, which was what mattered. Reacher could see another door in the corner, diagonally opposite. He started toward it. Made it halfway across the space, then the door opened. Reacher had the Glock in his left hand. He raised it. A man stepped into the room. He was heavy and stooped and he had a strange, angular head.

The man paused for a moment, then said, 'Reacher? No need for the gun. I'm here to help.'

Reacher didn't lower the gun. He said, 'Who are you?'

The man said, 'A friend. I saved you from the car wreck.'

'How do you know my name?'

'I found your things. Kept them safe. So the others wouldn't get them. I have them right here.' The guy gestured to his pocket. 'Do you want them back?'

Reacher nodded. 'Do nothing stupid.'

The guy pulled out Reacher's expired passport, his ATM card, some banknotes, and a folding toothbrush. 'You travel light, huh?'

Reacher said, 'Put them on the floor. Then step back.'

'No time,' the guy said. 'We've got to hurry. The man in the car with you? Who died? You remember him?'

'No,' Reacher said.

'Well, that's awkward. Because he was an FBI agent. Now he's dead all hell's going to break loose. There'll be

16

cops swarming everywhere. Hordes of agents, too, just as soon as they can get here. Every last one of them looking for somebody to carry the can for their buddy's death. And if you can't account for yourself, that *someone* is going to be you.'

FOUR

The guy with the angular head turned and ducked back out through the door, then reappeared a moment later when he realized that Reacher wasn't following. He threw up his arms in an exaggerated shrug and said, 'Why aren't you moving? Don't you get it? We need to leave.'

Reacher stayed where he was. He tucked the gun in his waistband, took his things back from the guy, then said, 'What is this place?'

'That's your question? Right now? Are you crazy? You should be asking, *What's the quickest way out of here?* And, *please, Ivan, can you save my ass again? Can you give me a ride to someplace where I won't get thrown in jail?*'

'Ivan?'

'Ivan Vidic. My name. Now come on. Move it.'

'I'm not going anywhere. Nor are you.'

'How hard did you hit your head? The police are coming.'

'Let them come. I've done nothing wrong.'

18

'How do you know? You can't remember anything. And have you seen yourself in the mirror lately? Do you think the police will look at you and assume you're some kind of choirboy?'

Reacher said nothing.

Vidic closed his eyes for a moment and sighed. 'OK. I get it. You wake up in a strange place. You don't know how you got here. You want answers. I can give them to you but this is—'

'I know how I got here,' Reacher said. 'Someone brought me. Darren Fletcher. I doubt he was working alone. So I want to know who else is involved. I want to know what is going on here.'

'How do you know about Fletcher?'

'We met.'

'You did? When? Where?'

'Just now. In there.' Reacher gestured toward the door he had emerged from.

'He let you out of the cuffs?' Vidic strode across to the door and peered into the room on the other side. 'Why would he—' Vidic spotted Fletcher's inert body lying slumped on the floor. He turned and backed away. 'Wait. Did you kill him? Is he dead?'

Reacher shrugged. 'He was breathing when I left him.'

'OK. That's good. I guess. Did you guys talk at all? Before you beat on him?'

'No. That's why I'm asking you. Who else is involved? I want names. I want locations.'

Vidic took a deep breath. 'Look, now I really get it. You're pissed. You want payback. *More* payback, I guess, now that I've seen what you did to Fletcher. I respect that. But let me ask you something. How much does your lawyer get paid?'

'I don't have a lawyer.'

'That's what I figured. But Fletcher? And his buddies? They do have lawyers. Ones who get paid five hundred an hour. Maybe more. Which means that if you're still here when the police show up and you all get thrown in the cells, Fletcher and the others will be on the street again before the public defender has even found out he has a new client. Then they'll disappear. You'll never catch up with them. If you stay here it'll be like you're choosing to let them get away. But if you come with me I'll help you. I'll tell you everything. The only thing I need you to do is come with me. Now.'

Reacher figured Vidic had a point. He'd gotten tangled up with the police in the past. More than once. Nothing had ever stuck, but getting cut loose always took time. More than it should. And wasting time was not going to help him get what he wanted. So he said, 'Fine. Just do me one favour.'

'What?'

'Drop the Good Samaritan act.'

'I don't follow.'

'You're not trying to help me. You're trying to save your own ass.'

Reacher followed Vidic into a kind of entrance hall. It was a large space. Octagonal, with a tiled floor; leaded windows either side of a heavy, studded oak front door; a crystal chandelier; wood panels on the walls; a bunch of oil paintings of outdoor scenes; and a staircase that divided three-quarters of the way up and branched off in two separate directions. Reacher expected Vidic to make for the obvious exit but when they reached the foot of the stairs he peeled away and headed for a smaller, plain door on the far side. He was moving fast and he placed his feet carefully to avoid making a noise. Reacher was slower and less discreet.

'Hey!' Vidic spun around. His voice was a low hiss. 'Quiet!'

Reacher said, 'Why?'

'So no one will hear us.' Vidic spoke slowly and stressed each word, like he was dealing with a child.

'No one, like who?'

'Well, for one, if Fletcher's here, you can bet Kane won't be far away.'

'Who's Kane?'

'Fletcher's buddy. His right-hand man. Acts like his bodyguard. A psychotic Neanderthal scumbag, essentially. Not someone you want to cross paths with.'

'Sounds like exactly who I want to cross paths with.' Reacher raised his voice. 'Kane? Can you hear me? Get your ass down here.'

Vidic stretched up and tried to put his hand over Reacher's mouth. 'What the hell are you doing?'

Reacher pushed Vidic away. 'Saving time.' He raised his voice another notch. 'Kane? This guy says you're a scumbag. Is that true? I kind of think it is.'

Vidic sank down until he was sitting on the third step and covered his head with his hands. 'Will you stop? You're going to get us both killed.'

'Kane!'

There was still no reaction. No angry voice. No heavy steps approaching from some other part of the building.

Reacher turned to Vidic and said, 'Seems like you're wrong. This Kane guy isn't here. So where else could he be?'

Vidic straightened up. 'Why do you care? This isn't your mess to clean up. I'm giving you a way out. Why won't you take it?'

'Because I have a rule.'

'A rule? What are you talking about?'

'People leave me alone, I leave them alone.'

'And if they don't?'

'I don't.'

'You know that bringing you here, this whole thing, it was Fletcher's idea, right? I didn't know what he was going to do. I was just trying to save your life. I thought that wreck you were trapped in was going up in flames.'

'Kane. Where is he? And everyone else who's tied up in this.'

'You're never letting this go, are you?'

'Now you get it.'

'OK. Give me a moment. I need to think.' Vidic's focus shifted to some distant, imaginary horizon and his eyes darted from side to side for a few seconds like a chess player planning his next moves. Then his gaze snapped back to Reacher's face and he said, 'Come with me. I have an idea.'

FIVE

Reacher expected that the door Vidic pushed through would lead to some kind of concealed exit, but it just opened onto another room. A small one. Not much bigger than a generous closet. The air inside it was stale. It was heavy with cheap aftershave and a hint of second-hand cigar smoke. A blackout blind was pulled across its window so the only light in the place came from a computer monitor on a battered metal desk that was shoved against the wall. The monitor looked bigger than normal, Reacher thought. More like a modest TV screen. Its display was divided into rectangles. There were three rows of four. Each of the images showed part of a building. Nine were interior shots. Three were exterior. Nothing was moving in any of them. There was no sign of any people. No one to capture and interrogate. Reacher was disappointed.

Vidic leaned down and fiddled with the computer's mouse until the display rearranged itself. Ten of the rectangles disappeared. The remaining pair expanded until together they filled the screen. Both showed an external view. The one on the left covered a white Jeep sitting on a curved gravel driveway that was hemmed in by tall bushes with large pale leaves. The one on the right showed a formal garden. Reacher assumed it would have been immaculate at one time, but now the various plants were running wild with neglect.

Vidic gestured to an office chair near the desk. One arm was missing and its mesh seat was saggy and loose. He said, 'Want to sit?'

Reacher shook his head.

'Smart choice.' Vidic kept his gaze on the screen. 'So you were right. I am trying to save my own ass. I can't have you anywhere near Fletcher or Kane. It's too big of a risk. If they find out I helped you, or if they figure it out, I'm dead meat. But there's something else you need to know.' Vidic lowered his voice to a whisper. 'I'm going to disappear. Very soon.'

'Why would I care?'

'Because when I do it won't matter what you tell Fletcher. It won't matter what conclusions he jumps to. So here's the deal. You sit tight for twenty-four hours. Forty-eight, tops. Then I'll give you Fletcher and Kane on a plate. With a cherry on top. They have a job planned. A big one. Not far from here. They're going to have to bring it forward now that we know the Feds are breathing down their necks. I'll find out when. Give you the address. You can catch them in the act. Deal with them yourself. Take the proceeds. Or not. Call the cops if you prefer. Lead the Feds there. Whatever you want to do. I won't care because I'll be in the wind. Nothing will be able to blow back on me.'

Reacher nodded his head slowly, like he was considering a

complex problem from every conceivable angle. 'So it costs me a day or two, but I get Fletcher. And you get away.'

'I get away. And maybe one other thing.'

'Which is?'

'Fletcher has a stash of cash. I know where it is. I figured there was nothing I could do about it. No way to get my hands on it before I go. Not on my own. But together we could take it.'

'Where is it?'

'Not far away. I could take you there. Then give you a ride afterward. Anywhere you want to go. Within reason.'

'How do we get it?'

'It's in a safe. A . . . the model doesn't matter. The point is, the lock's impossible to pick. Pretty much. Maybe three people in the world could do it and neither of us is one of them. The door, the top, the sides, they're all too strong and too thick to cut or drill or blow a hole in with explosives. But it does have a weakness. The back. It's thinner. Thin enough to make it vulnerable to a shaped charge. The manufacturer was looking to save weight, I guess. Or money. I don't know. They figured they could get away with it because the safe is supposed to be attached to the wall and the floor. No one should ever be able to get to the back.'

'But?'

'The safe isn't bolted down. Fletcher bought it cheap from someplace and just had it shoved against the wall. I can't move it. I've tried. It's too heavy. But Kane moved it. He installed it. And if Kane can move it, you can move it. Don't you think?'

Reacher looked at his wrist. He tried to flex it. A jolt of pain shot up his arm and down to his fingers. 'How much is in it?'

'Two point two million.'

'Split how?'

'Seventy/thirty.'

'In my favour?'

'Nice try.'

Reacher didn't reply.

'Sixty/forty. Sixty to me.'

Reacher said nothing.

'OK. Split fifty/fifty. What do you say?'

'Normally I'd say you were crazy.'

Vidic spread his arms out wide. 'Does this look normal?'

'So what's the plan?'

'I take you somewhere safe. Get you squared away, out of sight. Bring in a guy I know, a medic, who you can trust. He'll take care of your wrist. Then I'll get you some food. Some books, magazines, movies, whatever you want to pass the time until we need to move.'

'That could work. But I still need the full nine on Fletcher. And whatever kind of operation he's got going on.'

'I'll give you chapter and verse. But not here, OK?' Vidic pointed at the screen. 'We've pushed our luck far enough. The cops are bound to show up anytime now.'

Reacher nodded and took a step toward the door, but Vidic didn't follow right away. He leaned down, took hold of the mouse, and started fiddling with it again. The screen switched back to its original twelve rectangles. Vidic selected the image of the driveway and then a box appeared, demanding a password. Vidic hit a bunch of keys – four letters, eight numbers, then four more letters – and the screen filled with tiny versions of the same scene. Each had a time and a date under it. Vidic selected the most recent, did something else with the mouse, and a cartoon trash can appeared. He did another thing and the mini picture vanished.

'People say you can't erase history.' Vidic turned and flashed a smile. 'Maybe that was true before we had computers.'

Vidic took out his phone and tapped away at its screen for a moment. Reacher couldn't focus well enough to see exactly what he was doing. Vidic caught his eye and said, 'Don't worry. Just sending a message to the medic.' Then he moved the pointer to the top of the screen and a list of options appeared. He picked *Engage Privacy Mode* and selected *Fifteen Minutes.* 'Now I was never here,' he said. 'And we can leave together without being seen.'

Reacher said, 'What about the kitchen? And the hallway? There are cameras there, too, right?'

'Right. But the internal ones only record when the system is armed, and the system is only armed when no one is here. The external cameras are live all the time, in case anyone comes snooping around. Unless they're paused, like they are now, for another few minutes. So don't worry. We can go and there'll be no trace.'

Vidic locked the heavy front door behind them and ushered Reacher over to the Jeep. It had protective mesh cages fixed over its rear lights, and a wide bull bar covering the whole of the front. Its bodywork was gleaming white but its bonnet was finished with some kind of matte black coating. Reacher had seen vehicles set up that way before. In the desert. So that the sun wouldn't reflect off the shiny paint and dazzle the driver. He was no expert but judging by the tyres he guessed the Jeep had never been anywhere more challenging than a parking lot. He shrugged to himself. He was never going to understand car people.

Vidic drove fast but he had the vehicle well under control. The road was twisty and rough, with trees on both sides.

They were tall and close together with few branches within reach of the ground. All the action was up high where the leaves had to compete for the sunlight. The air in the Jeep was set low and the stereo was playing acoustic rock uncomfortably loud until Vidic switched it off and said, 'The place we were just in was built in the seventies by a guy named Arthur Grumann. He was a real estate developer from Manhattan. Crime was bad in the city back then, I guess, so he figured rich folk could be lured down here to the Ozarks, where it was safe and beautiful. He completed half a dozen mansions. All are within a couple of miles of one another. They did OK at first. The idea didn't stick in the long term, though. By the two thousands people could hardly give the places away. We got ours for a song in '09, after the crash. Turned it into our studio.'

'You're musicians?'

'Artists. Started out with four of us. Paris, Bowery, O'Connell, and Gibson. I joined later. Paris is great with computers so she handled the payments, that kind of thing. O'Connell dealt with the logistics. Art isn't easy to transport. You need special crates, things like that. They just did copies at first. Legitimate stuff. For collectors, mainly. People who don't want the real thing on their walls while they're on vacation or when they're having family with young kids to visit. But that morphed over time. They did a forgery for a gallery owner they met. Then they did a couple more. Then a lot more, until that was all they were doing.'

'Enough to get the Feds on your case?'

'Not at all. They were discreet. And careful who they sold to. There were no real victims. The buyers were all crooks themselves. No. The problems started when Fletcher came on board. He wanted contacts in the art world. But not so he could sell to them. So he could steal from them. He was aggressive. Pushed us in a whole new direction. Got us involved in disputes. Violence. O'Connell got killed. So did some old dude. A retired cop working security at a place they hit. That's when he brought in Kane, as muscle. Now Bowery's gone missing and Gibson turned out to be a Fed. What a fiasco. It's not the organization I joined. Not even close. You can see why I'm jumping ship.'

'You joined, when?'

'I kind of replaced O'Connell. So around the same time Kane joined. Only I'm not crazy and I'm not beholden to Fletcher. You can see why I'm leaving. It's not safe anymore.'

'You're sure Gibson was a Fed? Those guys generally don't advertise.'

'I'm sure.'

'How come?'

'Kind of a fluke, I guess. He always used to disappear for a few hours, one day a week. I didn't think much about it, at first. But when Bowery disappeared, I don't know, I got suspicious. So when I saw Gibson sneaking off today, I followed him. He went to a motel just off a highway exit. A big place with a gas station and a diner. I saw him go to one of the motel rooms. He knocked on the door, kind of in a funky rhythm, then went in. I caught sight of a woman, waiting inside. I was relieved at first. I thought he was there to see a hooker. But I crept up close and listened at the door. It felt a bit dirty but I needed to be sure. And that's when I heard her say it.'

'What?'

'Albatross.'

'Like the bird?'

29

'Right. Albatross.'

'So why's that such a big deal?'

'Because it's what she called him. *Albatross*. Not *Gibson*. It was a cover name, obviously. And who uses a cover name? An agent, when he's undercover. That's how those guys work.'

'You're sure about that?'

'A hundred per cent. Everyone knows.'

'If you say so. And how did I end up in Agent Albatross's car?'

'He offered you a ride.'

'Why would he do that?'

'To thank you, I guess.'

'Thank me? For what?'

'Two punks tried to steal his Lincoln. You stopped them. Laid one of them out. He was leaving the motel room. Saw what happened. He offered you some money. Looked like you turned it down and asked for a ride instead.'

'How do you know all that?'

'I was watching. From the diner. I was waiting to see him leave. You came in half an hour before. I heard you talking to the waitress.'

'What did I order?'

'A burger. A slice of pie. And black coffee. You had three refills.'

Reacher shrugged. He couldn't remember doing that, but it sounded about right. He said, 'So we drove off. What did you do?'

'Waited to see what Gibson's handler did.'

'And?'

'She hung back in the room for a couple of minutes. Maybe she was giving him time to get clear so no one saw them together. Maybe she was sanitizing the room. Or sending in some kind of report. I don't know for sure. Maybe all three things.'

'Then what?'

'She came out. Checked that the door was locked. Walked to her car. Drove away, too.'

'She didn't check out? Return the room key?'

Vidic shook his head. 'Just left.'

'What was she wearing?'

'She was dressed kind of casual. Jeans, white blouse, suit coat, flat shoes. Necklace, no earrings.'

'Hair?'

'Blond. Shoulder-length. Tied back in a ponytail.'

'Age?'

Vidic shrugged. 'Thirties?'

'Was she carrying anything?'

'A purse. Big enough to conceal a weapon. And a briefcase. Black leather. Slim.'

'What kind of car?'

'A Charger. It was flat blue. Poverty spec. Two extra antennas. Parked on the opposite side of the lot, well away from the room they were using.'

'What did you do after she left?'

'Got in my own car and headed to the house. Gibson's a slow driver. I'm not. I put my foot down, hoping to get there before him, knowing what I knew. But I caught up with him at the worst possible place. A switchback. A bad one. I startled him, I guess, and he lost control. The accident was my fault, if I'm honest. I stopped. Tried to help. But it was no good. Gibson was dead. I was able to pull you out alive, at least. That's something, right?'

31

SIX

Vidic kept going north, pushing hard, until they reached a string of tight switchbacks. Then he eased off the gas a little. The shoulder broadened as they approached a second turn and Reacher saw a set of skid marks snaking across the pale asphalt. The rubber looked dark and fresh, and beyond it he saw a half-demolished tree at the side of the road and a gap that had been torn in the safety rail.

Reacher said, 'This is where the accident happened?'

Vidic glanced across at him. 'You recognize it?'

'No. I just put two and two together. Now pull over. I want to take a look.'

'That's not a good idea. The police—'

'Pull over.'

The tone of Reacher's voice left no room for debate. Vidic did as he was told.

Reacher climbed out of the Jeep and moved closer to the

spot where the skid marks began. They were a curious shape. The tracks started out as one pair, straight and parallel. Then they divided. A loop ballooned to the right, all the way onto the shoulder, then curved back and rejoined the straight part. But only briefly. For maybe a foot. Then the marks careened to the left, winding up on the wrong side of the centre line. Finally, almost at the apex of the curve, the marks disappeared. All of them. The pattern reminded Reacher of a rock star from a few years back who had started using a weird symbol in place of his name.

'Come on.' Vidic appeared at Reacher's side. 'Let's get out of the road. It's not safe. You don't know how people around here drive.' He took Reacher's arm and tried to pull him toward the shoulder.

'The vehicle rolled?' Reacher gestured to the spot where the skid marks ended.

'Right.' Vidic pulled harder. 'The back end stepped out heading into the bend. Gibson recovered it – almost – but he overcompensated. Fishtailed the opposite way. Might have just slid off the road if he wasn't going so fast. Might have missed the tree.'

'You said he was driving a Lincoln?'

'Right. A Navigator. New-ish. I doubt there was anything wrong with it.'

'An SUV?'

'Yes. A tall one. Probably top heavy. That could have contributed to the rollover, I guess.'

'Was it four-wheel drive?'

Vidic shrugged. 'Maybe. Or all-wheel drive. Or only rear. I don't know. I'm a Jeep guy.'

'What colour was it?'

'Black. Why? What difference does that make?'

'Just trying to get the full picture. Maybe jog my memory.'
Reacher had hoped that a sight or a smell or just being at the accident site would shake something loose, but nothing was coming back to him. It was like opening a door and staring into a pitch-dark room. He could sense something was there, but he had no idea what it was.

Vidic didn't reply.

Reacher said, 'Where's the Lincoln now? Did it get towed?'

'No.' Vidic pointed to the gap in the safety rail. 'It should still be over there.'

Reacher walked across and looked down, but he couldn't see much. The whole gulley was in deep shadow.

Vidic caught up and tugged at Reacher's arm again. 'We shouldn't be here. If the police find us—'

Reacher said, 'You pulled me up from the bottom of that crevasse?'

Vidic shook his head. 'The Lincoln landed here, on the shoulder. On its wheels. Fletcher told me to push it over the edge after we were done saving you and recovering Gibson's body. I think he was hoping it would catch on fire.'

'You called him?'

'I had to.'

'When you found out about Gibson? At the motel by the highway?'

Vidic paused for a moment. 'You're thinking Fletcher set up some kind of ambush? Forced Gibson off the road?'

Reacher said, 'Did he?'

'No. The crash was an accident, like I told you.'

'You sure?'

'Positive. It had to be. I didn't call Fletcher until after the accident happened.'

'Gibson was dead by then.'

'He was.'

'So that's when you told Fletcher that Gibson was a Fed?'

'Hell no. I never said a word about it.'

'Why not? Isn't that the kind of thing a boss would want to know?'

'He would *want* to know. For sure. But I didn't tell him. Even if I'd wanted to I couldn't have done it over the phone. Fletcher was paranoid about his calls getting tapped. We were all banned from using phones for anything sensitive. Including landlines. He was dead serious about it. He'd have had my ass if I'd tried. So I'd have had to wait and do it in person. But it was his super-aggressive overexpansion bullshit that got the Feds sniffing around us in the first place. It was O'Connell getting killed that gave them the way in. Or the retired cop. And it was his fault that those guys got killed at all. So screw him. Like I told you, I'm out of here. He can take his chances. So can Kane. I'm done.'

'OK. So did you tell anyone else about Gibson?'

'Who would I tell? O'Connell's six feet under. Bowery's missing, presumed an asshole. There isn't anyone else.'

'You mentioned a woman. Paris.'

Vidic didn't reply.

Reacher said, 'You're jumping ship. A woman's involved. You've denounced everyone else but you're determined to keep the spotlight away from her. That math isn't hard to do, Ivan.'

Vidic closed his eyes for a second. 'I haven't told her. Not specifically. Just that something came up and we need to split, pronto. She doesn't know about you. Or about you helping me get Fletcher's cash. Or about me giving you Fletcher on a plate.'

'Is that wise? Keeping her in the dark?'

'How the hell would I know? I'm making this up as I go. The thing with Gibson only happened a few hours ago and I've been busy saving your ass ever since.'

Reacher and Vidic walked back to the Jeep together. As they got close Reacher acted like he didn't want to squeeze along the whole way between the vehicle and the safety rail. He moved ahead of Vidic and looped around the front of the Jeep, instead. Then when Vidic opened the driver's door and started to climb in Reacher took a moment to check the near-side edge of the bull bar. It was made of metal tubing, an inch in diameter, and it was powder coated solid black. The surface was mostly pristine but there was a stretch about six inches high with a series of parallel scratches. It was as if the bar had recently been jammed against a wall. Or another vehicle. The scratches were deep. They revealed the bright steel beneath the coating but Reacher could see no trace of any other shades of paint embedded in them. He thought about asking Vidic how the damage had been caused, but decided not to. There was no point. If he had anything to hide Vidic was bound to lie. And no good could come out of making him suspicious.

Vidic waited for Reacher to climb on board then he fired up the engine. But before he pulled back onto the road he took out his phone and typed a message. Reacher glanced at the screen. His sight was sharpening and he could read the text without much difficulty. It said, *ETA ten minutes.*

Vidic said, 'Don't worry. It's to the medic, again.'

Reacher said, 'Who is this guy?'

'His name's Buck Holmes. He's good people. Navy, retired. Runs his own practice now. Sports injuries, mainly.

Plus a few discreet jobs for people who don't want to generate any hospital records, if you know what I mean.'

'If you trust him, I'm happy.' Reacher had been treated by military doctors before. More than once. In his experience they were highly competent but less concerned about the cosmetic side of things than their civilian counterparts. And he had no problem with that. He said, 'Where's *there*?'

'What?'

'Where we're meeting this medic. Holmes.'

'Oh. The motel where Gibson saw his handler, and you hitched a ride. It's the only place around here a stranger can show up and not attract attention.'

The motel was on its own site, north of the highway, with entrances and exits fanning out to the east and west. The site was a large oval shape with a gas station at each end, a parking area in the centre, and the motel and the diner Vidic had mentioned plus a bunch of fast-food outlets spaced out around the sides. Vidic pulled into a space on the edge of the lot, midway along the motel's facade. Reacher counted twenty rooms. Ten, then an office, then ten more. The place had a fifties vibe, all neon and chrome and sputnik-shaped ornaments. It could have been cool, once, he thought, but now it looked tired and worn. The building's flat roof was in need of resurfacing and its wooden siding could have used a coat of stain.

'Stay here.' Vidic killed the engine and opened his door. He made sure to take his keys with him. 'I'll get you a room. Won't be long.'

Reacher watched until Vidic disappeared into the motel office then turned his attention to the diner. It was the next building in line. It had a vaguely cutesy-cottage appearance with window boxes and curlicues cut into the woodwork, but structurally it was nothing special. The place could just as easily have been a convenience store or a dry cleaner. Reacher was more interested in its position than its architectural merit. It was set at an angle of maybe thirty degrees to the motel. So it was feasible for someone to have sat inside and to have seen a person leaving a particular room, as Vidic claimed to have done. Possibly. If he had been in just the right position. At just the right time. And no vehicles or pedestrians had blocked his line of sight.

Vidic's story about watching Gibson's FBI handler leave the motel didn't pass the smell test easily, Reacher thought. But it didn't immediately fail, either. He resented the ambiguity. But more than that he resented the complete absence of recognition. Vidic said he'd been in this place before. The parking lot. The diner. That he'd been in a fight. Hitched a ride. Yet the whole scene was utterly alien to him. He could have sworn he'd never seen any of it before. He could have taken a lie detector test and passed with flying colours.

SEVEN

Vidic returned after five minutes. Reacher climbed down from the Jeep and Vidic handed him a plastic key card with a cartoon flying saucer printed on it in bright, primary colours.

'You're in room 20. All the way at the end.' Vidic locked the Jeep with his remote then started walking. 'The idea is to be invisible. Put the *Do Not Disturb* sign on the door, pull the drapes, and don't set foot outside. Not unless the building's on fire. And even then, only if the flames are actually heading your way. Are we clear?'

'Sounds straightforward enough. But tell me something. How did you register for the room without my ID?'

'No need to worry about ID. They're not hard to get. And anyway, here they're more interested in pocketing a few extra bucks than following a bunch of dumb rules.'

'Outstanding,' Reacher said. 'My kind of place.'

*

Reacher got to room 20 comfortably ahead of Vidic. He held the key card next to a black plastic rectangle below the handle, a red light turned green, and the door clicked open. Inside, there was a king-size bed against the right-hand wall. The cover had a picture of a lunar lander printed on it and the headboard was a giant semicircle, greyish white, and textured to look like the surface of the moon. The carpet was orange. The walls were inky blue. There was a pair of chairs that were covered with teal fabric, a metal desk/vanity, a flat-screen TV, stars painted on the ceiling, and a pendant light shaped like a satellite. A door at the far side of the room led to a bathroom with a separate shower stall, but the fixtures in there were all plain white twenty-first century standard-issue items. They were totally anonymous. Reacher wondered if that was a design choice or the result of some miserly investor tightening the purse strings.

Vidic followed Reacher inside and closed the door behind him. He took a moment to look around then said, 'Wow. What a place. I wasn't expecting this.' He pointed at the ceiling. 'I wonder if the paint glows in the dark? Then you'd have the whole Milky Way to keep you company.'

Reacher thought the painting looked nothing like the Milky Way. The constellations were completely wrong. He knew because he had gazed at them hundreds of times from dozens of countries in both hemispheres. But he had learned over the years to keep his more pedantic observations to himself, so instead he said, 'This isn't the room she was in?'

'Who?'

'Gibson's handler.'

'Oh. No. She was in 1. At the opposite end.'

'No space theme over there?'

'Maybe. I couldn't see. The door was only open for a second.'

'But you got a good look at her.'

'When she came out, sure. Why—'

There was a knock on the door. One sharp rap, a pause, then two softer taps.

Vidic said, 'Hide the guns. I don't want to put my guy in a jam.'

Reacher took the Sig and the Glock from his waistband and slid them under a pillow.

Vidic turned and opened the door and a man stepped inside. He looked to be six feet, even, and he was wearing dark chinos, a cream shirt, blue suit coat, and boat shoes. His hair was sandy-coloured and thinning and his face was pink from the sun. He was carrying a backpack in his left hand. It was made of black ballistic nylon with all kinds of pockets and flaps and straps. It was scuffed and creased and a little dirty. It lived a busy life. That was clear. Reacher wondered if the bulk of the guy's medical practice lay more on the unofficial side of the scale than Vidic had suggested.

'Buck, thanks for coming.' Vidic gestured toward Reacher. 'This is the friend I was telling you about. He got banged up in a car wreck. Guess he broke his wrist. Hit his head pretty good, too, so maybe you could take a look at it, as well, while you're here?'

'No problem.' Buck Holmes crossed to the bed and set his pack down on its back. He pulled the tag on a zipper that ran from the bottom left, around the top, and all the way down to the bottom right. Then he pulled the front of the pack, folding it over across its base so that it opened completely like a clamshell. The inside was full of small instruments in clear

41

packets and all kinds of bandages and dressings in white sterile packages. 'OK. Let's get started. Shirt off, please. Pants too.'

Vidic moved toward the door. 'I'm going to step out now. I'll get you some food. What do you like?'

Reacher said, 'Sandwiches. Four. Meat or cheese. Nothing green. Chocolate bars. Nothing fancy. Pie, if you can find any to go. Plus coffee, black, and a couple of bottles of Coke.'

Vidic closed the door behind him and Reacher turned to Holmes. 'You want me to strip? Is that necessary? I hurt my wrist and I'm wearing a T-shirt.'

Buck crossed his arms. 'Ever served in uniform?'

Reacher nodded. 'Army. Thirteen years.'

'So you've done basic life support training, as a minimum. Yes?'

Reacher nodded again.

'Cast your mind back to the final assessment. You find your victim. He's lying on the ground, screaming, writhing around, clutching his knee. You dive right in and start bandaging that knee. What happens?'

'You fail the course.'

'Correct. Because your patient would die from the internal bleeding in his abdomen that you missed when you only focused on the injury he told you about. See where I'm going with this?'

Reacher slipped off his pants and laid them on the bed, next to the doctor's pack. Then he took off his shirt and placed it on top of the pants.

Holmes stepped in closer and ran his eyes over Reacher's torso, shoulder to shoulder, neck to navel. He was silent for a moment, then said, 'This isn't your first rodeo, is it? I see bullet wounds. I see knife wounds. And what's this?' He

42

pointed at a long, curved scar just above the elastic of Reacher's shorts. 'Some other kind of blade?'

Reacher said, 'Shrapnel. Part of a man's jawbone. Happened in Beirut, a long time ago.'

'That's one I haven't heard before. Turn around?'

The doctor visually examined Reacher's back and legs then had him lie on the bed. He poked and prodded areas of soft tissue. Manipulated joints. Tested reflexes. Then finally said, 'OK. Everything seems fine, so get dressed and I'll check on your noggin.'

Reacher slid back into his T-shirt and pants, then sat on the side of the bed.

Holmes said, 'You hit your head in the car wreck?'

'Right.'

'Did you lose consciousness?'

'Yes.'

'For how long?'

'I don't know.'

'Any memory loss?'

'I can't remember the accident, and maybe an hour before it happened.'

'That's probably nothing to worry about. There's a good chance it will come back, given time. Now, who was the 44th President of the United States?'

'Barack Obama. Served two terms: 2009 to 2017. Born in Honolulu, Hawaii, August 1961. Married to Michelle. Has two—'

'OK. Your memory's fine. Have you thrown up since the accident?'

'No.'

'Any dizziness? Dropping things? Walking into furniture? Doorframes?'

'No.'

'Ringing in your ears?'

'A little.'

'Eye pain? Double vision?'

'No pain. Eyesight was blurry for a while. It's OK now.'

'Sensitivity to light?'

'No more than usual.'

Holmes pulled a slim flashlight from his pocket. He switched it on, held it out, and moved it slowly from side to side. 'Follow the light with your eyes. Just your eyes. Keep your head still. Does that hurt?'

'No.'

'Good. Your pupils are reacting normally. How's your depth perception?'

'Same as always.'

Holmes put the flashlight away. 'Obviously it would be better if you could go to the hospital, get checked out properly, but I'm not too worried. I think you have a mild concussion. I want you to take it easy for twenty-four hours. You can take Tylenol if you need to, but not aspirin or Advil. No alcohol, either. After that you can get back to light exercise. Whatever feels right. Just make sure not to hit your head on anything. That's very important.'

'Understood. Thanks, Doc.'

'No problem. Now let's take care of your wrist.'

Holmes selected a sterile package from his backpack. It was cylindrical, about twelve inches long and three in diameter. 'The pain is sharp, not dull, and eases when your wrist is still and not being touched?'

Reacher nodded.

'OK. Well, in an ideal situation the first step would be to

establish the full extent and location of the injury, but that would call for an X-ray machine and obviously we don't have one here. So I'm going to assume the radius or the ulna is fractured, or possibly one of the carpal bones.' Holmes tore open the package and took out a roll of some kind of tight, black, mesh-like material. 'Hold your hand up, pointing at the ceiling, fingers together, thumb out.'

Reacher did as he was asked.

'Good.' Holmes pulled out a bunch of rods from the middle of the roll and set them on the bed. The rods were round, made of plastic, and ranged in length from twelve inches to four. He straightened out the material, which made it look more like a mat, a half-inch thick, with long pockets let into one side. He held it up alongside Reacher's hand and forearm. Stared at it for ten seconds. Then rolled it back up, gripped it with both hands, and bent it double like he was trying to snap it in half. 'We have to move fast now. There are two chemical compounds in this sleeve and now that they're mixed, they're going to set. Rapidly. And harder than regular plaster. So I need you to be ready. Don't move.' Holmes grabbed some of the rods and started to feed them into the pockets in the sleeve. He started with an eight-inch rod in the first pocket. He slid twelve-inch rods into the next six and finished with another eight-inch in the last one. 'This will hurt at first. I'm sorry.' He held the sleeve up and wrapped it around Reacher's wrist, starting below his knuckles and extending to his forearm, his thumb protruding through the open side. Then Holmes pulled back four broad Velcro tabs – one above Reacher's thumb, three below – and wrapped them around to fasten the sleeve in place.

'Can I move now?'

'Go ahead. Take it easy for ten minutes but once it's set you can do everything you normally would. You can even take a shower. Just don't knock it against anything.'

Holmes had already left when Vidic got back with Reacher's food and drink. He set the paper sacks on the desk then stepped up close to get a clear look at Reacher's wrist.

Vidic gestured toward the cast. 'That thing working? You feeling better?'

Reacher nodded. 'Good as new.'

'How about your head?'

'Still attached.'

'And your memory? Does Buck think it'll come back?'

Something about the tone of the question put Reacher on the defensive. He didn't know why but something made him reluctant to turn his cards face up, so he said, 'He wasn't hopeful.'

'Oh. That sucks. Well, get some rest. I'll come back for you tomorrow. Maybe the day after. If so, I'll bring you some more food. Or send someone you can trust. But whichever day we leave, remember, no one can know you're here. Keep the drapes closed and don't leave the room. Not for a minute.'

'Leave here?' Reacher said. 'I wouldn't dream of it.'

EIGHT

Reacher leaned down so that his eye lined up with the peephole in the motel room door. He looked out into the parking lot and immediately caught sight of Vidic's back moving quickly away. The fish-eye lens made Vidic's body look swollen and round, like a balloon figure, and he seemed to be floating rather than walking. He was making for his Jeep. That was clear. Its white body and black bonnet made it easy to spot despite the distorted optics. Reacher saw the dome light suddenly glow. Vidic's angular head was silhouetted, just for a moment, then the Jeep's cab went dark again. Vidic must have closed his door. Reacher couldn't tell if he had started the engine, but the Jeep's headlights didn't come on. The Jeep didn't move. It stayed where it was for a minute. Two minutes. Reacher smiled. It was what he had expected. Vidic was watching in case he broke the terms of their deal and bolted. Then Reacher made a bet with himself.

He had Vidic pegged as an impatient kind of guy. He wouldn't last more than a quarter of an hour before he gave up and left. Reacher was the opposite. He would wait all night if he had to. A fifteen-minute delay barely registered as an inconvenience. Particularly when there were two other things he needed to do.

Reacher took the Styrofoam coffee cup from one of the paper sacks that Vidic had left and carried it to the bed. He sat down and took a sip. It wasn't the best he'd ever had. It was lukewarm, gritty, and it had a burnt, bitter aftertaste. But it contained caffeine, and that was what counted. It would be easier to persuade a heroin addict not to shoot up than to stop Reacher drinking coffee. His brother, Joe, had been the same way. On the rare occasions he gave it any thought Reacher blamed his genetics. Mostly he just looked forward to his next cup.

When he was done with the coffee Reacher picked up the phone from the table next to the bed, hit 9 for an outside line, and dialled a number from memory. The call was answered after two rings. A man's voice came on the line. It said, 'This is Wallwork.'

Ronny Wallwork was an FBI agent. His path had crossed Reacher's a couple of times over the last few years. Reacher felt their interactions had been pretty equitable. If anything, he would say Wallwork had got the fairer shake due to the regulations and bureaucracy he brought with him. Wallwork saw their encounters in a whole different light. Things had always panned out. He couldn't deny that. But he didn't look back on their exchanges with any degree of pleasure. Or even satisfaction. To him, they were like bullets he had somehow managed to dodge.

'Wallwork, this is Reacher.'

The line was silent for a moment, then Wallwork said, 'I told you to forget this number.'

'True. But you didn't hang up.'

'Because I have manners. But I can't help you. Whatever it is, find someone else.'

'I don't need help.'

'Then why are you bothering me?'

'I heard a rumour. It could be serious.'

'Call the tip line. You might get a reward.'

'It's most likely BS. But if it isn't . . .'

Wallwork resisted for a long moment, then said, 'Go on. What have you heard?'

'One of your guys has been killed. In a car wreck. While working undercover.'

'Damn. When?'

'Today. Around 1:00 p.m.'

'Where?'

'In the Ozarks. I don't know the name of the nearest town. I'll send you the coordinates.'

'You saw the body?'

'No.'

'Where is it now?'

'That's unclear.'

'Who told you this?'

'A member of the group this alleged agent apparently infiltrated.'

'Do you believe the guy? You said his story was BS.'

'Most of it is twenty-four carat BS, I'm sure. Like how he followed this agent to a meeting with his handler and eavesdropped on their conversation. Sounds about as likely as him spotting a fish wearing roller skates. But a couple of other things he said – I don't know. I can't rule them out.'

'Such as?'

'The place this alleged meeting took place is plausible. I asked what the handler looked like and he didn't miss a beat. The description he gave could hold up in court, right down to her wearing shoes she could run in and not having any jewellery that could get snagged in a fight. Same goes for the car he said she drove away in.'

'Why would he tell you those things, whether they're true or not?'

'He thinks I have a beef with his boss. He claims he's done with the outfit and wants to quit with more than his share of the ill-gotten gains. I think he's worried I'll burn it all down before he can do that. So he's trying to play it two ways. He wants me to help him. Failing that, he wants to scare me off.'

'Do you have a beef with the boss?'

'Most definitely. So here's the problem. If this group is the target of a sting, I'm happy to back off. I don't want to blow a bunch of undercover work. Especially if it cost one of your guys his life. But if the Bureau's not involved—'

'Stop right there. I know how you operate. Any plans, keep them to yourself. I don't want to hear them.'

'Fine. But there's another problem. Say my guy's telling the truth. An agent had infiltrated this group, and now he's dead. What happens next? Some kind of lost contact procedure, presumably. Which would take a set amount of time. Then a rescue team would have to be mobilized. When the net finally closes at least one of the assholes would be in the wind. Maybe all of them would be.'

'Which we don't want. I'll start digging. What's your guy's name?'

'Ivan Vidic. Could be an alias. I don't know.'

'Any tattoos? Distinguishing features?'

'He has a weird, square head, but no tattoos. Nothing else that stands out.'

'OK. I'll run his background, too.'

'Good. But there's one more thing. Vidic said he heard the handler use the agent's code name.'

'Really? Why would she do that? Doesn't make sense.'

'I know. But if it somehow is legit . . .'

'It could speed up the verification process. What name did she use?'

'Albatross.'

'Got that. OK. Got to go. Where can I catch you if I need you? Have you got a cellphone yet?'

'No cell. You can call this number. Leave a message if I'm not here.'

NINE

Vidic sat behind the wheel of his Jeep with one eye on the door to Reacher's motel room and the other on his phone. He dialled Fletcher's number but before he hit Call his phone began to ring. It was Fletcher calling him. Vidic smiled. He loved coincidences like that. He took them to be signs that the universe was winking at him. Letting him know he was on the right track. He hit the answer button.

Fletcher said, 'Where are you?'

Vidic said, 'At the diner by the highway.'

'What are you doing there?'

'Getting something to eat. I missed dinner.'

'Seriously? Gibson's dead and all you can think about is your stomach?'

'If I starve myself, will that bring Gibson back to life?'

Fletcher didn't reply.

Vidic said, 'I'm sorry. Scratch that. I know you guys were

close. But listen, I was about to call you. Losing Gibson, the stranger showing up the way he did, I've been doing some thinking. We need to talk. About what we do next. And when. We have some decisions to make. Urgent decisions.'

'Damn right we do. Meet me at the cave in an hour. We'll figure everything out then.'

'The cave? Why there?'

'You'll see.'

'OK. I guess.'

'One other thing. The stranger. Something weird happened. He got away.'

'How? You said you were going to tie him to a table.'

'I did. I cuffed him. Somehow he got the cuffs unlocked. Must have had a key hidden somewhere. But *how* is not important. Finding him is. So keep your eyes open. He and I – we have unfinished business.'

'Understood. Will do.'

'Good. Last thing. Is Paris with you?'

'No. Why should she be?'

'No reason. See you in an hour.'

The call disconnected and Vidic sat for a moment, staring at Reacher's door. He wasn't happy about what he'd just heard. Why did Fletcher want him to come to the cave? It was the most secluded place he could think of. And why did Fletcher want to know if he was on his own? To figure out if he needed to worry about witnesses? Vidic turned and looked over his shoulder as if he could see through the Jeep's back seats and into the trunk. His go-bag was there, as always. He had everything he needed. Including a copy of the report. He could leave that minute. Never be seen again. But then he thought about that wink from the universe. He figured he was overreacting. Maybe Paris was thinking along the same lines. He called her number but got bounced straight to voicemail. He hung up. Thought for a moment, then called her again. This time he left a message. Then he turned his attention back to Reacher's door. It was five minutes since he'd closed it behind him. He figured he'd give it another ten and then, if Reacher was still inside, it would be safe to assume he would stay there.

Reacher counted down ten minutes in his head after Wallwork ended their call then crossed to the door and peered out through the peephole. Vidic's Jeep had gone. The space it had been in was empty. Reacher scanned the lot just in case Vidic was playing it cute and had switched to a different spot, but there was no sign of the black bonnet anywhere.

Reacher grabbed the key card and slid it into his back pocket. He stepped outside, made his way past the row of rooms, listening at each door, until he got to the office. No one else was there but he saw that the colour scheme from his motel room was carried over. Orange. Lime green. Teal. But the design didn't extend to the fixtures. There was a vending machine, essentially the same as hundreds of others he'd seen in hotels and motels all across the country. A wooden dispenser holding leaflets with details of local attractions. A plain reception counter. And on it, a computer.

Reacher didn't care either way about the furnishings or the decoration, but he wasn't too happy to see the computer. He had been hoping for an old-fashioned ledger. He found those far easier to interrogate. He leaned across the counter and contemplated the keyboard and the mouse. He was wondering which one to start with when a door opened in the back wall. A woman came through. She was maybe five feet tall. Maybe twenty-five years old. Her hair had been dyed scarlet some time ago. It had long blond roots and it was sticking out at crazy angles like she had recently been electrocuted. Her skin was pale and pockmarked. She was skinny to the point of malnutrition and she was wearing bleached denim overalls and a plain white T-shirt. One strap was hanging down, unfastened, and a badge pinned to the other gave her name as *Mary*.

'Can I help you?' she said.

Reacher said, 'I hope so.' He attempted an engaging smile. 'Or more accurately, I hope you can help my sister.'

'We're not hiring.'

'That's not a problem because she's not looking for a job. She's looking for her husband.'

Mary shrugged. 'I haven't seen him.'

'I wasn't suggesting you had, but she heard he's been coming here. Maybe to see someone else. Every week, like clockwork. So I need you to tell me if anyone is renting a room on a regular basis?'

Mary shook her head. 'No. I can't.'

'It's not possible?'

'No.'

'Are you sure?'

'I'm certain.'

Reacher nodded toward the monitor. 'Aren't those kind of details stored in the computer?'

'Obviously. But I can't share them with you.'

'Can't? Or won't?'

'I'm not allowed to. There's like eight company policies stopping me. And probably the law, too.'

'You don't need to worry about those things.'

'Why? Are you a cop? You don't look like one.'

'I used to be one. But that's not what's important here. What's important is that the information does exist. Right there in the computer.'

'It does. But it's private. You're not getting it.'

'Life is a very uncertain thing, wouldn't you say, Mary?'

'I guess.'

'Well, this is a very unusual moment because right now the outcome is absolutely guaranteed. I'm leaving here with the information I want. There is no doubt about that. The only question is how we get to that point. There are two possibilities. One, you tell me what I need to know. Or two, I call my old cop buddies. Suggest they come visit. Now, I'm going out on a limb and guessing that you don't want those guys coming here with their dogs, sniffing around your locker. I'm guessing you don't want them stopping you on your way home and searching every last hiding place in your car. Am I right?'

Mary's eyes grew wide. 'Please. There's nothing I can do. You don't understand. I can't give you that information. I just cannot do it. You've got to believe me.'

'Let me tell you what we used to do back in the day when an investigator needed information from someone who wasn't supposed to give it to us. That person would leave the file or the records, or the computer, on their desk and step out to the bathroom, or to have a cigarette, or whatever else they felt like doing. While they were gone we got what we wanted. And technically they didn't tell us a thing. Does that sound like something we could work with here?'

Mary didn't reply.

'Or would you prefer the dogs and the traffic stops?'

Mary thought for a moment, then said, 'Two minutes.'

She worked the keyboard for a few seconds and fiddled with the mouse, then a display popped up on the screen. A grid. The squares across the top indicated the days of the week. The squares down the side showed the room numbers.

Reacher waited until Mary ducked out through the door behind the counter then turned his attention back to the screen. Vidic said that Gibson met his handler in room 1, earlier that day. The grid showed that room 1 had been booked by a corporate client. A company named Automotive Factors Inc., which had a contact number with a 312 area code. That would place it in Chicago. If it actually existed. Reacher picked up the desk phone and dialled the number. His call rang six times then diverted to a message that gave the correct company name and stated its standard business hours. He wondered how hard it would be to fake such a thing. He figured it would be pretty straightforward.

Reacher scanned down the screen and saw that four other rooms were occupied. His, under the name John Austin. Presumably the name Vidic had used when he checked in. And three other rooms. They were all under the names of apparent individuals. No way to tell if they were legitimate. Or what the clients were using the rooms for. He experimented with the mouse until he figured out how to make the display go back to the previous week. He saw the same company name – Automotive Factors – with the same 312 phone number, but this time registered against room 4. The other three individuals all had the same rooms. He went back another week. Automotive Factors was booked into room 6. The individuals had the same rooms. The week before Automotive Factors had room 2.

Mary reappeared after three minutes. She said, 'Got what you need?'

Reacher clicked random parts of the screen with the mouse until the display changed to a high-level menu. He said, 'I don't know. We'll see.'

TEN

The diner was Reacher's next port of call. He stepped inside and found the interior didn't match the outside at all. Instead of cutesy and affected, it was plain and simple, just as he liked it. There were sixteen four-top tables in two parallel lines, one large rectangular table at the far end for larger groups, and a hatch that led into the kitchen. The place was deserted, which wasn't surprising given the time. It was a minute shy of 1:00 a.m. Reacher moved across to the window and picked the seat that gave the best view of the front of the motel. He could easily see the door to room 1. He could see the doors to all the rooms except 20. The diner was an excellent observation point. Vidic's claim about seeing Gibson's handler could have been true.

It could have been. That didn't mean it was.

A door to the side of the serving hatch opened and a waitress appeared. She was tall and thin with grey hair tied up in a bun on top of her head and a kind expression on her face.

The name tag on her apron read, *Hannah May.* She said, 'Back so soon? You must've liked us. You can't stay away.'

Reacher said, 'You've seen me before?'

Hannah May tipped her head to one side. 'That's not much of a pickup line and this isn't a bar so I don't really know what to do with that.'

Reacher held his hands up, palms out, as if to apologize for the confusion. 'I was in a car accident this afternoon. I can't remember anything that happened this morning. The guy who pulled me out of the wreck told me he saw me here, earlier. I'm trying to figure out whether he was shooting straight or if he's trying some kind of angle.'

'You were here. No doubt about that. I never saw anyone drink so much coffee in so short a time.'

'When I was here, did you see another guy? Kind of stooped with a strange square head?'

Hannah May nodded. 'A guy like that was sitting where you are now.'

'Ever seen him before?'

'No. A head like his I'd remember.'

Reacher wished he could ask her about Gibson, but he didn't know what the guy had looked like. He had no idea how to describe him. He swallowed his frustration and got to his feet. He said, 'I'm going to switch seats. I don't like this one.' He moved to a table near the wall, where he could keep an eye on the kitchen door, the main entrance, and all the other tables. The waitress followed. The look on her face said, *Weird. But not the weirdest thing I've seen on this job.* Out loud she said, 'Want any food while you're here?'

Reacher said, 'What did I have before?'

'A cheeseburger and a piece of pie.'

'Did I like it?'

'There was none left on your plate when you were done, so I guess you did.'

'OK. Sounds good. Let me have that again.'

Hannah May stepped away and was back a minute later with a mug of coffee. 'Don't worry. I'll keep them coming.'

The food arrived after another ten minutes. Reacher picked up his fork, then said, 'Tell me about this place. I heard a bunch of crazy houses were built somewhere nearby in the seventies.'

Hannah May shrugged. 'Guess so. Some fancy architect trying to lure people away from New York and places like that back when crime in the cities was out of control.'

'Did it work?'

'I couldn't say. I don't know much about real estate. I know that there are people living in one of them.'

'What kind of people?'

'I don't know. But when you drive past the place, sometimes there are SUVs parked outside. Pickup trucks. Box vans, a couple of times.'

'And the other houses? Anyone living in those?'

'You thinking of buying?'

Reacher smiled. 'Absolutely not. Just interested.'

'Well, they were all vacant for a few years but I heard a couple have been bought. Maybe more. I don't pay too much attention.'

'When did they get bought?'

Hannah May glanced up at the ceiling for a second. 'I'm going to say, maybe January twenty-one. Around then. After the worst of the COVID madness, anyway.'

'Ever see the people who live in them?'

'I don't know if people even do live in them. The lights are always off. No vehicles to be seen. They're some kind of investment, I heard. Someone else said it's to do with money laundering, but I don't know about that. Is there anything else I can get you?'

'Not right now. But I'll be back for breakfast.'

Vidic was waiting for five minutes before Paris's Land Rover pulled up alongside his Jeep. He had picked the meeting spot carefully. It was ten minutes from the place they had been summoned to by Fletcher – the cave – so it was convenient. And it was hidden from the road by a screen of dense trees, so it was discreet. If Fletcher had a helicopter Vidic would have worried. Or a drone. But as things were, he was confident they wouldn't be seen.

Paris climbed down from her Defender and got into the Jeep's passenger seat. She said, 'What's going on? Why does Fletcher want to see us?'

Vidic said, 'Guess we'll find out.'

'Why so late? And why at the cave? This doesn't feel good.'

'Two possibilities, as I see it. One, Fletcher has found out about us and Bowery and he's going to shoot us in the head.'

'Don't joke about that.'

'Who's joking? Or two, he's cooking up something else.'

'Like what?'

'No idea. That's why I wanted to talk before we see him.'

Paris was silent for a moment, then said, 'What if there's a third option? What if he's found out about the report and he wants a piece of it? What would we do?'

'Shoot him in the head.'

'Ivan, this is serious. We're looking at a fortune. We could easily give him a chunk and not even notice the difference.'

'No way, no how. I hate that asshole. He's not seeing a penny.'

'How do we say no?'

'We don't know he's found out. Don't jump to conclusions.'

'But if he has? We should be prepared. We should have a plan.'

'I do have a plan. You know the stranger that was with Gibson?'

'What about him?'

'Fletcher let him escape.'

'Seriously? How?'

'The guy overpowered him would be my guess. But that's not the point. The point is that Fletcher doesn't know where he is. I do. And he's going to help us. I had something else in mind but we could use him for this, too.'

'Why would he help us? He doesn't know us.'

'He thinks there's something in it for him.'

'Is there?'

'Of course not.'

'So what do we do?'

'We make sure the Russian job goes ahead. Soon. It needs to be wrapped up tomorrow. The day after tomorrow at the latest. So if Fletcher balks, I need you to back me up. We still do the job. We just alter the timetable, OK?'

'And the stranger? Another loose end? How does that help?'

'Don't worry about him. He won't be a problem at all. Not for us, anyway.'

ELEVEN

Reacher stepped out of the diner and took a moment to scan the parking lot. He didn't expect that Vidic would have come back but he was a cautious man. A teacher in shop class had drummed into him, *Measure twice, cut once*, back when he was barely a teenager. He had never forgotten. He had foreseen little use for woodworking in his life but he appreciated the sentiment, all the same. So he adapted it. Made it into something more relevant. *Look twice, act once.* That became a key principle. It had served him well over the years. It had helped him stay alive while the fools who rushed in had wound up six feet underground.

There was no sign of the Jeep but one shape did attract Reacher's attention. A man's silhouette. He was in front of the motel office, ten yards from the door. He was maybe six feet two or three. He was wearing jeans and a black leather vest and the light from the office window was reflecting off his shaved head.

It wasn't so much the size of the guy, or his clothing, that caught Reacher's attention. It was his movement. He seemed agitated. He was pacing from side to side. Fifteen feet one way, then fifteen feet the other, back to where he started. Over and over. He didn't pause. He didn't change his pace. It was like he was mad about something and was looking for someone to take his aggression out on. The direct route to Reacher's room led right past the guy. That was fine by Reacher. He wouldn't bother the guy. Not as long as the guy didn't bother him. It was his rule.

The guy in the leather vest turned and started to walk away from Reacher. Reacher set off at the same time. In the same direction. The two men were sixty feet apart. They stayed that way until both had covered fifteen feet. Right on cue the guy turned and started walking back toward Reacher. Reacher continued, directly toward the guy. The gap closed to fifty feet. Forty. Thirty. Then the guy broke his routine. He didn't turn. He stopped and stood still with his head tipped to one side. Reacher kept moving but adjusted his course slightly so that he would pass the guy on his left-hand side. The guy stepped across to block Reacher's path.

Reacher thought, *Mistake*. He shifted back to his original course. The guy stepped over to block him again.

Bigger mistake.

The guy stood with his arms bowed and his fists clenched. He scowled for a moment, then said, 'You the one who's been bothering my girl Mary?'

Reacher said nothing.

'Don't deny it. It was you. She described your ugly ass. You were asking questions. Poking your nose where it doesn't belong.'

Reacher said nothing.

'Questions about girls and missing husbands. That stops now. Get it?'

Reacher said, 'Rooms.'

'What?'

'I asked about rooms. Not girls.'

'Same thing.'

'You think that, you're doing something very wrong, my friend.'

'Whatever. The point is, the questions stop. You leave. And if you ever come around here again, you'll regret it.'

'Regret it, as in I would wish I'd chosen to spend my time somewhere else? Where the company's more engaging?'

'I'm warning you, smart-ass.'

'You're warning me?'

'Damn straight.'

'You're not doing a very good job. Warnings have two parts. If you do X, the consequence will be Y. I'm not hearing about any consequence, other than some vague idea of regret. Spell it out for me. Say I don't leave. What are you going to do about that?'

'Stick around and you'll find out.'

Reacher spread his arms wide. 'Here I am. Sticking around.'

'I'm warning—'

'Enough. I've used up all the time I have for your nonsense. Go back to your boss or whoever sent you and tell them I have no interest in whatever you've got going on here. I'm not looking for trouble. Stay away from me and no one needs to get hurt.'

'As soon as I see you leave . . .'

'That's not going to happen. I'll leave when I'm ready.'

'Leave now.'

'Make me.'

'Happy to.'

'Go ahead. Try. But before you do, think about this. You can still walk away. You should. While you still can.'

'What are you going to do? You've only got one working arm.'

'If I only had one working finger that would be enough. Be smart. Walk away.'

Reacher could see the guy weighing up his next move. A twitch of his right arm. A shuffle on his left foot. He was slow off the mark. That was for sure. Reacher guessed the guy usually got by through intimidation. But that had already failed. Reacher felt his neck muscles flexing. He was ready to drive his forehead into the guy's face. It would be a brutal move. Vicious. Devastating. One of his favourites. A kind of Pavlovian response to being confronted by an asshole. But Reacher stopped himself. He remembered the doctor's words. *Don't hit your head on anything. It's important.* So he decided to play it safe. He watched the guy draw back his right fist. Then he stamped on the guy's front foot. He used all his weight. He felt the little delicate bones beneath the guy's instep crush and shatter. He stepped to the side. The guy screamed and doubled over. Reacher drove his left knee up into his face. For a moment the guy looked like an acrobat on a balancing pole, hanging in mid-air, then he landed on his back. His legs slammed into the ground a moment later. And after that he didn't move.

Reacher looked around. He could see no one in the parking lot. He checked for cameras. Didn't spot any. He checked that the guy was still breathing, then walked over to the office door. He shoved it open and stepped inside. Mary, the woman with the red hair, was standing behind the counter. She looked like she'd seen a ghost.

Reacher said, 'Mary? Come with me.'

Mary stood still. She didn't respond.

'Come here.'

Reacher's voice had become a low rumble. Mary could feel it in her chest. She closed her eyes for a moment. Reacher could see her lips moving but he couldn't hear any words.

'Come here. Now.'

Mary crept around the end of the counter. Her arms were rigid by her sides and her legs were straight and stiff.

'Who did you call?'

Mary's eyes widened. 'How did you find out?'

'Who?'

'I don't have a name. Just a number. For the man who rents the three rooms. For the girls who . . . you know what they do in there. Listen, I'm sorry. I had to call. I need money for . . . you can probably guess. And he said if I go against him he'll put me in one of those rooms. And I figured, with your questions, you must be some kind of rival. A newcomer looking to muscle in.'

'I'm not.'

'I'm sorry. I didn't know.'

'Here's what you're going to do to fix it. Look out of the window. When I'm gone, call that number again. Tell whoever answers what happened to the guy he sent. Tell him that if he sends anyone else, the same thing will happen to them. Then, when I have a spare five minutes, I'll come for him. And he won't send anyone, anywhere, ever again.'

*

If a chivalrous man suspected he was walking into a possible ambush, he would volunteer to go first. Give his partner a chance to escape if things went south. Vidic was not a chivalrous man. He killed his Jeep's headlights. Coasted up to one of the heaps of spoil that hid the approach to the cave. Checked that his dome light was switched off. Opened his door. Climbed out. Crept forward until he could see the entrance. Waited for Paris to pass him. And watched to see what kind of reception was in store for her.

The place they called *the cave* wasn't really a cave. It was the entrance to a gold mine. Only it wasn't really a gold mine, either. A local guy, fresh back from California in 1856, had taken a gamble. He used his last few ounces of black powder to blow a hole in a rock face, planted the few miserable gold nuggets he'd been able to find out west in the rubble, and sold the mineral rights to a wannabe millionaire from Chicago. A few months and a couple dozen yards of fruitless excavation later, the venture was abandoned. It was briefly reactivated in the 1940s in the pursuit of uranium, but that search proved futile, too. The entrance was shuttered. Metal rusted. Weeds grew. People forgot that the place existed. Until Fletcher arrived. He was looking for somewhere remote to store any wares that were too hot to sell right away. When he spotted the place on a satellite image online he figured they could build something secure. But when he visited for the first time and prised open the rusty barricade he realized the hard work had been done for him. All he needed was a new set of doors. Something substantial. With keys that couldn't be duplicated. And a security camera linked into the existing system at the house, just to be safe.

The doors to the cave were open when Paris arrived. The nose of a panel van was sticking out. Paris had never seen the vehicle before. She pulled up next to Fletcher's Cadillac Escalade and jumped down from her Land Rover. She looked around, saw no one, then heard footsteps crunching on the gravel. Fletcher appeared from the cave's entrance and strode toward her.

Paris said, 'Darren, what's going on? What happened to your hand?'

Fletcher glanced at his splinted fingers but ignored her question. He said, 'Good. You're here. Kane's inside. We just need Vidic to show up.'

'Why?'

'All hands to the pumps: 911.'

'What's happened?'

'We've been targeted by the FBI.'

'Are you sure?'

'Sure enough to get the hell out of Dodge.'

TWELVE

Reacher waited until he saw Mary's face disappear behind the blind in the office window then he leaned down, grabbed the unconscious guy by his belt, and dragged him through the gap between the office and the diner. He moved deep into the shadows, stopped, and looked around. A dumpster was sitting in the centre of the space behind the office. It was small. Not a suitable place to deposit a body. The area behind the diner was much more promising. There was a large dumpster for regular waste. Another for recycling. A tall, cylindrical container for collecting used cooking oil. And another shallower, rectangular container. It was painted green and it had a bunch of symbols stencilled on its side. Reacher didn't recognize them so he lifted the lid and looked inside. The thing was full of food. Lettuce. Tomatoes. Onions. Various other vegetables that Reacher wasn't familiar with. Hunks of bread. Scraps of meat. All in different stages of decomposition. All giving off a disgusting stench.

Reacher weighed his options. He came down in favour of the food container. It was long enough. Deep enough. And it was the lowest, which made it the most convenient to throw the guy's body in using only his left hand.

Reacher emerged from between the buildings and started to turn left, toward his room. Then he stopped. He turned right instead. Went back to the diner and saw Hannah May sitting at the table he had used, drinking coffee.

Hannah May started to get to her feet. She said, 'Breakfast time already?'

Reacher gestured for her to stay in her seat. He said, 'Not yet. I have a question. The green dumpster out back. What happens to all the waste food that's in it?'

Hannah May shrugged. 'Goes to a farm, I think. Gets fed to the pigs. They'll eat anything, those critters.'

'How often does it get emptied?'

'Every two or three days. Unless it gets full quicker than that. Then the boss calls someone. Gets them to come an extra time.'

'When's the next collection?'

'Tomorrow, I think. Why? Want me to check?'

'No need. I'm just curious.'

Vidic kept his eyes on Paris's hands. If she clasped them low down behind her back, that was the emergency signal. It would mean Fletcher was on to them. That the meeting was a trap. It would be Vidic's cue to charge in, guns blazing, and rescue Paris. He was ready to jump back into his Jeep if she gave the sign. That was for sure. Only he wouldn't drive toward the danger. He would drive the opposite way.

Vidic watched for five minutes. He saw Fletcher approach

Paris. Saw them talk. Saw plenty of arm waving on both sides. Something major was being discussed. That was clear. But Paris's hands stayed far apart. And they stayed in front of her body. So when Vidic was sure he was safe he drove around the heaps of ancient spoil and parked next to her Defender.

Fletcher waited for Vidic to jump down then turned and started toward the cave entrance. 'Come on,' he said, over his shoulder. 'We have things to talk about.'

Reacher left the diner and strolled back to his room. He locked the door behind him, stripped off his shirt and pants, placed them under the mattress so that they would get pressed while he slept, then went to the bathroom. He brushed his teeth and thought about taking a shower. It was late but his body was sore. His right shoulder hurt. So did his arm. His rib cage. All probably as a result of the accident, earlier in the day. And his head was aching. He figured a little warmth and some steam might help. But before he could decide, the room phone started to ring. Normally he ignored calls late at night. They were usually bad news. He knew. He had made plenty of them himself over the years. But this time it could be Wallwork calling. Or Vidic. He could be checking that Reacher was still there. Or giving word that it was time for the next step in the plan. So to be on the safe side, Reacher picked up.

'Mr Austin?' It was a woman's voice. Mary, from the motel office.

Reacher said, 'Yes.'

'Mr Austin, I thought you should know, a couple of detectives were just here looking for you.'

'Really?'

'Yes. A minute ago.'

'Were they wearing suits? Or undercover clothes?'

'Undercover, I guess.'

'Which division were they from?'

Mary paused. 'I'm not sure. They just said they were detectives. They showed me their badges and everything.'

'What did they want?'

'They were asking all about you. Where you were? If you were in your room? Like that.'

'What did you tell them?'

'I said I didn't know.'

'Why are you telling me this?'

'I thought you'd want to know. I would, if the police were looking for me in the middle of the night.'

'Mary, is someone there with you?'

'No.'

'Did someone get you to make this call?'

Mary was silent.

'Mary?'

'Remember the thing with leaving the files or the computer or whatever and me not saying anything, but you finding out, anyway? Can we pretend we're doing that?'

'Understood. Goodnight, Mary. Thanks.'

Reacher put the handset back in its cradle and retrieved his clothes. He put them on but he didn't go outside. There were no detectives looking for him. He was sure about that. He guessed that a couple of buddies of the guy he'd thrown in the pig slop had shown up. Maybe in response to the call he had told Mary to make. She must have given up his room number. But if these guys were friends of the motel, and needed it to run their business, they wouldn't want to risk causing damage. They would want to lure Reacher outside before starting whatever trouble they had in mind. And if they wanted trouble, Reacher had no problem with giving them some. But it was going to happen on his terms. On his timetable. And it could wait till morning. That would be best from a tactical standpoint. It would leave plenty of time for their adrenaline to drain away. They would be much less brave in a few hours' time. Reacher was confident about that. But he slept with his clothes on, just in case. And he kept his left hand under his pillow with his fingers against the Glock's grip.

The entrance to the cave was twenty feet wide by ten feet tall. The opening was square and true, and Fletcher had installed a metal frame to carry the weight of the doors. The first fifteen feet of the excavation was also relatively neat and smooth, but beyond that the floor became ragged and the walls and ceiling began to slope and weave at crazy angles until they met to form a rough shelf another twenty feet back. Fletcher had rigged up a lighting system that ran off a series of car batteries. He'd set up shelves along the left-hand side, constructed a mesh cage in the centre for securing the most portable valuables, as well as adding an old safe against the right wall. He'd also dragged in three old couches. They were arranged in a U shape between the cage and the safe, and when Fletcher led Paris and Vidic inside, they saw that Kane was already there, sprawling on the central one. He had a can of beer in his hand and when he caught Paris scowling at him he let out a huge belch.

Paris took a seat as far from Kane as she could get. Vidic sat next to her. Fletcher remained standing. He moved to the centre of the U and said, 'All right. Listen up. There's no easy way to put this. We always knew this day could come. We hoped it wouldn't, but hope doesn't keep you out of jail. It looks like the Feds have finally picked up on our scent.'

Paris said, 'Because of this stranger showing up? How can you be sure that's what it means?'

'I'm not *sure*. The people who wait around to be sure are the people who get locked up. But look at the facts. The stranger targeted Gibson. To do that he must have known Gibson's routine. Which involves surveillance. Manpower. Resources. Then he set up an incident – the failed carjacking – so that he could gain Gibson's trust. If it wasn't for the accident, which Ivan witnessed, he could be sitting here with us now.'

'You can't know that the stranger set the carjacking thing up. Sometimes a crime is just a crime.'

'He was making out to be a bum. A drifter. Who just happened to be carrying a Glock? That's an expensive weapon. Where would he get the money for one? And look at how he escaped. He was cuffed to a table. Then – gone. Disappeared. Not a trace. Does that sound like the skill set of a random hobo?'

Paris shrugged. 'I guess not. But the setup thing. The carjacking. I still don't buy it. The simple explanation is usually the accurate explanation.' Like with the bruises on Fletcher's head and throat, Paris thought. It was more likely the stranger kicked his ass than pulled off some magical escape.

Fletcher said, 'What are you driving at?'

Paris said, 'Maybe the stranger didn't need to gain Gibson's trust. Maybe he already had it. Maybe they didn't run into each other at the motel by chance. Maybe Gibson went there to collect him. Maybe the car bozos were just in the wrong place at the wrong time.'

Fletcher took a step closer to her. 'That would mean . . .'

'. . . that Gibson was a Fed. Yes.'

Kane crushed his can and tossed it aside. He sat up straighter in his seat.

Fletcher took another step. 'No. Gibson was my friend. I brought him in. Do I need to say any more?'

Paris looked away. She shook her head. She got the picture. If Gibson was a Fed, and Fletcher had brought him in, then the ultimate screwup lay at Fletcher's door. And that was something he would never accept. Just like he'd never admit he'd gotten his ass kicked.

Fletcher said, 'Good. Now this is an emergency. There's no doubt about that. The only question is, level one or level two?'

The different levels of emergency had been laid down long ago. One was measured in minutes. It meant drop everything and run. Two was measured in hours. It meant tie up loose ends, grab what you can, and run.

Vidic shuffled nearer to the front of the couch cushion. He said, 'Level two. For sure. The Feds needed to send a guy in undercover, which shows they were fishing. They didn't have anything solid to justify an immediate bust. They still don't. The stranger was unconscious when you brought him to the house, and groggy when he somehow got out. He certainly didn't have time to search the place. And he didn't come here.'

'Good points. So what do we do?'

'You have a van here, so clearly you're ready to load up. Fold the tents. Which I agree with. But we should give ourselves twenty-four hours. Do the Russian job. Take what's already arrived. Forget the final delivery. Split directly from there.'

'Paris?'

Paris said, 'Works for me.'

'Kane?'

Kane grunted. 'We can't leave without doing the Russian thing. I don't care what is there and what isn't. We need to teach them a lesson. That's the priority.'

Fletcher nodded. 'Good. We pack up here. We do the Russian job. But that's not all.'

Paris said, 'What else is left?'

'Two other houses. Some Russians own those as well.'

'You're not suggesting—'

'I am. We take all three.'

'It's not justified. We don't know if anything's there. Whoever bought them might not be using them yet. So we'll spend time, maybe for nothing. And we've done no surveillance. Which means it's dangerous. There could be booby traps. Guards, even.'

Fletcher nodded again. 'Fair points. We might waste time. We might face opposition. But there's a way to mitigate those risks. When Bowery disappeared I called in reinforcements. I was worried someone was moving in on us. That's moot now. So we use the extra manpower to help with the additional properties. And to help find the stranger.'

Vidic threw up his hands in an exaggerated shrug. 'Wait a minute. Reinforcements? You should have told us. Who are they? How do we know if we can trust them? When will they get here?'

Fletcher said, 'Sometimes decisions have to be made on the fly. It's called *leadership*. I brought in four guys. All vouched for by Kane. He's worked with them before. And they're already here. They arrived this evening.'

'Arrived where?'

'That weird motel by the highway. They can stay there till they're needed.'

'This is a mistake. You should have—'

'Enough. It's done. Accept it. OK?'

Vidic shrugged.

'Good. Next. We need a new schedule. How long to get this place packed up?'

Kane scratched his armpit. 'Couple of hours, max.'

Fletcher nodded. 'Then we'll sleep now. Pack up in the morning when we have more light. Everything except for the industrial metals. They're too dangerous to transport. Too hard to sell. We'll hit the first Russian place at noon, followed by the other two. Then we'll split.'

Paris said, 'What time do you want us back?'

'Back? No. We're not leaving. We'll sleep here.'

'All of us?' She couldn't help shooting a scowl at Kane.

'All of us.'

'OK. And we clear our house when? After we're done here?'

'No. We don't go back to our house. None of us. Assume it's blown.'

'But I need to get something.'

'What?'

Paris was silent for a moment. 'My books.'

'You can buy new books.'

'I want my old books. They have sentimental value.'

'The answer is no. It's too dangerous. Any other questions?'

Vidic cleared his throat. 'This is a delicate one. Speaking of the house. Gibson's body is there. Aren't we going to retrieve it? Give him a proper funeral, or something?'

'We're not going to retrieve his body. Too much risk, too little reward. Assume the house is under surveillance, twenty-four/seven, from now on. But we are going to give him a funeral. A Viking funeral. The moment we're finished with the Russians I'll light the house up like a pyre. We'll say goodbye to Gibson. Destroy everything that could come back and bite us. And create a diversion while we split. A perfect triple play.'

'How can you light the house on fire if you can't go near it?'

'I don't need to go near it.' Fletcher pulled out his phone and held it up. 'Smart switches. Tap a couple of buttons. The deep fat fryer overheats. The dryer malfunctions. A table light short-circuits.'

'A home-arson app. Who knew? It was only a matter of time, I guess. We could license it. Make a fortune.'

'Already been done. Some guy out of Pensacola, Florida.' Fletcher paused. 'Anything else?'

'Just one thing.' Vidic swivelled and pointed at the safe. 'You said pack everything up, apart from the metals. That, too?'

'What's inside it, sure. We'll split it five ways. Gibson had a kid. She'll get his share.'

'That's fair, I guess.'

'But we'll do that last. After the Russian thing's a wrap.'

'What if something happens to you? No one else knows the combination.'

A smile crept across Fletcher's face. 'Guess you better take care that nothing does happen to me. I know how you'd hate to lose all that cash.'

THIRTEEN

Reacher slept, but lightly. Part of his subconscious remained active, on the alert for the slightest sign that somebody was trying to pick the lock. Or tamper with the bathroom window. He was disturbed at one point by noises from room 19, next door. Someone must have checked in while he was at the diner. He listened for five minutes, then dismissed the threat. It was just aimless voices. A couple of guys settling in for the night. Then he was woken finally a minute after 6:00 a.m. by a knock at the door. It was loud and confident and it was followed by a woman's voice. It said, 'Mr Austin? Room service. I have your breakfast.'

Reacher pulled the Glock out from beneath the pillow, stood up, and tucked it into his waistband. He rolled up the pillow to make it more rigid and carried it to the door. He moved to the right-hand side and lifted the pillow until the top was covering the peephole, in case someone was standing on the other side with a gun, waiting to pull the trigger when the little lens went dark. A second crawled by. Two. There was no gunshot. No shattered wood or shredded fabric. Reacher risked a quick glance. He saw a woman. She was slim. Maybe five feet eight. She had dark brown hair, tied back away from her face, and she was wearing an apron over her clothes. It was the kind he had seen the waitresses wearing at the diner the day before, but with no name tag. The woman was carrying a rectangular tray with a coffee mug on it alongside a plate that was covered with a silver metal lid. But she was only supporting the tray with one hand. Her left. Her right arm was tucked in tight against her side and her hand was hidden behind her thigh.

Reacher said, 'I didn't order any breakfast.'

The woman said, 'You did. Kind of. You told Hannah May that you would be coming in but she's gone off shift now. She asked me to take care of you. She's sweet on you, for some reason. So I thought I'd go the extra mile. Bring your food to your room.'

'What did you bring me?'

'Coffee, obviously. She told me you like it. Only one mug, but I can get you a refill anytime. Plus I got bacon, eggs, and some toast.'

Reacher assumed that this was the next step in the attempt to lure him outside. He guessed a couple of guys, minimum, would be waiting, hidden from view on either side of the doorway. He decided to test the theory. He said, 'OK. Sounds great. Bring it in.'

Reacher started to open the door. He moved it slowly and when it was two-thirds of the way through its arc he heard the clink of crockery on the other side. He slammed the door back the other way. He put all his weight behind it. The leading edge smashed into the tray. Then the woman. Then it crashed into its frame. The wood shuddered. The handle rattled. Reacher pulled the door open again. He did it fast this time. He saw the woman on the ground, sprawled on her back. A gun was lying four feet from her head. The mug had shattered. Brown liquid was pooling on the ground. The plate had landed upside down. But there was no sign of any other people. Reacher grabbed the woman by her foot and dragged her into the room. Then he stepped past her, ducked down, leaned out, and scanned to the left and the right. There was still no sign of anyone lurking near his room. He retrieved the fallen gun, shut the door, and turned to check on the woman. She had moved. She was on her feet. Her arms were out in front, fingers extended like claws, and her body was taut, like a cat about to pounce on its prey.

She said, 'Found you at last, you son of a— oh. You're not . . .' She dropped her arms and stepped back.

Reacher waited for a moment, then said, 'I'm not what?'

The woman looked down at the floor. Then she raised her eyes to meet Reacher's and said, 'You're not the man who killed my father.'

Vidic barely got any sleep. He lay awake on one of the couches in the cave for most of the night, cursing Reacher for not having a cellphone. He could have sent him a text silently. But he couldn't call. Not from inside. Not with Kane stretched out on another couch. And he couldn't risk going outside, even if he pretended to need the bathroom. Fletcher was there. Spending the night in his Cadillac. Maybe asleep. But maybe watching.

Fletcher came back into the cave at a quarter after six. He slammed the door behind him and said, 'Big day today. Who wants breakfast?'

Kane stretched and said, 'Me. I'll have a burrito.'

Vidic said, 'Croissant. Coffee.'

Fletcher said, 'I want sausage and biscuits. Paris?'

Paris shrugged. 'I'm not very hungry. Maybe some yogurt. A little fruit.'

Fletcher grimaced. 'Sounds gross. But hey, your funeral. You heard what everyone else wants?'

Paris nodded.

'Good. Now go fetch. Be quick.'

Paris shot daggers at Fletcher, hauled herself off the couch, and made for the door. Vidic waited until she was out of sight then jumped up and went after her. He looked at Fletcher as he hurried past and said, 'Changed my mind. I want a pain au chocolat instead.'

The woman's gaze dropped to Reacher's motel room floor. She said, 'This is really embarrassing. Clearly I made a mistake. Now if I could just get my weapon back, I'll leave you alone. I won't disturb you again.'

Reacher said, 'I don't get it. Do I look like the man who killed your father?'

'Like I told you. I made a mistake. This isn't on you. I should have checked you out more carefully.'

'Did your father live around here?'

'Look, assuming the ground won't open up and swallow me, which believe me I'm praying for right now, I just want to go. I'm mortified. And I'm wasting time. So please, give me my weapon. I'll get out of your hair. You'll never see me again.'

The woman held out her hand. Her fingers were trembling. Her eyes were red. She wasn't telling the whole story. Reacher was certain of that. But he didn't believe she was lying. And he didn't see her as a threat. He hit the catch to release the magazine from her gun. Thumbed out the bullets and slipped them into his pocket. Checked that the chamber was empty. Reassembled the weapon. And handed it to her. He said, 'The man who killed your father? I hope you find him.'

Vidic slipped between his Jeep and Paris's Land Rover and ducked down so that he wouldn't be visible from the cave's entrance. Paris had been about to start her engine but instead she rolled down her window. She said, 'What are you doing? Are you trying to get us caught?'

Vidic said, 'Don't move. Give me a minute. If Fletcher comes out, stall him. Cover for me.'

Vidic pulled out his phone and dialled the number for Reacher's motel. The call rang. And rang. Vidic pictured the clerk asleep in the back office. He imagined her waking up. Stretching. Remembering where she was. Recognizing the ringing sound. Then strolling to the reception counter like she was moving in slow motion. He was struggling to catch his breath. His heart was beating so hard he could hear it. Finally the clerk picked up. Vidic asked for room 20. There was a pause, a click, some more ringing, then Reacher's voice came on the line.

Vidic said, 'Reacher? Listen. I've got to be quick. Two things. One, Fletcher's last job will be tomorrow morning, 4:00 a.m., so you and I are going to hit his stash this afternoon. Maybe around 2:00 p.m. I'll call when I'm on my way to pick you up. Two, Fletcher has called in extra muscle. Four guys. Kane's buddies, so undoubtedly psychos. They've checked in to your motel. They have your description. So it's even more important than ever that you keep the drapes closed and don't leave the room. Understood?'

'Why did Fletcher bring in these extra guys? Because of Gibson? Or what happened in the kitchen, yesterday?'

'Neither. When Bowery disappeared Fletcher got twitchy. Turns out he was worried about getting jumped at the job, tomorrow. He had Kane call them a couple of days ago.'

There was silence on the line for a moment, then Reacher said, 'What does Kane look like?'

'What?'

'Describe Kane.'

'I don't have—'

'Describe him.'

'He's big. Scary-looking. Six-six. Three hundred pounds. Mad eyes. Hair kind of like yours.'

'What's his first name?'

'Zach. Why?'

'No special reason.'

'You . . . forget it. I've got to go. You, rest up. Be ready for this afternoon.'

Reacher tucked the two guns into his waistband and left his room. This time he turned left, away from the motel office. He looped around the back of the building and continued for the full width of the diner so that when he emerged he approached its door from the opposite direction. He stepped inside. The woman who had tried to trick her way into his room was sitting in the nearest seat. The one with the view of the first nineteen motel rooms. Just as he had expected. She was wearing black leather boots with low heels. Jeans. A fitted black T-shirt. A tan leather jacket. And she had a small purse hanging from its shoulder strap across the back of her chair.

Reacher took the seat facing hers. He said, 'Zach Kane.'

The colour drained from the woman's face. She said, 'Who?'

'Zach Kane killed your father.'

'Who told you?'

'No one. I joined the dots.'

'How?'

'Four guys checked into the hotel yesterday evening. They're Kane's associates. You followed them, hoping they'd lead you to him. You saw me. Apparently Kane looks similar. You jumped to the conclusion.'

'The fact you beat the living ... whatever out of some random lowlife and threw his body in the pig swill might have had something to do with that.'

Reacher shrugged.

The woman thought for a moment. 'Now I get it. You're looking for Kane, too. Are you a PI?'

'Yes, I'm looking for him. No, I'm not a PI. My name's Reacher.' He held out his hand.

'Jenny Knight.' She gave his hand a firm shake. 'So why are you looking for him?'

'I'll come to that. But first, we have two problems.'

'Only two? My luck must be improving.'

'We can't go after him separately. There's too much chance of tripping each other up. Do that at a vital moment, one of us might not live to tell the tale.'

'True. So what do you suggest?'

'Kane is only of peripheral interest to me. It's his boss and the rest of his crew I really want. Let me handle this. Stay out of my way. And I'll give Kane to you when I close their operation down.'

Knight frowned. 'I'll think about that. What else?'

'You were a cop?'

'What makes you think that?'

'The phone call from the clerk in the middle of the night. You put her up to that?'

'What if I did?'

'That's a classic cop trick. You thought Kane was in my room. He has a history of violence. You were trying to make him bolt. Run to a vehicle. Flee on foot. Whatever. You just wanted him out in the open. To gain the element of surprise. And reduce the risk to yourself. Because you have no one backing you up. You're too young to be retired. You don't seem like a quitter. You don't have a line-of-duty disability. Which means you were fired.'

'You're wrong.'

'Am I?'

'Absolutely. Because I wasn't fired. I'm on suspension. I'm a detective out of Phoenix, Arizona.'

'You're on suspension because of Kane?'

Knight nodded. 'My father was a cop. He was retired from the job and working security at a private gallery in Tempe. One night it got hit. He took a bullet in the chest. Got taken to the Emergency Room, unconscious. He came around for two minutes, a couple of hours before he died. I was there. He told me Kane was the shooter. He recognized him from his time on the job. Kane has a jacket two inches thick but nothing has ever stuck. Another detective caught the case but Kane disappeared off the map. Just vanished. The detective tried to get the Feds involved but they blew hot, then cold. In the end they wanted nothing to do with it so I ran with the case myself. Evenings. Weekends. Every spare minute I could find. My LT didn't like it. He said it was a conflict of interest. A distraction from other investigations. He told me to stop. I didn't, and here I am.'

'I can't blame you. So what will you do when you find Kane?'

'I expect you want me to say something banal like *make sure justice is done,* or promise to turn him over to the local cops, unharmed. But you know what? I can't do that. What I'm going to do when I get my hands on the miserable son of a bitch is make sure he knows who I am, then shoot him in the gut and watch him die. Slowly. And in agony. That's the truth, but you're probably horrified now. In which case, so be it.'

'I'm not judging.' Reacher thought about his own response when someone murdered his brother. He was many things, but he wasn't a hypocrite. He said, 'It's something else.'

'Such as?'

'What if I told you that the FBI could be investigating Kane, after all? And they maybe lost a guy along the way?'

Knight leaned forward. 'What makes you think that?'

'I'll explain in a minute. But until I know if it's true I'm not going to do anything that could spook these guys. I'm hoping that as a cop you'll respect that. Agree to do the same.'

Knight took a moment. 'Why should I trust you? You know a lot about cop tricks. Maybe a few have been used on you?'

Reacher shook his head. 'Not used on me. Used by me.'

'You're a cop? I don't believe it.'

'Was. A military cop. For thirteen years.'

'Get out of town. Where were you based?'

'Pretty much everywhere in the world the army has a presence.'

'What rank?'

'Terminal at major.'

'OK then.' Knight nodded like she was acknowledging some kind of kinship. 'So how are you going to find out if the FBI thing is true?'

'I know a guy at the Bureau. He's looking into it. I should hear pretty soon.'

'That's good. But I'm not going to do nothing while you sit around waiting for an email from this buddy of yours. Assuming you can even trust what he says. Assuming he won't change his tune in ten minutes' time.'

'We can trust him. He won't be emailing. And I won't be sitting around.'

'Then what will you be doing?'

'Learning more about Kane and whoever he's in bed with. Making sure they don't hurt anyone. Making sure none of them vanish. Then if the FBI thing turns out to be bogus, I'll close them down.'

'I can get behind that. On one condition.'

'Go on.'

'I'm not going to wait on the sidelines while you do the heavy lifting. We'll do it together.'

'No.'

'Yes. Look at you. Your arm is in a cast.'

'That makes no difference.'

'Of course it does. Listen. Finding Kane? I want to succeed. I have more skin in the game than you, I'm sure. But I'm not too proud to say I stand a better chance if I work with a partner. I'm hoping that as a former military cop you'll respect that. And admit you're in the same boat.'

FOURTEEN

Vidic ran the numbers in his head, over and over. How long to get to the breakfast place. To stand in line. To place the order. For the food to come out. To pay. To drive back. And every time he came up with the same conclusion. Paris was taking far too long.

Every time he reached that conclusion his mind set out in a different direction. First, he got worried. He pictured Paris's Land Rover fishtailing into one of the switchbacks. Rolling. Her neck breaking as she slammed against the windshield, just like Gibson's had. Then he got anxious. He imagined her speeding, or driving erratically. Getting pulled over. Giving herself away somehow and getting arrested. He ran through one possibility after another until he was left with nothing but raw fear. In that final scenario he saw her running, like Bowery must have done. But in Paris's case the consequences were different. They weren't irritating or inconvenient. They were catastrophic. Because she had a copy of the report. She could put it on the market. Undercut his price. Be more convincing when the questions started coming in about how the report had been obtained. And be more credible when it came to establishing its provenance.

A car horn honked outside the cave's entrance. Four times. One long beep. Two short. Another long. Vidic silently thanked God then set down the crate he had been carrying and said loudly, 'That'll be Paris. She'll need help bringing in the food. I'll go.'

Paris was standing at the side of the Land Rover when Vidic reached her. The rear door was open and she was trying to stack four cardboard carry-out boxes into a manageable pile in the footwell.

Vidic said, 'What the hell happened? You were gone so long. Are you OK?'

Paris stepped closer to him and lowered her voice to a whisper. She said, 'I went to the house.'

'Why on earth ... ? What's so important? Fletcher was right. You can get new books. Soon you'll be able to get anything you want.'

'I didn't go for my books. I went for my ledger.'

'You didn't already have it?'

'Obviously not. Or I wouldn't have had to go back for it.'

'I told you to—'

'Ivan. Is this really the time?'

Vidic was silent for a moment, then said, 'So did you get it?'

'No. I didn't go inside. Fletcher was right. But not about replacing stuff. The house is being watched.'

Reacher ordered coffee and a full stack of pancakes with bacon on the side. Knight asked for Earl Grey tea, hot, with milk. The waitress headed for the kitchen and Knight dropped a twenty on the table. She said, 'In case something happens. I don't want to skip out on the bill if we have to leave in a hurry.'

Reacher nodded.

Knight walked Reacher through everything she had done since the FBI passed on her father's case. She had run computer searches on all of Kane's known aliases. Posted BOLOs for him, and the truck and the motorcycle that were registered in his name. Requested an alert on his passport. Set flags for any activity on his credit cards. Initiated traces on his phone numbers and email addresses. None of those actions bore fruit so she broadened her net. Started looking at his known associates. Interviewed the ones who were in jail. And watched the guys who were still on the loose. When four of the five names at the top of that list all suddenly packed up and left town, together, and made for the same location, she figured she'd hit pay dirt. That location was the motel by the highway. Which wasn't promising, in itself. The place felt like a staging point, not a final destination. But she had to believe that Kane was close by. She could see no other reasonable explanation.

Reacher had a shorter story to tell. He began with how he had woken up handcuffed to a table and ended with details of the deal he had struck with Vidic.

Knight drummed her fingers on the table. 'Am I getting this straight? If you're able to move the safe, and if Vidic is able to break into it, and he keeps his word, he's going to tell you where Kane will be at 4:00 a.m. tomorrow? What kind of deal is that?'

'Kane, Fletcher, and Paris. The other surviving member of their crew. That's the deal. Yes. But you're missing the point.'

'So what is the point? The million in cash?'

'No. The point was to make sure that all four of them are still here. I could have put Vidic on ice. Easily. Fletcher too. But what about the others? I had no idea where they were. Or how many I was looking for. By the time I tracked them down at least one was bound to have heard that his buddies were MIA. Maybe both would have. Then they'd have disappeared, too. They're all as nervous as a cat in a room full of rocking chairs. Kane is only still in play because I made that deal.'

Knight leaned back in her chair. She said, 'Fair point. So what's your plan from here?'

Reacher said, 'I told you. And it hasn't changed.'

'So do you—'

The waitress hurried back to their table but instead of a tray of food she was carrying a cordless phone. She said, 'Are you Mr Reacher?'

'Just Reacher.'

'Sorry to interrupt but the guy on the phone described you. He was very insistent that I ask.'

The waitress held out the handset. Reacher took it and she discreetly walked away.

He said, 'Reacher.'

'This is Wallwork.'

'How did you know I was here?'

Knight got out of her seat and moved next to Reacher, close enough to hear both sides of his conversation. He whispered, 'My FBI guy.'

Wallwork said, 'I didn't know, but you weren't picking up in your room. I got the address from the number you left. Googled the place. Saw there was a diner next door. Diners have coffee. It didn't take long to figure out. Anyway, I talked to my friend and she said her nephew has been on vacation in your area recently. She hasn't spoken to him for a while – he does a lot of cave exploration and there's not much signal underground, apparently – but she did mention she's planning to come down there with the extended family for some kind of a reunion. They should arrive by dinnertime. I thought I should let you know because if they recognize you and start talking, you could be detained for quite a while.'

Reacher said, 'Good to know. Thanks. I don't fancy dinner but you could tell your friend there's a breakfast place in the neighbourhood that does interesting specials. I'll call you back with the address. Tell her it's so popular it opens crazy early. Like, at 4:00 a.m. Which is extreme, but the dishes on offer should make it worth the effort.'

Reacher ended the call and set the phone down on the table. Knight remained standing. She said, 'What's with the weird code?'

Reacher said, 'We could talk freely before. I was just reporting a rumour I'd heard. But now we're further down the line. He's worried about increased security. If an agent's cover was blown they'll have to worry about a leak.'

'Did he mean what I think he meant? The dead guy really was an agent?'

Reacher nodded.

'Wow. I wasn't expecting that. From what you told me, I thought Vidic was bullshitting, all day long.'

'I've got to admit, I'm surprised, too.'

'So the cavalry is coming.'

'It is. And that means leaving Kane to the Feds. Are you OK with that?'

Knight shrugged. 'If I get to see him taken away in cuffs, I'll be happy. But if they blow cold again and turn their backs on him I'm not going to stand still and let him get away.'

'That's fair.'

'What about you? The cavalry's not due till this evening. Vidic's coming at 2:00 p.m.'

'So I go with him. Taking care of the safe won't take long.'

'You think he'll stick to the deal? I can see you shoving the safe. Manhandling it around and getting it where he wants it. You'll be tired and out of breath. And he'll have a choice. Give you a million dollars or put a bullet in your head. I'm betting he'd prefer the latter. And you get that he's essentially been profiling you, right? He thinks you're a drifter. Which means no friends. No family. No bills to go unpaid if you disappear. No mail to pile up. No one to raise the alarm if you don't call or email or show up somewhere. To him you're totally disposable. You're the perfect patsy.'

'I get that. But if I'm not here when Vidic shows up he'll split. If he thinks he's getting the money there's a chance he'll give up the address for the others. Then I'll put him on ice. If he tries to double-cross me, I'll make him give up the address. Either way, we get what we need.'

'I don't like it. You'll be too exposed.'

Reacher shrugged. 'Have you got a better idea?'

'No.' Knight was silent for a moment, then broke eye contact. 'Say you're successful with Vidic. What happens to the money from the safe?'

'This isn't about—'

Knight put one hand on Reacher's shoulder and pointed through the window with the other. 'Look. Kane's guys are leaving. They're carrying their bags. They might not be coming back. Come on. Let's see where they go. We might not need Vidic and the safe.'

Reacher shook his head. 'Bad idea. A single car tail on roads like these? They'll make us inside of a mile.'

'I won't get close enough to get made. I don't need to. They have two cars. I hid an AirTag in both of them. That's how I tracked them all the way here.'

'What's an AirTag?'

'What kind of rock do you live under? It's a location device. Originally made for people to stick on keychains and in wallets and luggage in case they got lost. Pet owners attach them to dog collars in case their furry buddies stray. And wives slip them in husbands' pockets for the same reason.'

'What's the range?'

'Pretty much worldwide.'

'OK. We'll see where they go. But first let's take a look in Kane's guys' rooms.'

FIFTEEN

Kane was the first to finish breakfast. He wolfed down his burrito, scrunched up the wrapper, and tossed it on the ground. Fletcher took a little longer to get through his food. Vidic fussed with his pastry and dropped half of it on the floor. Paris stirred her yogurt around for a while and toyed with a couple of chunks of strawberry, then snapped her plastic spoon in two and shoved the pieces into the pot. Vidic got to his feet and started to collect everyone's trash. When he reached Paris he said, 'Get the door for me?'

Kane sneered at him and said, 'Why bother? Leave it. Who cares if rats come in now? Or more rats.'

Vidic glared back. 'Maybe this whole thing with the Feds will be a false alarm. Maybe we'll need this place again. And anyway, don't tell me what to do.'

Paris held the door then Vidic led the way to the back of

his Jeep. She opened the tailgate for him. He dropped the trash onto the load bed floor, checked that no one had followed them outside, and said, 'I've been thinking about the house. Are you sure someone was watching it?'

Paris said, 'Certain. Why?'

Vidic shrugged. 'The timing seems off. It's too soon for the Feds. And I can't see who else it could be.'

'Too soon? How? If they have an agent missing . . .'

'Think about it. Gibson died yesterday. He could only have missed one contact, maximum. There could be all kinds of reasons for going dark like that. The Feds wouldn't send backup immediately. What if Gibson changed his routine because he thought Fletcher was on to him? He could be lying low deliberately. And if Fletcher was already suspicious and then spotted a bunch of strangers running surveillance, that could blow Gibson's cover. There must be some kind of emergency procedure they would go to. Alternative contact arrangements to try. No one would show up, physically, for a couple of days, surely.'

'I guess. Don't ask me. How would I know? All I know is that the house was being watched.'

'How many people were watching it?'

'I didn't see any people.'

'What kind of vehicle were they using? Or was there more than one?'

'I didn't see a vehicle.'

'I don't understand. If you didn't see any people, and you didn't see any vehicles, how can you be certain anyone was watching?'

'I could feel it.'

'Are you serious? That's all you have? A feeling?'

'Don't question me. I know what I felt. Someone was watching. It's a fact.'

Vidic couldn't keep a smile from spreading across his face. 'If you say so.'

'Don't laugh at me. This is serious. What if they do more than watch? What if they break in? Find the ledger?'

'The ledger's hidden, right?'

'Right.'

'And you wrote it in code.'

'I did.'

'So if somebody broke in, they wouldn't find it. And even if they did find it, they couldn't read it.'

'I guess. And by the end of the afternoon Fletcher's going to burn the place down, right? So I'm probably worrying over nothing.'

Vidic looked away. The house was going to burn. That was for sure. Only the fire wasn't going to be set by Fletcher. He said, 'You are worrying over nothing. And there's something more important than the ledger, anyway. The phosphorus. Did you get it?'

Paris covered her mouth with her hand. 'Oh my God. I totally forgot. I did get it. Yes. But I left it at the house, too.'

'Whereabouts?'

'In its container. It's full of water. I checked. But the container is glass so I left the thing in its crate full of sand to make sure it didn't break.'

'Where's the crate?'

'In the closet in my bathroom. Under a bunch of towels.'

Vidic smiled. 'Excellent. Then we have no problem at all. Trust me. By the end of the afternoon we'll be free and clear.

And we won't be leaving empty-handed. We're taking Fletcher's two mil.'

Knight finessed a passkey from the guy who had replaced Mary behind the motel reception counter, then set off toward the door to room 18.

Reacher caught up and easily kept pace beside her. He said, 'These guys are Kane's known associates, right? So you must have pulled their jackets.'

Knight nodded. 'All four are ex-military. Infantry. Dishonourably discharged.'

'Together?'

'Two were. The other two, separately.'

'And they haven't learned the error of their ways?'

'They have not. They've become what I call *secondary players*. They don't initiate anything. Their speciality is providing muscle or backup for anyone who needs it. And can pay for it. Typically they get involved in raids on high-value targets, kidnapping, extortion. Things like that.'

'Is Kane ex-military?'

'No. He crossed paths with one of the guys in jail. Kept in touch on the outside. Then the one introduced Kane to the others. They worked together a half-dozen times, we think, but nothing could ever be proved.'

They stopped talking when they were ten feet from the room. Reacher checked the parking lot and the surrounding area. No one was watching. No one was sitting in any of the nearby vehicles, so he stepped to the handle-side of the door. He took the Glock from his waistband and nodded to Knight. She held the key card to the lock, pressed down on the handle, pushed the door, and spun away to the

101

opposite side. They waited. No shots were fired. No one emerged. No one shouted a challenge. Reacher stepped inside. The Glock was raised in his left hand. He checked that the room was unoccupied, then moved on to the bathroom.

A moment later Reacher called, 'Clear.'

Knight joined him and took her time to look around. The décor was just like Reacher's room, but this one had a pair of queen beds in place of a king. She said, 'There's nothing left behind. Not even any trash. The place hardly looks used. The beds are even made.'

'Old habits,' Reacher said, then handed her a towel he had picked up in the bathroom. 'In more ways than one.'

Knight saw it had a row of black stains across the centre. She sniffed it and immediately her nose wrinkled. 'Hoppe's No. 9. They spent their evening cleaning their weapons, and now they're backing Kane's play. Great.'

'Want to stand down? Leave this to the Feds?'

'Hell no. We'll just need to take extra care.'

Their search of room 19 yielded no further information so Knight led the way to the parking lot. She stopped next to a silver sedan. A Toyota Avalon, several generations past current. It was in a space at the end of the front row. She had chosen a good location, Reacher thought. The spot gave her a good view of the motel as well as a clear shot for both of the exits to the highway. He was less sure about the vehicle. It looked ancient. There was a dent in pretty much every body panel. The wheels were all scuffed around the rims. Part of the lip beneath the radiator grille was hanging loose. And there was a foot-long gash in the back of the rear seat like a knife fight had recently broken out in there.

Knight caught the way Reacher was looking at her car. She said, 'Meet Trevor. He might not be pretty, but he'll run forever.'

Reacher said, 'Looks like he already has.'

Knight unlocked the doors with her key because the remote wasn't working, then opened the trunk. There were four plastic tubs inside, with lids. She moved one aside. It was labelled *Plastic Cuffs*. A metal lockbox was behind it, bolted to the frame of the car. She said, 'Feel free to use it.' Reacher handed her the Sig. She squared it away. He fished the bullets he'd taken from her in his room and handed them back. She dropped them into her purse, slammed the trunk lid, and moved around to the driver's door. Reacher climbed in on the passenger's side. He was pleasantly surprised by how much space he had. Knight fired up the engine then slotted her phone into a holder that was hooked onto an air vent. She fiddled with its screen for a moment and a map appeared with two dots superimposed on it. They were close together over a road and moving steadily toward the top of the screen.

'There they are.' Knight shifted into Drive and eased the car forward. 'Let's see where they go.'

Reacher settled back in his seat. He wondered what the odds of the car's ancient radio being able to pick up a good blues channel were. Not great, he figured. Which was a shame. He could have used a little John Primer or Junior Wells right around then.

SIXTEEN

Knight was silent for the first half mile, then said, 'There's something I don't understand. I get that you were in an accident. Gibson was driving. And he got killed. But how did you wind up in his car in the first place?'

Reacher said, 'I can't be sure. It's one of the things I don't remember. According to Vidic it came from some random encounter. He says he saw me help Gibson out of a bind with some assholes who were trying to steal his car. Apparently he gave me a ride as a thank you.'

'OK. Back up. First, why did you accept a ride with the guy? Had your car broken down or something?'

'I don't have a car.'

'You don't? So how do you get around?'

'I take the bus. Or I hitch rides. Although that's getting harder these days.'

'You were an army major and now you have to hitch rides? What happened? If that's not too personal.'

'It's fine. And I don't have to hitch rides. I choose to.'

'You choose to? Why?'

'Because I don't want to stay in one place and I don't want to own a car.'

'Weird, but OK. You do know how to drive though, right?'

'I did the training, back in the day.'

'All right. It sounds like maybe you wanted a ride. But why would Gibson offer you one? I get that you did him a favour, but I can't see an agent doing that.'

'It seems odd to me, too.'

'How long had Gibson been working this case?'

'I don't have a date. Why?'

'Maybe he was undercover too long. He could have been getting sloppy. Or maybe he knew that Vidic had seen what happened with the assholes in the parking lot. Felt like it would look wrong if he didn't do something for you in return for helping him.'

'Possible, I guess.'

'Or maybe he was going off the rails. Trying to deliberately screw up so he'd get pulled out. He could have just asked, of course, but a lot of people don't like to admit defeat. Specially men.'

'We'll never know, unless some other witness comes out of the woodwork. Or my memory comes back.' Reacher closed his eyes, but it didn't help. He still felt like he was staring into a darkened room when he tried to remember the wreck.

Knight's driving was smooth and efficient. Fast on the straights, easy through the bends, no grumbling from the transmission or squealing from the tyres. The morning sun was softening the faded blacktop with the shadows of leaves and branches and the gentle breeze was making them sway and dance. Reacher settled back in his seat. He was enjoying the view and playing a little music in his head. Then he noticed that an arrow had appeared on the phone screen. It was below the two dots, but getting closer. Knight pointed to it and said, 'That's us. We'll—'

The turn into the first of the switchbacks near where Gibson had crashed was tighter than Knight had expected. The back of the car twitched. Reacher closed his eyes. Knight lifted off the gas and corrected her line with a neat flick of the steering wheel. Then she said, 'I'm so sorry. I should have seen that coming. I didn't cause some kind of flashback, did I?'

Reacher opened his eyes. He felt like the first shaft of light had penetrated the darkness. He said, 'Don't apologize. That made me remember something. Just a fragment. When Gibson approached that bend he looked in his mirror. He said something like, *How did he catch up so quick?* Then he hit the gas. Too hard, I guess.'

'Reacher, that's great. Anything else?'

Reacher closed his eyes for another moment. 'No. Nothing more yet.'

'It will come. This is just the beginning. I have faith. Meantime, who do you think Gibson saw in his mirror? Vidic?'

'Seems likely. Vidic was at the crash scene. We know that. He says he was following Gibson and saw what happened. There's no reason to think he's lying.'

'OK. Then why did Gibson try to lose Vidic? What scared him so badly he wound up wrecking his car and killing himself?'

'Some of Vidic's story is true. Maybe all of it is. Perhaps he did see Gibson meet his handler at the motel. Maybe Gibson knew that. He could have been desperate to get to Fletcher first. To lay down some kind of pre-emptive defence.'

'What kind of defence, though? It would be an if-you're-explaining-you're-losing situation, all day long. Not convincing. Not worth dying for. It had to be more urgent. Maybe he thought Vidic was going to kill him. Shoot him. Or run him off the road. He might have been trying to escape.'

'Possible. Gibson's Lincoln was black, and I saw flakes of black paint on the bull bar on Vidic's Jeep.'

'Could be something.'

'Could be nothing.'

'The FBI evidence guys will get samples. Their lab will figure it out.'

Soon after Fletcher got his operation up and running at the cave he arranged to have a porta potty installed, just out of sight of the entrance. Everyone in the crew used it – reluctantly, in the warm weather – except Kane. He preferred to go behind one of the heaps of rocks. And not all the way behind if Paris was nearby. She knew what he was thinking when he smirked at her, slid a crate into the back of the van, and continued out into the fresh air. She hurried away from the entrance, deeper into the cave. Then she saw Fletcher heading outside, too, with his phone in his hand.

Paris grabbed Vidic by the arm and pulled him close. She said, 'Quick. We only have a minute. What do you mean we're taking Fletcher's two million? Are you crazy?'

Vidic glanced toward the entrance. 'I have it all figured out. It's perfect. The cash will buy us time. Take the pressure off selling the report if there's any problem getting the gold lined up. The alternative is to take something from the Russians, and I don't want to do that. I don't want those mad vindictive bastards on our asses for the rest of our lives. It's better if they think Fletcher and Kane were the only ones involved.'

'Right. But how? We can't move the safe. And Kane's not going to do it for us.'

'The stranger's going to. He's big enough. I hope.'

'How will you get him here? What's in it for him?'

'He's on some kind of crazy revenge kick. I promised that if he helps me with the safe, I'll give up Fletcher and Kane in return.'

'All he wants is Fletcher and Kane? He doesn't want any money?'

'Well, yes. He thinks he's getting half. But that's not going to happen.'

'How—'

'Go. Quick. Kane's coming back.'

Knight went easier on the gas after the scare at the switchback. The arrow on the phone screen slowed so that it only just kept pace with the two dots. Knight made no further attempt to draw attention to it. She glanced across at Reacher a couple of times, then said, 'No more recollections?'

Reacher shook his head.

'You can't rush these things, I guess. How about your long-term memory?'

'It's fine.'

'Good. So, like, for example, you could tell me your address?'

'Actually, no.'

'Oh. That's not so good.'

'It's not a problem. I don't have an address.'

'You must have an address. Everybody has one.'

'Not me.'

'How come? Are you in the middle of moving? Lease ran out, haven't found a suitable alternative?'

'I don't rent a place.'

'So you sold your old house and haven't moved into the new one yet?'

'I didn't have a house to sell.'

'Then what happened? Was it the market crash in '08? Interest rates going up? That crazy inflation we had after COVID? Sorry. I don't mean to be intrusive. But I'm a detective. It comes with the territory.'

'No problem.'

'So . . .'

'I did have a house, once. Briefly. But I got rid of it.'

'Why?'

'It confirmed something I had suspected for a while. You don't own a house. A house owns you.'

'That's ridiculous.'

'Is it? Where do you live?'

'Scottsdale, Arizona. Nice little condo. It's on the thirteenth floor, so I got it cheap.'

'Have you been there long?'

'Ten years, give or take.'

'Ever fancied a change?'

'I've thought about it.'

'What stopped you?'

'I see where you're going. Getting it ready for the market. Finding an agent. Viewings. Negotiating. Finding a new place.

It's a lot. But at the end of the day a person needs a place to call home.'

'Not me. I spent thirteen years going where the army told me. Now I go wherever I want. Whenever I want.'

'I get that. I think. But what about your stuff? Where do you keep it?'

'In my pocket.'

'I'm serious. Your clothes, for example. Shoes. Your TV. Books.'

'I'm wearing my clothes. And my shoes. I don't often watch TV. And when I finish a book, if it was any good, I leave it on a bus or in a motel room so someone else can read it.'

'Wait. Rewind. You must have more than one set of clothes.'

'Why?'

'How do you wash them? What do you wear while they're in the laundry?'

'I don't wash them. I wear them for a couple of days, then get new ones.'

'That's crazy.'

'Is it? Because I'd say owning a building and buying a machine and hooking up electricity and water and paying taxes and getting insurance and being tied to one place? That's crazy.'

Knight pointed to her phone. 'Look.' One of the dots had stopped. The other was still going. 'Is that its destination, I wonder? Let's see if it moves again.'

Reacher pointed to a driveway they were about to pass. 'That's where they took me after the accident.'

Knight slowed down. The driveway was empty and there were no vehicles parked on the road. She said, 'No one there, I guess. Let's continue. Stick with Kane's guys.'

*

110

Reacher kept an eye on Knight's phone and when they were close to the stationary dot he tipped his seat back as far as it would go and hunkered down.

Knight continued, smooth and steady. A minute later she said, 'We're clear.'

Reacher raised the seat. 'What did you see?'

'The car was positioned with a good view of the front of a house. A large place. Fancy. Half-timbered, like it was trying to look European. Only the driver was visible.'

'They're running surveillance. The passenger will be watching the rear.'

'That would be my guess, too.'

'Vidic said Fletcher wanted the extra muscle because he was worried that Bowery sold him out. The missing guy. This must be the target. They're thorough. The job's scheduled for 4:00 a.m. Could you find out who owns the place?'

'Possibly. I'd have to call in a favour or two, given that I'm persona non grata right now. It would take a while. And assuming something fishy is going on, I doubt we'd learn much. Just the name of some shell corporation out of the Cayman Islands or somewhere. That would be my bet.'

'The waitress at the diner told me a couple of these places got bought by Russians, in early twenty-one. What are the odds this is one of them?'

Knight pulled over to the side of the road. She pointed to her phone. 'The other car has stopped, too.' She did something to the screen that caused the map to zoom in. The outline of a building appeared next to the stationary dot.

'Is that shape accurate?'

'Pretty much. I think.'

'It's another house. Another surveillance job?'

'Let's find out.'

Reacher tipped his seat back again when they were near the second car and straightened up when Knight gave him the all-clear.

She said, 'Carbon copy. They're watching both places. No doubt about it. The question is, why? Are they going to hit both? Or is it an either-or situation? Maybe they'll make a late decision depending on what the watchers report?'

Reacher said, 'Or maybe it's neither. Fletcher wanted to avoid getting hit. I assumed that meant he wanted backup at the target location. Which works if the origin of the threat is unknown. But what if the Russians, the owners of these properties, are connected? Offence is the best defence. These guys' job could be to make sure they don't make it to the target at all.'

'How can we confirm that?'

'There's no point hanging around, watching the watchers. They won't give anything away. And it's not like Fletcher or Kane will show up and talk to them. Anything develops, they'll call them on the phone.'

'So what do we do?'

'Go back to Fletcher's house. He had a bad day yesterday. Maybe he didn't square everything away properly.'

'How will we get in? If they figure out someone's been messing with the locks, they'll run, for sure.'

'Not a problem.' Reacher pulled a set of keys out of his pocket. 'We can use these. They're Fletcher's. He lost them.'

'Lost them?'

Reacher shrugged.

Knight said, 'He must know they're missing. What if they changed the locks?'

'Then we think of something else. But for that to happen Fletcher would have to admit to his people how badly he screwed up. Does that sound like the way a boss would behave?'

SEVENTEEN

There were still no vehicles parked outside the house. Knight pulled into the wide gravel driveway and turned the car around so that it was facing the exit. Reacher took a moment to study the windows. He was looking for telltale silhouettes, or anything that was moving. He saw nothing that worried him so he approached the door. Fletcher's keys still worked the lock. He stepped into the octagonal hallway. Knight followed him. She moved to the bottom of the staircase and turned around 360 degrees.

Knight said, 'What a place. You don't see it and think about settling down? Just for a second? Imagine living somewhere like this.'

Reacher said, 'I'd rather sleep in a ditch.'

'Suit yourself. Start upstairs?'

'No. In here.'

Reacher led the way to the small room with the security camera setup. The computer monitor was back to showing twelve live images. Knight's Toyota was clearly visible at the top left. Reacher took hold of the mouse and managed to move the pointer, but he struggled to click in the right place. He was working left-handed and his fingers were too big for the buttons.

Knight elbowed him in the ribs. 'Move. Let me do it.' She used the mouse to select the driveway view and the password box popped up. She said, 'Problem.'

Reacher closed his eyes. His vision had still been blurred when he'd watched Vidic use the system, and his head had been hurting. He set those echoes aside and tried to focus. He concentrated on the keys Vidic had pressed. Remembered there were sixteen. Worked on recalling them, one by one. He said, 'Not a problem,' and recited four letters. Knight tapped on the keyboard. He gave her eight numbers. And four more letters. Then the screen filled with tiny pictures.

Knight said, 'Now what?'

'You can do something with the mouse. A trash can will appear. Put the most recent record in it.'

Knight figured it out, then Reacher told her how to put the camera into privacy mode. She selected a sixty-minute window. 'Long enough?'

Reacher nodded, then said, 'Now do that for all the other cameras. They record inside the house as well when no one is home.'

Knight started pointing and clicking with the mouse. She said, 'No problem.' Then, 'Wait. Look at this.'

She had worked through the views of the front and rear of the house and now another exterior image was filling the screen. It was coming from a camera mounted somewhere high up, looking down. It showed the roof of a panel van. It was parked on a rough, stony surface. It was facing away from the lens and its rear doors were open. A man appeared behind it. He was carrying a box the size of a tea chest. Even from above it was clear he was huge. His head was like a boulder. His shoulders were like a bull's. He slid the box into the van, turned, and disappeared from the shot.

She said, 'Holy hell. That was Kane. They must have some kind of storage facility. He's clearing it out.'

Reacher said, 'Looks like Vidic isn't the only one planning to go AWOL. Can you tell where the storage place is?'

Knight slid the mouse around for a couple of seconds, then said, 'No. There's no location info. Just time. Date. And temperature. Which is weird. Why would anyone want to know that?'

They watched Kane dump another couple of boxes into the van, then Knight switched the view to one of the inside cameras. She said, 'We should take some time with this thing. It could be a gold mine. These archived files – we can see who's been here. When. Who with. What they brought. What they took.'

'You do that. I'm going upstairs. Take a look around. We'll rendezvous down here when we're done. Share what we find.'

Reacher started on the second floor. There were four doors leading off the left-hand branch of the landing, and four leading off from the right. He figured they would all have been bedrooms, originally. The ones at the front of the house were larger. They had more closet space, too, and bigger bathrooms. A quick triage suggested that four were definitely in use. Two could be, or might have been recently abandoned. One looked like it was mothballed. And the last – the smallest – had become a storeroom. It was full of luggage and boxes and crates and other random junk.

Paris's room was easy to identify. It was the only one with women's clothes and toiletries in it. A fluffy robe was hanging on the back of the door. The walls were painted pale blue. The bed was made. There was a half-full glass of water on the nightstand. A phone charger, but no phone. A wooden table under the window that was clearly being used as a desk. It was old with spindly legs and leaves that extended on either side to provide extra workspace. There was a charging cable but no computer. A stack of paperbacks. A mug full of pens. A notebook with a turquoise cover. It was spiral-bound. About half the pages were missing and the ones that were left were blank. There were more books on a shelf against the far wall. Reacher scanned the titles. He saw textbooks covering painting. Sculpture. Jewellery. Furniture. Cars. Watches. Precious metals.

Reacher moved across to an old-fashioned wardrobe and looked inside. Dresses and blouses were hanging from a rail. Sweaters and hoodies were piled up on a shelf. Underwear was neatly folded in a set of built-in drawers. Throughout the room the floor was made from hardwood. It looked like it hadn't seen any polish for a good few years, but it still had a rich patina. The developer had used quality materials. That was clear. He must have been serious about seducing the disaffected city folk. Although Paris wasn't fully on board with that particular choice, Reacher thought. She had covered most of the centre of the room with a rug. A thick, heavy, multicoloured thing covered with garish abstract patterns. Reacher noticed a pair of slippers tucked against the side of the bed. A pair of hiking socks was lying next to them. Reacher figured Paris didn't like to feel the cold wood on her feet at night.

Paris's bathroom was functional with a few touches of

luxury. She had an electric toothbrush. Dental floss. Plastic pots and tubes with all kinds of liquids and gels in them. Another robe. More towels than Reacher thought one person could possibly need. A line of glass bottles along the side of the tub, full of different sizes and colours of grains and crystals. There was another glass container shaped like an hourglass with an open end. Thick, viscous liquid was pooled at the bottom and a half-dozen skinny wooden sticks were poking out of the top. It was giving off a faint smell of lavender. A medicine cabinet was set into the wall above the sink and there was a closet full of spare towels and backup cosmetics. It was less well organized than the rest of the room. Some of the towels had been dumped on a coarse wooden crate. Reacher moved them and lifted the lid. The crate was full of sand. He started to dig with his fingers, carefully. He came across something hard. And cold. It was glass. Full of clear liquid. More of the perfumed oil, Reacher guessed. Ordinarily he would have pulled it out and opened it, to be sure, but he figured there was too much chance of dropping it or spilling a bunch of sand, as he only had his left hand to work with.

Reacher had searched many people's rooms over the years. It wasn't something he had ever come to enjoy. He always felt awkward and uncomfortable, like a trespasser, but he knew it had to be done. Sometimes the rooms belonged to people who were suspected of a crime, and evidence was needed to confirm or deny their guilt. Sometimes the room's owner had fled, and clues were needed to help track them down. Reacher felt like Paris's room was the second kind. Because of her things. No entire category was missing. But in each place he looked he saw gaps. Empty hangers in the wardrobe. Half-full drawers. Spaces on the bookshelves. It felt like someone had grabbed up the bare minimum and wasn't expecting to come back for the rest.

Reacher checked the time in his head. He knew that if they found nothing definitive he would have to be back at the motel before Vidic or he could forget about keeping the gang intact for the FBI to scoop up. He ran through the top hiding spots he had encountered in his years as an MP. The seams of the curtains. The folds of the towels on the rail. Behind the frame of the bathroom mirror. Beneath the lips of the windowsills. He tried the obvious ones as well. Under the mattress. In the underwear drawer. On top of the doorframe. He came up with nothing. But when he turned for a last look before closing the door behind him, he was left with a feeling he was missing something.

The other bedrooms belonged to men. Reacher identified the owners of three of them by the size of the clothes he found in the closets. Fletcher's were tall and slim. Vidic's, almost as tall but broader. Kane's, enormous in every direction. Too big even for Reacher. Then he found two sets he couldn't place. The first was in a room that looked like it had recently been slept in, so he guessed it was Gibson's. The next was in a room that felt like it hadn't been occupied for a few days, so Reacher guessed they belonged to Bowery, the guy who Vidic said had just disappeared. The last room felt like no one had lived in it for some time. It reminded Reacher of rooms he'd visited that belonged to dead people. The kind of places that relatives or friends couldn't bear to clear out after someone was taken early by illness or accident. Vidic had mentioned a guy who died, O'Connell, so Reacher guessed the room had been his.

Reacher checked each room as thoroughly as time allowed. They all shared a weirdly disjointed sense that

Reacher chalked up to the contrast between the opulent architecture and the sparse, meagre possessions. Vidic's room in particular seemed very lightly stocked. But aside from that, Reacher could find nothing useful. Nothing incriminating. No clue as to what the target for the upcoming job could be.

Fletcher locked the panel van's back doors and joined the others out in the open. They were standing in a loose circle. Kane inched closer to Paris. Paris shuffled toward Vidic. Vidic looked lost in thought.

Fletcher looked at each person in turn, then said, 'Somebody told me something once. I can't remember who it was, but I guess that doesn't matter. They said it's impossible to do a thing, knowing it's for the last time, and not feel sad. I thought they were talking crap at the time, but you know what? I think it's true. Look at us. We haven't always seen eye to eye. We've lost people along the way. But we've had more successes than failures. How many jobs has it been?'

Paris said, 'Seventy-four. This'll be seventy-five.'

'And seventy-six. And seventy-seven. Our last jobs together. And you know what? I feel genuinely emotional. It's the end of an era. We had a good run. We made money. We kicked ass. So let's be careful today. Take care of business. Meet back here. Split the cash from the safe. Go our separate ways.' He nodded toward the van. 'Then the only time you'll hear from me again is when everything in there is sold and I need to send you your checks. Or your crypto. Or whatever else you want. OK. Any questions?'

Vidic looked up. He said, 'I know we'll only be gone a few

hours, but am I the only one who's not comfortable leaving the van here, out in the open, all packed up?'

'What's the problem? Who's going to steal it?'

'Said everyone who's ever gotten anything stolen. Sorry. It just seems like asking for trouble. Especially when there's an easy solution.'

'Such as?'

'One of us stays here.'

'Who?'

'Paris.'

Paris said, 'No way. You patronizing asshole. I set up this job. I'm just as capable—'

Kane started talking over her. 'Like hell. We get back here. She's gone. With the van. You act all outraged. Then you lovebirds meet up later. Grow fat and happy together after you've sold all our stuff. Forget about it.'

Vidic held up his hands like he was surrendering. 'Guys. Please. Take a breath. One, we're not lovebirds. Look at Paris. She would happily strangle me right now. Two, Paris, of course you're totally capable. But when you planned this job we were expecting another delivery. That hasn't arrived. There's less stuff to carry. So we can get by with fewer people. You staying here to guard the van is a better use of resources. That's just a fact. And three, Kane, the van's locked. You take the keys. Or Fletcher can take them. Then there's no way Paris can drive it anywhere. All she can do is protect it. Which benefits all of us. Right?'

Kane and Paris and Vidic exchanged sullen glances but no one spoke for a long minute. Then Fletcher said, 'It makes sense. Paris, you stay. Kane, Vidic, get ready. We go in fifteen.'

EIGHTEEN

Reacher heard Knight calling his name. She was on the ground floor. Reacher put his hand on the Glock in his waistband and took the stairs, two at a time, as quietly as possible. He paused in the hallway and heard her voice again. She said, 'Reacher? In the kitchen.'

Reacher found her standing next to an open door. It was about fifteen feet further into the room than the door Reacher had come through after his encounter with Fletcher. Reacher moved up next to her and looked inside. It was a walk-in refrigerator. There were plastic containers of beef and chicken. Wooden crates of carrots and green beans. And on the floor, with pale skin and blank eyes and one ear resting on his shoulder, was a man's body.

Knight said, 'Is it Gibson?'

Reacher said, 'It must be. We know they brought him here. And there's another shirt just like the one he's wearing in a closet, upstairs.'

'You don't recognize him? You were with him when he died.'

Reacher crouched down and took a closer look at Gibson's face. His hands. His clothes. His shoes. There were a few things that were unnatural. The angle of his neck. The pallor of his skin. The utter, unworldly stillness that only settles on the dead. But as far as his features went, he appeared totally normal. Anonymous, even. There was nothing remarkable about his nose. His eyes. His mouth. His fingers. Reacher took it all in. He willed himself to remember something about the guy. Anything. His manner. His voice. Whether they had talked during the drive from the motel. Whether he had seemed confident. Happy. Scared. But nothing came. Reacher stood up and a question popped into his head. What if he hadn't stopped the car thieves from stealing Gibson's Lincoln? Would the guy still be alive? He pushed the thought away and turned to Knight. 'It's like I never saw him before.'

Knight took Reacher's place by the body. 'Don't worry. I'm sure it'll come back.' She pulled out her phone, experimented for a moment until she found the best angle, and took two pictures of Gibson's face. Then she stood up and took a bunch more shots to show his full body and the place where it had been dumped.

Knight moved to the regular refrigerator and took out a pack of butter. She said, 'Have you seen any paper in the house?'

Reacher said, 'On its way.' He made his way back to Paris's room and took the spiral notebook from her desk. He took a pen, as well, just in case. And as he closed the door he again picked up the feeling that he was missing something.

Reacher handed the notebook to Knight. She opened it and set it down on Gibson's chest. Then she took the butter,

123

smeared some on Gibson's thumb and each finger on his right hand, and pressed a greasy version of his prints onto the first page.

Knight stood and caught the look on Reacher's face. She said, 'I know. You're horrified. You think I've contaminated the crime scene. Which in a way I have. But we're not going to be here all the time until the Feds show up. Anything could happen in the meantime. Fletcher could move the body. Kane could do God knows what to it. The house could burn down. And we want the Feds to be able—'

Reacher said, 'Stop. Come with me.'

Reacher led the way back to Paris's bedroom. He took the notebook from Knight, tore out the page with Gibson's prints, and put it back in its place on the table. He returned the pen to its mug. Continued to the bathroom. Opened the closet. Moved the tangle of towels out of the way, and lifted the lid off the crate.

Knight said, 'Sand? What the . . . ? What kind of bathroom product needs that kind of protection?'

Reacher said, 'Like I'm an expert on bathroom products. Pass me the trash can?'

Knight grabbed it from next to the toilet, then realized what Reacher wanted it for. She said, 'Move aside. I'll do it.' She knelt down and started scooping out the sand and dumping it into the trash can. She moved carefully, beginning in the centre, and working her way around in a circle. She soon came to the glass object Reacher had found earlier. She exposed more of it. Kept digging. Got down another three inches. Four. Then she stopped. Something silver-coloured was nestling in the liquid at the bottom of the vial. It was bright. Shiny. Metallic.

Reacher said, 'The house is going to burn down. That's for sure. Only it won't be any kind of an accident.'

'That metal is phosphorus. They must figure if it makes the fire hot enough it'll destroy Gibson's DNA. Prevent the Feds from identifying him.'

'Is that possible? I didn't work much with DNA.'

Knight nodded. 'Sufficient heat can make it impossible to recover usable DNA. Obviously the fingerprints will be gone long before that. So will the teeth. It should be possible to tell that there are human remains in the heap of ash, but that'll be about it.'

Knight picked up the trash can and started to pour the sand back into the crate. She worked it all the way around the vial, packed it tight, then smoothed it down at the top. She said, 'Can you fix the lid on properly? Make it secure?'

Reacher said, 'It was loose to start with. That's how we should leave it.'

'Is that safe? I don't want the damn stuff falling out in my car.'

'Jenny, we can't take it.'

'We have to. We can't let them destroy an agent's body.'

'We have no choice. Think about it. They can come back and burn the house down with the phosphorus. Or they can come back, find the phosphorus is missing, and do what? Run. And probably burn the place down anyway, hoping the fire will still get hot enough. Either way, the body is destroyed. But there's only one way the assholes don't escape.'

Knight was silent for a moment. Then she said, 'I guess you're right. Damn it. I hate to think of the family. No body to bury. No chance to properly say goodbye.'

Reacher said nothing. He figured it was how you treat a

person while they're alive that counts, and he couldn't quite banish the thought that he had made Gibson's accident possible, even if he had been trying to help the guy.

Knight said, 'Could we switch the phosphorus for something else? Something that looks the same, but is harmless in a fire?'

'Like what?'

'I don't know. Could we sabotage it? Fix it so it doesn't burn? Or at least, not so hot?'

'Do I look like a chemist?'

'Damn. You're right. OK. So let's finish this search. Maybe we can find something that will help us catch them before they can set the fire.'

'Any rooms left to check downstairs?'

'Just one.'

Knight left Paris's room and made for the stairs. Reacher got as far as the doorway then stopped and called her back.

She said, 'What? Come on. We're wasting time.'

Reacher said, 'There's something else wrong here. I could feel it before but I've only just figured out what it is. Look at the rug.'

Knight came back as far as the threshold. She said, 'The colours are awful. The pattern is gross. The woman obviously has no taste. But I don't see any other major problem.'

'Look at where it is.'

'On the floor? That's where rugs are supposed to be.'

'It's off centre. People only put a rug off centre if there's a reason. Like they want it close enough to the bed that they don't have to step on the cold floor with bare feet when they get up. But this one isn't close to the bed. And look where it is in relation to the desk. And how thick it is. You pull the

126

chair out far enough to sit on and the back legs will snag on the rug, every time. It would drive you crazy.'

'Maybe she just has a weird sense of the aesthetic.'

'Maybe. But let's make sure.'

Reacher went back into the room and rolled up the rug. He pushed it to one side and systematically examined the entire space it had been covering. Left to right, near to far. He saw nothing problematic. Then he got on his knees. He bent down and tipped his head to the side so that he was looking parallel with the floor. Nothing seemed out of place. He focused on each board. Each joint. And spotted something. A piece of black hair, about an inch long. It was sticking up between a regular-sized board and a shorter section, almost level with the nearest table leg. He moved closer and tugged at the hair. It was stuck fast. He bent down again and checked the join. The gap on one side was wider. Not by much. A fraction of an inch. But there was a difference. Reacher could see it. He worked his thumbnail into the crack. Pressed against the small board. Levered it upward. Felt the wood shift. Just a little. He levered it again. It moved a tiny bit more. A sixteenth of an inch. Then an eighth. A quarter. Enough for Reacher to grip on to. He pulled and twisted. The board raised up further, then came free. Knight had crowded in close and was ready with the flashlight on her phone. She shone it into the space Reacher had revealed. It was maybe a foot deep and spanned the whole width between the floor joists. It was a great hiding place. Plenty could be concealed in there. But Reacher could only see one thing. A notebook. He took it out, stood next to Knight, and opened it.

The first page was blank. Reacher turned it over and saw that the second and third pages had been combined. They had been divided into columns. There were nine. The first was relatively narrow. It looked like it contained a list of dates. The fifth was the same. The entries in the ninth all included @ signs, so must have been email addresses. And the other columns all contained groups of three digits, all separated by commas. There were twenty rows, plus twenty more on pages four and five, twenty more on pages six and seven, and fourteen on pages eight and nine. The next pages were blank. Reacher flicked through all the way to the end and only found one other set of entries. They were on the final pair of facing pages, and were written the other way up. Reacher turned the book around. If there were multiple sets of pages, they would work back to the centre from the opposite end, but only one pair of pages was used. They were divided into eight columns. Not nine, this time. Three looked like dates. One, email addresses. And the rest, more groups of three digits. The entries at this end seemed to be newer. The ink was darker, and there were only two rows.

Reacher handed the notebook to Knight. He said, 'Can you take pictures with your phone?'

She said, 'Sure. All the pages? Or just a sample?'

'All of them.'

Knight worked through, page by page. She checked the images were legible then passed the notebook back to Reacher. She said, 'What does it mean? Any idea?'

'It's a book code. Each group of digits represents a word. The first digit tells you the page number. The second, the line. The third, the word itself.'

'How do you know which book to look in?'

'You don't. Not unless the person who did the encryption tells you. That's why it's so simple, yet so hard to crack. Even if you find out the title of the book you still need to know which edition, and whether it's the hardcover or paperback.'

'So we can't read it?'

'Not immediately.' Reacher pointed to the books on the desk and the shelf. 'My guess is one of these will be the key.'

'I'll get pictures. We can identify the right one and order it online.'

Reacher said, 'Or we could go to a bookstore.'

NINETEEN

Reacher put the notebook back in its spot in the space beneath the floor. He replaced the piece of board, including the hair in case Paris was practising old-school field craft to reveal if her cache had been discovered, then rolled out the rug and followed Knight downstairs. He found her in what he guessed was originally the dining room. It was a large, rectangular space with a long table in the centre, panels on the walls, and a bay window. The drapes were closed and a projection screen was hanging down in front of them. A projector was fixed to the ceiling at the opposite end of the room. There was a rose in the centre of the ceiling. Reacher imagined it was designed for an elaborate chandelier but now a low profile LED light was wired into it. Anything hanging lower would get in the way of whatever was being beamed onto the screen.

Knight was sitting at the head of the table. There was a

laptop computer in front of her. It was plugged into a power supply and another cable snaked away and disappeared through a grommet at the centre of the tabletop. The computer's screen was filled with a picture of a yacht under full sail. A box had popped up across its spinnaker with a message stating that either a password or a Touch ID was required to proceed.

Knight sighed. 'Any ideas?'

Reacher said, 'How about the password from the security system?'

'First thing I tried. No luck.'

'Whose computer is it?' Reacher had a pretty good track record at guessing passwords and PIN numbers. He had a technique. But to make it work he needed to understand the individual who had chosen them. To know their tastes and priorities and habits and hobbies. Without that kind of detail he'd be shooting in the dark.

'It's wired up to the projector so it's probably shared. Anyone who wants to present anything probably loads up whatever files they need. It's not networked so they'd need to use a thumb drive. So either they're behind the curve, technology-wise, or they've gone full *Battlestar Galactica*.'

'Meaning what?'

'It was a TV show. Sci-fi. Bad things happened because of connecting computers together. Anyway, the details don't matter. I just mean either they're out-of-date or they're paranoid about security. Probably paranoid, because this computer is actually pretty new.'

Reacher said, 'We don't need to project anything, so why would we care?'

Knight said, 'Think about what kind of things Fletcher or

131

Vidic or whoever would want to present. Probably not vacation photos, right? I'm guessing they use it for briefings. Probably about forthcoming jobs.'

'Makes sense.'

'If I'm right, there's a good chance they load their presentation files onto the computer itself, rather than run them off the thumb drive. Now, they might delete them afterward. But they might not. There could be all kinds of details in here. That's why we need the damn password.'

'It says password or Touch ID. What's that?'

'Just a fingerprint, basically. The on/off key has a sensor in it. If you have clearance you touch the key, and boom, the computer unlocks.'

'Which of them has clearance?'

'No way to tell.'

'If you don't have clearance, does it do any harm to try?'

'No. The system would just refuse to unlock.'

'Do you have to be alive to try?'

Knight unplugged the computer and carried it to the walk-in refrigerator. She set it down on Gibson's chest, just like she had done with the notebook when she took his prints. Then she looked up at Reacher.

'Is he a righty or a lefty?'

Reacher said, 'His watch is on the left.'

Knight took hold of Gibson's right hand and twisted it around until the tip of his index finger made contact with the computer's key. The screen unlocked. She mouthed a silent *thank you* and took the computer into the kitchen. She rested it on the counter and set about scrolling through a list of files until she found one she liked the look of.

*

Paris was sitting behind the wheel of her Land Rover. Her arms were crossed. Her lips were pressed together. Her purse was on the passenger seat next to her, propped open. Her Walther PPK was within easy reach. She caught sight of Vidic hurrying toward her and she was tempted to grab it. And use it. But instead she just locked her door and turned away.

Vidic tapped on the window.

Paris didn't look at him. She said, 'Go away.'

'I'm here to apologize. You're right to be mad at me. Just not for the reason you think.'

Paris didn't answer.

'Open the window. Come on. We've only got a minute. Don't ruin everything now.'

'Don't tell me what to do.'

'Open the window. Please. It's important.'

'Fine.' Paris cranked the handle until the glass dropped halfway down into the door. 'What?'

Vidic leaned in closer and lowered his voice. 'Listen carefully. I told the stranger we were going to rob the safe first and Fletcher's job would be second. Truth is, the job happens first. Fletcher and Kane are not coming back from it. I'll bring the stranger here. He'll move the safe. His eyes will be on me as I make a big show of breaking into it. He'll be dreaming of his million dollars. And you'll put a .38 in the back of his head.'

'Me?'

'What? You just said you were capable. You shoot him, we take all the cash, and we dump his body at the Russians' place. It's another layer of insulation. We were never there. We jumped ship with Bowery. Fletcher and Kane ran the job. They brought in the stranger. That was a mistake. Everything went to hell.'

Paris blinked her eyes four times. Five. 'How do you know Fletcher and Kane aren't coming back?'

Vidic didn't answer.

'Oh. That's why you want me to stay here?'

'No point both of us getting blood on our hands.'

'Do you have to kill them?'

'I'm not leaving hostages to fortune. We have too much at stake. We leave them alive, either one day they come after us themselves, or they get caught and use us as bargaining chips. We need a clean break. No risk of blowback. This is it.'

'I guess.'

'I'll text you when I'm fifteen minutes out. Hide in the cave. Be ready.'

Paris thought for another moment. 'We'll have to leave my gun at the Russians' place.'

'Correct.'

'Shame. I like this gun.'

'You can get another.'

'What about Fletcher's? And Kane's?'

'They both use 9mm Parabellum. They like the same brand. Hornady. I'll make it look convincing. And it's not like the Russians will be in a rush to call 911. There'll be no ballistics labs working their magic on this one.'

TWENTY

The computer file Knight settled on turned out to be a PowerPoint presentation. Not her favourite format after all the hours of briefings she'd sat through over the years, but useful in some circumstances. She checked to see if the slides contained the kind of information she was hoping for. She scanned the thumbnails a second time. Then she turned to Reacher and said, 'You're going to want to see this.'

She took the computer back to the dining room, reconnected it, and fired up the projector. 'We have the facilities. We might as well use them.'

Reacher didn't look convinced.

Knight took the seat in front of the computer. Reacher stood behind her.

She said, 'Ready?'

Reacher said, 'As I'll ever be.'

Knight hit a key and an image filled the projection screen.

It was a picture of a house, nicely framed and perfectly lit. It looked like it could have been taken from a real estate listing. The place was the same kind of age as the house they were in. The same kind of size. And style. It was pretty much indistinguishable from the ones that Kane's guys were watching. All four must have been part of the same development. If you were in the market it would be hard to pick between them.

Knight waited a moment then moved on to the next slide. This showed a satellite image, heavily cropped to focus on the house and its immediate surroundings. Its roof looked in good shape. The gravel driveway was tidy. No vehicles were parked there. At the back the formal garden had received some recent attention. All the plants and hedges had been trimmed back, hard, like whoever had done it was more concerned with keeping the maintenance in check than worrying about its appearance.

One other thing in the picture caught Reacher's attention. He pointed at the centre of the screen and said, 'What's that?'

Knight called up the next slide. It was a shot of the house from the road, and it showed that the driveway was closed off by a gate. It was black. Wrought iron. Maybe eight feet tall at the centre. The top was curved and it had the kind of heraldic-style emblems and flourishes that are designed to look classy, but really are shaped and sharpened to make it hard to climb.

Reacher said, 'Can we see the lock?'

Knight moved on to the next slide. It was a close-up of the centre of the gate. Where the two halves joined, three feet from the ground, there was a keypad. Knight hit the space-bar again and a box appeared on the screen, superimposed over the shiny black bars. It contained a string of six digits, then the hash symbol.

Reacher said, 'Interesting.'

'Isn't it?'

Knight hit the spacebar again. The next slide showed the front door. The next was a close-up of its handle. It showed another keypad. The next click brought up a text box. It showed another string of digits followed by a hash symbol. Knight stayed on the image for a moment, then clicked again. The next image was different. It was a diagram, not a photograph. It showed how a battery of deadbolts extended from the frame into the top and the sides of the door. It gave the specification of the metal that was used. It was too hard to be cut. Too thick to be bent. And it was complemented by even thicker strips that braced the door's entire height and width. A two-headed arrow indicated that the door opened out, not in.

Knight checked that Reacher had finished absorbing the detail then hit the spacebar another time. A picture of one of the ground-floor windows appeared. It was a little grainy, like someone had zoomed in on the image too aggressively.

Knight said, 'What are we looking at here?'

It took Reacher a moment, then he realized. 'Bars, behind the glass. For security.'

Knight shivered. 'Not very homey. You probably like it.'

'I doubt it's being used as a home.'

'No kidding.'

Knight hit the spacebar. Another diagram appeared. It showed an armoured panel suspended above a door. Knight hit the bar again. The panel dropped down, blocking the exit.

She said, 'What the . . .'

The next slide showed a painting hanging on a wall. It was

137

a Van Gogh-style landscape in an ornate, gilded frame. The next slide showed it pulled away from the wall, hinged at the left like an open cupboard door. Behind it was another keypad. This one was slimmer than the others, with a touch-screen instead of regular keys. The next click of the spacebar brought up another textbox, with another code.

Knight said, 'So what does this mean? You need a code to get through the gate. You need a second code to get through the front door. Then if you don't know to use a third code on the pad hidden behind the picture, a cage drops down and locks you in?'

Reacher said, 'That's how it looks.'

'And then what? The owners are in Russia. How do they know if someone is trapped in the house? And if they do know, what do they do? They can't fly back, surely. Do they have someone local to take care of it?'

'They don't need to do anything.'

'They do. Or . . . oh.'

'Exactly. The door is blocked. The windows are barred. I'm guessing there's no food in the fridge. The water will be shut off.'

'So . . . my God, that's awful. Think of it. You can't eat. You can't drink. You can't even flush the toilet. You'd go mad, if you didn't die first.'

Knight was still for a moment. She was silent. Then she hit the spacebar again. A slide appeared that showed a pair of floor plans. One was for the ground floor. The other was for the first floor. The layout was unremarkable, but some of the rooms were labelled with coloured stars. There was a blue one in the first bedroom on the right-hand stretch of the landing. Green, orange, and purple stars all together in the first room on the left-hand stretch. A yellow one downstairs in the living room. And a red one in the dining room. The colours were all rich and bold, apart from the red, which looked pale and washed-out.

The next slide showed a table with three columns. For each colour of star it gave a category and a value. Yellow represented paintings. They were worth $480m. Blue was statues, $27m. Green, industrial diamonds, $124m. Orange, precious metals, $13m. Purple, jewellery, $41m. Red was for wine, $19m, and it was shown in the same weak shade as its star on the floor plan. A pale asterisk matched up with a date. It was for the following Tuesday.

Knight sat for a minute in silence, staring at the screen with her arms hanging down by her sides.

Reacher said, 'You OK?'

'I'm fine. It's just . . . look at those numbers. How can a bunch of art be worth half a billion dollars? You know what a police department could do with that kind of money? A school? A hospital?'

'I hear you. But it's not art we're talking about.'

'It is. It's paintings. Statues.'

'But it's not on display. No one can see it. It can't provoke thought. Emotion. Any of the things art is supposed to do.'

'So it's not art because it's hidden away? What does that make it, then?'

'A financial parachute. Metaphorically speaking. It's there so that if the guy who owns it gets shot down, he won't crash and burn. He can flee Russia. Come here. Liquidate the assets. And continue to live in obscene luxury. The question isn't how much it costs. It's what did the guy do to be able to afford it. Nothing legal, I guarantee. And now it's here, taking up space in a perfectly good house, at the same time we have veterans sleeping on the street.'

'Damn. You're right. Almost makes me wish someone would steal it. Anyone but Kane, anyway.'

'Someone should do something with it.' Reacher nodded toward the screen. 'Is there more?'

'Just a bunch of detail about how the valuations add up. Screenshots of spreadsheets, mostly, based on the peek I took in the kitchen. Want to see them?'

'Not especially. How did Fletcher get all this detail?'

'Best guess, he has a hacker working for him.'

'Vidic said Paris was good with computers.'

'If she's good enough she could have started with the buyer and worked back from there. Dug through the shell companies that are bound to be involved. Got into the guy's personal records. Found out what he owns. Where it is. Where he's moving it to. And when. Weird that he'd keep the codes to the gate and the front door locks somewhere so vulnerable, though.'

'I doubt those got hacked.'

'Then where did they come from?'

'Think how the operation must work. There are three hurdles. Getting the goods into the country. Getting them across the country. And getting them into the house. The first two are easy. You can pay customs guys. You can pay transport guys. But, assuming you're not there to open the door in person, what are you going to do to grant access to the building? You don't want to mail a key. Keys can be stolen. Copied. Sold. Reused. You'd be asking to get ripped off. So you use a keypad in place of a regular lock. Its code can be changed. Probably remotely. Activated a minute before the delivery guys arrive. Updated the moment they leave.'

'So Paris hacked the delivery guys? No. That doesn't work. They wouldn't keep that kind of information on a computer.

And if the code is changed the minute they're done delivering, what use is it, anyway?'

'Fletcher's guys didn't hack anyone for the code. They used their home field advantage.'

'I don't follow.'

'They steal art, and similar valuable things. They use other people to transport it. Stealing and transportation is a symbiotic relationship. They'll have been working together for years. A new player shows up, especially a foreign player, they hear about it. They find out about the deal with the code. Then they look for someone at the lock company who has a sick kid. A gambling debt. Some other urgent need for money.'

'They hack, and they bribe. New school, and old school.' Knight glanced across at Reacher. 'Could be a good combination.'

Reacher glanced back. 'Could be a great combination.'

Silence filled the room for a moment, then Reacher said, 'So we agree? This is what Fletcher is planning to hit?'

Knight nodded. 'It's the newest file. The values are ridiculous. Worth sticking around for even if they think the FBI is getting close. And it looks like one of the assets isn't here yet. The wine. Looks like it's coming next week. Which shows the operation is still active. Nothing is ever guaranteed but I wouldn't bet against it. Would you?'

'No. Is there anything to confirm what day they're planning the hit? What time?'

'Nothing. You don't trust what Vidic told you?'

'I'd like a way to validate it. That's for sure. What about location? Can we narrow down the address?'

'We can do better than that. I hope.' Knight scrolled back to the first slide and hit a button on the keyboard. The image shrank and a bunch of words and icons appeared in a band across the top of the screen. Knight put the pointer over the picture of the house and did something with the track pad, but nothing happened. 'Don't worry. Just means this picture wasn't taken with a phone.' She scrolled to the close-up of the gate and tried again. This time a panel appeared. It showed an address and some technical details about the photograph. Knight clicked on it and a map opened with a blue dot showing the location. She said, 'Here it is. It's less than a mile from here. I'll send it to your FBI friend if you give me his number. Vidic said 4:00 a.m. tomorrow, right?'

'Right.'

'Strange time, but OK.'

Reacher paused. He had raided dozens of houses over the years at that kind of time. Nothing about it struck him as unusual. It was when you had the best chance of catching your targets in bed. In the deepest state of sleep. And at their groggiest when they woke up. When they would be least able to think clearly. Or resist effectively. He thought about the research he'd read from armies and secret police forces going all the way back to the Soviets and the Nazis. And how it matched his own experience. Then he said, 'Messaging Wallwork can wait. Sanitize the computer. Shut it down. We need to leave.'

Knight checked her watch. 'We have plenty of time to get back to the motel.'

'No,' Reacher said. 'We don't.'

TWENTY-ONE

The keypad was mounted at the centre of the gate so it appeared at the front of an approaching vehicle, rather than being mounted on a post or wall on the driver's side, where it would be easy to reach. Fletcher pulled up just shy of the mouth of the driveway and glanced down at the note on his phone to check that he had remembered the code correctly. Then he climbed out, tapped in the digits, and waited. Nothing happened for a moment then the two halves of the gate started to swing open, slowly, without making a sound.

Fletcher got back in behind the wheel, drove through the gap, turned, and backed his Escalade until its tailgate was three feet from the door to the house. Vidic followed him in. He backed his Jeep, keeping Fletcher's Escalade to his left and leaving room for another vehicle to park on his right. Kane came in last and took the final space in the line.

Fletcher waited for the others to join him then entered the code into the keypad on the door. There was a heavy *clunk* as the bolts retracted into the frame, then Fletcher leaned on the handle and pushed the door. It didn't move. Then he remembered it opened outward and pulled it, instead. He held it open, turned to Vidic, and said, 'Go ahead.'

Vidic said, 'Me? Why?'

'Why do you think? If anyone's getting trapped in this place, it's not going to be me.'

Vidic swore under his breath then stepped inside. The door closed behind him. He crossed the hallway and stopped in front of a painting in a gold frame. It was a Turner seascape. Vidic reached for the frame, then corrected himself. He moved over to a painting on the wall to the right. A Van Gogh. He pulled the frame away from the wall. Revealed a keypad that was hidden behind it. Entered a code. And held his breath.

The keypad beeped. The words *Arming – Wait* appeared on its LCD display. They were replaced by an asterisk. It flashed four times, then scrolled across the screen from left to right. It did the same thing again, a little faster. And again, faster still.

Vidic said, 'What the . . . ?'

He glanced toward the exit. The door was still closed. For a moment he wished he'd asked Fletcher or Kane to hold it open, then realized there would be no point. The door opened outward. The steel mesh was on the inside. It could crash down regardless of the position the door was in. He would get more fresh air. Maybe someone could pass him food and water through the bars so that he wouldn't starve or die of thirst. But he would still be trapped. There was no way to tell how long for. He'd have no choice. He would have to wait for the Russians to show up. And then he'd no doubt wish he had died.

With the door closed there was no way for Fletcher and Kane to see what was happening. No chance of anyone helping him so Vidic took a gamble. He entered the code again. The asterisk froze, then disappeared. The pad beeped twice. Then the word *Disarmed* popped up in its place.

Vidic breathed out slowly then crossed back to the doorway. He opened it and said, 'Guys, you should have seen what happened. The system wasn't even active. I almost locked myself in here when I entered the code. The last delivery guys must have screwed up. Forgotten to do it when they left.'

Fletcher shrugged. He said, 'Not our problem,' and moved into the hallway. Kane followed him. The door closed again behind them. Vidic jumped at the sound it made, then stepped across and joined them in a little huddle. Fletcher pulled three sheets of paper from his jacket pocket. A list of items was printed on each. Some of these were highlighted in yellow. Fletcher handed one page to Kane. One to Vidic. And kept the last one for himself.

Fletcher said, 'You know what we're looking for. Portable. Valuable. In demand. Check the list if you're not sure. Find everything. Bring it here. Then we'll load the vehicles together. Questions?'

Kane shook his head.

Vidic said, 'Nothing from me.'

Fletcher and Vidic headed up the stairs together. Fletcher took the branch to the left. Vidic went right. Fletcher moved along the corridor and opened the door to the first bedroom he reached. He went inside. There was no furniture in the room. The drapes were closed and only a little light was seeping in around the edges. Most of the floor space was taken up with wooden crates. None were very large and they varied in height and width and depth. A piece of paper was attached to the side of each one. Fletcher could see writing, but the light was too dim for him to be able to read it or the entries on his sheet of paper. He turned to look for the light switch.

And saw Reacher leaning against the wall.

Fletcher's uninjured left hand darted toward his waistband.

Reacher pushed away from the wall and said, 'Stop.'

Fletcher's hand was in limbo, hovering an inch above the grip of his Ruger.

'Use your thumb and finger only. Take it out. Drop it. Kick it away.'

'You're not in a position to give orders.'

'Aren't I?'

'No. For a start, you don't have a gun. I do.'

'Does that help you?'

'Obviously.'

'Remember last time we met? You had two guns. I was cuffed to a table. How did that work out for you?'

'Fool me once . . .'

'I'd fool you a hundred times if I could stand your company.'

Anger flashed across Fletcher's face. His hand moved. His fingers closed around the Ruger's grip. Reacher stepped forward. He pinned Fletcher's hand, still holding the gun, with his left. But then he was short of options. He couldn't hit Fletcher with his right hand, because of the cast. He couldn't headbutt him because of the concussion. So he drove his

146

right knee up into Fletcher's abdomen. It was an inelegant move. But it was effective. It rocked Fletcher up onto his toes for a moment and forced all the air out of his lungs. He gasped for breath. Gravity took over and dropped his heels back onto the floor. Reacher let go of Fletcher's hand, dodged around behind him, and smashed the side of his foot into the back of Fletcher's knees. The joints jackknifed and he crashed down, then flopped forward. Reacher stepped around and kicked him in the side of his head.

The endgame was the same as when they first met. And it had the same result. Fletcher, face down on the ground, still as a fallen tree.

Reacher pulled Fletcher's arms up behind his back and secured his wrists with a set of plasticuffs he had taken from the improvised crime scene kit in the trunk of Knight's Toyota. He secured Fletcher's ankles, then checked his pockets. The pickings were slim this time. There was no new wallet. No cash. Just a phone and one key. It was on a leather fob with a Cadillac dealer's contact information embossed in gold leaf. Reacher dropped it on the floor and retrieved Fletcher's Ruger. He released the magazine, put it in his pocket, and worked the slide to make sure the chamber was empty. Then he moved to the door. Checked that the corridor was clear. And made his way to the first room on the opposite side of the staircase.

Vidic wasn't even trying to match the labels on the crates in his room with the list Fletcher had given him. He had no interest in the sculptures that were packed inside them. He didn't care about their value, or the ease of selling them. He had no intention of taking any with him. All he cared about was finding a crate that was a suitable weight and size. He needed one that was light enough to carry in front of his body, supported with just his left hand, and large enough to conceal the gun he would be holding behind it in his right. He would identify the crate then listen to Fletcher's progress. Let him make two or three trips down the stairs and back up, hauling boxes of jewellery or diamonds or whatever he had set his sights on. Then, when he figured Fletcher would have settled into the routine and his edge would have dulled, he would follow him downstairs. Stay behind him as he approached the front door. And wait for him to lean down and add his current armful to his pile of spoils.

What happened next would depend on Kane. If he was in the hallway at the same time, Vidic would shoot him first. He was the bigger threat. That was for sure. But if Kane wasn't there, Vidic would put a bullet in Fletcher's chest, then wait. Kane would hear the sound and come rushing in to investigate. A target so big in a space so enclosed, at such short range – it would be the easiest shot Vidic had ever taken. It would be impossible to miss. After that he would just have to stage the scene, which wouldn't be difficult. He would have to take a bullet from each guy's gun, assuming their magazines were full to start with, place the weapons in their hands, and make sure they were in a position to have shot each other. Two minutes' work. Three, tops. Then he would have plenty of time to get to the motel and collect Reacher. Take him to the cave. And open the safe.

Vidic smiled. He had been dismayed when he realized that the huge stranger had survived the car wreck. And now the guy was going to gift him two million dollars. God truly does move in mysterious ways.

Vidic heard a sound behind him. It was soft. High pitched. Metallic. A door hinge opening. He spun around. Fletcher interfering wasn't something he had anticipated. They had worked a couple of jobs together recently and the M.O. had been the same. Their roles were agreed in advance. They carried them out. They left. The only exceptions he'd heard about had been when something went catastrophically wrong, like when O'Connell had been shot by a security guard. But there were no security guards here. Vidic was certain about that.

'What . . .' he started to say, then a sudden realization stilled his tongue before he could form another word.

Reacher moved to within an arm's length before he spoke. 'This is the part where you swear that it was all Fletcher's idea. He sprung a change of plan on you at the last minute. You tried to tell me. You couldn't, through no fault of your own. But there's no need to worry because you'll find a way to hold up your end. I'll get what you promised and we'll all live happily ever after. Right?'

Vidic's jaw was slack. His mouth sagged open but he didn't speak.

Reacher said, 'But here's the problem. I don't have the stomach for any more of your bullshit.'

Reacher raised his right arm. Vidic instinctively leaned away. He started to lift his left hand, ready to attempt a block. Then Reacher pulled his right shoulder back and swung his left fist out and around, accelerating all the way through its arc until it crashed into Vidic's temple. Vidic cartwheeled sideways, tumbling over a waist-high stack of crates, crushing another, and landing, crumpled, pressed up against an enormous jade Buddha that had been nestling inside.

Reacher moved to the side of the door and listened. No footsteps came racing up the stairs. Not heavy. Not light. He waited another minute to be sure, then crossed back to Vidic and checked his pockets. The contents were standard fare. Keys. Phone. And wallet. The only thing that interested Reacher was the stack of driver's licences tucked away in a section designed for coins. There were five. Reacher spread them out on the ground. Each had an identical photo of Vidic, a gentle smile on his face, taken straight on to soften the distinctive shape of his head. Each was issued in a different state. One was from Michigan. One from Alabama. Washington. Nevada. Rhode Island. And each had a different name. Cameron Archer. Daniel Ings. Dean Saunders. Dalian Atkinson. And Kevin Richardson. Reacher examined each in turn. He was no expert but he figured they looked pretty authentic. He gathered the IDs up, then replaced them. He figured the FBI would be interested when they finally showed up. They might have questions about where the licences had come from. And they would definitely want to know what else they'd been used for.

Reacher secured Vidic's wrists and ankles with plasticuffs, took the bullets from his gun, then left the room. He drew his Glock and started down the stairs. Two down, two to go, he figured. Kane and Paris were still unaccounted for. According to the floor plan in the presentation he had seen, two other rooms were designated for storing valuable contraband. The dining room, for wine. And the living room, for paintings. If the other information was correct, the wine wouldn't be there yet, and the paintings were the most valuable category. So it made sense that Kane and Paris would be working together in the living room.

Reacher decided to clear the other rooms first, to be safe. He started in the kitchen. The room was empty. There were no people. No crates stacked up on the floor. No appliances parked on the countertops. No dishes lined up, waiting to be washed.

The only thing not fixed to the wall or the floor was a wooden rack hanging from the ceiling above an island counter. A bunch of copper pans was attached to it with S-shaped hooks. Reacher had seen similar collections before. He had never been sure if they served any purpose. The fact that these had been left behind when the rest of the kitchen clutter had been taken away made him think they were just for decoration.

Reacher moved back into the hallway. He saw that two crates had been moved to a spot near the front door. They were rectangular. Their height and width were of regular proportions but they were exceedingly shallow. Four inches, max. Designed to protect delicate oils or watercolours, no doubt. Then Reacher heard a sound. An angry grunting. It was coming from the living room. The door wasn't closed all the way. Reacher crept forward and peered through the gap. He couldn't see anything. He pushed the door open a little wider. A man came into view. He was at the far end of the room, wrestling with a giant version of one of the crates in the hallway.

Reacher said, 'Need a hand?'

The guy pushed the crate away. It fell and knocked three others over like massive dominoes. He spun around and opened his mouth, but before he could say anything his lips curled into a smile. He stepped forward. It was the guy, Kane. He was maybe an inch taller than Reacher, and definitely heavier. He must have weighed fifty pounds more, at least. Reacher had no doubt about that. But it wasn't Kane's height or weight that stood out. It was his eyes. They were like narrow slits, and the part surrounding the pupils seemed more yellow than white. They radiated menace, like a stuffed wolf Reacher had seen in a museum in Germany when he was a kid.

The guy took another step and looked beyond Reacher for a moment, into the hallway. He called, 'Darren. Come down here. And bring your fifty bucks.'

Reacher gestured to the crates that lay all around and said, 'Short of cash in a place like this? How ironic.'

'It's a bet, dumbass. The other guy thinks you're a Fed.'

'And you don't?'

Kane shook his head. 'I think you're a random asshole who just stuck his nose where it's not wanted for the last time.'

Reacher's neck was beginning to tingle. His back was exposed. He knew Fletcher wouldn't be showing up, but he still hadn't located Paris. He didn't want a bullet in the head or a knife in the ribs while he stood listening to Kane's nonsense. He said, 'I'll take that bet. Turns out you both owe me fifty.' Then he stepped back into the hallway, closed the door behind him, and ducked into the kitchen.

He'd taken a good look at Kane. The guy was heavy, all right. He maybe had a slightly longer reach. But he seemed slow. The way he had been wrestling with the crate indicated a poor temperament. Reacher hadn't seen anything that worried him, but he didn't want to get involved in a brawl. Not just then. Not one with the potential to be long and drawn out. Not when there was a second opponent, probably armed, still unaccounted for. Plus he had to be careful with his right arm. And his head. Two of his favourite weapons. So he decided to cut the proceedings short. He stepped across to the island. Grabbed the biggest of the copper frying pans that was hanging from the rack. Moved back to the doorway. Tucked in tight against the wall. And waited.

Kane appeared after another thirty seconds. He took one step into the kitchen and paused, looking around. That put him exactly where Reacher wanted him. He swung the pan backhand, like a tennis player looking to bury match point against his greatest rival. The base caught Kane clean on the temple. He staggered sideways. Reacher came after him. He stepped around and swung the pan back the opposite way. It smashed into the other side of Kane's head. Kane's legs turned to jelly. He sank down onto his knees. Reacher whirled the pan around in a giant circle so that it crashed up under Kane's chin. His head whipped back. His eyes rolled into their sockets. His body collapsed, legs bent under him, and he settled into a solid heap, silent, and still.

Reacher secured Kane's ankles and wrists, then searched his pockets. He worked fast but turned up nothing useful. Then he stood and left the kitchen. *Three down, one to go,* he thought. The question was, where would he find her? He had heard Fletcher and Vidic talking when they came in and failed to realize why the alarm wasn't set. He'd listened to Fletcher give his briefing. But he hadn't picked up a woman's voice the whole time the others had been in the house. And he hadn't heard an extra set of footsteps moving around anywhere.

Reacher thought about the way Fletcher had deployed his resources. There were three kinds of merchandise. He had three people selecting and carrying it. Maybe Fletcher had figured the fourth would be better employed as a lookout, or to safeguard their escape route. Reacher made his way along the hallway, shoved Kane's crates aside, and eased the front door open. He could see three vehicles lined up, side by side in the driveway. Fletcher's Escalade. Vidic's Jeep. And Kane's truck. Paris wasn't in any of them. She wasn't near any of them. She wasn't by the gate. She wasn't watching from across the street. If the three men had brought their own cars, why hadn't Paris? Had she gotten a ride with one of the others, for some reason? Or was she not there at all?

Reacher went room by room, starting on the ground floor. He checked the kitchen and living room even though he had already been there minutes ago. He tried the dining room. The pantry. The utility room. He looked in the powder room and the study. He stuck his head into the little closet-like room off the hallway. There was no camera equipment in this one. And no sign of Paris.

Reacher climbed the stairs and checked each bedroom in turn. He started at the rear end of each corridor and worked forward, smaller rooms to larger. None were furnished. And none were occupied. He checked the bathrooms. It was the same story. There was no sign of Paris. Nothing to suggest she'd ever been there.

Reacher returned to Vidic's room and picked his phone up off the floor. He used Vidic's face to unlock the screen then dialled Knight's number from memory. He wasn't sure of her exact location but knew it would be somewhere close. They had worked out the plan in her car, on the fly. That came after the penny dropped in Reacher's head about Vidic's agenda. 4:00 a.m. was a great time to raid a house. Reacher knew that from experience. But he realized it would be a terrible time to burgle one. Especially if you knew for a fact that it would be empty all day long. If someone drove by in the afternoon and saw a removal truck outside they would think nothing of it. But if they passed in the early hours of the morning and saw guys hauling out a bunch of crates and loading them into random SUVs, their imaginations would go into overdrive. That was for sure. Their fingers would be itching to dial 911. Which meant Vidic had lied. Fletcher's job was happening before the attempt on the safe. Not after.

Which had left very little time. Reacher's rendezvous with Vidic had been set for 2:00 p.m., which meant the break-in must have been scheduled for before then.

Knight had suggested calling the police. It was a natural reflex for a detective. But Reacher had balked at the idea. Vidic had told him on the phone that the police had done nothing about Gibson's accident, despite his earlier prediction that they'd be all over it. Reacher added their looking the other way to the fact that Fletcher's crew had been operating in their backyard for years and no one had even taken a sniff, and he didn't find a reason to have much confidence in the local law enforcement. Instead he called Wallwork. Agents were coming, Wallwork promised. But there was no way they'd arrive in time. So Knight had dropped Reacher at the gate and continued toward the other houses they'd driven by earlier in the day. Her idea was to find a discreet place to wait and, if necessary, block off Kane's guys if they somehow received an SOS and came racing back to help.

Knight picked up on the first ring. She said, 'If this is a sales call, I'm hanging up.'

Reacher said, 'It's me.'

'You have them?'

'I have three of them. I can't find Paris.'

'How can I help?'

'You can come meet me. Look for places to hide. And if she's not holed up here, help me figure out where else she could be.'

'Don't worry. We'll find her. I'll be there in five.'

Knight ended the call but Reacher kept the phone to his ear. He moved out of Vidic's room and onto the landing. He raised his voice and said, 'Understood. You're right. That's a better plan. I'll be out front in thirty seconds. You can pick me up there.'

Reacher slipped the phone in his pocket in case Knight called back, and made his way down the stairs. He covered the length of the hallway and opened the front door. But he didn't go through. He stayed where he was and slammed the door closed. Then he stood completely still. He slowed his breathing and didn't make a sound. He wasn't optimistic, but he had drawn people out of hiding places that way more than once before.

A minute ticked by in Reacher's head. Then another. And another. The house remained completely silent. Reacher stayed where he was. Another minute passed and he heard tyres crunching on the gravel driveway outside. A car door slammed. Footsteps approached, light and fast. He looked out and saw Knight. He let her in and she said, 'Three cars outside? I don't think Paris is here. But let's find out for sure. I'm going to need Kane's phone. Then Vidic's.'

Reacher led the way to the kitchen. Knight paused for a moment and stared at Kane's body. She stretched out and held the doorframe for a moment to steady herself. She took a deep breath then looked up at Reacher and said, 'I'm sorry. This is the closest I've ever got to him. I didn't think it would hit me this way. What did you do to him?'

Reacher pointed at the dented copper frying pan lying discarded on the countertop.

'You hit him with that?'

Reacher nodded.

'Is he . . . ?'

'Dead? No. He can still stand trial.'

Knight shrugged and scooped up Kane's phone. She leaned over to hold it near his face and when it unlocked she straightened up and opened his messages. She searched through his conversations for a moment then selected the one she wanted. It was between Kane and four other numbers. No names were attached. Knight scrolled back through the last few days' worth to get a sense of Kane's style and vocabulary, then she typed: '911. Return to base, stat. Confirm receipt then radio silence, 48 hours. Full compensation to follow regardless of abort.'

She hit Send, then waited. The first reply came in after thirty seconds. It was a cartoon thumbs-up. A second came a moment later. It showed a round, cartoon face with a hand at its temple like it was saluting. Reacher found it in poor taste.

Knight said, 'Good. That rules out unwelcome guests.' She dropped Kane's phone onto his chest. 'Now, where's Vidic?'

Reacher said, 'Upstairs. But his phone is here.' He pulled it out of his pocket and handed it to Knight.

She said, 'That's some spooky kind of ESP.'

'Not really. He was the nearest when I needed a way to call you.'

Reacher showed Knight which room Vidic was in so that she could use his face to unlock his phone. She called up his messages, then shook her head. She tried his call log. His contacts. And she shook her head again.

She said, 'He's a sneaky asshole, this guy. He deletes everything. His phone's like it's never been used. But don't worry. I have a couple of other tricks up my sleeve.' She called up a menu and spent a moment sliding her finger up and down the screen, then shook her head for a third time. 'Damn. There's a way to see the places a person's been, if you know where to look. Not many people do. He does, apparently. And he knows how to disable that feature. OK.

Let's try one other thing.' She swiped and prodded at the screen for another moment, then a smile broke out on her face. 'Look at this.' She held the phone out for Reacher to see. The screen was filled by a map with a dot on it, like the one she'd used to track Kane's guys earlier.

Reacher said, 'He has a phone tag thing in her car?'

Knight smiled. 'Don't be an idiot. They're sharing their locations. They haven't been doing it long.'

'That's a thing?'

'Of course. Lots of people do it. Couples. Relatives. Co-workers. Creepy stalkers in abusive relationships.'

Reacher took another look at the screen. 'That dot is Paris?'

Knight nodded. 'Her phone, anyway. It's not like she has a chip implanted in her.'

'How do you know?'

'Implanting chips? That's not a thing. Not yet, anyway.'

'How do you know it's Paris's phone? We don't have any messages or call logs to compare the number with.'

Knight didn't reply right away. The smile faded from her face. 'I mean, they're a man. A woman. They're absconding together. Who else could it be?'

Reacher said nothing.

'You got a better way to track her down?'

'No. I'm coming up empty. So let's give this a try. The location's not far away. It won't take long to get there. And if we find someone else, not Paris, maybe they'll be connected somehow. They might know where she is.'

Reacher was first down the stairs and by the time he was halfway along the hall he realized Knight was hanging back. He said, 'You coming?'

Knight crossed her arms. She said, 'I think it's better you

go alone. I'll stay here. Handle things if the agents get here before you're back. Or the police. Or Kane's guys, if they see through my message standing them down.'

'You sure?'

'I think it's best.' She held out her keys. 'Here. You can take my car.'

Reacher shook his head. 'I'll take Kane's truck. That way if it is Paris, and she sees me coming, I'll have an extra couple of seconds before she figures I'm not a friend.'

Reacher didn't have to adjust the driver's seat in Kane's Ford when he climbed in, which was a pleasant change. He fired up the engine and took his time to manoeuvre around Knight's car, which she'd left perpendicular to the other three vehicles and centred on Vidic's Jeep. He figured she'd be pissed if he damaged it, and he wasn't sure how much more punishment it could take. He didn't want to leave it in pieces on the driveway. That would take some explaining. He made it to the gate without incident then looked back toward the house. Knight was framed in the doorway, waving. Reacher couldn't tell what kind of wave it was. It could have been saying, *good luck and come back soon*. Or it could have meant, *so long – you're never going to see me again*. That made Reacher wonder if Knight would be there when he got back. And if she wasn't, whether Kane would still be breathing.

TWENTY-TWO

Reacher fixed Vidic's phone into a bracket on the truck's dashboard, the way he'd seen Knight attach hers in her car, earlier. The map was still displayed on its screen, but Reacher didn't pay it much attention. He had memorized the route before leaving the house, which wasn't difficult. The place he was heading was barely five miles away.

The further Reacher got from the house, the narrower and twistier the roads became. The tarmac got rougher. The dips and potholes were deeper and more frequent. The incline grew more aggressive and the trees on either side thinned out, exposing coarse, scrubby dirt beneath them. Reacher saw no houses or dwellings of any kind. He guessed it was no coincidence that the fancy developer from the seventies had invested his building dollars elsewhere.

Reacher kept going until he could see where the road dead-ended. Rough rocks rose on the left, and their profile

160

was mirrored on the right by heaps of man-made spoil. Reacher cut the engine and coasted until the truck slowed to a stop. He climbed out, taking care not to slam his door. He could see a track winding its way through the spoil heaps. It was wide enough for SUVs and regular-sized trucks. Or larger ones, in skilled hands. And it would also be the perfect place for an ambush.

Reacher selected the spoil heap on the left of the track. Its incline was shallower. Easier to climb. He moved slowly, placing his feet deliberately and trying to dislodge as few stones as possible. He crept on up, steadily, until he made it to the top. It was domed, maybe twenty feet across. Reacher got down on his stomach and crawled forward until he could see down to the far side. There was a clearing. It was semicircular and covered with gravel. A metal door was set into the rock face beyond it, like the entrance to a mine. It was shiny and incongruous against the hulking grey slabs. And there were two vehicles. A panel van and a Land Rover. Reacher couldn't see if either was occupied, due to his angle of view. He couldn't tell how big a space lay behind the metal door. And he had no idea if anyone was waiting there with hostile intent.

Going back down was harder, especially on the loose surface, so the descent took Reacher longer than he would have liked. Every second made the scant intel he had gathered increasingly worthless. He made it without causing a rockslide, which he figured was something, then he hurried back to Kane's truck. He knew the smart move would be to leave. The area could be booby-trapped. And if the mine was defended to even a minimal level he would be crazy to attempt an assault with the equipment at his disposal.

Reacher didn't like to take unnecessary risks. But neither did he like to change course or abandon an objective. The likelihood was that Paris was in the mine or one of the vehicles. It was only a matter of time before Vidic missed a contact. She would realize something was wrong, and run. Maybe they had a contingency plan already figured out for this kind of situation. Or maybe she would wing it. But either way, she wouldn't be there for long.

Reacher knew what he should do. But he also knew that an FBI agent had died trying to build a case against this woman and her buddies. He had three of them under wraps, but that wasn't good enough. There was no way he was about to let the fourth go free.

Reacher fired up the truck and took the track between the spoil heaps. He made the final bend and caught movement inside one of the parked vehicles. The Land Rover. A woman was behind the wheel. She was pale, with black hair, and there was a look of thunder on her face. Reacher pulled up in front of the two vehicles, parallel with the door to the mine, with the rock face to his right. That way if any shooting started he could bale out and put the engine block between himself and anyone with a gun.

Ten seconds crawled by. No shots were fired. The metal door to the mine remained closed. But the woman jumped down from the Land Rover. She took two steps toward the truck and stopped, hands on her hips, head tipped slightly to the side. Reacher climbed out, too. He left the engine running and circled around to face her.

The woman was wearing a sky-blue blouse over jeans and sneakers. She had a jacket styled like a man's blazer and a broad black purse was slung over her shoulder.

Reacher said, 'Are you Paris?'

Paris snorted. 'Like you don't know who I am. What am I

supposed to think? You strayed in here by chance and pulled my name out of the air?'

'Is that a *yes*?'

'If you like.'

'Good. My name's—'

'I know who you are. Your name's Reacher. You're the guy who was with Gibson when he died. You beat up Fletcher in the kitchen at our house.'

Reacher held up his hands. 'The first was an accident. It had nothing to do with me. The second, what can I say? He cuffed me to a table. He had it coming.'

'You don't get it. I'm not mad at you. Gibson was a snitch. I'm glad he's dead. I'd prefer it if someone had killed him. And Fletcher's a despicable turd. If I thought for one minute you didn't mean it when you kicked his ass, I would have shot you before your feet hit the ground. Now, what are you doing here? And why are you driving Kane's stupid truck?'

'Vidic sent me. We're working together. The thing with the safe. He didn't tell you?'

Paris waited a moment. 'Go on.'

'Something happened. An accident. Vidic is hurt. Pretty bad. He sent me to fetch you. To take you to him. He needs you.'

'Seriously? Damn. You could have led with that. Come on, then. Let's get going.'

Reacher nodded toward the passenger seat of Kane's truck and turned to get back in on his side.

Paris shook her head. 'No. I'm not riding in that piece of garbage. I don't care how bad Ivan is hurt. We'll take my car.'

Reacher shrugged. He continued to his door, leaned in, and killed the engine. Then he made his way around the bonnet and started toward the passenger side of the Land Rover.

Paris said, 'No. You drive. I can't. This news about Ivan? I'm too upset.'

Reacher changed course and made for her driver's door.

Paris said, 'Thank you.' She turned and took a step toward the back of the vehicle like she was going to loop around to the other side. But when she figured Reacher would be about to climb in she stopped. She spun around. She had a gun in her hand. A small one. A Walther PPK. She said, 'On your—'

Reacher wasn't where she expected him to be. He hadn't paused to open the driver's door. He had kept on going, hard on her heels, and now he was right on top of her. He grabbed her right hand with his left and moved it aside so that the muzzle was almost touching the Land Rover's side window. He said, 'Nice try. Now drop it.'

Paris held on to the gun. She tried to pull it back in line with Reacher's head but her arm didn't move an inch.

Reacher said, 'Think about what you're doing. You seem like an intelligent woman. The gun is metal. Your fingers aren't. What's going to happen when I start to squeeze?'

Paris pulled again, harder, twisting from the waist and using all her weight.

Reacher started to apply pressure. 'Does a broken hand sound good to you? Because that's what you're going to have in about thirty seconds.'

Paris held on. She tugged and heaved and pitched from side to side, then accepted the inevitable. She relaxed her grip and said, 'Fine. Do whatever you want.'

Reacher slipped the gun out of her fingers and stepped back. He said, 'What I want is for you to get in the vehicle. We're going to where Vidic is. I wasn't joking about that. He is hurt.'

Paris started moving around the back of the Land Rover. 'If you say so. I still don't believe you.'

'Turn around.'

Paris stopped. 'Why?'

'You're going to drive.'

'I am? What kind of kidnapper are you?'

'A smart one. You'll be in the front. I'll be behind you. You won't have a seatbelt on. I will. See how that works?'

Paris let out a long, deep sigh. She said, 'I get the picture. Come on, then. Let's get this over with. But I'm warning you. You better not be lying.' She was silent for a moment like the full implication of her words was just dawning on her. 'I mean, you better not be lying about him being alive. He better be OK when we get there. If he's dead and you know it and you—'

'I'm not lying. He is hurt but he's going to make it.'

'Then let's go. We're wasting time.'

'Tell me about this place first.'

'What about it? It's a filthy hole in the ground that no one should spend a second more in than absolutely necessary. What more do you need to know?'

'Who found it?'

'Fletcher.'

'What do you use it for?'

'Parties. Wedding receptions. What do you think we use it for?'

'Storage. Or hiding out. A place like this would be easy to fortify.'

'Fortify? What kind of world do you live in? We use it to dump all the crap we steal but no one will buy. Fletcher thinks it's like a bank. I say it's like your mad auntie's basement. Or it would be if she had industrial-scale kleptomania and very poor decision-making skills.'

'Sounds picturesque. Show me.'

'Now?'

'You want to come back later?'

'What about Ivan? We shouldn't keep him waiting, right?'

'Another minute or two won't kill him.'

'Don't use that word. *Kill.* And there's no point going in. Not anymore.'

'Why not?'

'See that van? We spent basically all morning loading it with everything that wasn't a complete turkey. It's ready to burst. And before you ask, I don't have the key. Kane took it. They left me here to make sure no one else stole it but they didn't trust me not to take it myself. I have the best co-workers, right?'

'Why pack it up?'

'We're leaving.'

'All of you?'

'Obviously.'

'But not all together.'

'How . . . ? Oh. Ivan? How much did he tell you?'

'He said you and he were going your own way. Ditching the others. Starting over.'

'That's correct. It was supposed to be a secret. But we weren't being disloyal. Not really. You don't know how bad things had gotten. The early days were golden. Then Fletcher showed up. He was OK once. I guess. But after Kane arrived? Forget it. Unbearable. The pair of them, together? Talk about a toxic environment. And Gibson was OK, looking back. Which is ironic, given that he wanted to put us all in jail.'

'And Bowery?'

'He was with us. Or I thought he was. He's gone now. I have no idea where.'

'Vidic?'

'What can I say? Things changed when he joined. He has a

different way of thinking. I felt like I was trapped by the status quo. I was sleepwalking over a cliff. He sensed that. Showed me that I have a choice.'

'When did he join?'

'When I was at my lowest ebb. Kane had just killed a guard on a job. It was completely unnecessary.'

'OK. So the mine. Show me.'

'We call it *the cave*. And it's empty now, like I said.'

'You put the safe in the van? I heard it was too heavy to lift.'

Paris looked at the ground. 'I had nothing to do with that whole scheme. It was Ivan's idea. I told him he was overcomplicating things. But two million dollars? Split two ways? You can see the appeal.'

'Actually, no. I can't.'

'Really? What are you? A monk?'

Reacher said nothing.

'Look, don't be mad at Ivan. He really thought it was a win-win. You were obsessed with getting Fletcher and Kane. He was happy to give them to you. For obvious reasons. Who wouldn't be? And with them gone there was no point in the money sitting in the safe, rotting away. Someone had to benefit from it. You can see that, right?'

'So after I moved the safe for him he was going to give me Fletcher's whereabouts?'

'That's what he told me. I know it sounds fishy now with the timing and everything but circumstances change. Situations are fluid. And the two of you are good now, right? Otherwise you wouldn't be helping him. You wouldn't have come here for me. And speaking of him and me, we should go. He's hurt. I need to see him.'

'We'll go. After I see the inside of the cave.'

*

167

Reacher hadn't expected to find much in the cave but he couldn't leave without confirming what was there. The years had taught him to never take shortcuts. To turn over every rock. So he checked out the safe. Inspected the ratty old furniture. Poked through the boxes of weird metals that had been left behind. Sifted through the trash. Checked the floor and the walls for hidden compartments. Searched for concealed exits. And in the end Paris's claims had been basically borne out. The place had been stripped. Nothing of value was left. It was essentially abandoned. But Reacher didn't feel like he'd wasted his time. Two things had become clear. Fletcher and his guys were smart operators, to have found and used a place like that. And the effort it took to keep them off the street would definitely be worthwhile.

Reacher decided not to sit behind Paris while she drove. She seemed sold on the need to get to Vidic as quickly as possible. He collected Vidic's phone from Kane's truck and climbed into the Land Rover's passenger seat. Paris fired up the engine and stamped on the gas. The big SUV pitched and wallowed around the bends between the spoil piles. Reacher thought it felt more like a boat than a car. Then it rattled over the blacktop and bounced and swayed through the potholes until they reached the wider sections of road. Progress was calmer after that. Not exactly poised, but there was less danger of being shaken to death.

Paris found the Russians' house and pulled straight through the open gate. She stopped alongside Knight's Toyota. Reacher was happy to see it. Paris switched off the engine and jumped out. She rushed to the keypad and entered the code. She pulled open the front door and scampered inside. Reacher followed. He caught the door before it swung all the way closed. Stepped into the hallway and called to Knight to let her know they'd arrived. Then he figured he'd catch up with Paris, presumably in the bedroom Vidic was in, and offer her a choice. Conscious or unconscious. Because she was getting tied up, either way.

Reacher made it to the bottom of the stairs, then stopped. Something was bothering him. Knight hadn't answered. She hadn't come out to greet him or check who had arrived. A picture formed in his head. He saw her standing over Kane's body. His corpse. A knife in her hand, or a gun. Too immersed in the situation to react. He hurried to the kitchen. Knocked on the door in case she was in some kind of rapture. Pushed it open. Went inside. And saw only Kane. Tied up, on the floor, just as he'd left him. He checked for a pulse, to be sure. There was no doubt. Kane was still alive, and Knight wasn't anywhere near him.

Reacher stepped back into the hallway at the same time Paris came running down the stairs. He moved to block her path to the front door but she didn't seem to notice. She dodged into the kitchen. Came back out. Made for the dining room. The living room. Then she spotted Reacher and marched right up to him. She said, 'What kind of bullshit stunt is this? Is Ivan in on it? It was his idea, right? He thought it would be funny to scare the daylights out of me. Well, it's not funny. Not one little bit. Where is he? Tell me. Right now. I'm going to kill that son of a bitch.'

Reacher held up his hands. He said, 'Slow down. What stunt? Vidic is upstairs. First bedroom on the right. It wasn't exactly an accident, but he did get knocked out. You get the gist.'

'He's not there. That room's empty. I found Fletcher. I found Kane. No one else.'

Reacher paused. 'You didn't come across a woman? Same height as you? Same kind of age? Brown hair, tied back?'

'No. Where's Ivan?'

Reacher said, 'Go upstairs. Now. I need to see that room.'

TWENTY-THREE

Pieces of wood were still scattered around from the crates that had been broken in the scuffle. The jade Buddha was still sitting there, half on the floor. But Vidic was gone. The patch of floor where Reacher had left him was bare. There was no doubt about that. Reacher stayed still for a minute. He cast his eyes over every square inch of ground. Over the intact crates. Over the wrecked ones. Then he turned to Paris.

Paris was smiling. More than that. She was grinning. She looked triumphant. She said, 'I bet you feel pretty stupid now.'

Reacher said, 'Stupid, no. Worried, yes.'

'Worried because you're going to get fired? Because you screwed up. Big-time. You failed. Admit it.'

'What are you talking about?'

'Fletcher was right. Gibson wasn't the agent. You are. You wormed your way in. Got Ivan to trust you. Showed up at the raid. Thought you'd caught everyone. But I wasn't here. You

171

had to come and find me. And while you were gone, Ivan escaped. You'll never catch him again. Your career is toast. There's only one way out of this that I can see. Give me one of those planks. I'll knock you out. You can say Ivan did it. You'll still look pretty incompetent, obviously. But if you're injured, they may take pity on you. Send you to Alaska or make you spend the rest of your career doing cavity searches on drug mules. Face it. You're not getting out of this without some kind of stink on you.'

Reacher looked at her and shook his head. He said, 'Wow. You're actually crazy.'

'Ivan escaped. He's smarter than you. And you just can't admit it. OK, that's your funeral.' Paris turned and made for the door.

Reacher said, 'I'm not an agent. Vidic didn't escape. And if you don't help me, you'll never see him again.'

Paris stopped, turned back, and said, 'He didn't escape?' She made a show of looking around the room. 'Where is he, then?'

'That's what I'm worried about. You see any plasticuffs anywhere? The remains of any?'

Paris glanced at the floor. 'No. So?'

'He couldn't escape without removing the cuffs. You think he hopped out of here? So where are they? No one cuts their cuffs off and then throws them in the trash. They drop them and run. That's Human Nature 101.'

'So, what, then? He got rescued?'

Reacher shook his head. 'Think again.'

'That has to be it. Someone rescued him.'

'Who?'

Paris was silent for a moment. Then she said, 'Kane's guys. They were watching the other houses. Two minutes away.'

'Kane's guys? Then why did they leave Kane?'

'OK. Not Kane's guys. Someone else.'

'Not possible. How would anyone else have known Vidic needed to be rescued? This plan only came together minutes before I showed up here.'

Paris went quiet again. Then she nodded her head, vigorously, like she'd come upon an absolute certainty. 'I know. It was Bowery.'

'You said you didn't know where Bowery was.'

'I didn't. I still don't. I just know he rescued Ivan. Who else could have gotten into this house? Bowery knew the code for the gate. For the door. And he knew about the cage that slams down.'

'How would he have known Vidic was here? He'd have had to be watching the house.'

'He was. I went to our place, yesterday, to collect something. But I didn't go in. Because I could feel someone watching me. I didn't know who, at the time. I thought it must be the FBI because that's all anyone was talking about. But now it's obvious. It was Bowery.'

'You could feel someone watching?'

'Get off my back. Ivan didn't believe me, either. I bet he feels stupid now. And lucky.'

'You say you felt someone watching, I believe you. But why do you think it was Bowery?'

'There are things you don't know about.'

'So tell me.'

'No.' Paris started toward the door again. 'Why should I? You're not an agent. You said so. And you're not a cop. You can't keep me here.'

'Can't I?'

Paris reached for the handle. 'Why would you? You said

you wanted Fletcher and Kane. You have them. You've got no quarrel with me. I've done nothing to you.'

'If you're wrong then Vidic is in trouble. And not just him. A woman was here. She's missing, too.'

'Why was another woman here? Who is she?'

'Her name is Knight. She's working with me.'

'Working with you? So you didn't tie her up?'

Reacher shook his head.

Paris said, 'Then it's obvious. She took Ivan.'

Reacher said, 'No. She's involved because Kane killed her father. If Kane was missing, I'd agree. But she has nothing against Vidic. And what you need to understand is that I like her. So I'm not playing games here. Tell me what you know.'

'Then you'll let me go?'

'When you give me what I need.'

'Fine. It's like this. It's true, what I said. Ivan and I, and Bowery, were planning to split. Even before we found out about Gibson and Fletcher hit the panic button we were going to start again, on our own, asshole free. But here's what you have to understand. Businesses change. Things move on. Like Henry Ford said, what gets you to the top doesn't keep you there. So we weren't going to do the same thing over again. We evolved. Found a new model.'

'Hacking. Like you did here.'

'Not exactly. We're taking it a stage further. Here, we only hacked the basic details. What was here. What it was worth. How it was secured. The same kind of information we used to buy from art dealers and insurance agents. Which meant we still had to do the physical stealing. The dangerous part. As you demonstrated. The new model is different. It's better. I hack information that has value in itself. Then we sell it back to its original owner. It's quicker. It's lower risk. And it's more efficient because you don't need the manpower that's involved in a heist.'

'Sounds like old-fashioned blackmail.'

'Call it what you like.'

'How do you know who to target?'

'We don't. It's like going in on the prowl, only electronically. It's random. I spend hours every day online, searching. Sometimes a company name catches my eye. Sometimes a website looks creaky and vulnerable.'

Reacher thought for a moment. 'Let me guess. You did a trial run. Bowery went to collect the payoff.'

'Right. He went, but he didn't come back. Ivan thought he stiffed us. But what if that's not what happened? What if he got stiffed and thought we wouldn't believe him? Or he got hurt and needed time to recover. Or the guys we hit came after him. He dropped out of sight, then came back to warn us. Which is why he had to lay low and watch. To make sure they weren't already on to us. And when he saw what you did, and then knew you'd left . . .'

'So he'd be working alone?'

'I guess.'

'Vidic was still unconscious. His cuffs weren't removed, because rescuers don't waste time throwing away their trash, either. I can just about see Bowery leaving the cuffs on. He could have figured Vidic would be easier to carry that way. Or that cutting them off would waste a few seconds. But here's the problem. He's alone. He's carrying Vidic. So how did he get Knight to go with him?'

'He surprised her when he came in. Took her hostage.'

'And kept her subdued while he searched the house and then carried an unconscious body down a flight of stairs?'

Reacher shook his head. 'There's no chance that happened. Zero.'

'What, then?'

'Talk me through the process. Everything that happened from making contact with your mark and losing touch with Bowery.'

'It wasn't complicated. It was agreed that Bowery would meet their guy at a diner and exchange the information for the gold.'

'Gold? Why not crypto, or whatever you tech guys use?'

Paris shrugged. 'That was Ivan's idea. He wanted gold.'

'What for?'

'He didn't say. I didn't ask. I didn't care. I just wanted to prove the concept.'

'How long between first contact and the sit-down at the diner?'

'Seventy-two hours, give or take.'

'Who picked the venue?'

'They did.'

'After Bowery dropped off the map, did you visit the diner? Speak to the waitresses? Other customers?'

'No.'

'Did Vidic?'

'He thought about it. But when Bowery didn't come back, Fletcher got all hysterical. He thought every shadow was an agent. Every passing car was a spy. Ivan figured dropping out of sight to investigate would be too risky, at the time.'

'OK. One last question. The guys you tried to rip off. What kind of business are they in?'

'Property development. It's a young company. Very active in the market. Constantly acquiring rivals. Taking on new projects. Their growth is phenomenal. So's their profit. Investors can't get enough.'

'Sounds too good to be true.'

'It is. I found their skeletons. They're booking their new assets for what they think they're going to be worth at the end of the following year. If they meet the projected valuation, great. They take the credit early, make it look like they're growing faster than they are, attract more investment, rinse, repeat. And if they take on a dud that doesn't live up to the forecast, which obviously can happen, they should book the loss. But they don't. They have a whole complex web of subsidiaries and sister companies, and they bounce the toxic asset around between them, hoping that if they keep it moving no one will spot it. But I did. They've built a house of cards and I had the proof.'

'And that's what you were going to sell back? The proof?'

'Correct. And for a fair price, considering the hit they'll take if the truth comes out.'

'All right. You know what? I think you're half right. Bowery is involved. He did come back. But not voluntarily.'

'Why, then?'

'The guys you tried to blackmail didn't want to pay. Or they didn't want the message getting out there that it was OK to rip them off. Maybe both things. So they brought someone in to take care of the problem. Seventy-two hours is plenty of time to get the ball rolling. These problem-solvers had no intention of giving Bowery any gold. They lured him to a location they were familiar with. Captured him. Took him somewhere. And made him give you up.'

'No. I don't believe it.'

'Everything fits. Bowery tells them who else was involved. Vidic. And you. A woman. Then who did they find in the house? Vidic. He was unconscious, but he's a recognizable guy. And Knight. A woman. Who looks broadly like you. They took her in your place.'

'That's awful.' Paris clutched her hands and twisted her fingers together. 'Do you think they'll come back?'

'It won't take them long to figure out that Knight isn't you.'

'Then I better go. Run. Like now.'

Reacher stepped across and pushed the door shut. He kept his palm flat against its surface and said, 'Do you have a pen in your purse?'

'What? Yes. Why?'

'Leaving your friend to get tortured to death is one thing. He chose to be part of this. But Knight didn't. Turning your back on her is unacceptable. So either you stay and help me figure out how to find her, or I'll knock you out. Write your name on your forehead in massive letters and leave your body in the hallway. It'll be the first thing those guys trip on when they come in here looking for you.'

Paris swallowed hard. 'You wouldn't do that. You're bluffing.'

Reacher said, 'Am I?'

Paris swallowed again. 'And anyway, when I said run, I didn't mean, like, *run*. I meant, take a moment. Regroup, perhaps in a more secure location. And absolutely figure out how to find your friend. And Ivan, too. No way would I abandon him in his hour of need.'

'I'm glad to hear that.'

'So what do we do next?'

Reacher thought about Knight and all her tricks for tracking people with their phones. He wondered about calling Wallwork and asking him to trace hers. If she had it with her. If it was switched on. But he decided against it. Even if it worked it would take too long. Then he remembered how she'd used Vidic's phone to pinpoint Paris's. Through location sharing, she'd said. *Sharing.* That implied a two-way street. He could use Paris's phone to find Vidic's. Except he couldn't. Because Vidic didn't have his phone. Reacher did. It was right there in his pocket. It was like he'd learned long ago. There are no shortcuts. So he said, 'The property developer guy. How did you communicate with him?'

She said, 'Email.'

'Does your phone send email?'

'Of course. This isn't the Stone Age.'

'OK. Use it to contact the guy. Tell him you're the fourth member of the group. A sleeping partner, brought on board to handle emergencies. Tell him we know his guys are nearby. That's obvious. And now they need to release Bowery, Vidic, and Paris. They need to bring them to the cave. They need to be there in an hour or you'll release the incriminating information to every newspaper and financial website in the western hemisphere.'

'I can't. There's no point. It won't work.'

'Why not?'

'It's part of the concept we set out to prove. The information we sell is formatted in a special way. The best way I can describe it is that it's similar to an NFT.'

'In English?'

'Similar to a non-fungible token. In layman's terms, it means a unique computer file, like an original painting. There can only be one version. There's no point if it can be copied. We could keep going back for more money. The marks would know that. They wouldn't pay.'

'Did you use all the information you hacked? Or do you have any left? Even a tiny bit.'

'Maybe a snippet.'

'Good. Include that. Tell them you have a second tranche that you kept, for insurance. Tell them you're giving them a taste, to prove you're serious, and the rest will go out far and wide if you don't get your people back.'

'That might work, I guess.'

'Try it. Send the email.'

'I can't.'

'You just said you could.'

'I said my phone could. In theory. But I need an address.'

'You sent messages to the guy before?'

'Obviously.'

'Then you must have his address.'

'Had. I *had* it.'

'How could you lose it? Don't phones and computers remember that kind of thing?'

'Usually. Unless you tell them not to. Which I did.'

'Why?'

'Because what I was doing was illegal, Einstein. I didn't want a paper trail leading back to me.'

'I thought email addresses are supposed to be easy to remember?'

'They can be. If you want them to be remembered, like the guy's corporate email that I used for our first contact. Then he blocked me from that one and set up a special address for us to use. It's not like he's john-dot-smith-at-blackmail-target-dot-com. There was no name. The domain was disguised. And the rest was just a long string of random numbers and letters.'

'It was impossible to remember, and you never wrote it down?'

'Oh yes. I did.'

'Where?'

'In my ledger. It's at my house.'

TWENTY-FOUR

Knight's first priority was trying not to be sick.

She was in the back of a van, on the floor, in the load space. It was totally dark. There were no windows. No ventilation. The van was moving. Fast. On a twisty, bumpy road. She couldn't change her position easily because her wrists and ankles were tied. And she was sandwiched between two people. Both men. Vidic was on her right. He was still unconscious. One of the guys who had captured her had carried him down the stairs at the house, slung over his shoulder like a sleeping child, while the other had held a gun on her. They'd thrown Vidic in first. Then her. The other man was in the van already. He was the main problem because of how he smelled. He reeked of blood and stale vomit.

Knight was feeling too miserable to worry about where she was being taken, or why. She was focused on breathing through her mouth. Although if there had been a way to stop breathing altogether she might have seriously considered it. Then she pushed the thought away. She tried to summon happy memories. Sun-soaked meadows or breezy beaches. Her mind refused to cooperate. And then the stinky guy started to poke her in the side.

The guy said, 'Paris? That you?'

Knight tried to ignore him.

He said, 'Paris? I saw them throw Vidic in here. Is he next to you? Is he OK? He looked like he was out cold.'

Knight turned her head away.

The guy said, 'Paris. It's me. Bowery. Can't you hear me?'

Knight closed her eyes and clenched her teeth. She wanted to scream.

'Listen. This is important. There's something you need to know.'

Knight turned her head to face him. 'What is it, for God's sake?' She kept her voice to a low hiss. On a surveillance course years ago she'd been told that if you whisper, and your subject can't see you, it's next to impossible for them to recognize your voice. She remembered being dubious at the time, but in the circumstances it seemed worth a try. She figured she might learn something. And failing that, the guy should finally shut up.

'I screwed up. I'm sorry.'

'Tell me what happened.'

'Well.' The guy took a breath. It was ragged, like maybe a few of his front teeth were broken. 'I made it to the diner, no problem. Went in. Gave the hostess the name they said I should use. She took me all the way in back. To a booth. I sat. Waited. The guy was late. When he showed up it was weird. He was wearing tennis clothes. I remember feeling pissed, like he kept me hanging around so he could play some dumb game.' Bowery's voice faded and he stopped speaking.

Knight said, 'So the guy arrived?'

Bowery coughed then said, 'Right. He sat down. Unzipped the bag he was carrying. Took out his racket and a laptop. Then told me to look inside. It was unbelievable. Gold. So much of it. I was kind of mesmerized. I gave him the memory stick and he fired up his laptop. Checked it out. It passed muster, like we knew it would. And he told me I was free to go.'

'OK. And?'

'The guy was in the way. I couldn't get past him. So I had to go the other way around the booth. It was like a horseshoe. I shuffled on my ass all the way to the other side, dragging the bag behind me. Then a guy's head appeared from the next booth. He knelt on the seat. He leaned over. I felt something on my neck, like a bug had bitten me. I tried to shoo it away but nothing was there. Then I saw the guy's hand. He was holding a syringe. The plunger was all the way down. The vial was empty.'

'It knocked you out?'

'Right.' Bowery went silent again, aside from the rough wheezing sound as he breathed.

Knight said, 'How long were you out?'

Bowery said, 'Don't know. When I woke up I was in a weird space. Best I can make out it was a transport container, but it wasn't moving. The inside was split in two by a glass wall. My half was empty. I was lying on the floor when I woke up. It was hard. Cold. The light was harsh. There was no shade. Nothing to soften it. I was dizzy. My mouth was dry. I managed to raise my head and look through to the other half. Another man was there. He was strapped to a chair. Kind of like a dentist's. Or a barber's. There were thick leather straps. Metal buckles. The guy wasn't moving. His head was tipped toward me. His eyes were gone. So were his teeth.

His arms were hanging down. His nails had been pulled out. I couldn't see his feet.' Bowery drifted away again.

Knight said, 'Was he dead?'

Bowery said, 'Not yet. Eventually one of the guys I'd seen at the diner came in. The one who roofied me. He was wearing goggles. Rubber boots. Leather apron. He was naked under it. He had a scalpel in his hand. He checked to make sure I was watching. Then he grabbed the guy by his hair. Straightened his neck. And sliced. Just once. That's all it took.' Bowery spluttered and didn't say anything else.

Knight said, 'The guy killed him?'

Bowery said, 'The blood hit the ceiling. It covered the glass wall. It was jetting out like a fire hose. Pulsing. Then it got weaker. The guy's heart gave up, I guess. Finally the blood stopped. They left him like that for hours. Eventually one of them took the body away. I don't know what they did with it. Then they came for me. Dragged me around to the other side of the glass. Made me clean. Scrub up all the blood. If I didn't work fast enough, they hit me. Or kicked me. When I was done cleaning, they made me strip. Put me in the chair. Fastened up the straps. And offered me a choice. Give you two up or get the same treatment as the last guy.'

'So you gave us up. That was the right thing to do. Either of us would have done the same.'

'I guess. But that's not all. I'm not stupid. I knew they were going to kill me, anyway. At first I just hoped it would be quick. But then I had an idea. I figured I had something I could trade.'

'What did you offer them?'

'The report. I'm sorry. I was desperate. I told them I could get it for them if they let me live.' Bowery's breathing grew lighter and shallower.

Knight paused. 'I need to know exactly what you told them. Every word. Think carefully.'

Bowery said, 'I told them the expected value. Where it came from. Cone Dynamics. And that they would have to move fast because we have an offer on the table.'

'Did you tell them who the offer was from?'

'No. I don't know who it's from.'

'Vidic told you there's an offer?'

'Not exactly told. But I did find out from him.'

'What kind of timescale is on the offer?'

Bowery groaned but didn't reply.

'Hey, come on. Don't give up on me now.'

Bowery still didn't answer.

Knight closed her eyes and nudged him with her elbow.

There was still no response.

Knight jabbed harder. She held her breath and moved her face closer. She saw that Bowery's chest was still rising and falling. He was alive, but consciousness had finally deserted him.

Knight realized that the ride had become smoother. The van's heading was straighter. It was no longer careening around bends or racing over sudden crests. She was growing used to Bowery's stench. She risked sitting up. Her stomach felt more settled. So she raised her hands. Started to run them along the metal fins that lined the walls. She just needed one stretch with a jagged edge. She didn't know that the guys who were up front, driving, were the ones Bowery had described with the aprons and the scalpels. Not for sure. But she had a strong suspicion, and no desire to have it confirmed.

*

185

Paris parked on the gravel driveway outside her home. She took her favourite spot. The one she always used except for when Kane got to it first. He knew she liked it so he blocked it whenever he could, just to annoy her. She wasn't going to miss that kind of nonsense. But she was going to miss the house. This was going to be the last time she set foot in it. Maybe Fletcher had been on to something about the way nostalgia gets triggered.

Paris turned and took her laptop from a tote bag wedged behind the passenger seat, then climbed down. She crossed to the door, unlocked it with the keypad and led the way inside. She climbed the stairs and paused outside her room. She looked at Reacher and said, 'Sorry. You can't come in. Not for a minute.'

Reacher said, 'Why not?'

'My ledger is hidden. No one can see where.'

'You're leaving this house. You're never coming back. Why would it matter if I see your hiding place?'

She glared at him. 'Fine. Come in. But stay back. Don't get in the way.'

Reacher stood by the door while Paris dropped her laptop on the bed and then rolled up her rug. She closed straight in on the loose floorboard and pried it up. Leaned into the cavity. Retrieved the notebook. Crossed to the bookshelf. Took down the third volume from the left on the top shelf. It was a book on military strategy from Rome to Vietnam. Then she collected her notepad and pen from the table and returned to the bed. She sat down, cross-legged. Flipped the ledger over to its back cover. Opened it. Checked the groups of digits in one of the columns she had created. In its second row. And cross-referenced them with pages of the book. Reacher watched closely. He realized she was picking

186

atypical entries. Tables, mainly, plus a few sets of chapter endnotes. Which meant she wasn't selecting whole words. Just numbers and letters. The kind of things you need if you want to re-create an email address, he guessed.

When Paris was done she opened her laptop and selected her email program. She began a new message. Entered the address, then typed rapidly for a couple of minutes. She read what she'd written then turned the screen so that Reacher could see.

Reacher shook his head and said, 'No. I've changed my mind. There's a problem. If the property guy sees this he'll talk to his hired help. They'll realize that we're bluffing.'

'We're not. If they don't let Ivan go I'll send that document out in a heartbeat. I'll dig up more dirt and send that, too.'

'Not about that. About the timing. Our goal is obvious. We want our people back. Releasing the material is a means to that end, not the end in itself. They'll see that. So if they demand twenty-four hours to comply, what can we do? Forty-eight hours? We'd have to agree. Which would give them plenty of time to set up an ambush, like they must have done with Bowery.'

'So are we giving up?'

'No. We're streamlining. I want you to send them something simpler. A picture of the snippet of information that we have with your phone number splashed across it.'

'That's all?'

'That's all.'

'Why?'

'The lack of context will imply a question. Humans are hard-wired to seek answers. So he'll call the number to find out what's going on. I'll talk to him. Convince him of the urgency.'

'You sure that will work?'

Reacher nodded. 'One question first. Is it possible to preset an email to send at a certain time in the future?'

'Of course.'

'OK, then. Put the image together.'

Paris turned back to her keyboard and trackpad and after a couple of minutes' work she showed Reacher the screen again. This time he said, 'Good. Go ahead. Send it.'

Paris hit a key. 'Done. Do you think he'll call?'

'He will. In the meantime, here's another question. The little icons you get on computer screens that represent documents. Can you name them anything you want?'

'Pretty much.'

'What's the property company called?'

'Nechells Property Partners, LLC.'

'Could you make a document called something like, *NPP false accounting tranche 2*?'

'Easily.'

'Could it be empty?'

'Of course. Documents always start off empty.'

'OK. I want you to write an email with a pretty innocuous message. *To whom it may concern, please see the attached file.* Something like that. Add the empty NPP document. Just its icon. Address it to the finance desks at all the major papers. Set it to send in, say, three hours. And take a picture of it on the screen.'

'A screenshot?'

'If you say so.'

Paris got back to work but before she had anything to show Reacher, her phone began to ring. She checked the screen. She said, 'Number's blocked,' and passed him the handset.

Reacher hit the answer button and said, 'Yes?'

The voice on the line said, 'Who is this?'

'My name isn't important. What I want is. And what I'll do if I don't get it? That's critical.'

'You're wasting my time. Tell me—'

'You saw the sample on your email. Unless I get what I want within three hours, the entire file will be sent to all the national newspapers.'

'And what do you want?'

'You, or someone you control, has taken three of my associates. You know the people I'm talking about. They are to be released. I'll send you the coordinates of the place where they are to be left.'

'Three hours? That's not possible. I—'

'No. We both know what happened last time. We gave you seventy-two hours. Our man didn't return. We didn't get paid.' Reacher pointed to Paris's laptop. She nodded. 'Look at your email. You're about to receive a message. Look at it closely. You'll see that the clock is already ticking. The only way to stop it is to release my people. You know where we live. You could call an airstrike on our position and it would make no difference. The email will be sent. Your life, and your company, will be destroyed. Any questions?'

There was only silence on the line.

Reacher said, 'Good. Now for the full terms. Your guys are to leave a vehicle at the coordinates you will receive, within three hours. My people will be in that vehicle, safe and well. Your guys will drive away. If they do not have a second vehicle of their own, they can take the white Ford F-150 that will already be there. We don't need it back. No one else will be present on site, but we'll be watching. Remotely. If you comply, the email will be cancelled. If you don't, you can look forward to public humiliation, bank-ruptcy, and a couple of decades in the Federal pen.'

Paris closed her laptop and put it and the ledger and the strategy book in a bag she took from her wardrobe. Then she said she needed the bathroom before they got back on the road. Reacher told her he'd wait downstairs. But not out of any sense of modesty. Because he was half expecting her to climb down a drainpipe and make a break for her Land Rover.

Paris made her way down the stairs a few minutes later but she didn't head straight for the front door. She said, 'Give me a minute, OK?'

Reacher said, 'What is it now?'

'There's something I need to do. In private.'

'What?'

'Say goodbye to Gibson. Fletcher stuck his body in our walk-in refrigerator. The unsanitary asshole.'

'You said you didn't like Gibson. He was a snitch. You wished someone had killed him.'

'So what if I didn't like him? I worked with him. And he's dead. That's enough. We have to be civilized, or what do we have left? Did you love everyone whose funeral you went to?'

The van that Knight and the others were being transported in belonged to the Mount Pleasant Tennis Club, from just outside Wichita, Kansas. The club was indeed pleasant. It had six courts, a clubhouse, a convenient parking lot, and a line of mature trees that separated the site from the nearby highway. The trees also screened off the pair of old shipping containers that had sat on the adjacent lot for so long that most of the members had ceased to notice they were there.

190

The two guys in the cab were the owners of the tennis club. They were looking forward to getting back, especially since they now had two extra guests. The driver turned to his partner and said, 'Worth it?'

The guy shrugged. 'The property developer thing? Easy money. This side gig? I don't know. The jury's out. Seems too good to be true. How can one report be worth so much? And Cone Dynamics? What kind of a company name is that?'

'You might be right, but where's the harm? Nothing ventured, nothing gained.'

'We're going to—' The passenger's phone started to ring. He picked it up, glanced at the screen, and answered. He listened for a moment then hit the speakerphone key.

The voice on the line said, 'We have a problem. You have to go back. Return the goods.'

The passenger said, 'Really? Why?'

'That's need to know, and you don't. But you do need to go back. Now. Today. The goods need to be returned in three hours.'

'Not possible. We're already on the road.'

'Then go back.'

'Tell whoever's squeezing your nuts that we need more time. A couple of days, minimum.'

'You have three hours. Not a minute more.'

'We're not actually returning anything, right? We're playing along and adding to the collection. That takes time to prepare.'

'No. We're returning everything. In two hours fifty-five, now. Sooner if possible.'

'What's gotten into you? If there's some kind of problem—'

'Just do it. No debate.'

The passenger sighed. 'OK. I guess. But it's going to cost extra.'

The line went silent for a moment, then the voice said, 'How much?'

'Fifty per cent.'

'Thirty.'

'Fifty. Or we keep driving.'

'Fine. Now listen up. There are some special instructions this time. They need to be followed to the letter or all hell's going to break loose.'

TWENTY-FIVE

The Tennis Club guys arrived at the cave twenty-five minutes ahead of their deadline. They bounced along the track between the spoil heaps, skirted around another panel van and a Land Rover that were parked close together, and pulled up a couple of feet shy of a white Ford truck. The driver shut off the engine. He left the keys in the ignition and climbed out. The passenger joined him. They looked around for a moment, taking in the rock and the gravel and the shiny metal door. The driver nudged the passenger and pointed to a spot above the centre of its frame. He mouthed the word *camera*.

The passenger nodded and said, 'Come on. Let's go.' He climbed up into the Ford.

The driver got in behind the wheel and turned the key. The engine took a moment to catch. He said, 'What a piece of garbage. I can't believe we're stuck with this.'

'Don't worry. I'll tell the property guy he owes us a bonus.'

'A big bonus.' The driver nodded toward the back of the van. 'I was looking forward to some fun.'

The driver swung the truck around and started toward the exit. The passenger was fiddling with the stereo. It wouldn't make a sound. Then the silence was shattered by a gunshot. The truck bucked a little. Steam started to pour from somewhere at the front. There was another shot. More steam gushed out. A hole was ripped in the dead centre of the bonnet. The windshield shattered. A bullet tore through the wheel arch at the side of the load bed and the left-hand rear tyre exploded. The truck pulled to the side. The driver hit the brake and tried to correct the steering but he was too late. He couldn't avoid planting the truck's nose six inches deep in the side of the spoil heap.

The driver climbed out. He was shaking. The passenger tumbled down at the other side. They both looked around, stunned, trying to figure out who had fired on them.

'Up here, gentlemen.' Reacher got to his feet at the top of the right-hand spoil heap. The Glock was in his left hand. 'Now move back behind the vehicle. Get down on your knees and lace your fingers behind your head.'

Neither man moved.

Reacher put a bullet through the roof of the truck's cab. He said, 'The next goes through one of you.'

The driver started to shuffle away from the truck. The passenger followed. They moved ten feet clear of the tailgate then slumped down. Reacher stayed still. The cave door slid open a couple of feet and Paris appeared. She was holding half a dozen plasticuffs. She hurried toward the Ford and stopped when she was behind the driver. She guided his arms behind his back and looped a cuff around his wrists.

She pulled it tight then repeated the procedure with the passenger.

Paris called, 'They're good.' Then she started toward the van the guys had brought.

Reacher made his way down the spoil heap. He took his time, gun in hand, switching his glance back and forth between the two guys and the rocks and pebbles beneath his feet.

Paris made it to the van. She took the keys from the ignition, looped around to the rear, and unlocked the double doors. She pulled the first one open. Then, from Reacher's viewpoint, it looked like a giant, invisible hand had flung her onto the ground. Knight appeared in the open doorway. She jumped down. Stepped across to Paris. Grabbed her by the blouse. Lifted her head and chest. And punched her square in the face.

Reacher herded the two guys across to the van. Neither would go near Knight, who was rubbing her bruised knuckles. Reacher said to her, 'That's Paris. Not one of the guys who grabbed you.'

Knight shrugged.

'Solves a problem, though.' Reacher pointed to the plasticuffs Paris had dropped.

Knight scooped up a couple and secured Paris's arms and legs. She said, 'In the van?'

Reacher nodded. Knight was favouring her left hand but she was still able to haul Paris into a sitting position, lift her under the armpits, and push her through the open door.

Knight looked at the two guys. She said, 'Which of you assholes took my phone?'

The passenger said, 'It's in the front.'

Reacher opened the second of the van's rear doors and turned to the driver. He said, 'Sit on the edge. Lift your feet. Do anything stupid and my friend will work out some more of her anger on you.'

The driver did as he was told and Knight slipped a cuff around his ankles. She tightened it and then shoved him in the chest. He toppled back into the van's load space. She repeated the process with the passenger, told them both to bend their knees, then slammed the doors, closing them in.

Knight breathed out heavily and stepped away from the van.

Reacher said, 'You OK?'

'My hand's been better. The rest of me's fine. A little bruised, maybe, from being bounced around on the metal floor.' She gestured to the truck and the wrecked Ford. 'This was all you? How did you do it?'

'A phone call. A couple of emails. Nothing to it.'

'You sent emails?'

'Not personally.'

'I was worried for a minute. I thought you must be a ringer.' She rubbed the skin on her wrists. 'But seriously, Reacher, thank you. Bowery's in there. He's in bad shape. Mistook me for Paris and told me a bunch of things. Including how those two guys made him watch them torture a man to death. They have a whole setup for it. A torture chamber with a viewing gallery for their next victim. If they'd got me there . . .' She turned away and shivered.

'What else did Bowery say?'

'He got captured. Was forced to give up Paris and Vidic. Then he promised to give them some kind of stolen document in return for his life. It's worth a fortune, he said. A report from a company called *Cone Dynamics*. Ever heard of them?'

'No. I wonder what their big secret is?'

'I can't imagine. Probably some boring finance thing.'

Reacher retrieved Knight's phone from the passenger's door pocket in the Tennis Club van and used it to call Wallwork. He wrapped up his summary and said, 'So unless you know where I can get ribbon around here, to tie a bow around everything for your agents, this is me signing off.'

Wallwork said, 'Good. Go. The agents are only a half hour out now. Maybe less. And if I've learned anything it's that the more daylight there is between you and the Bureau, the better I sleep.'

'You don't mean that.'

'I do. And Reacher?'

Reacher didn't respond.

'Lose my number. Don't call me anymore. I mean it.'

'Until next time, Wallwork.'

'There won't be any next time.'

'Then let me ask you one last thing. Have you heard of a company called Cone Dynamics?'

'No. Why?'

'It's Paris's next hacking victim. I don't know anything about them. She stole a report. Apparently it's worth a fortune. And that makes me curious. How could one document be so valuable?'

Reacher checked the van's doors one last time then climbed into the Land Rover's passenger seat. Knight was already in the vehicle, waiting for him behind the wheel. She started

197

the engine and took off slowly, threading her way through the gap between the spoil heap and the wrecked Ford. She picked up speed once they reached the smoother road and drove the rest of the way to the Russians' house in silence. Reacher watched her out of the corner of his eye. The expressions on her face kept changing. She looked angry one moment. Then sad. Then scared.

Knight left the Land Rover on the street to save having to manoeuvre it into the space Kane's truck had been in. She finally smiled when she saw her old Toyota. Reacher jumped down, made his way through the gate, and climbed in. Knight followed but diverted to the car's trunk. She popped the lid, leaned in, then a moment later straightened up and started for the house's front door. Reacher saw that she had something in her hand. A gun. It was the Sig he had taken from Fletcher and later stowed in her lockbox.

Knight worked the keypad and pulled the handle. Reacher went after her. He caught the door before it closed and followed her into the hallway. She kept going straight. All the way to the kitchen door. She paused outside it long enough for Reacher to catch up. She took hold of the handle, turned to him, and said, 'Give me a minute?'

Reacher said, 'Whatever you need. But are you sure about this? Some things can't be undone.'

'Am I sure? When did you become a comedian?'

Kane was conscious. He had rolled over and pushed himself up into a sitting position then shuffled back until he could lean against the wall. His phone and wallet were lying next to him on the floor.

Kane's head snapped around toward the door. 'What . . . Who the hell are you?'

A smile crossed Knight's face, but it was full of sadness, not humour. She said, 'Who am I? You don't know me. For weeks I've dreamed of finding you. Making sure you know my name. I've pictured dozens of scenarios. Hundreds. None like this, though. In my dreams, any time you'd been dumped on your ass and tied up, it was me who'd done it.'

'Did I knock you up? Sleep with your sister on prom night? You're pissed about something. I can see that.'

She took a step closer. 'I'm Jenny Knight.'

Kane glanced at the gun in her hand. 'You say that like it should mean something to me.'

'My father was Dennis Knight.'

'Are you going to run through your whole family tree? Because I can save you the trouble. I don't care who you are. I don't care about your relatives.'

'Dennis Knight. My father. You killed him.'

Kane shrugged. 'If you say so.'

'You shot him down like a dog when all he was doing was his job. Earning an honest buck.'

'Well, there's his mistake. Honest jobs don't pay for shit. Means you have to work long hours. Increases the risk of a workplace accident.'

Knight looked around for a chair but there were none in the room so she sat on the floor, cross-legged, six feet in front of Kane. She raised the gun so that it was lined up on his stomach. The muzzle was rock steady. She said, 'You shot my father in the chest. Left him to bleed out. It took hours. I came to return the favour. Only *you* ran away after you pulled the trigger. *I'm* going to stay. I'm going to watch until the last breath has left your body.'

Kane swallowed. 'Don't do that. Let's talk. There must be something—'

'What I *came* to do. Past tense. I've changed my mind.' Knight lowered the gun and got to her feet. 'See, if I shoot you, it'll feel good for maybe an hour. But then I'd regret it. I know I would. Because you wouldn't die fast. Oh no. But it would still be too fast. Faster than spending the rest of your life in jail. Which is what's going to happen. The FBI will be here in minutes. They have a dead agent.' Knight looked Kane in the face and winked. 'I hope no one meets them outside. Tells them you're to blame for that.'

Knight was quiet until they were safely through the set of switchbacks. Then she glanced at Reacher and said, 'So what's next for you?'

Reacher shrugged. 'I'll get back on the road, I guess. You?'

'Go home. Get my job back. With Kane out of the picture there's no reason not to.'

'I wish you luck.'

'Thanks. Where are you heading?'

'New Orleans.'

'What's in New Orleans?'

'A new club opened. A band I like got a residency. I helped them with a thing, a while back. Thought I'd catch a couple of shows. See how they're doing.'

'Some good clubs in Phoenix. You could come there.'

'Maybe I will, one day.'

'You'll head out in the morning?'

'Maybe. Or tonight.'

'Tonight? So soon?'

'Why not? There's nothing to keep me here.'

'I guess not.' Knight glared at him then leaned a little harder on the gas.

*

The four guys hadn't taken much of a bite out of the drive back to Phoenix when they got the call from Kane. They had set out heading north on US 65 and then looped clockwise around the outskirts of Springfield. But instead of continuing until they hit I-4 like their phones told them to, they dived south-west onto US 60 and kept going until they reached a roadside bar between Monett and Yonkerville. The place was owned – indirectly – by a guy they had met in the state pen in Tucson. A live band was playing. The food was cheap. The portions were generous. The beer was cold. But the most attractive feature in their minds was the barmaids. As the neon sign above the door promised, they were all topless, all the time.

The conversation got off to a rocky start. Kane didn't know that Knight had sent the guys a text from his phone telling them to stand down so he was expecting them to still be a couple of miles away, watching the other Russian houses. He was expecting them to be sitting in their cars, keeping a low profile. So he couldn't understand why there was so much background noise. And why, when he told them to come to his location, stat, they said they would need such a long time to get there. It took a moment to straighten things out. Kane couldn't argue with them following 'his' instructions, but he still wasn't happy. There was only one reason he could think of for Reacher to have tied him up and left him in the house. Fletcher had been right. Reacher was working for the FBI. Agents must be on their way. He told the guys not to spare the horses.

Kane didn't say he was worried about the FBI showing up but the guys weren't stupid. They could listen between the lines. When they got back they drove past the house twice to be sure there were no nasty surprises waiting for them. Then one guy stayed in each car. One car was facing one way, one the other, and both had their engines running. The other two guys hurried to the house. One of them entered the number Kane had given them into the keypad. Panicked for a moment when the door wouldn't open. Then the other guy remembered to pull it. They hurried inside. Ran down the hallway. Found Kane in the kitchen. Cut his ties. And helped him to his feet.

Kane led the way out of the house. He moved slowly at first. His joints and muscles were stiff after being tied in an unnatural position for so long. He was back to something like full pace when he reached the front door. But after he took one step out onto the driveway, he stopped.

He said, 'Where the hell is my truck?'

The two guys looked at one another and shrugged.

The first one said, 'This guy, Reacher. Maybe he took it?'

The other said, 'Why not take the Caddy? Or the Jeep? That truck was a dog. You're better off without it.'

'Do you need another vehicle? We can take you wherever you need to go.'

Kane said, 'I don't need the truck. But I do need the tools that are in it.'

Kane figured he had two decisions to make. Whether to see if Fletcher and Vidic were still in the house. And whether it was still worth going to the cave, even without his tools. He decided not to go back inside. The FBI could arrive at any moment. And if they found Fletcher and Vidic that could work to his advantage. They would be occupied with arresting them.

Processing them. They would have questions to ask. Procedures to follow. Those would all take time. If they found the place empty that would leave more agents free to search for him. He checked his pocket. He still had the key to the box van. Not as convenient as a heap of cash, but better than nothing.

TWENTY-SIX

Knight slowed down to a regular speed after a couple of miles, but she didn't say anything until she reached the motel by the highway. She pulled into the same space she had used before and left the engine running. She turned to Reacher and said, 'Is this where you need to be? Or do you want me to leave you somewhere else?'

Reacher said, 'This is fine.'

Knight was silent for a moment. Then she nodded toward the diner. 'Want to at least get a coffee before you go?'

'Sure. Coffee is always good.'

Knight switched off the engine. They both got out and Reacher led the way past the line of motel room doors, to the diner's entrance.

Hannah May was working that evening. She smiled when she saw Reacher and Knight walk in and offered them a table by the window. Reacher declined. He preferred the one he'd used before, tucked away at the back.

Knight talked about her childhood, growing up in Arizona. Reacher told her about the different military bases he had lived on as a kid. The different countries. What was the same. What was different. Knight shared her favourite memories of college. Reacher told her about West Point. The place he'd remained in for the longest time, and for more than three decades his principal experience of the United States.

Hannah May arrived with a second coffee refill. She said, 'Want anything to eat with that? We have a special pie today. Rhubarb.'

Knight said, 'I'll try some of that.'

Reacher said, 'I'll stick with peach. I'll take a burger, too. With fries.'

Knight said, 'I'll have a BLT. Heavy on the bacon. Light on the rest.'

They shared war stories from the early years of their careers while they waited for their food. They talked about their best cases. Their worst. The ones that got away. The ones they couldn't forget.

They settled into a comfortable silence as they ate, and when Hannah May tried to top up their coffee mugs for a fourth time Reacher stopped her. He dropped some cash on the table. Knight matched it. Then they stood up and stepped outside.

The sun had gone down by the time they came out. The lamps mounted on tall poles in the parking lot cast long shadows. There was a chill in the air. Reacher noticed Knight shiver.

Reacher scanned the parking lot. No vehicles were moving.

Knight saw what he was doing. She said, 'Could be hard finding a ride at this time.'

Reacher said, 'Could be.'

'I'm going to get myself a room. Walk with me to the office?'

Kane was riding up front in the lead car. The driver made the turn into the track between the spoil heaps a little fast, jinked to the left, and slammed on his brakes. He had come within an inch of hitting another vehicle. A Ford F-150. Its nose was buried in the dirt, there were bullet holes in its windshield, and its rear tyre was blown.

Kane jumped out of the car and hurried around to take a closer look at his truck. It was in the last place he had expected to find it. And he couldn't understand how it had come to get shot up. The only thing he could figure was that Reacher had taken it from the Russians' house. Driven it here looking for Paris. And that Paris must have gotten away on foot, climbed the heap, and shot at Reacher as he tried to chase her. There was no body in the cab, though. Which was a shame.

Kane looked up. It was too dark to make anything out at the top of the heap. He called out, 'Paris? You up there? You OK?'

There was no reply so he climbed back into the car. The driver pulled away and headed for the cave's metal door. Kane saw the van that was full of their loot, still parked where he had left it. And next to it, another van. One he had never seen before.

The driver pulled up next to the new van and switched off his engine. The second car pulled in next to him. Kane got out. He checked the new van's cab and saw its keys were in the ignition. Then he heard a voice. A man's. Kane didn't recognize it. It was coming from the back of the vehicle. It was calling for help.

Kane took the keys and unlocked the rear doors. He saw the soles of five pairs of shoes. He recognized three of the bodies they belonged to. He pulled Paris out. And then Vidic.

Kane said, 'What the hell is going on here?'

Vidic looked at Paris, then said, 'To make a long story short, those two guys captured Bowery. They forced him to tell them about this place, then showed up here to rob it.'

Kane crossed his arms and said, 'Then who stopped them? Not you, since you were locked up, too. How did you get here?'

'Reacher jumped us in the middle of the job. He realized Paris was missing. Forced me to show him where she was.'

'He took my truck.'

Vidic nodded. 'He was with a woman. She had a silver Toyota. He figured that if Paris saw a strange vehicle approach, she would be suspicious.'

'So why not take your Jeep?'

'It was Reacher's call. He wanted your truck for some reason.'

'How did it get wrecked and shot up?'

'Reacher got into it with these new guys. They ran. Took the truck. Reacher stopped them.'

Kane turned to the driver of the car he'd been riding in. 'Got a knife?'

The driver handed him a switchblade. Kane popped it open and cut the ties from Vidic's wrists and ankles. He said, 'Start walking.' Then he turned to Paris.

Vidic said, 'Walk? Why? There's plenty of space in your cars.'

'Better get going. The FBI will be here soon.'

'You're leaving us here?'

Kane turned his back.

Vidic said, 'Wait. What if I tell you I can make you a very rich man?'

Kane said, 'I'm giving the stuff in the van to my boys here.'

'I'm not talking about the van.'

'Oh. You're thinking about the two million in the safe.'

Vidic didn't reply.

'You look surprised. Yes, I know about it. And yes, I know how to get it. Everything I need is in my truck.'

Vidic said, 'No. Not the cash in the safe. That's pocket change compared to what I'm talking about.'

'I'm not keeping you around so you can waste my time on some dumb pipe dream.'

'This is no dream. It's reality. It's something Paris and I have been working on for a while. It's already up and running. And it's set to bear fruit very soon. We'll cut you in if you help us now. And I'm not exaggerating. It will make you rich beyond your wildest dreams.'

'Are you sure? My dreams are pretty wild.'

'I'm sure.'

'Then tell me more. Make me believe you.'

Reacher and Knight set off together, strolling, taking their time. When they were halfway across the gap between the buildings a shadow broke away from the side of the motel. It split into four separate shapes. Arms and legs and heads came into focus. The guy who had tried to run Reacher off the day before was at the left-hand end of the line. He was wearing a black bike jacket, with sleeves this time, and jeans. The three other guys were dressed the same way.

The familiar guy looked at Knight. He said, 'You can leave. Go back to your car. Drive away.'

Knight said, 'While you boys have all the fun? Not a chance.'

The guy turned to Reacher. He said, 'I told you if you came back you'd regret it.'

Reacher said, 'Shows what you know.'

'What?'

'I'm having a great time.' He glanced at Knight. 'And the evening isn't over yet.'

'It is over.' The guy gave a signal with his right hand. The other three took a step forward. 'For you.'

'Really?' Reacher looked at each of the other guys in turn. He said, 'You don't have to do this. You can walk away. Right now we're in a no-harm, no-foul situation. But when the first one of you tries something, all bets are off.'

None of the three new guys said anything.

Knight said, 'This is ridiculous. Where do you guys get off? Attacking a guy with a broken arm. You're pathetic.'

The guy from the previous night pointed at Reacher. 'That's on him. He should have thought before he came back.'

A line of deep creases appeared along Reacher's forehead. He leaned toward the guy. 'You have something in your hair. Is it lettuce? Didn't you shower after I threw you in the pig swill?' He stretched out his right arm as if he was going to brush something away with his finger. 'Did you make it all the way to the farm before they let you out of that dumpster? Did you feel at home with the hogs?' The guy went to push Reacher's hand away but before he made contact Reacher jerked it back. He twisted his shoulders and transferred the momentum to his left arm. It shot out and around and his fist caught the guy on the hinge of his jaw. He fell sideways into his buddy and wound up sprawled on the ground at the guy's feet.

Reacher said, 'Last chance. You can leave now, if you take your garbage with you.'

The guys closed ranks and stepped closer to Reacher and Knight.

The one on the right said, 'Or we could stay, and take your chick.'

The guy stuck out his tongue and leaned forward, like he was going to lick Knight's cheek. She kicked him in the balls. He jackknifed at the waist and made a sound somewhere between a cough and a scream. Knight punched him in the face. He staggered back like he was trying to find his footing on an icy sidewalk, stayed upright for another moment. Then crashed down on to the ground in a position that was almost the mirror image of the guy Reacher had hit.

The guy who was closer to Reacher held up both his hands. He started to slink away backwards. He said, 'This wasn't our idea. We don't want any trouble.'

Reacher said, 'You want to leave in one piece, you clean up. Take your trash with you.'

The guy leaned down. He grabbed the original guy's arms. Hauled him up. Flipped him over his shoulder. And started toward the parking lot. His buddy did the same with the guy who had wound up on the ground nearer him.

Reacher said, 'You're going the wrong way.'

'What?'

He pointed to the gap between the diner and the motel. 'Take them through there. Throw them in the pig swill.'

'You don't mean it.'

'Don't I?'

The Ford wasn't going anywhere under its own steam. That was clear. So when Kane had finished using his tools he took them to one of his guys' cars and started loading them into the trunk. Paris grabbed Vidic by the sleeve and pulled him aside, out of earshot.

She said, 'Why the hell did you bring Kane on board? He's an oaf. A disgusting piece of crap. You know I can't stand him.'

Vidic said, 'All that is true. But he's a useful oaf. We would be heading to jail without him.'

'Fair point. But telling him about the report? Cutting him in? I'd rather set the money on fire than give any of it to him.'

'Don't worry, he won't see a cent. We're going to use him one more time. Then we'll dispose of him.'

'How?'

'I have a plan. Similar to what we were going to do with Reacher.'

'OK. And what are we going to use him for?'

'We have a problem. Those maniacs who snatched me from the Russians' house? They grabbed a woman at the same time because they thought she was you. They already had Bowery. He was really messed up. He also thought this woman was you. He started blabbing about the report. How it's worth a fortune so he promised it to the guys in return for his life.'

'So this woman knows about it?'

'She does.'

'Who is she?'

'I don't know for sure, but she's working with Reacher. Which means very soon, the FBI will find out about the report, too.'

Paris turned and started toward the van.

Vidic said, 'Stop. There's no point. Bowery didn't make it. He slipped away half an hour ago.'

'On his own? Or did you help him?'

Vidic didn't answer.

Paris said, 'You knew he was dead and you didn't say anything?'

'We were locked in the back of a van. If you'd known there was a corpse in there with us, what would you have done?'

Paris was silent for a moment. 'I can't believe this is happening. We're so close. We can't fail now.'

'We won't. I have a plan. A framework, anyway. I need to think. The time. The route. The location. They all have to dovetail perfectly. There's no room for error. And I need the answers quickly. This has to be done tomorrow.'

Reacher and Knight waited for the guys to reappear. They watched them scuttle to the parking lot and jump into a beat-up old Chevy Camaro. Its motor was reluctant to start. It eventually caught, rough and raw, but it kept going long enough to get them out of sight.

Knight nodded toward the office. She said, 'I'm going to get that room. It's kind of late. Do you want to stay? Try for a ride in the morning?'

Reacher said, 'Sure.'

'Good. I'll take care of it. But we're getting two rooms, OK?'

Reacher nodded. He watched her disappear through the

212

door, then something else caught his eye. A triangle of light suddenly appeared in room 2's window. A corner of the drape had been pulled back. It fell back into place and the window went dark again. Reacher figured a motel guest must have been disturbed by the noise. Not a problem in itself. But there was always the risk a nervous person might call the police.

Reacher stepped across to the door and knocked.

There was no response.

He knocked again and said, 'Hey. I know you're in there. I just want to talk. No need to open the door all the way. Use the chain. Open it just a crack.'

There was still no response.

Reacher knocked again. 'Come on. I can do this all night. Can you?'

The door opened wide. A young woman was standing at the threshold. She had on a pink nightdress. She had long red hair and heavy makeup.

Reacher said, 'You OK, Miss?'

'Why wouldn't I be?'

'I noticed you peeking out from a corner of the drapes. I thought maybe you saw what happened with those guys. I wanted to reassure you. There's nothing to worry about. We're old friends. We've known each other since second grade. It was some harmless fun that got a little out of hand. You know how guys are. We'll shake hands and it'll all be forgotten in the morning.'

'A, that's bullshit. B, you're way off base. And C, you want to make sure I didn't just dial 911.'

'Did you?'

'That would be about the stupidest thing I could possibly have done. So no. I am a little pissed though.'

'How so?'

'You had a great chance. They were asking for it. You're obviously capable. But you didn't touch two of them. You let them walk away.'

Reacher thought for a moment. 'Are you working?'

'Not at this very moment.'

'But you do work from this room.'

'Is that why you're here? To save my soul?'

Knight emerged from the office. She saw Reacher and came over to his side. She said, 'What's going on?'

Reacher said to the woman in the nightdress, 'I need to know if you saw someone, yesterday.' He turned to Knight. 'You got that photo of Gibson?'

Knight pulled out her phone. She fiddled with it for a moment. Found the picture. And said, 'I have to warn you. This is an image of the victim of an accident. It shows a person who is no longer alive. Are you OK to look at it?'

The woman said, 'You think I'm a blushing flower? Show me.'

Knight held up the phone.

The woman said, 'It's possible I saw him, I guess. My memory's a little foggy.'

Reacher pulled out his bundle of banknotes and peeled off two twenties. He held them out. But he didn't let the woman take them.

She said, 'I more than saw him. And not just yesterday.'

Reacher said, 'He was a regular customer?'

'Not one of my best. Not one of my worst.'

'When you say you saw him yesterday, do you mean walking by? Going to another room?'

'He wouldn't dare. And the other girls wouldn't take him. No. I saw him in here. For the full ninety minutes.'

Reacher let the woman take the two twenties. He peeled another two off his roll. 'I have a couple more questions. They may sound strange but I need you to answer. There's no right or wrong. Nothing that can hurt you in any way. Just tell me what you remember, OK?'

'Go for it.'

'When you were done, before he left, did you come to the door with him?'

'Sure. I gave him a kiss on the cheek and sent him on his way, like I always do.'

'What were you wearing?'

'I wear whatever I get paid to wear. That particular guy likes – liked – me to be smart. Kind of like I was his boss at an office, or something. Like he was having an affair with a co-worker. Not – this. Weird, I know. But hey, I'm not judging.'

'You took time out of the ninety to change?'

'It's all part of the fantasy. What he wanted. We finished up. Chilled for a few minutes. Then took a shower together. Got dressed. And pretended we were taking separate cars back to wherever we worked.'

'What did you do after he left? Get ready for the next guy?'

'Not yesterday. I didn't have another appointment until the evening. So I went home for a while, did some laundry.'

'What kind of car do you have?'

'A Crown Vic. Former cop car. Ironic, huh?'

Vidic walked over to one of the cars and opened the passenger door. Paris hurried after him. She grabbed his arm and said, 'Wait. I'm still not sure about this. I think maybe I should do the flight. You do the drive.'

Vidic smiled at her. He said, 'Admit it. You just don't want to be in a car with Kane.'

'Would you? But that's not the point. You were unconscious. Your IDs were in your wallet. Do you think Reacher saw them? Do you think he told anyone?'

'There's no way to be certain.'

'Mine were in my purse. I think they're a safer bet. We should use one of mine.'

'This is the sketchiest part of the plan. I get that. But I know how these guys work. It's better if I do it.'

'You think?'

'There are no guarantees in this life, Paris. You know that. But this is our best shot. Trust me. Suck it up. A car ride with the asshole. Then a flight. That's all. Then we'll be free and clear.'

Reacher thanked the woman and gave her the other two twenties. He turned and walked away. Knight kept pace and slipped her arm through his. She said, 'I have a confession.'

'What did you do?'

'I only booked one room.'

TWENTY-SEVEN

Reacher woke first the next morning. He got dressed, slipped out of the room, and went to the diner. He got coffee. Two carry-out cups. He brought them back and when he got to the room Knight was awake. She was sitting up in bed with a sheet pulled up to her chest.

She said, 'Is everything OK?'

Reacher said, 'Yes. Why wouldn't it be?'

'Your expression. You look worried.'

'I'm not worried. I thought I smelled smoke, is all. Very faint. I was trying to figure out where it came from.'

'Maybe it came from in here? Things did get pretty hot last night.' She folded back the covers on Reacher's side of the bed. 'Maybe we should re-create the conditions. See if it happens again. Purely in the interest of science.'

Reacher set the coffee cups down on the desk and stepped toward her.

Her phone began to ring.

Reacher said, 'Ignore it.'

Knight checked the screen. 'It's your buddy, Wallwork. Shouldn't you see what he wants?'

'Damn.' Reacher took the handset and hit the answer key. 'Yes?'

Wallwork's voice sounded hoarse. He said, 'Where are you?'

'At the motel where Gibson met his handler. Although we have new information about that meeting.' Reacher looked at Knight. Her sheet had slipped down a few inches. He had a feeling that wasn't an accident.

Wallwork said, 'Shame. I was hoping you'd be far, far away by now.'

'Why?'

'Two agents are on their way there. To look for you and Detective Knight.'

'Us? Why?'

'Pretty much everything you touched yesterday has gone to shit. When the agents got to the Russian place, Kane had escaped. At the cave, Vidic and Paris had gone missing. Bowery was dead. And when they searched the gang's house an agent tripped a booby trap. A vial of phosphorus had been propped up behind a door, right by Gibson's body. The entire place burned down.'

'Sounds like a fiasco.'

'No kidding. Although it's not a total loss. They have Fletcher. And several vehicles, including Gibson's, which was recovered from the crash site. His cellphone was still inside, wedged down the side of the driver's seat. They pulled prints and DNA from all over the place. The DNA will take a while but the prints were confirmed as his. And when the fire department releases the house, I'm sure our techs will confirm human remains. Probably won't be able to pull DNA from them, though.'

'So why are the agents coming after us? None of this is our fault.'

'They want to talk to you both. I guess Knight is about to find out what happens to people who help you.'

'Talk to us about what? We didn't lose any suspects. We didn't light anything on fire. And we only left the scene because you asked us to.'

Reacher heard a rustling sound from the bed. He glanced over and saw that Knight was kneeling up, now. The sheet was pulled right up to her chin and her face was suddenly pale.

Wallwork said, 'I know. But the loss of Gibson's body complicates the formal ID. And with a couple of the other guys in the wind the bosses want as much information as possible to help kickstart the search. And Reacher?'

'Yes?'

'I need you to do me a solid here. Go along with these guys. Don't resist. Don't run. Answer their questions. And don't get smart. Can you do that?'

Reacher didn't reply.

Wallwork said, 'This is important. You know how the politics work. If we had gotten a result I would be a genius for thinking outside the box. That's kind of my thing. But if this goes south all the blame will land on me, instead. For sharing sensitive information with an unauthorized person. You. I could be in seriously hot water. I could get fired. I could lose my pension.'

Reacher didn't respond.

'They'll only need you for twenty-four hours. Forty-eight, max.'

Reacher laughed.

'What's funny?'

'That's exactly what Vidic said to me at the start of all this. I didn't believe him, either.'

Reacher was standing at the window, looking out for the agents' cars. Knight was sitting on the bed, lacing up her shoes. 'I'm so pissed at myself. So pissed. I should have seen it.'

Reacher said, 'Take it easy on yourself. You weren't the only one there. I saw it. I didn't figure it out.'

'I don't mean seen it literally. I should have seen the implication. The possibility. The blindingly obvious certainty. How could you have done that? You're a Luddite. You don't even own a phone. What do you know about Siri? Virtual assistants? Voice control?'

Reacher shrugged.

'Exactly. How could you know. But I do. I use Siri all the time. And I was so taken up with wanting to put the fear of God into Kane, to making sure he knew I could have killed him if I wanted to, I didn't make the connection. His phone was right there by his side. It didn't matter that his hands were tied behind his back. He could have called anyone he wanted.'

'The four guys we sent away, presumably. We must have missed them by minutes.'

Knight threw herself back on the bed. 'So it's even worse. I should have kept his phone when I sent that text. Or smashed it. But he was unconscious then. I didn't think about him waking up and being able to talk. And I figured the Feds would want the phone when they showed up. Maybe there was something useful in it. And I had no idea we'd be coming back to the house.'

Reacher gave her a minute to clear her head, and then said, 'What did you make of the hooker's story? The woman from room 2. I meant to ask you last night. But I got . . . distracted.'

Knight sat up again and said, 'It was kind of strange, wasn't it? Do you think Vidic could have been confused? He said he was watching the rooms from the diner. We don't know what his eyesight is like. There could have been people in the way, milling around. He could have mixed up the door numbers. Rooms one and two are next to each other.'

'Possible.'

'The woman said she was dressed smart. As smart as a typical agent, maybe, from a distance? She said she left the room a few minutes after Gibson. And if she drives an old detective special that could easily be confused for a Bureau car by a layperson.'

'I could buy Vidic being confused. Or paranoia playing a part. But here's the thing. The Bureau confirmed that Gibson was an agent. Now they've ID'd his prints from his Lincoln, too. If Vidic actually saw him with a hooker, not a handler, and jumped to the right conclusion for the wrong reason, isn't that a little coincidental?'

'Not necessarily.'

'No?'

'No. Here's an example. Were you good at math at school?'

'I got by.'

'See, I was terrible. But I remember this one time, in sixth grade, we got a new math teacher. She came in early, her first morning. Wrote a problem on the board. Told us to try to solve it. It was super difficult. She was sure no one would be able to. It was supposed to be a motivational thing for the

221

rest of the year. Work hard, and you'll get it in the end. But the funny thing is, when I tried, I completely scrambled the method, but somehow got the answer right. It was a total fluke. A mistake. The teacher was so mad at me. Maybe Vidic did something like that?'

'Maybe. But I guess the clincher is whether there actually was a handler at the motel that day. We have some quality time coming up with the Bureau. Let's see if our new friends will share.'

Reacher saw a pair of vehicles approaching. Chevy Suburbans. Both black. They were close together, one in front of the other, and hints of shiny paint glinted through a thick coat of road dust. They ignored the open spaces in the parking lot and drove right up to the motel room door. Reacher stepped outside. Knight followed him. An agent jumped down from each of the SUVs. Hands were shaken. IDs were checked. Then the agent from the lead Suburban helped Knight into his back seat. He climbed in and pulled away. The second agent opened his back door. Reacher stayed where he was. He said, 'Where are we going?'

The agent said, 'I'm not at liberty to—'

'I am at liberty. Literally. And I'm going to stay that way unless you lighten up.'

The agent thought for a moment then said, 'Fine. You'll see for yourself soon anyway. It's a house. One of the crime scenes. Owned by some Russians and crammed full of smuggled goods. Everything's been confiscated now and the building's been commandeered. There's nothing else suitable nearby.'

'Do you have a coffee pot there?'

'I don't know. I don't drink coffee.'

'Think. This is important. I can't be sequestered somewhere with no available caffeine. That wouldn't end well for anyone.'

'One of the agents brought something. Not a pot. One that works with pods.'

'As long as it makes coffee, it'll do.'

Reacher walked around the Suburban and got into the passenger seat. The agent shrugged, climbed in himself, and headed for the exit. He hit the gas a lot harder than the agent who was driving Knight had done. Reacher thought it was maybe a good job that the guy had no caffeine in his system. He knew firsthand what happened to drivers who took the upcoming switchbacks too fast.

Fletcher's Escalade was gone when Reacher arrived at the house. So were Vidic's Jeep and Paris's Land Rover. Their places in the driveway had been taken by three more black Suburbans. Knight was standing by the front door. She was talking to a guy Reacher hadn't seen before. He was tall and thin. He was wearing a plain black suit. His head was shaved and the morning sunlight was reflecting off it. He was wearing small, round, wire glasses which made him look studious. And he was gesticulating enthusiastically with his hands. Reacher pegged him as the local guy in charge. Probably looking to make a good impression with his people before the bigger hitters arrived from Quantico.

Reacher waited for the agent to come around and open his door. Then he climbed down and made his way toward Knight and the tall guy.

'I'm Supervisory Special Agent Dokonaly,' the guy said. He offered his hand. 'Thanks for coming. We'll take up as

223

little of your time as possible.' He nodded toward the door. 'Let's get started.'

Inside, the house was fundamentally the same as it had been the day before, only all the crates and packages had been removed and it had already picked up the vibe of an office or an institution rather than a home. Dokonaly led the way to the dining room. A picnic table had been set up in the centre. It had a plastic top and folding metal legs. Four collapsible chairs were arranged around it. They looked like they'd been bought from a camping store, Reacher thought. Maybe this was an example of the kind of out-of-the-box thinking that Wallwork aspired to.

Dokonaly ushered Reacher through the door. He said, 'Wait here, please. Someone will be with you in a minute.' Then he guided Knight toward the kitchen.

Reacher looked at the chairs and decided to sit on the floor. Five minutes ticked by. Ten. He smiled to himself. The accommodations may have been unconventional and the furnishings improvised, but the Bureau's tactics were still the same. That was clear. Make the suspect wait, alone, and in silence. Isolation ratchets up the tension. Silence breeds the urge to speak. And speaking in a tense situation can easily lead to a confession. Reacher assumed they would be doing the same with Knight. He hoped she could keep a lid on the guilt she felt about not realizing Kane had summoned help, which had led to his escape. Especially since it looked like her interview was going to happen in the place Kane had escaped from. It was possible that a smart agent could connect those dots without her saying anything. If that happened, they would deal with it, down the line. But there was no point in inviting trouble by incriminating yourself.

Reacher lay down. His mind wandered back to the drive

from the motel. Figures floated into his head. Speeds. Distances. Given a spell of downtime he could never resist running random calculations. The shapes and patterns that numbers form themselves into always soothed him, like the harmonies in a perfectly constructed musical phrase.

He started with distance. The stretch of road from the motel to the house was roughly ten miles long. He had been driven on it by three people, that he could remember. Vidic. Knight. And that morning's agent. The agent had been the fastest. He had averaged a whisker over sixty miles per hour, making the journey last ten minutes. The agent driving Knight had left two minutes earlier. Knight was already talking to Dokonaly when Reacher arrived at the house, so he assumed that she must have arrived at least a minute before him. That meant the slowest her agent could have driven was 54.5454 miles per hour. Reacher liked that. He enjoyed coming across quirky results, like prime numbers or recurring decimals. He shifted his focus to the split time from the motel to the switchbacks, hoping for more of the same. But he came to a much less satisfying conclusion. Not because of the numbers involved. Because of the people.

The distance from the motel to the switchbacks was roughly five miles. According to Vidic he had left the motel five minutes after Gibson, and he had caught up with him just before the switchbacks. There was a problem with that, Reacher realized. Even if he assumed that Vidic had raised his game and had driven as fast as the agent had done that morning, all Gibson would have had to do was average above thirty miles per hour. Then he would have been through the switchbacks before Vidic got to them. Gibson was a trained agent. He knew his cover was blown. He was effectively running for his life. Was it reasonable to believe

225

that he would drive at less than thirty miles per hour? When it was possible for people with the same training to do fifty-five or sixty on that stretch of road? Reacher didn't think so. It was another anomaly in Vidic's story. And Reacher didn't like anomalies.

TWENTY-EIGHT

Reacher had moved on from math in his head to music when the door to the room opened. He was halfway through a live version of 'You Done Me Wrong' by Shawn Holt. He was enjoying it. He was inclined to make whoever had finally arrived wait until the end of the song before he acknowledged them. But in the end he didn't, because of something he smelled.

He sat up and saw a woman in a dark pantsuit and cream blouse settling into one of the collapsible chairs on the far side of the picnic table. She had dark hair, cut short. Minimal makeup. Flat shoes. And no jewellery. A disposable plastic cup was sitting on the table in front of her. She pushed it toward Reacher and said, 'I heard you like coffee. This is from my own supply. If you enjoy it, let me know. I have plenty.'

Reacher stood and crossed to the table. The woman's expression turned to concern. She said, 'Are you all right?'

Reacher said, 'I'm fine. Thank you. Why?'

'No back issues? Sciatica?'

'No.'

'That's good. I was worried when I saw you lying on the floor. That's what a lot of people do when they have back problems.'

'Not me. I was worried about having a chair problem. Conserving tax dollars is admirable but maybe next time spring for the adult size.'

'You have a point. These look a little delicate. But they're stronger than they appear.'

Reacher eased his weight down onto a chair on the opposite side of the table to the woman's. The material sagged. The leg joints groaned. But the structure held. He picked up the coffee cup she had brought and sampled the aroma. He nodded, then took a taste. He smiled. 'This is excellent. Thank you.'

'I'm delighted you like it. My name is Agent Devine, by the way. Laura. I'm here for a rather sombre reason, unfortunately. We have a personnel file to close. That's the diplomatic way to put it, according to our training unit.'

'Agent Gibson's file. I'm sorry for your loss.'

'Let's call him Albatross for now. Gibson wasn't his real name. Agents use pseudonyms when they're undercover, obviously. They're supposed to be recorded in the file, but that doesn't always happen. Some handlers are more accommodating than others and turn a blind eye or put in a place holder entry. Some agents are more security conscious – or paranoid, in the original English – and don't want anything in the computer at all. We have a saying. There are old agents. There are bold agents—'

'But there are no old, bold agents.'

'You know that. Of course. Thirteen years in the Military

Police. Lots of overlap between our worlds. Anyway, his real name needs to remain confidential for the time being. The family. Privacy. You know how this works.'

'I do. So what do you need from me?'

'I want to home in on the identification. We have the technical side covered. We took prints and DNA from the wreck of his vehicle. The prints are already back and they confirm it's him. The DNA is at the lab, and it's being expedited. I have no doubt that it will corroborate what we already know. But this is a dead agent we're dealing with. We have to keep one eye on the future. When we catch the assholes who are responsible – and you can bet your house we will – we need to make sure we don't leave any cracks in our armour. Nothing that a defence lawyer could exploit.'

'Makes sense.'

'So I don't just want the testimony of machines. I want warm bodies involved. People who can stand up in front of a jury and win their hearts and minds. Normally we would start with the agent's handler. Have him or her identify the body and swear to it if necessary. But this time we can't do that because we don't have a body.'

'It got burned up in the fire.'

'Correct. Which further reinforces what we know. The point of the fire was obviously to prevent the body being identified as an agent's. Hence the phosphorus. To destroy the DNA and avoid a match being made. Which leaves, who?'

Reacher didn't answer.

Devine said, 'Fletcher. But he's no use. Uncooperative and unreliable. Your basic evidentiary nightmare. There's no reason to believe that Kane, Paris, or Vidic will be any better when we recapture them. Detective Knight never met him.'

'She took pictures of him. Of his body, when we found it.

She got a couple of good shots of his face. And she took his prints. Give me your info and I'll get her to send them to you.'

Devine took a stainless-steel case from her purse, pulled out a business card, and slid it halfway across the table. 'She can if she wants. No rush. It could be interesting background, I guess, but we couldn't bet the farm on it. There's no chain of custody, so it would be no use in court. Which just leaves you.'

'I have no memory of meeting him. I can't recall anything. Not the crash. Not the hour before.'

'You can't recall yet. But let's be positive. Let's assume you will. Maybe the best thing is to take it easy for a couple of days. Give your memory a chance to heal. And when it does, think what an asset you'll be to the case. A decorated army major as an eyewitness.'

'I'm retired.'

'Doesn't matter. You still scrub up just as well, I'm sure. And in the meantime we'll do our best to take care of you. We really are grateful for what you've done. The time you bought us has made all the difference. Without that we'd have responded to Albatross's missed contact in the regular way and found Fletcher and co. blown to the four winds and nothing else apart from a burned-down house.'

'And the Lincoln. With the prints and the DNA.'

'Yes. That was their only mistake. They probably thought it would burst into flames when it hit the bottom of the gorge. Just goes to show. There's no such thing as the perfect crime.'

'What's happening with funeral arrangements? That kind of thing?'

'Too early to say.'

'Did you know Gib . . . Albatross personally?'

'No. I only knew him by reputation.'

'What about his handler? Must be tough on her. I bet she has all kinds of survivor guilt now. She's probably thinking, *What if I'd kept him talking five minutes longer? What if I'd wrapped the meeting up ten minutes sooner?*'

Agent Devine smiled and wagged her finger. 'Come on, Major – Mr – Reacher. You know better than that. I was born at night. But not last night. I'm not going to reveal any details about Albatross's handler, or his or her location, or movements.'

Reacher shrugged. 'You can't blame me for trying.'

'Any other questions?'

'Just the standard ones. Food? Billet?'

'You'll find basic refreshments in the kitchen, twenty-four seven. We'll get you guest access to our portal so you can order main meals. Oh. Wait. You're the one who doesn't have a phone?'

Reacher nodded.

'Not a problem. I'll arrange for a pad of paper and a pen. You can write down what you want. We'll have a delivery once a day, for the duration. As for sleeping arrangements, we're using the bedrooms, upstairs. You're in room 6. Number cards are going up on the doors. Then we're just waiting for some furniture to arrive. Nothing fancy. Just a bed, really. More of an army cot. So I guess you'll feel at home.'

'Honestly? I never liked those things. Never could get comfortable. So I'll just go back to the motel. Stay there for another couple of days. Then you'll know where I am if you need me.'

'No. Better you stay here.'

'I'll be more comfortable there. I'll get better rest. Improve the chance of my memory coming back.'

Devine shook her head. 'I'll make a call. Get you a better bed for upstairs. This is where you need to be. Just for a couple of days.'

'Am I being detained?'

'Detained? Of course not. Why so dramatic?'

'Then why do you care where I sleep? One minute you say you're grateful. The next you're putting me under house arrest.'

Devine leaned forward and lowered her voice. 'We're doing this because we're so grateful. There's a delicate aspect to this situation. The way you brought the information to us was . . . unconventional. It put another agent in a position where he had to make a choice about how to proceed. Unfortunately, the choice he made was . . . suboptimal. So we're trying to massage the records to show that your report of a rumour of a dead agent came through the proper channels. That isn't easy with all the oversight we have to work around these days. I'm confident we can get there. It just takes time. And while we're dealing with it, it's important that we keep a handle on every part of the narrative.'

'Then I guess I'm sleeping here.'

'Thanks for your understanding. It won't be for a moment longer than necessary. I promise.'

'Is there anything else for me?'

'No. Just remember that I'm here for you twenty-four seven. I gave you my card . . . which won't help much if you can't call. Anyway, you'll see me around. And if you need anything out of hours, I'm in room 4.'

Devine got up and made for the door, then turned back with one hand on the handle. She said, 'There is one other thing, actually. Nothing official. Just investigator to investigator. What did you think of the report?'

'My days of report writing are long gone.'

'I'm talking about the Cone Dynamics thing.'

'I don't know anything about that.'

'That's not what you told Wallwork.'

'I just told him what I heard. That Paris and Vidic had stolen a report from Cone Dynamics – whatever that is – and that Bowery was trying to use it to trade for his life after a previous blackmail target – Nechelles Property – hired some fixers to make an example out of the three of them. I've never seen the report, or read it, and I know nothing about its subject or its contents. I just told Wallwork because if Paris and her buddies are segueing into some kind of cyber-crime organization, I figured the Bureau should know about it. And stop it.'

'Absolutely we should. I would have done the same thing, passing on the information. Do you know how Paris targeted Cone Dynamics? How she even heard of it?'

'She didn't target them. It was random. She was just fishing.'

'It's intriguing though, isn't it? Cone Dynamics. That's a weird name. Did Bowery or whoever say anything about what it does?'

'No.'

'Any theories?'

'Why would I care?'

'Once an investigator, always an investigator. And investigators are inquisitive. It's in our natures. You hear about some obscure thing that's supposed to be super valuable and it's just been stolen, and that doesn't pique your interest?'

'I was in an apartment one time where there was a plant that looked like a dead twig. The owner had paid fifty grand for it. So I've long since given up trying to understand why people think certain things are valuable.'

'That's fair, I guess. Still, if you think of anything . . .'

'There is one thing. A detail that might help you track down Vidic. Although I did come by the information in an . . . unconventional way. I don't want to push you into any suboptimal choices.'

'Don't worry. Go ahead. Any records that need to be massaged, we can do that.'

'I looked in Vidic's wallet yesterday. He had a bunch of spare IDs in there. Pro quality, I'd say. If he's flying, or renting a car, or booking a hotel, he might be using one of them.'

'Can you remember the names? The states where they were issued?'

'Have you got paper and a pen?'

TWENTY-NINE

The 'army' cot that Reacher found in room 6 was not genuine. He was pretty sure of that. The standard issue item was designed to provide enhanced stability when assembled and optimum storage when folded down. This object pitched and rolled like a hammock when Reacher lay on it. But it didn't collapse, so he figured it might be good for a night or two if Devine was slow coming through with a replacement.

Reacher had been lying down for fifteen minutes when there was a light tap on the door. It was Knight. He sat up and she came in.

Knight said, 'You OK?'

'Fine. You?'

'I feel like I'm getting cabin fever already. Did they question you yet?'

'An agent pretended to. She was basically laying out a

bogus justification for keeping me here. When that didn't hold water she switched to emotional blackmail. Suggested that if I left they would hang Wallwork out to dry for keeping me in the loop.'

'That sucks. It was the same kind of story in my interview.'

'What carrot did they use? What stick?'

'Getting my shield back. The guy threw a bunch of questions about Kane at me. Superficial nonsense, mostly. He made out that the chance of me getting reinstated was hanging by a thread. He said they were grateful for my help and were prepared to pull some strings and get me my shield back. But to stand the best chance of that working I need to stay under the radar for a couple of days. And the only place they can be sure I'll do that effectively is here.'

'Did he mention Cone Dynamics?'

'Yes. At the end. He went full Columbo on me. *Just one more thing . . .*'

'Same with me. She slipped it in when she was already halfway out of the room. Tried to make it casual, like she wanted my help with some innocuous puzzle.'

'You get the feeling that's what this is really about?'

Reacher nodded. 'If all they wanted was for me to identify the body, they could have shown me a picture from his file. They could help you get your job back wherever you are in the world, and whatever you're doing. No, I think they're panicking and trying not to show it. I think they want us on ice until they figure out how bad this report is. And where it is.'

'I think you're right. The agent who drove you from the motel? He wasn't exactly outside your door just now, but he wasn't far away. When I came up the stairs he acted like he was waiting to talk to someone. The agent who drove me.

236

And they let me keep my phone. No doubt to see who I contact.'

'They're keeping tabs on us. They drew the short one. Babysitting duty.'

'The question is, what are we going to do about it?'

'What you do is your call. Me, I'm going to hang around a day or two. I brought Wallwork into this. He's a decent guy. I don't want his career to get ruined because of me. And speaking of Wallwork, can I borrow your phone? There's no harm in talking to him. They already know we're in touch.'

Knight passed Reacher her phone and he dialled Wallwork's number. Wallwork picked up on the first ring and said, 'How's it going? Are you hanging in there? Behaving yourself?'

'No one's been hospitalized yet. I need one favour, though.'

'I've already stuck my neck out too far. Don't ask me for anything else, Reacher, please.'

'I need one more thing. This is important for both of us or I wouldn't ask.'

Wallwork sighed. 'OK. What is it?'

'I need to know if Gibson's – Agent Albatross's – handler was at the motel on the day of the crash.'

'No way. Absolutely not. I can't share that kind of operational information.'

'What harm can it do? It's in the past. I'm not asking for someone's future whereabouts.'

'No. I'm hanging up now.'

'You need to find a way. I need that information. It's vital.'

'Why is it vital?'

'Find out for me. If my suspicion is right, then I'll tell you. If I'm wrong, you want no part of it. Trust me.'

*

237

Reacher handed the phone back to Knight but she didn't put it away. Instead she called up its browser and started tapping away on the pretend keyboard. Reacher said, 'What are you doing?'

She said, 'Googling Cone Dynamics. I want to see if it's even a real company.' She tapped and swiped a little more, then held the screen up for Reacher to see. 'I guess they do exist.'

Reacher took a moment to read the text. It said that Cone Dynamics was an audio consultancy specializing in the design of high-end loudspeakers for home and professional use. He touched an underlined word, *Gallery*, and a bunch of pictures came up. They showed scenes from houses. Offices. Concert halls. Nightclubs. A diverse set of venues, but all with one thing in common. Loudspeakers with a distinctive royal blue grille. Reacher thought about all the bands he'd seen in all the bars and clubs and halls around the world. He tried to remember if he had ever seen any speakers like them. He didn't think he had. But he couldn't swear to it. He was more about the music than the equipment.

Knight took the phone back and tapped a bunch of horizontal lines in the top right corner of the screen. The words *About*, *Products*, *Services*, *Customer Care*, and *Contact Us* appeared. Knight hit *Contact Us*, touched the call option, and put the phone on speaker. A machine picked up after six rings. A recording of a woman's voice said, 'Thank you for contacting Cone Dynamics. All our consultants are tied up helping clients right now but your call is important to us so please leave a message after the tone.'

Knight said, 'This is Alicia Taylor of Taylor Design Partners, Manhattan. I'm rehabbing a property for a client on Central Park West and they have some pretty specific requirements for audio. I need to go bespoke because nothing off the shelf is acceptable to them, so please call me back to discuss. Budget's no issue on this one so we could really have some fun.'

Reacher said, 'Think they'll call?'

'I do. I think they'll ask a few pertinent questions, say they need some time to pull a proposal together, then a week or so later say they're too busy to give the project the time it deserves and back out. We'll most likely have moved on by then. And if we haven't, we'll still be no closer to knowing if they're legit or not.'

Reacher figured there could be a different kind of response altogether, but he didn't say anything.

There was a tap on the door and right away Agent Devine burst into the room. She was breathing hard and her eyes were wide. She said, 'Grab your gear. We leave in five minutes. And Reacher, this is thanks to you. One of the aliases you gave me has panned out. Vidic has booked a plane ticket. He's flying from Oklahoma City to St Louis. Today. We will have someone watching to make sure he gets on the plane and we'll be at the other end when he gets off.'

Reacher and Knight waited together in the hallway but when the Suburbans arrived outside the agents separated them. They insisted they ride in different vehicles. Reacher knew it was standard procedure to keep suspects separated but he was disappointed, all the same. He was allocated to the second Suburban in a line of four. He climbed all the way through to the back seat. He had to fold his legs almost to his chin and stretch out sideways in order to fit. Four other agents rode ahead of him. He saw Knight climb into the Suburban behind his. The convoy left a moment later. The drivers took it easy on the twisty local roads then cut a little looser once they made it to US 63.

The trees on either side of the road began to give way to scrappy fields. The vehicles stuck together like they were joined by an invisible rope as they surged past. The drivers settled into a steady speed, and Reacher relaxed his body and closed his eyes. But he didn't sleep. The agent in front of him had a laptop open on the next seat and she spent most of her time on the phone. Reacher got the impression that plenty of people must be focused on Vidic and his trip. Updates came in regularly. Information was being gleaned from his email. His text messages. His credit card use.

The data set the agents were interested in went back two weeks. That was when contact was first established with someone using an email service based out of Switzerland. It was highly encrypted, one of the agents said. Almost impossible to hack.

Almost.

The correspondence was banal on its face. One party had something to sell. The other wanted to buy. A price was agreed. And that's where things got interesting. Slang terms were used, which an agent translated as meaning *$2,000,000*. Terms were set. Cash was insisted on. The date and the time fell into place. St Louis was agreed upon. The only thing missing was the precise location. There was nothing to indicate whether it was somewhere in the airport. In the city. Or just somewhere in the general vicinity.

The convoy swung north-east onto I-44. Reacher knew that was part of the original Route 66. And before he knew it the song was playing in his head. The frequency of the agents' reports slowed down. Evidently all available hands were trying to nail down the place where the transaction was due to occur. There seemed to be no lack of effort. But no result, either.

After another half hour Reacher heard Agent Devine on the phone. He guessed she was talking to people in the other three SUVs. They agreed that if no firm information was received before they reached the city they would rendez-vous in the parking lot of the World War II Museum and wait for updates from the team that would pick Vidic up at the airport.

Reacher said, 'He'll go somewhere outdoors. Somewhere with plenty of people. One of the parks or the area around the Arch.'

Devine said, 'Or maybe he wants privacy. He's about to commit a crime. He might not want a bunch of witnesses.'

'Witnesses are exactly what he wants. Last time out was a dry run with the property sharks. Their guy Bowery went to collect their payment. The buyers picked the venue. A diner. And it was a disaster. Bowery was kidnapped. Their mer-chandise was stolen. They didn't get paid. They were naïve, but they're not stupid. They won't make the same mistake again.'

'Maybe. We'll see.'

They were within sight of the museum when Devine's phone rang. She put it on speaker. A man's voice said, 'Vidic has just left the airport. He's in the ride share pickup area. He's calling an Uber. We have eyes on his screen. 4145 Main Drive. That's Tower Grove Park. Humboldt North Pavilion. We have roving teams deployed. One is rerouting to that spe-cific area of the park as we speak. We'll follow him all the way and company will be waiting for him when he gets there.'

The line went dead. Devine turned to the driver. She said, 'Figure out the most likely route a cabdriver would take to the pavilion from the airport. Then take us to the opposite side of the park. Two streets back. When we get there, find somewhere to wait. We'll see how this plays out from there. And hopefully we'll be close enough to join if we're needed.'

Devine called the agents in the other Suburbans. She outlined the plan and told them to each find a spot on a separate street. One black Suburban is suggestive enough. Parking four together would be like taking out an advertisement in the *Post-Dispatch. The FBI is here . . .*

Devine's phone rang again. She hit the speaker key. It was a woman's voice this time. She said, 'Vidic is mobile. He's in an Uber. A silver Prius. Still on I-70. We'll watch him all the way to the park. He'll likely arrive on the north side. ETA sixteen minutes. Out.'

The driver pulled over to the side of the road. Reacher figured they were two streets from the south side of the park. He was starting to get twitchy. Back in the day he would have been the one running an operation like this. He was itching to get out of the SUV. To get into the park. To be involved. But he knew there was no chance of that happening. The agents had only brought him along to keep him on ice until they were sure he wasn't mixed up in the fallout from the theft of the report.

A quarter of an hour crawled by, then Devine's phone rang. It was the woman's voice again. She said, 'Slight delay. Nothing to worry about. ETA now two minutes. Out.'

Devine's phone rang again almost immediately. It was the man's voice. He said, 'The roving team in Tower Grove spotted a man, mid-twenties, wearing a hoodie, with the hood pulled up. He approached Humboldt South Pavilion. If you're not familiar with the area, Main Drive cuts through the park.

At the centre it divides and runs round each side of an oval that is filled with trees. The pavilions are opposite one another on either side. They're maybe thirty seconds apart on foot. There's a large trash can just adjacent to the South Pavilion. The man deposited a black backpack and then strolled across and sat on a bench. He's still there, looking at his phone. We have eyes on the trash can and on the individual. It looks like this is a live one. Out.'

The woman called and reported that Vidic's Uber had reached the park. Vidic had exited and was heading for the North Pavilion.

The man called. 'We have eyes on Vidic. He's approaching the North Pavilion. Going inside. Glancing around. He ... has not made us. Repeat, not. He's sitting on a bench. He's leaning down like he's tying a shoelace. He's taken something from his sock. A tiny envelope. He's peeled the backing off an adhesive patch. He's stuck the package onto the underside of the bench. He's sat up straight. He's looking at his phone. Maybe sending a message. He's getting up. He's walking around the oval. He's heading for the South Pavilion. Is he? Yes. The man in the hoodie is on his feet. He's moving. He's heading the opposite way around the Oval. Heading for the North Pavilion. Going straight for the bench that Vidic just left. He's sitting on it. He's reaching underneath. We're moving. We have him. We have the envelope. Vidic is sitting on a bench. He's looking around. Hold on. I don't like his body language. He's getting squirrelly. Now he's standing. He's going for the trash can. He's going to pull out the backpack. We're— Wait. No. He didn't stop. He's still going. He's abandoned the backpack. He's running. He's—'
The call dropped out.

There was silence in the Suburban. The agents looked at

one another. Reacher felt like the temperature had dropped ten degrees.

Devine's phone rang. A new woman's voice said, 'Confirming one male suspect in custody. One package secured. Contents: One USB computer memory stick.'

Devine said, 'What about Vidic? Do you have him?'

The line went dead.

Five minutes crawled past. Six. Then the man called. He said, 'We're still looking, but as of now we do not have a visual on Vidic. We'll keep you posted.'

Two more minutes crawled past. Then Devine turned to the driver and said, 'Take us right up to the park. We're not doing any good here. It's time to get our hands dirty.'

The driver turned right at the end of the block, crossed two streets, then bumped up onto a footpath and parked at the side of a softball field. The agents all piled out. Except one. The one who had driven Reacher that morning. He said, 'We're staying here.' He didn't sound any happier about the prospect than Reacher was.

It was more than an hour before the other agents returned to the Suburban. By then Reacher had memorized every detail of the trees and walkways that surrounded the softball pitch. He had calculated the number of trees per acre in the park, assuming the sample he could see was representative. And he had tried to put himself in Vidic's shoes. He wondered what had spooked him. Caused him to run without collecting the money. And he wondered how much there could have been in one backpack. Everything he heard about the Cone Dynamics report suggested untold riches. That made him think in terms of wheelbarrows full. Not bags.

Maybe Vidic was guilty of overpromising, as well as so many other things.

Reacher didn't need to ask the returning agents about the outcome of their search. It was clear from the looks on their faces that they had been unsuccessful. Vidic had given them the slip. Reacher moved back to the tiny back seat without saying a word. The agents climbed in. No one spoke for a moment. Then Devine clapped her hands. She said, 'Come on, people. Chins up. Vidic got away, and that's disappointing, I'm not going to lie. The man who left the backpack will most likely turn out to be a cheap stooge. But let's focus on what's important. We have the money and we have the USB. If we're lucky, the money will lead us to the buyer and the USB will contain the report.'

Devine gave a signal and the driver backed up onto the street and set out into the evening traffic. No one spoke. The agents sat limp and despondent in their seats. Dejected from the loss of Vidic, Reacher guessed. Regardless of Devine's brave words. Nine minutes later they pulled up diagonally opposite the Gateway Arch. None of the agents were paying it any attention. Reacher couldn't take his eyes off it. He had heard you can go inside, which he certainly wouldn't want to do, but he was mesmerized by the shape. He could only imagine the kind of calculations that went into creating its flawless curves.

One of the other Suburbans was already there when they arrived and the other two joined them within a minute. The agents climbed out and trudged over the street and into the lobby of a hotel. Reacher saw Knight in the middle of the group. The lobby was plain and sparsely decorated, but that was fine with Reacher. The view of the Arch more than made up for any stylistic deficiencies, which he probably wouldn't have noticed, anyway. The agents hung around in a loose knot while Devine dealt with the clerk. No one spoke. No one made eye contact with one another. Reacher thought they looked like members of a high school sports team who had just been on the wrong side of a particularly heinous drubbing.

Devine returned to the group a couple of minutes later. She was struggling to hang on to a handful of shiny key-card wallets. She finished distributing them, apparently at random, then said, 'OK. That's a wrap. Eat something. Get some sleep. Get your heads back in the game. Tomorrow's a new day.'

Vidic was in another hotel, two hundred and thirty miles away. He was propped up in bed. An episode of *Breaking Bad* had just finished on his TV. He took a last bite of his room service steak. Drained his wineglass. And picked up his phone. He wanted to check in on Paris. See how her journey had gone. How close she was to stabbing Kane in the head. And most important, to make sure she was ready for the next day.

Vidic had hit the first two digits of Paris's new number when his phone began to ring. It was Paris, calling him. The universe was winking in his direction again. Clearly he was still doing something right.

Paris opened with 'I hate you. I'm going to kill you.'

Vidic smiled to himself. He said, 'What's he done?'

'It's like travelling with a child. Kane is a complete moron. An actual imbecile. He kept asking me about how the exchange is going to work tomorrow. I gave him an overview.

Nothing too specific. And he couldn't even understand that. He was more interested in making fart jokes and trying to rub up against the flight attendants on the plane. Being around him is so embarrassing.'

'Sounds pretty much par for the course with that guy.'

'And that's not even the worst of it. We had to change hotels.'

'Why?'

'We were in the bar and—'

'You went for a drink with him? What were you thinking?'

'I didn't mean to. He asked if I wanted to get something to eat. I said I was getting room service. He said he was going out somewhere so I went to the bar on my own. Then he showed up. I couldn't get away. He started up with his stupid jokes. Some other guy took offence. So Kane followed him to the bathroom, made him strip naked, apparently, and threw his clothes out of the window. Seriously, it's like being shackled to a juvenile delinquent. I hate it.'

'Are you in your room now?'

'Yes. Finally.'

'Then relax. Forget about him. Because in twenty-four hours he'll be on a mortuary slab and we'll be in paradise. In our own little fortress. With more money than we'll ever be able to spend.'

THIRTY

The FBI was paying for a lot more bedroom than Reacher needed. That was for sure. The key Agent Devine had handed him belonged to a suite on the eighth floor of the hotel. Reacher had let himself in and explored the space. There was a bathroom with enough gels and liquids to open a store. A living room, full of couches and chairs and cushions, plus a desk and a TV. And the bedroom itself. Reacher walked around the area, then stopped between a pair of ornate king-sized beds near the window. They were giant pieces of furniture but they seemed barely present against the expanse of floor all around. Like islands in an ocean, Reacher thought. He mentally compared them with the army-style cot he had lain on earlier. The contrast was laughable, but he wasn't about to complain. Anything that offered the opportunity to sleep was OK by him. *Sleep when you can so that you won't need to when you can't.* That was his rule.

Except that when he got into bed he couldn't sleep. That was very unusual for Reacher. He could generally drop off within a couple of minutes, pretty much anywhere, if he put his mind to it. But that night a thought was lurking, indistinct and out of focus, just beyond the boundary of his consciousness. Not just frustration at the lingering gap in his memory. A symptom of some kind of problem. But not something that could be forced into sharpness. Clarity would come. He was sure of that. But it would take time. And until it did, the waiting was evidently going to cost him an unknown number of restless hours.

Reacher was edging closer to pinning down what was bothering him when the room phone rang. It was Knight. She said, 'I tried to come find you.'

'I'm in 810.'

'I know. But I couldn't get off my floor. I'm on seven. The agent from this morning – the one who's apparently my babysitter now – was lurking in the elevator lobby. He sent me back to my room like I was a naughty freshman on a high school field trip.'

'Shame. I could use the company.'

'What are you doing?'

'Lying in bed, not sleeping.'

'Something bothering you?'

'Aside from our babysitters?'

'Maybe I should hit the fire alarm. We could sneak away in all the confusion.'

'I like how you think.'

'Seriously, though. What's wrong?'

'I don't know. But it has to do with Vidic. I'm asking myself, why is he free?'

'That's obvious. Because the agents did a crappy job of tailing him.'

'No. That seems like the obvious answer, I know, but something else is going on here.'

'Like what?'

'It's . . . I'm thinking it's a case of fundamental attribution error.'

'The agents made a fundamental error? That's what I said.'

'No. Step back. Look at the situation from a distance.'

'We were at a distance. We heard the play by play, on speakerphone.'

'That's not what I mean. Here's an example. A car ferry leaves port with its cargo doors open. It sinks. The investigation finds that the guy who was supposed to check that the doors were closed was asleep in his bunk when the ship set sail. Whose fault is the accident?'

'The guy who was asleep instead of doing his job.'

'What if you found out that the ship's owners had fired a bunch of people to save money? The guy who was supposed to check on the doors was doing three people's jobs. He'd been up for seventy-two hours straight. He was exhausted. He collapsed. He couldn't have checked on the doors. It was physically impossible. Was that his fault?'

'No. The owners were to blame for being tightwads.'

'Right. So in our case Vidic isn't free because the agents didn't tail him effectively. He's free because he was able to go to St Louis in the first place.'

'Because someone released him from the van we left him in at the cave.'

'Right.'

'That had to be Kane.'

'But why? Vidic hated Kane. He was about to split. I bet he

was planning to kill Kane during that burglary, then lure me there after the fact to take the blame. I bet he was going to kill Fletcher, too. So why would Kane help him?'

'Kane was having some kind of bromance with Fletcher. Maybe he saw Vidic as a rival. Wanted him out of the picture. They could have made a deal. Kane let Vidic out of the van if Vidic promised to leave and never come back.'

'Then why release Paris, too? And why leave Fletcher tied up at the house? No. It feels like Kane didn't set out to rescue anyone. Something happened at the cave to make him change course.'

'It's obvious what must have happened there. Money. I bet Vidic told Kane about their big cash cow. The Cone Dynamics report. He promised him a piece in return for setting him free.'

'That's where I keep winding up. But something doesn't fit.'

'What?'

'I don't know. Yet. But there is one other positive from your point of view.'

'Go on.'

'If Vidic offered Kane big bucks, Kane is going to stay in Vidic's shadow until he gets his hands on the cash. So we find Vidic, you find Kane.'

Reacher figured that since a federal agency had dragged him to the hotel, it was only fair to order room service breakfast on the government's dime. Pancakes, bacon, and coffee. He dragged the desk over to the window and gazed out while he ate. He could see the Arch. The swell of the river beyond it, heavy and thick and dark. And all the way over into Illinois, far away on the eastern side. He finished the food. Emptied the coffee jug. Took a shower and got dressed. He had been back at his vantage point for ten minutes when there was a knock at his door. It was his babysitter. The guy said, 'Time to move. Agent Devine is holding a debrief in a conference room, second floor, starting now. You're invited. Come on.'

The conference room was like a scene from a business furniture catalogue, Reacher thought. The walls were panelled with cherry wood. It was polished to a deep shine. There were framed oil paintings hanging every six feet, showing well-stocked wagon trains setting out from the historic heart of the city, bound for the West. The tables were formed into a horseshoe. They were perfectly aligned and exactly parallel with the walls. The chairs were made of black mesh material and shiny chrome. A projector was mounted to the ceiling and a screen had been lowered in front of the window, which was hidden by vertical blinds.

Devine was sitting at the head of the table. The agents Reacher had last seen in the lobby the evening before were lined up along both sides. The downtime had done them good. That was clear. There were no more scowls. No more sagging shoulders or slouching backs. Determination was evident on most of the faces. Enthusiasm, even, on a couple.

Knight had taken a chair midway along the far side of the table. The one opposite was open so Reacher lowered himself into it and poured himself a glass of water.

Devine cleared her throat and said, 'Folks, let's get under way. I have information for you. There are some tired eyes in Quantico this morning, I can assure you. I've asked Detective Knight and Mr Reacher to join us for a few minutes out of respect for the contribution they've made to this case. We'll share what we can, then let them take their leave so that we can move on to some of the more official aspects. Any questions before we jump in?'

No one raised their hand.

Devine said, 'Some people like to keep good news until the end, but not me. So here's our headline. The techs worked all night with the data they pulled off the memory stick that was recovered from the bench at the pavilion. The one Vidic left, and the man in the hoodie tried to take. It contained one thing. A document that was stolen when a server belonging to a company – Cone Dynamics – was illegally accessed. The techs were able to confirm that the document is genuine. All I can say in this forum is that the contents are extremely – and I mean *extremely* – sensitive from a national security standpoint. In other words, we were up to our eyeballs in the worst kind of shit. Now we're not. We're free and clear. The nature of our work means that the public will never know what you've done for them. But the Bureau does know, and it will not forget. You should all feel very proud of yourselves.'

The agent who was sitting next to Reacher raised her hand. She said, 'I don't want to sound like Debbie Downer here, but Vidic is still free. His sidekicks are still free. So what's to stop them from copying this document onto another memory stick and hitting the market again? We could be back at square one by lunchtime.'

Devine shook her head. 'I'm not a techie so I can't give you the specifics, but this document was formatted in a very unusual way. It uses technology similar to what underpins NFTs, apparently. Non-fungible tokens. I don't know how, but the good news for us is that it means we can be sure it's the original, and no copies have been made.'

'What if they hack Cone's computers again? Steal something else?'

'You can never say *never*. But this incident was a major wake-up call for the company. I'm not exaggerating when I say they have executives facing jail time over it. As soon as the breach came to light, they pulled all their systems off-line. They're still offline and that won't change until they get the green light from the Department of Energy. They'll need Secretary level authorization.' Devine let that thought hang in the air for a moment. 'Any other questions about the memory stick?'

Heads shook all around the table.

Devine said, 'OK, then. Let's move on to our second piece of good news. We've picked up a record of a plane ticket that was booked in the name of Kevin Richardson.'

She was met with a wall of blank faces. Everyone's except Reacher's.

She said, 'Kevin Richardson is one of the aliases Vidic set up for himself. A seat has been booked in that name on a flight from Chicago Midway to Anchorage, Alaska. One way. This afternoon. And get this. Only two other seats on that flight are one-way. One is in another man's name. One is in a woman's name. Both were booked within a minute of Richardson's. And all three bookings came from the same IP address.'

Devine caught the look on Reacher's face and said, 'That means the same computer was used. Or phone, or iPad, or whatever.'

An agent at the far end of the table said, 'We're thinking this is Vidic, Kane, and Paris?'

'We are. Vidic used another name from the same set of aliases for the flight into St Louis. We located him at both the arrival and departure airports on that occasion. We're going to do it again at Midway. The three of them will be off the street by dinnertime.'

Devine wrapped up the first phase of the meeting and escorted Reacher and Knight to the elevator lobby at the end of the corridor. Before either of them could hit the call button she crossed her arms and said, 'First, thank you, again. Without you that report would not be sitting safely in a locked drawer in Quantico. It would be in the possession of goodness knows who. Someone with a very poor disposition regarding the United States, I'm certain.'

Reacher said, 'Do you know who the wannabe buyer was?'

'No. Not yet. The man in the hoodie was a local loser who thought he was getting a year's pay for an hour's work. It didn't take long to find him, but he hasn't spilled anything useful yet. We have people working with him. Sketch artists. Hypnotists. Our counterintel guys are all over this now. Don't worry. One way or another we'll figure it out. But the most important thing is, our secrets are safe.'

'I'll drink to that.'

'Now, one last thing. This doesn't need to be said, but I'm going to say it, anyway. Everything connected to Cone Dynamics is top secret. You need to forget you ever heard the name. And you absolutely must not breathe a word about a report getting stolen or a network getting breached. Are we clear?'

Reacher nodded.

Knight said, 'Got it.'

Devine said, 'Thank you, Detective. I'm sure you'll find your shield waiting for you when you get back to Arizona. And I'm sure you'll hang on to it this time. As long as you don't do anything stupid. Anything *else* stupid, I should say. Like googling Cone Dynamics again. Or leaving them any more convoluted messages.'

Knight blushed.

'Well, I hate goodbyes.' Devine turned to head to the conference room.

Reacher said, 'Wait. I have a question.'

Devine turned back and did her best not to frown.

Reacher said, 'The document on the memory stick, that we know nothing about. Was a password needed to open it?'

Devine thought for a moment. 'No. The tech guy I spoke to was surprised about that. He put it down to the document being copy-protected. Is that important?'

'I don't know. It's certainly sloppy. What if the memory stick got lost? If someone found it, plugged it into their computer, and got served up the secret report right there on their screen? Whether it could be copied would be beside the point.'

'Vidic must have been confident he wouldn't lose it. And he didn't care what happened after he got paid for it.'

'That's another strange aspect. Vidic is new to this, I guess, but he was missing a step in the process. A safeguard. I've been involved in dozens of cases where things were getting sold that shouldn't have been. Guns. Grenades. Documents. Plans. IDs. Booze. And whoever is in the driver's seat invariably wants the final say.'

'In what way?'

'Imagine you're looking to trade item A for payment B. You make the exchange, but you leave A inoperable. You don't provide the key to work it until you're sure B is legit. It's weird that Vidic wouldn't work that way. What if the backpack was empty? What if the cash was counterfeit, or marked in some way? He'd have no recourse.'

Knight said, 'They already got stiffed once, by the property guys. Maybe he's a slow learner. Not all criminals are very bright.'

Devine said, 'You're right. But it is weird. I'll make sure to ask Vidic about it when we catch up with him.'

Reacher said, 'One other thing. At the old mine. The cave, where Vidic and Paris got released. Was a second van there, full of contraband?'

'No.'

'Inside the cave, was there a safe?'

'Yes.'

'Was it intact?'

'No. It had been broken into. It had been pulled away from the wall and a panel on the back had been cut through. Apparently the equipment that was used had been stored in a toolbox mounted on a truck that was found there. A white one, full of bullet holes. I have no idea what its story is.'

'Was the safe empty?'

'Not completely. Some jewellery, I think, and a few other trinkets. They didn't sound valuable. Some papers as well.'

'Any cash?'

'Not a penny.'

THIRTY-ONE

Reacher and Knight were silent until they were outside the building, on the pavement. Pedestrians hustled by. The streets were busy with traffic and a helicopter was coming in to land on a narrow strip next to the river.

Knight said, 'I'm going to Chicago. I want to be at Midway when they catch Kane. Will you come with me?'

Her phone rang before Reacher could respond. She checked the screen. It was Wallwork. She held the phone out and said, 'You really ought to get one of these. I'm not your damn assistant.'

Wallwork didn't have time for any pleasantries that morning. His voice was a low whisper. He said, 'Albatross's handler was at the motel. That's it. Got to go. Don't call me back. Ever.'

Reacher said, 'Thanks for the intel. Now, one more thing.'

'No. Never. We're done. No more things.'

'This is even more important. Even more urgent. I need to know if anyone of interest to the Bureau has been acquiring quantities of gold. If so, where is it? And I need the answers yesterday.'

'How am I going to find that out?'

'I don't know. Think outside of your box.'

Knight waved to a taxi that was stuck on the far side of the lights then turned to Reacher. She said, 'Why are you asking about gold?'

Reacher said, 'Something about the way Vidic's deal went south. It doesn't ring true.'

'So what does gold have to do with it?'

'I don't know. Maybe nothing. But for the test run with the property guys Vidic insisted on payment in gold. I thought that was weird at the time. If he changed what he wants now, that's weird, too.'

'Maybe he changed because asking for gold the first time was a fiasco. Or maybe because this deal was set up in a hurry. Not a lot of people have a ton of gold lying around.'

'Like I said, it could be nothing.'

The light changed. The cab crossed the intersection and pulled up next to them. Knight opened its rear door. She said, 'The airport, please.' Then she turned back to Reacher. 'Are you coming?'

Reacher said, 'I'll ride to the airport with you. But I'm not going to Chicago.'

The cabdriver set his meter running then pulled away from the kerb. He tapped a white plastic device in his right ear and began talking, soft but fast, in a language Reacher didn't recognize. Reacher watched the Arch until it disappeared from view then turned to Knight. He said, 'Ever had a case that

259

came together like dominoes falling? One fact after another, neat and tidy, nothing out of place?'

Knight nodded. 'Once or twice.'

'How did they turn out?'

'Badly. One was a murder case. A rich guy strangled his wife after an argument over a pair of shoes got out of hand. He paid some poor guy who had terminal cancer to take the fall in return for putting the guy's four kids through college. The other was a woman who was running for her local school board. She planted porn on a rival's computer to try and knock her out of the race.'

'So when a case seems too good to be true?'

'It usually isn't true. I have to admit, the Bureau melting down over this report and a lead popping up the very next day? That's a little convenient.'

'Paris is such a skilled hacker, she can get into the computers of a defence contractor with top level clearance, but she can't keep her email secure?'

'A woman who encrypts her private records with some complex code but doesn't put a password on a priceless document?'

'And why did Vidic set out driving in the wrong direction, then turn around and fly to St Louis? It would have been quicker to drive directly there from the house, like we did. And more discreet. No passenger manifests or credit card transactions for the Bureau to comb through.'

'He did use a fake ID for the flight, though.'

'Right. Which could be the smartest part of the plan. He had the IDs in his wallet when I knocked him out. He guessed that I would have searched him while he was unconscious. And that I would have seen the selection of names he could use.'

'He couldn't be sure you'd do that.'

'True. But most people project their own actions onto others when they're trying to anticipate what they might do. So the question is, what would Vidic do in that situation? And we don't even have to speculate. We know the answer because of what he did when he pulled me out of the car wreck. He looked in my wallet. My passport. The first thing he did when I ran into him was use my name.'

'So Vidic wanted to be followed to St Louis.'

'I think so.'

'Which means he wanted the deal to tank. He wanted the FBI to retrieve the report.'

'Looks that way.'

'Because, what? He realized how hot the report is? He figured that as long as it was unaccounted for the Bureau would never stop looking for him. Which would put a dent in his plan to start over somewhere new with Paris and set up their hack and blackmail racket. Maybe he figured the smart play was to burn the report. Trade the short-term pain for the long-term gain.'

'That's possible. No doubt about it.'

'But you don't think I'm right.'

'I think you could be. But it's more likely you're half right. Vidic wanted the Bureau to retrieve the report. Or to believe they'd retrieved it.'

'But they have retrieved it. Do you think it's a fake? Quantico said it was real.'

'I believe it's real. I believe all the non-copying gobble-dygook. I just don't believe it's all Vidic and Paris took. Everyone keeps referring to it as a report, right? Think about how reports are written. They always have summaries and extracts and conclusions and appendixes. All kinds of places where the important stuff is mentioned and repeated and reiterated. If I was in Vidic's shoes I'd have trimmed off enough to look compelling, use that as a decoy, and sell the bulk of the thing as originally planned.'

Knight tipped her head one way, then the other. 'How do we figure out which one it is?'

'For me it comes down to the money. The report is supposed to be worth a fortune. Is two million a fortune these days? Divided three ways?'

'Six hundred and sixty-six grand? I wouldn't turn it down. But I wouldn't quit my job, either.'

'Then there's also the coincidence. They steal two million in cash from Fletcher's safe, and the next day the asking price for the report is two million in cash? Plus one of them flies, to attract our attention, while the others drive. What can you take in a car that you can't take on a plane?'

'A giant sack full of twenties. You think the whole setup was a fake. They were providing both ends of the transaction.'

'Walking away from that kind of money makes their position more authentic. It makes it look like they lost everything, not gained something. And it's easier to snub two million bucks if you know you've got a bigger payday just around the corner.'

'So you think the main part of the report is still out there?'

'I don't have proof. Your theory could be right. You should go to Chicago. If they catch Vidic there I'll be the first to cheer. I'll call you tonight. You can tell me if you're celebrating.'

'I will. But if there's any chance you're right, you should talk to Devine. If the report is as sensitive as she says, with all the national security stuff, you can't take chances with that.'

*

262

The cab driver continued his conversation until the moment he pulled up outside Departures. Knight settled the bill in cash, climbed out of the car, and stood on the sidewalk. She turned to Reacher and said, 'Is this it, then? Is this goodbye?'

Reacher said nothing.

She said, 'Can we make it au revoir, at least? Promise you'll come out to Phoenix and visit.'

Reacher said, 'That's not a promise I'm sure I can keep.'

The corners of Knight's mouth curled down and she blinked, twice. 'That's honest, at least. OK. Bye, Reacher.'

'Look after yourself. Get that shield back.'

Knight took two steps toward the terminal entrance, then turned back. She said, 'I don't get it. You ride in the cab with me. You lay all that stuff about a second report on me. Then you dump me? That's an asshole move, Reacher. And I didn't have you pegged as an asshole.'

'Dump you? No. You're the one who's leaving. And I didn't ride with you to talk. I shared a cab because I needed to get here and that was the most efficient way.'

'Where are you going? You didn't say anything about flying anywhere.'

'I'm going back to the city. To Tower Grove Park. Just like Vidic did. I need to see the route through his eyes.'

'How come?'

'It'll help me figure out how dire the situation is.'

Knight shrugged. 'Well, have fun with that.' Then she turned and walked away.

Reacher found his way to the ride share pickup area on the Arrivals level. Twelve people were waiting there. A mixture of men and women, young and old. They were spread out, apparently at random, no sign of forming an orderly line.

Some had multiple suitcases with them. Others, just a purse or a briefcase. The only thing they seemed to have in common was that they were all staring at their phones. A car pulled up to the kerb. A black Tesla. A woman in a business suit waved to the driver then climbed inside. Reacher knew that the phones had something to do with summoning cars, and with pairing the drivers and the passengers, but he had no idea how the system worked. He scanned the remaining eleven faces to see which seemed most approachable when he sensed someone walking up behind him. He looked around and saw Knight. She pointed at a yellow plastic hut, about twelve feet by eight, that looked like it had been abandoned in the middle of the sidewalk, twenty yards away. She said, 'Come with me.'

Knight got to the hut first. It had no windows. Its edges were rounded and a sign above the single door said, *Smoke Shack.* Knight opened the door, looked inside, coughed, then said, 'Come on.' She stepped inside. Reacher followed. The interior of the hut stank of cigarette smoke. The walls and ceiling were stained orange. There was nowhere to sit, and the ashtrays which ran along the walls at waist height, like narrow troughs, were all overflowing.

Knight said, 'Horrible place. Let's make this quick. Tell me what you think the report is about.'

Reacher said, 'Everyone just calls it *the report.* I don't even know its title.'

'That's not what I asked. Listen, a penny dropped just now when I was walking to security. Something Devine said. Or let slip. I think she gave the game away. If we're on the same page, I'll stay. I'll help.'

Reacher took a moment to think. Then he said, 'Department of Energy.'

Knight nodded.

Reacher said, 'The report's about nuclear weapons. Specifically, I think, the design for a new warhead.'

'I got the weapons part. The Department of Energy is responsible for the nuclear arsenal, for some odd reason. Where do you get the new warhead from?'

'I'm speculating. It could be anything. But something about the name Cone Dynamics has been bugging me. This morning I realized why. In World War II the Brits began an atomic weapons programme that wound up getting swept into the Manhattan Project. They needed to keep it top secret so they had to find a way to account for all the expenditure. So they created a fake company as a front. It was called *Tube Alloys*. They figured it was innocuous. Boring. Not the kind of thing to attract attention. Cone Dynamics strikes me as similar.'

'You know what this means. We have to call Devine. Right now. You can't go rogue on this. It's too important.'

'I'll call her. There's one thing I need to nail down first. To make sure she gets the full picture. If she doesn't have it already.'

Reacher was first out of the hut. He hadn't enjoyed the atmosphere inside, but he hadn't hated it. And it had made an impact. It had been decades since he'd smoked a cigarette. Years since he'd thought about having another one. But right then, he could have been tempted.

Reacher led the way back toward the pickup area. As they came close, he turned to Knight and said, 'I guess you've done this before? Used the Uber app?'

She said, 'I'm not dead, and I'm not a hermit, so yes.'

'Good. I want you to—'

Knight's phone rang. She glanced at the screen, then held it out for Reacher. She said, 'Do I need to start billing you for the airtime?'

Reacher hit the Answer key and Wallwork's voice came on the line. He said, 'This is awkward. Before I tell you what I found, I need to ask you something, but it's something I can't ask you about. I'm right up on the limit of crossing a line, here. Truth is, I might have crossed it already.'

'I can't tell you what to do, Wallwork. If you're worried, hang up the phone. I don't want to put you in a bind. All I can say is, I bet that if someone could have provided information that stopped the Rosenbergs before they passed information to the Soviets, even if they had to cross a line, I bet they wouldn't have regretted it.'

'Did you pick the Rosenbergs at random?'

'No.'

The line was silent for a moment, then Wallwork's voice returned. 'A few days ago a request came in for information relating to the sales or shipping of gold. It came from counterintelligence. I called a buddy who works there. He told me three shipments had been traced to an address in Fort Lauderdale, Florida. I'll give it to you. It's basically an aircraft hangar at the executive airport. Belongs to a little outfit that hops between the mainland and the Bahamas. Passengers, and cargo.'

'Thanks, Wallwork. We'll be discreet, but this could be critical.'

'Don't thank me. Just leave me alone. I'm going to lie down now and have a heart attack.'

'Before you do, there's one more thing I need.'

'I've told you, stop this. I'm not going to keep—'

'I have a name. An alias. I think Vidic is using it. I need to

266

know if any transport has been booked for the next couple of days that corresponds. The name is John none Austin.'

'You know you'll get a million hits.'

'Filter by destination. Fort Lauderdale, or anywhere less than two hours away in a cab.'

Knight took her phone back. She said, 'John Austin? That's the alias Vidic used when he booked your room at the motel.'

Reacher said, 'Right. But he didn't mention it at the time. He doesn't know that I know about it. I'm thinking, if he's using the IDs he left in his wallet to lead the Bureau by the nose, what is he using for himself? It has to be one he believes is still under the radar.'

'OK. And why Fort Lauderdale?'

Reacher told her about the gold.

'You think someone is building a stash of gold to trade for the report?'

'I think it's possible.' Reacher started moving toward the ride share area again. 'Now, I want you to do whatever you would normally do if you wanted to get a ride to the park.'

Knight moved closer to the edge of the sidewalk and pulled out her phone. She opened her Uber app, entered the address for the park, confirmed her current location, and picked a luxury car. She figured she'd find a way to bill Reacher for the extra cost later.

Reacher was on the sidewalk behind Knight. The height difference between Vidic and any agent who was likely to be tailing him was probably significantly smaller, so Reacher factored in an estimate. He moved up as close behind her as he could without attracting attention. He stood beside her and pretended to check the licence plate of a car that had just pulled up. He moved to her other side and acted like he was watching for any new cars arriving. A couple of minutes later a car did pull up. An Audi A8. Knight opened the rear door and climbed in. Reacher looped around and got in at the other side.

Knight said, 'What could you see?'

Reacher said, 'Nothing. Were you trying to hide the screen?'

'Not at all. I was holding it like I always do. Unless I was talking to someone, or texting with them. And then the Uber app is hidden, anyway.'

They made good time into the city. The traffic was kind and the driver took detours around the parts where congestion was starting to build. He checked his mirror at one point to make sure Reacher was watching him, then said, 'This is my own route. I'm not following the phone. I could get in trouble, but I want you guys to get where you're going without any delays.'

Reacher had nothing to say to that.

Knight said, 'Thank you. Very good. We'll make sure that's reflected in the tip.'

Reacher figured the spot they got out at was close enough to where Vidic would have been dropped off the day before. The park didn't look exactly as he had expected. It was wide and open, with bushes and shrubs surrounding neatly trimmed grass. The air was heavy with the scent of tree blossoms. They set out along a path opposite the mouth of Thurman Avenue. It was a straight shot south. Reacher figured that if they kept going they would come out to the east of the softball field he'd waited next to last time, so instead they took a diagonal fork that cut through a stand of mature trees. A moment later he caught a glimpse of the North

Pavilion. They moved closer and he saw it was an open structure with eight pillars supporting an octagonal roof. A cupola perched on top and a weathervane sprouted from its peak. The whole thing was painted green and cream, and the centre was full of picnic tables with attached benches. A half-dozen more were scattered around the outside.

Reacher circled the pavilion, observing it from all angles, then continued around the oval to the south, the way Vidic had done after he had deposited the memory stick. Knight followed. They came to the second pavilion. It was just like the first, except for the shape of its cupola. This one had a rounded dome and no protruding vane. Reacher didn't like it. He would have made them identical.

Reacher spotted the trash can where the man in the hoodie had dropped the backpack full of money. He walked toward it, picturing himself executing a covert exchange. He imagined something had spooked him. He stopped and turned 360 degrees, checking his escape routes, looking for places to hide. Then he turned to Knight and said, 'Enough. We need to talk.'

She said, 'To Devine?'

Reacher said, 'To each other. We have a decision to make.'

THIRTY-TWO

Reacher and Knight selected a picnic table that was well away from any other pedestrians. Reacher faced north. Knight faced south and they sat slightly offset so that they could make sure no one crept up on them and eavesdropped. Neither of them spoke for a moment, then Knight said, 'So what was that all about? The cab from the airport and the walk in the park.'

Reacher said, 'I like to find patterns in things. Harmonies. If something is out of whack it rings alarm bells.'

'What's out of whack about taking an Uber? Covering the last part on foot when there isn't a road for it to drive on?'

'Nothing. Not in itself. But take the broader view. Vidic drove the wrong way, then flew. He used an alias. Either that was an attempt to elude the FBI, or to get their attention. Either way it was a ruse. Then he picked up a tail in the airport. Let himself be followed to the pavilion. Performed some incredibly clumsy pseudo fieldcraft with the memory

270

stick. Waited until it had been intercepted. Then disappeared into thin air. Look at this place. Losing a tail here would not be easy.'

'So he's better at some things than others. That's not a crime. Especially if he's self-taught.'

'I think he's good at all these things. And I think he's been very well trained.'

'I don't follow.'

'I think Vidic is an FBI agent.'

'He can't be. The Bureau's not incompetent. They wouldn't have infiltrated two agents into the same team.'

'I'm not saying they did.'

Knight stood up and took a step away from the table. She said, 'What the hell is wrong with me? I should have gone to Chicago to make sure the man who killed my father gets hauled away in handcuffs. Instead I stayed here with a crazy person. We know that Vidic isn't an agent.'

Reacher said, 'Do we?'

'We just agreed, there can't be two. We know Gibson was an agent. Therefore, Vidic isn't one.'

'Are you sure about Gibson?'

'Your friend Wallwork confirmed it.'

Reacher shook his head. 'Wallwork confirmed there was an agent. Not who it was. And Devine told me the agent's cover name was omitted from the file. That's a breach of procedure, but too common to raise any eyebrows before it was too late.'

'Who cares about the cover name? Gibson's prints proved it. They were pulled from the wreck of his car and matched with FBI personnel records. You can't fake that.'

'Walk it back. Vidic pulled Gibson and me out of Gibson's

271

Lincoln. Then he was alone with it before he pushed it through the guardrail. He could have wiped Gibson's prints and planted his own. Some DNA, too. A drop of blood, something like that. Easily accounted for by the accident. And he knew they'd be found. Devine told me that modern cars have a thing that shuts off the fuel supply in an accident to stop them from catching on fire or exploding. If Vidic is an agent, he'll know that, too. So it was a calculated risk, not a fluke.'

Knight was silent for a moment, then she sat back down. 'There's a way the pieces could fit, I guess.'

'There is. Start at the motel. Who was there?'

'Gibson. Vidic. The agent's handler. And the hooker.'

'Right. Vidic said he saw Gibson leaving a meeting with the handler in room 1. But that can't be true because Gibson was with the hooker in room 2.'

'You think it was Vidic with the handler in room 1. And Gibson who saw him leave.'

Reacher nodded. 'They were both going to regular meetings at the motel. Both were flying under the radar, but for different reasons. The hooker always had the same room. The handler switched hers up. It was only a matter of time before they wound up next door to each other.'

Knight said, 'That's how Vidic was able to describe the handler so well.'

'And her car. And why he lied about when he left the motel. He needed a plausible explanation for knowing those things so he claimed to have hung back and watched.'

'So Vidic was scared that Gibson was on to him. He probably followed him to the parking lot. But he couldn't confront him because you were there, dealing with the wannabe car

272

thieves and hitching a ride. Can you remember how Gibson seemed at that moment? Was he freaked out? Angry?'

Reacher paused. He closed his eyes, then nodded. 'Yes. I can remember. He was pissed about the car thieves, but not scared or agitated or impatient.'

'Doesn't sound like someone who just discovered a spy in his camp.'

'And it explains why he gave me a ride. The idea of an agent doing that never sat right.'

'Remember what you said about people projecting their own actions onto others? That goes for thoughts, too. And fears. Vidic would have assumed that Gibson would be suspicious when he saw him leaving a woman in a motel room. But Gibson would have thought Vidic was just there for some hanky-panky of his own. This whole thing could have been caused by a horrible misunderstanding.'

'A lot of tragedies are. Gibson's behaviour at the switchback fits that theory, too. He hit the gas when he saw Vidic closing in, sure. But in a regular macho, not-wanting-to-be-seen-as-a-slow-driver type way. Not in a serious attempt to run for his life.'

'So the crash was an unfortunate accident?'

'Unfortunate for Gibson. A godsend for Vidic.'

'How so? A civilian was dead.'

'Vidic wanted to get away and start over with Paris. Ditching Fletcher and Kane was one thing. Killing them, even, so that they couldn't describe him to anyone if they ever got busted in the future. But the Bureau? If they knew he was MIA they'd never stop looking. He had to make them believe he was dead.'

'Hence the fire. We assumed it was to make sure the body

couldn't be identified as an agent's. But we had it backwards. It was to make sure the body couldn't be identified as a civilian's. So the Bureau would have to go with the circumstantial evidence and order a new star for the Wall of Honor.'

'It all fits.'

'Not quite. There's one piece missing. The most important piece. This all depends on Vidic not only being an agent, but also deciding to turn his back on the Bureau. On the law. On what's right. That's a lot to accuse a person of when you don't have a shred of real evidence. We need to know more about his state of mind.'

'I don't think we do. Here's the clincher. If Vidic isn't an agent, how did he know the code name *Albatross*?'

Knight didn't reply.

Reacher said, 'In a way revealing it was a smart play. He apparently watched me intervene when I saw some guys trying to steal a car so it was a decent bet that I'd drop a dime to let the Bureau know about a dead agent. Using the real code name made it more likely they'd take it seriously and follow up, which he wanted them to do, so that he'd be officially recorded as DOA. But how did he know the real name?'

Knight said, 'He claimed he'd heard the handler say it to Gibson. But she couldn't have. Gibson wasn't with her. He was with the hooker in the next room.'

'There's no other explanation. Vidic turned.'

'I was wrong before,' Knight said. 'Vidic wasn't under too long. He was in too deep. He couldn't get back to the light. It's kind of tragic, honestly.'

Knight handed her phone to Reacher and he dialled Devine's number. She picked up after five rings. She said, 'Detective?'

'It's Reacher.'

'Oh. What do you need?'

'After we spoke back in the Ozarks, Knight sent you the picture she'd taken of Gibson's face. I'm guessing you haven't passed that on to his handler yet?'

'I'm not . . . I'd need to check on that. Lots of plates spinning here, Reacher.'

'You need to show it to her. Immediately.'

'Why?'

'Show her. Then pull the CCTV from the Oklahoma City or St Louis airport. Find some footage of Vidic. Show that to the handler as well.'

'I don't see where you're going with this.'

'You will.'

'OK. Then I'll get right on it.'

'Why don't I believe you?'

Devine didn't answer.

Reacher said, 'I'm not going on record as having drawn any kind of conclusion here. Or as having any knowledge of this situation. But you asked for my advice in that meeting. And my advice is that every investigation needs a solid foundation. You need to be sure of the identities of your principals. You should look to that. Right now. You have the tools. Knight sent them to you. Use them. Don't waste any more time.'

'OK. Well, thanks for your advice. Now, if there isn't anything—'

'There are four other things. First, the document you recovered in St Louis isn't all of Vidic's material. He split the report, let you retrieve part of it to buy himself room to operate, and is going to sell the rest.'

The line went silent for a moment, then Devine said, 'That's a mighty big claim. Can you back it up?'

Reacher said, 'Think about it. How hard was it to get wind of the sale? To track Vidic to St Louis, and then the park? Why did he fly when he could have driven? How did he disappear so easily as soon as the memory stick was intercepted? And here's the key. The report was supposed to be worth a fortune. You know what's in it. I don't. So tell me, is two million a fair price?'

'He was short of time and—'

'The price was two million because that's all they could put their hands on. They stole it from the safe at the cave.'

'How can you be sure?'

'If I'm wrong, so what? You throw more resources at catching Vidic, who needs to be caught, anyway. You save a little time. If I'm right, he's out there right now hawking the rest of that report. You can stop that from happening.'

Devine didn't respond.

Reacher said, 'Second, forget about the flight from Chicago to Alaska. Forget about those aliases I gave you for Vidic. They're junk. He wants you to think he'll be on that plane. He wants you on a wild-goose chase.'

'What makes you—'

'Send Gibson's picture to Albatross's handler. Pull the airport CCTV. Then you'll understand.'

'Damn it, Reacher, just tell me.'

'You wouldn't believe me. You need to join the dots for yourself. Third, I think Vidic is using a different alias. John none Austin. You should check flights, car rentals, hotels. You know the drill.'

'Where did—'

'Finally, someone has shipped a bunch of gold to an airplane hangar in Fort Lauderdale, Florida. I'll send you the address. It's possible that another section of the Bureau is watching it. You should tell them to be on the lookout for Vidic. It's a long shot, but we know from past deals he has a preference for gold and is selling something very valuable.'

'What other section?'

'Counterintelligence.'

'I can't just butt into their investigation, out of the blue, and start making requests.'

'Why not? What's more important? Retrieving the report or following protocol?'

'Fine. I'll think about it.'

'Don't think. Do.'

'Reacher, you've done the right thing bringing these issues to me. Don't think I'm not appreciative. It's just that there are a lot of moving parts here. I need to keep the machine working efficiently. Not stick a spanner in the works, even if it's with the best of intentions. Which brings me to a very important point. You need to let me run with it from here. I get that these kinds of things used to be in your wheelhouse. They're not anymore. Don't go meddling in areas that are beyond your sphere. Understood?'

Reacher said nothing. He hung up and dialled Wallwork's number. He wanted to check on flight records for John Austin but got dumped straight into voicemail.

Knight took her phone back and said, 'What does your gut tell you? Is Devine going to act?'

Reacher shrugged. He said, 'It's fifty/fifty. If she shows Gibson's picture to the handler, then the dominoes will fall pretty fast. If she soft-pedals that, maybe nothing will happen.'

'No luck with Vidic's plane tickets?'

'No. And we don't know if he's planning on flying, anyway. Hey, you had tags in Kane's guys' cars that you could track on your phone. Are they still in place?'

'You think those guys are still around? I bet Kane stood them down. He must be trying not to draw attention. The smaller the group, the better in this situation.'

'I'm sure he stood them down. He sent them away in the van full of contraband from the cave. As a reward. As a cover. Who knows. But I think he kept their cars. Vidic needed to get to Oklahoma City so that he could fly here. Kane and Paris needed to drive here with the two million. I want to know where those cars are now.'

'The guys could have found the tags by now and ditched them.' Knight opened her phone then swiped and tapped the screen. 'Vidic might be more observant. Wait. No. Here they are. Both of them. The first is at . . . the Oklahoma City airport. Just as you thought. And the second is . . . OK. Interesting. It's at the Indianapolis airport.'

'Pass me your phone? We need Wallwork to factor Indy into his search as the point of origin.'

Reacher got Wallwork's voicemail again. He left a message then turned back to Knight. He said, 'So. Decision time. Stay here and wait for intel, or roll the dice and head to Florida?'

Knight shrugged. 'This is a good location. Reasonably central. But I hate sitting still. What do you think?'

'An investigation needs momentum. We should go.'

THIRTY-THREE

They were closer to the south exit from the park than where they'd come in so Reacher and Knight hustled along the nearest path, which led diagonally to Arsenal Street. Knight used her phone to call an Uber. A car arrived after three minutes. A silver Toyota Camry. The driver was maybe twenty-five. He was from the Gambia and he talked incessantly about trees. His dream was one day to return home with seeds from every species of tree in the United States and plant a whole new forest. *Good luck with that,* Reacher thought.

While the driver talked, Knight switched apps and bought plane tickets to Fort Lauderdale. Reacher paid her back in cash. A lot of cash. First class, one way, last minute. They were every airline's dream customers that day.

At the airport Knight led the way to the airline's check-in desk and had the agent print paper boarding passes for them both. She didn't need one but Reacher had no phone and she didn't want to draw attention to the fact. He had enough strikes against him when it came to security screening.

Knight breezed through pre-check security and went in search of coffee. Reacher dragged through the regular line. When the TSA guy saw Reacher's expired passport he raised an eyebrow but he knew the rule and waved him through. Reacher caught up with Knight and grabbed a large cup of coffee for himself. Then they made their way to the gate and waited for boarding to begin. Reacher had forgotten how much he disliked airports. There were people everywhere, milling around, stopping for no reason, dawdling aimlessly, dragging unwieldy suitcases. He suspected that if hell exists, it resembles an eternal trek through a departure hall.

Reacher's pass said he was in boarding group one but four other categories of customers were called before him, which offended his sense of order. Things looked up once he was on board. He had a window seat with sufficient legroom, and once they were airborne the flight attendant brought him regular refills of coffee without needing to be asked.

Knight fell asleep but Reacher used the two and a half hours they were in the air to think. He was basing a lot on one slip from Devine. Her mention of the Department of Energy. He ran back over his conclusion that the Cone Dynamics report was connected to nuclear weapons. He had no reason to believe he was wrong. But no evidence that he was right. That seemed appropriate, in a way. Nuclear weapons always seem to conjure fear and paranoia in people. The rational part of Reacher's brain found that hard to understand. Only two had ever been used in anger. Fewer people had been killed by both of them combined than had died in many fire bombings during World War II. Or had starved and frozen in Leningrad. Or had been murdered after the siege of Nanjing. Or starved in Stalin's famines. He figured the reaction came from the unknown. The danger of dying, years later, of some hideous disease you had no idea you were incubating.

Reacher didn't share that fear, but he did feel some unease. For him it came down to the risk of human error. And the consequences. There weren't just two bombs now. There were vast arsenals, capable of destroying the world many times over. And they were only a hiccup in an early warning system away from doing just that. Or a tired eye mistaking a blip on a screen somewhere. He thought about all the near misses he'd read about. A Soviet guy named Petrov who had suppressed an early warning report because his gut told him it was false. A miscalibrated upgrade to a radar system that made flocks of birds look like missiles in flight. And error wasn't the only danger. There was foul play. The Rosenbergs. And after them, the guy who stole the design for a centrifuge that could refine uranium, which doubled the number of nations with nuclear capability. He thought about Vidic, the rogue agent with secrets to sell, and wondered if he'd be remembered in the same way.

Knight woke up as the plane started its descent. She switched her phone off airplane mode the moment the wheels touched the ground and checked for texts or voicemails. There was nothing.

Reacher spotted a cluster of empty seats near a gate that was out of service. He steered Knight toward it, borrowed her phone, and tried Wallwork. Again he got no reply.

Knight said, 'I hate this not knowing. Should we get a hotel? Or go straight to the hangar?'

Reacher said, 'Hangar.'

Knight led the way along another long corridor. They slalomed around the slower-moving travellers and dodged the knots of people spilling out of the little stores and cafés and bars that lined the route. They passed a sign warning them that they were leaving the secure zone, then started down an escalator. It was a long one and it moved slowly. Reacher could see a series of baggage carousels stretching out along the hall at its base and a wall of glass to its right with doors every few yards that led out to an access road.

Reacher had to push his way through a gaggle of people at the bottom of the escalator. They were hanging around a stationary carousel. A monitor suspended above it flashed a message warning passengers to check luggage carefully before removing it in case they were taking someone else's.

Reacher said, 'Does that really happen? Surely people know what their luggage looks like.'

Knight said, 'It happens all the time. A lot of bags look similar. Some are identical. That's why some people attach coloured straps, or bright ribbons. To make their things easier to identify. Plus people could be tired after a long flight. Or stupid. Or careless.'

Reacher shrugged. It seemed to him like another reason to avoid getting bogged down by possessions.

They continued past the last carousel, looking for signs for the taxi area, and Knight's phone rang. It was Wallwork. Reacher answered.

Wallwork said, 'Got a hit. *John Austin* is due into Fort Lauderdale from Indianapolis in thirty-five minutes.' He paused, then read out a flight number.

Reacher thanked him, then took Knight's arm to stop her.

They moved to the side and Reacher dialled Devine's number. This time she answered with a curt, 'Yes?'

Reacher said, 'Did you show Gibson's picture to Albatross's handler?'

Devine took a moment, then said, 'I did.'

'So you know.'

'I know. And I'm not happy.'

'I didn't think you would be. Did you deploy to Fort Lauderdale?'

'I'm not at liberty to—'

'So, no. Why not?'

'The justification was too thin. And thanks to you I'm standing in the path of a category 5 shitstorm.'

'I'm not to blame. You should be thanking me for finding out before things got any worse. And as for justification, Vidic will be landing in Fort Lauderdale in half an hour. Send the police, at least. Notify TSA. Airport security. Someone.'

'I'll do what I can. And Reacher? Stay clear of this. Leave now.'

'Leave where?'

'The Fort Lauderdale airport. I know you're there.'

Reacher looked around for a trash can. He said, 'Time for a new phone. Devine is using this one to track us.'

Knight said, 'What's the point? Are you going to buy another one every time you need to call her? Are you ever going to buy one?'

Reacher didn't reply.

Knight grabbed the handset from him and said, 'Give that to me. I need to buy more plane tickets. Whatever's the cheapest, just to get us air-side. To see what happens with Vidic. Watch Kane get arrested. And if no one else is there to do that . . .'

They had drawn level with the last carousel and Reacher was watching a lone suitcase rattle slowly around the oval.

Knight said, 'How did Devine seem? Is she going to do anything down here?'

Reacher said, 'They know they have a major PR disaster on their hands. That means people will fall into two groups. Those who will roll up their sleeves and try to fix the problem. And those who will do whatever it takes to shift the blame onto someone else. I think Devine will roll up her sleeves, given the chance. But she's not in for an easy ride.'

'I guess not. A couple of dirty cops came to light while I've been at the department. No work got done for weeks afterward. It was a festival of ass covering, both times. No reason to assume it's any different at the Bureau.'

'We'll soon know. If she can pull the right levers, Vidic and the others won't even make it off the plane. They'll have all the passengers stay in their seats after the plane has landed, then send in the local police. Maybe Homeland Security if they have anyone close enough.'

Knight looked away. Reacher thought she looked disappointed at the prospect.

The suitcase continued to circle the carousel.

Reacher said, 'What's up with that? Could someone have forgotten to collect it? Left the airport without picking it up?'

Knight said. 'Obviously. Why do you think they have left-luggage offices? Anyway, who cares about some dumb suitcase?'

Reacher did, for a reason he couldn't quite put his finger on. He said, 'Anyone could pick it up now, right? I could.'

'I thought you were anti-belongings. Why would you need a suitcase? You don't have anything to put in it.'

'What about the other carousels?' Reacher pointed to the

next in the line. People were swarming all around it and the belt was jammed with bags and suitcases of all sizes and colours. 'What's to stop me taking that silver one, right there?'

'Maybe the owner? Or airport security. Come on. Focus. We have to get air-side. Find Vidic's gate before his plane lands. So, enough with the questions. Back to security. There could be a line.'

'You go. I'm staying here.'

'What the . . . Why?'

'Bizarre idea. I'll explain later if it pans out. Rendezvous here if we both strike out. Otherwise, at whatever hotel is closest to the airport.'

Knight checked her phone and said, 'There's a Courtyard not far away.'

'Good as any, I guess. Good hunting.'

Reacher stationed himself near the baggage reclaim monitor and waited for Vidic's flight number to join the list. After half an hour he saw it, next to carousel 4. That was the carousel to his left. He checked the area around it. What he saw was not encouraging. There was no effective cover anywhere in the vicinity, other than a bunch of people, and Reacher was not built to blend into a crowd. He kept looking and spotted three yellow janitor's carts lined up in an alcove next to an accessible bathroom. One of them had a yellow bib hanging from a broom handle. Reacher strolled across. He glanced around. He saw no sign of any janitors so he stepped in closer, took the bib, and slipped it on. There was no way it was going to fasten around his chest, but he figured that wouldn't matter. He had the perfect disguise. Everyone would look at him but no one would see him. He could be wherever he needed to be. He released the cart's wheel lock and pushed it slowly to the far side of carousel 5. It wasn't moving. No one was waiting nearby, so Reacher took a sweeper on a long handle from its holder at the side of the cart and began to make his way forward and then back, gathering litter as he went, all the time keeping carousel 4 in his sight.

As Reacher swept the floor, the crowd around carousel 4 steadily grew. Soon it was two or three deep in places. Reacher scanned the faces methodically, left to right, front to back. And spotted Vidic. He was wearing a Pirates ball cap and had done something to his face to alter its contours. He had stuffed his cheeks with cotton wool, Reacher thought. Vidic had done the same kind of thing with his stomach. Rather than tall but stooped, he looked paunchy and squat.

A klaxon sounded and the belt began to move. A suitcase appeared at the top of a ramp in the raised centre section, like the top tier of a wedding cake. It slid down and joined the main ramp. It was made of ribbed aluminium and all kinds of bright stickers were plastered over its surface. A guy stepped forward and grabbed it. Vidic took out his phone. He did something to its screen then held it low down by his side. A bunch of other bags tumbled down. Some were claimed right away. Others made their way around the circuit, ignored by everyone who was waiting. A couple were grabbed, then put back. Vidic didn't move. He made no attempt to take anything or make contact with anyone.

The stream of new cases gradually slowed. Around half the people were still waiting, including Vidic. Then a backpack appeared. It teetered at the top of the ramp for a moment, then slid down. A rainbow ribbon was tied to one of its straps and it had a Real Madrid baggage label hanging from a handle at the top. Vidic kept his arm by his side but cocked his wrist so that his phone was facing out. Reacher guessed he was taking a photograph. Vidic relaxed his wrist, lowered the phone, watched the backpack as it made a complete circuit of the carousel, then turned and threaded his way through the crowd. Reacher saw him raise the phone again as he walked. He tapped the screen a couple of times then slipped the phone into his pocket.

Reacher slotted the sweeper back into its place on the cart and slipped off the bib. He took a step in the same direction as Vidic, then stopped. He could follow Vidic, or watch the backpack he had been so interested in. Letting Vidic escape after all the trouble he'd taken to find the guy seemed massively counterintuitive. But Reacher did it, anyway. He stayed where he was and kept his eyes on the moving belt.

The backpack made another circuit. Fewer bags joined it. More were taken. No one approached it. Reacher scanned the hall around him. He spotted Knight heading down the escalator. She reached the bottom then headed straight for him. She took a spot by his side. Her shoulders were sagging and she couldn't drag her gaze up from the ground. She said, 'You struck out, too? Let's hope our luck changes at the hangar.'

Reacher said, 'Vidic was here. Heavily disguised. I guess he slipped by you at the gate.'

'Vidic was? Where is he now?'

'He left.'

'And you didn't follow him? Are you crazy?'

Reacher pointed out the backpack. 'Vidic waited till he saw that bag. He sent a picture of it to someone.'

'Why would he do that? And why did you stay here? What's wrong with you?'

'Watch this.'

A man had stepped forward. He was around six-two and was wearing a blue pin-striped suit and smart black shoes. He had blond hair, cut short, and combed into a neat style. A tan leather briefcase was slung over his left shoulder. He watched the backpack as it approached, glanced around, then picked it up and walked away.

This time Reacher did follow. Knight kept pace at his side. The guy in the suit was making for the escalator. He stepped onto it. Stood politely to the side until he reached the top. Then he turned left and started across an enclosed bridge that led to a multistorey parking garage. At the far end the space opened out into a square lobby to accommodate a trio of payment machines as well as three doors leading to respective restrooms. The guy dodged to his left and disappeared through the centre door. The accessible restroom. Reacher tried the handle. It didn't move.

'Hey,' a voice said from behind the door. 'Occupied.'

Reacher looked at Knight and said, 'Got a quarter?'

Knight pulled out her wallet, rummaged for a moment, then handed a coin to Reacher. He waited a couple of minutes then forced it into the plastic groove beneath the door handle. He turned it, releasing the lock, opened the door, and stepped inside.

The guy was sitting on the closed lid of the toilet. His phone was in his hand. He had a computer on his lap. A memory stick was attached on one side. The backpack he had taken from the carousel was lying at his feet with its main compartment unzipped. His briefcase was perched on the edge of the sink.

The guy said, 'You can't come in here. This bathroom is occupied.'

Reacher thought he could pick up a hint of an Eastern European accent.

The guy's phone made a whooshing sound.

Reacher closed the door behind him and said, 'Who are you texting with?'

The guy said, 'Leave. Now. You can't be here.'

Reacher stretched out his left hand and took the phone. It made a different sound. A ping. The guy grabbed Reacher's wrist and gripped it tight. He pulled something from his suit coat pocket with his right hand. It looked like a pen until he hit the button at the top of its barrel. Then a spike shot out in place of a nib. It was three inches long, needle sharp, and made of some kind of laminate. Nothing that would raise any suspicions on an airport X-ray. The guy got to his feet, pushing with his legs to propel himself forward. His laptop slipped down and landed on the backpack, then slid onto the floor. He jabbed at Reacher's stomach. Reacher twisted his right hand around and blocked the blow with the back of his forearm. The sharpened tip bit into the dense material of his cast. A jolt of pain ran through his wrist. Reacher pivoted on his right heel and used the guy's own momentum to spin him into the wall. Reacher slipped the phone into his pocket then brought his left hand back up, driving his fist into the underside of the guy's chin. The guy rocked back on his heels. His head smashed into the wall. He stayed upright, swaying on his feet. Reacher grabbed him by the throat. He squeezed, crushing the guy's larynx, and simultaneously lifted. The guy raised up on his toes. He couldn't breathe. He grabbed Reacher's wrist with both hands and tried to wrench it free. He failed. His eyes began to bulge. He flailed wildly with both arms. His hands were trying to grab Reacher's head. His fingers were searching for his eyes. Reacher brought his right knee up and crashed it into the guy's stomach. The remaining air was driven out of his lungs. Reacher twisted and pushed the toilet seat up with his foot. He relaxed his grip on the guy's throat. The guy slumped forward. Reacher slid his hand around to the back of his neck, pulled the guy forward, then pushed his face into the toilet bowl. He leaned down with all his weight. The guy's forehead was crushed against the porcelain. The tip of his nose was touching the water.

Reacher said, 'Who do you work for? Who bought that memory stick?'

The guy pressed down against the floor with both hands. He was in good shape. Wiry rather than outright muscle, but even so he had no chance of lifting Reacher's weight.

Reacher said, 'A government? A middleman? Who?'

The guy kicked and scrabbled with his feet but couldn't get any purchase.

Reacher pressed the lever with his right hand. The toilet flushed. Water flooded down, filling the bowl. The guy's head was mostly blocking the pan so the water almost overflowed. It took a good thirty seconds to work its way around the U-bend. The guy bucked and heaved and twisted but Reacher didn't let up the pressure on the back of his head.

Reacher said, 'Who?'

The guy coughed and gurgled but said nothing intelligible.

'Want me to do that again? I can keep going all day.'

The guy spat, then said, 'Why not? Now I know I won't drown.'

Reacher pressed down on the lever again. The bowl filled.

The guy struggled, but less violently than before. When the water subsided he said something. Two words. Reacher didn't recognize the language but their meaning was clear. Reacher took a handful of the guy's hair, pulled him up into a kneeling position, then drove his knee into the guy's temple. The side of the guy's head smashed into the wall and he slumped down into the gap alongside the toilet bowl. Reacher dragged his body into the middle of the floor to make it easier to search him. He checked everywhere, right down to the heels of his shoes. He found a wallet with some paper money and four credit cards. An Australian passport, half full of stamps, which he guessed was a forgery. Some keys. And that was it. Nothing useful, which wasn't unexpected. Reacher checked the briefcase. Then the backpack. Neither was helpful. Finally he took the phone out of his pocket. He held it in front of the guy's face so that it unlocked, then read the conversation that unfurled on the screen. It started with a photograph of the backpack on the carousel, along with four digits. The combination for the bag's lock, Reacher guessed. It must have been sent by Vidic, although no name was displayed. Next was the guy's reply. An address. It was for the aircraft hangar at the executive airport that Wallwork had previously given as the location of the suspicious gold. Vidic had replied with a whole string of letters and numbers and symbols. A password, Reacher guessed. He memorized it, then dropped the phone and smashed it with his heel. He took the memory stick and slipped it into his pocket. Then he propped the guy's computer against the base of the wall to form a triangle with the floor and snapped it in half with the side of his foot.

When Reacher came out of the bathroom, Knight had moved to the side to make it look like she was waiting for someone to finish in the men's room. A guy in a wheelchair was in line. He saw the guy in the suit lying on the floor and said, 'What the . . . ?'

Reacher said, 'Call 911. He was looking at kiddie porn on his computer. Wanted me to join in.'

The guy wheeled away, fast. Reacher used Knight's quarter to relock the door from the outside then beckoned her over. He borrowed her phone and called Devine.

Devine's tone was no warmer than before. She opened with, 'What?'

Reacher said, 'Vidic is in Fort Lauderdale. Probably heading to a hangar at the executive airport.' He gave her the address. 'And send some guys to the regular airport as well. Vidic's contact is in the accessible bathroom at the end of the bridge leading to the parking garage. He slipped. Hit his head. He won't be awake for a while.'

THIRTY-FOUR

The executive airport complex is easy to find your way around if you've been there before. It's less straightforward for first timers because the buildings all look basically the same. They're lined up along one side of the runway and their individual signs are small and use the same font and colours due to some local regulation.

Vidic used the fact to his advantage. He gave his cabdriver the address for the building next to the one he wanted and as the guy crept along looking for street numbers, Vidic checked the parked cars and trucks for anyone keeping watch on the place. He only spotted one he was suspicious of. A panel van with a business name stencilled on the side: Crabtree and Watson Landscape Contractors. He googled and found a website with the same name, but it felt a little generic to him. More like a placeholder than a real resource. He was happy about that. Assembling 720 gold bars in one place was the kind of thing that drew attention. That was to be expected. A couple of agents keeping an eye open was fine. A heavier presence would have been more worrying.

Vidic stood in the shadows of the next hangar in line and waited for a suitable vehicle to come by. It was hot and humid outside of the cab's air-conditioning and his shirt was soon sticking to his back. A UPS van trundled into sight after a couple of minutes. He broke cover and kept pace with it, using its bulk to shield him from the landscaping van, and made it to the right hangar unseen.

The building was divided into two sections. The left-hand part was smaller. About an eighth of the overall floorspace. It was a combined reception and waiting area. There was a desk immediately inside the door where all the check-in and destination paperwork was taken care of. Beyond that were three discreet seating areas, each with eight chairs, so that passengers could be grouped together by flight. And at the back there was a self-serve bar with coffee, tea, and snacks.

Vidic smiled at the woman who was on duty at the desk and handed her a driver's licence. He said, 'Hi. John Austin. I'm here to check on a freight consignment.'

The woman checked the ID, looked up a record on her computer, then got to her feet. She passed the licence back, took a bunch of keys from a drawer, and said, 'Follow me, please.'

She led the way through a door in the right-hand wall, into the hangar itself. A large scales was set up for weighing cargo, and behind that a plane was standing with its engine cowling removed for maintenance. The section Vidic was interested in was behind the plane, along the far wall. There was a line of mesh cages for securing freight that was awaiting transport or collection. Eight, altogether. Three were empty. He scanned the others as he approached. He identified the one that must be his. The one with thirty wooden crates, seven inches deep by five inches wide by six inches tall. Small, but heavy. Vidic knew they would weigh more than fifty pounds each.

The woman unlocked the padlock holding the cage door closed and said, 'Take your time. Lock it when you're done.'

Vidic waited until the woman had left the hangar and crossed to a toolbox on wheels near the front of the plane. He took a screwdriver and went back to the cage. He opened the door and used the screwdriver to lever the lid off the nearest crate. He brushed back the packing straw and couldn't keep himself from grinning.

Gold. Universal. Indestructible. Eternal. Twenty-four bars per box. Seventy-eight thousand dollars per bar at current rates. Now all he had to do was move it before the untrustworthy bastards he'd sold the Cone Dynamics report to decided to double-cross him and take their assets back. He took one of the bars from the crate, replaced the lid, worked the lock, and went back to the reception area. He said to the woman, 'Is Mr McLeod available?'

She said, 'He's around somewhere. Outside, checking on one of the planes, probably. Take a seat. I'll find him for you.'

Andrew McLeod was a short, squat man in his thirties who still hadn't learned that as the manager of the operation he was supposed to delegate. He appeared in the hangar doorway five minutes later. He was wearing coveralls rolled down to the waist with the sleeves hanging loose and a white shirt with a tie poked through between two buttons.

Vidic followed him to the cargo area so that they could talk in private. He nodded toward the cage full of crates and said, 'I need all those gone inside of thirty minutes.'

McLeod said, 'No can do. Sorry. They weigh, what? Sixteen hundred pounds? Can't add them to another load, and I don't have a spare plane to take them on their own.'

'Are you sure?' Vidic pulled the gold bar out of his pocket. 'Is that what I think it is?'

'If you think it's a new Porsche, then yes.'

McLeod was silent for a moment, then said, 'Any passengers?'

Vidic said, 'Three.'

'How much do you all weigh?'

'Two hundred. One thirty, maybe. And around three hundred.'

'OK. I can make that work. Where to?'

'The Bahamas. Andros Island.'

'Fresh Creek?'

'No. I'll give you the coordinates. It's a new strip. Private. You won't find it on any maps.'

'Good deal.'

'There's one other thing. I want you to send your receptionist home, right away.'

'Why? What did she do wrong?'

'Nothing. She seems like a good person. One of my crew isn't. She doesn't need to be exposed to that.'

'If your guy's such an asshole, why do you hang around with him?'

'Call it a marriage of convenience. One that's not going to last very long.'

When Vidic texted the hangar's address to Kane and Paris, he told them to take the kind of precautions he had, because the place was being watched. Kane did not do that. He got out of the cab, crossed the street, and knocked on the rear door of the landscaping van. He got no response so he took hold of the handle and wrenched the door open. Two guys were inside, sitting at a console with cameras hooked up to computer monitors and microphones feeding compact speakers. They were in their mid-thirties, wearing shirts, ties, and shoulder holsters. They both went for their guns, but they weren't fast enough. Kane shot them both in the head with a silenced .22.

Kane walked into the hangar and crossed straight to the cargo cage. He looked in at the wooden crates and said, 'That's $56 million? I thought it would be bigger.'

Paris stopped in front of Vidic. She put her hand on his chest and said, 'Everything went OK?'

Vidic said, 'Like clockwork. We're just waiting for the pilot to switch over one of the planes. We should be loading in ten minutes. Out of here in twenty. It would speed things up if we could drag those crates over to the door. I tried, but they're crazy heavy.' He turned to Kane. 'Mind giving me a hand?'

Kane shrugged.

Vidic moved to the side of the cage door and waited for Kane to move.

Kane didn't move. He said, 'So let me guess. Vidic, you make like you're going to push. I pull. I don't get anywhere because these damn things must weigh a ton, but while I'm giving it the good ol' college try, Paris whips out her little Walther and pops a .38 behind my ear?'

Paris pulled her PPK out of her purse and said, 'That's pretty much what we were thinking, yeah. But if you'd rather take it straight in the face, that's fine, too.' She raised the gun and lined it up on the bridge of Kane's nose.

Kane said, 'If today's my day to go, then so be it. But maybe hold that thought for a second. Wait till you have all the facts.'

'I have all the facts I need. I pull the trigger, the world has one fewer asshole in it, and I'm nine million dollars richer. Am I missing anything?'

'Only that your boyfriend is an FBI agent.'

Paris lowered the gun. 'Wait. What? I don't have a boyfriend. Who's an agent?'

Kane stepped to the side. 'Vidic.'

Vidic reached for his gun, but he didn't have it. He'd come directly from the airport. So he said, 'Paris, shoot him already.'

Kane said, 'Notice he's not denying it.'

Vidic said, 'Of course I'm not denying it. It's a joke. You're just desperate to save your own miserable skin. You'd say anything.'

Paris raised her gun and pointed it at Kane. Then she lowered it again. She said, 'I want proof. You have thirty seconds.'

Vidic said, 'This is ridiculous. Gibson was the agent. We all know that.'

Kane said, 'Gibson was on board way before you. How could he have been an undercover agent so long and not have done anything?'

Vidic said, 'Not an agent, then. An informer. Whatever they call it. He flipped. Wanted out, did a deal.'

Kane shook his head. 'I knew Gibson. He was no rat. But you?'

Vidic took a step toward him. 'I'm no rat.'

Kane said, 'You know what they say. If you're explaining, you're losing.'

Paris said, 'Stop this. I want proof. Not insults.'

Kane said, 'Ask your boyfriend how he was able to set this deal up so fast.'

Paris said, 'He's not my boyfriend.'

Vidic said, 'Easy. I have connections.'

Kane said, 'What kind of connections? You deal with fences. Fences sell art. Not nuclear secrets.'

Vidic said, 'Right. Fences sell art. And they know people who sell all kinds of other things. Including secrets. Like I said, it all comes down to connections.'

'Connections, like foreign spies?'

'Any kind of connections.'

'Warhol one day, warheads the next? I call that bullshit.'

Paris put the gun in her purse and walked up to Vidic. She said, 'Ivan, look me in the eye. Tell me it's not true.'

Vidic said, 'It's not true.' Then he looked away.

'Liar!' Paris slapped him across the face. 'What happens next? A bunch of agents kick the doors in and drag us off to jail? Or will they wait till we're in the Bahamas? Where it'll be easier for us to get shot resisting arrest.'

'Nothing like that.'

Paris didn't reply. She couldn't bear to look at him.

Vidic said, 'OK. I was an agent.'

Kane said, 'You still are an agent.'

'Actually, no. As far as the Bureau is concerned, I'm dead.'

Paris said, 'That's why you wanted the phosphorus. So they'd think Gibson's ashes were yours. And you tricked me into helping you. This situation just keeps getting better.'

'Look, does any of that matter? We're here. The gold is here. We did that together. Let's not throw it away over some stupid—'

'It's not stupid—'

A red dot appeared on Vidic's forehead and the next instant the back of his skull was torn off. The cage next to theirs was sprayed with blood and brain. Then Paris heard the sound. A gunshot. She spun around and saw Kane holding his .22.

Kane said, 'There's your extra nine million. I never liked Vidic. But you? I can see a future for us. On the island. On the beach. In the bedroom . . .'

'I'd rather eat crushed glass.'

'You'll come around.' Kane took out his phone and took a picture of Vidic's body. 'An FBI agent selling nuclear secrets? It's the ultimate Get Out of Jail Free card. Go find a container. A jar or something. We need his blood. His DNA. Find something with today's date. And get me his phone.'

Paris picked up Vidic's phone, handed it to Kane, turned, and started toward the reception area.

'Paris?'

She stopped. 'What?'

'Your Walther. Drop it and kick it away.'

THIRTY-FIVE

Paris returned a couple of minutes later. She had a folded newspaper under her arm and she was carrying a tiny glass jar and a teaspoon. She said, 'This had jam in it. From the snack counter. I washed it.'

Kane said, 'Fill it.'

Paris took a deep breath, stooped down, scooped three spoonfuls of Vidic's blood into the jar, then screwed on the lid. She handed it to Kane. 'You say gross things, but it's an act, isn't it? It has been all along.'

Kane shrugged. 'You started it. I played along. You thought I was big and dumb. You were only half right.'

'Then be honest. You're not taking me to Andros. You're going to kill me here. No roll in the hay is worth twenty-eight million dollars.'

'I could take you there and have you and the money.'

Paris didn't reply.

'But no, you're right.' Kane raised his gun. 'You're not coming.'

'Wait.' Paris pointed to the crates in the cage. 'What if I could get you double that? Maybe more?'

'I'm listening.'

Paris unbuttoned her blouse, lifted the hem, gripped it in her teeth, and pulled. She made a hole in the stitching and worked an object out through it. A memory stick. She passed it to Kane.

'What's this?'

'A copy of the report. Exactly the same as the one Vidic had. I duplicated it in case the plan changed on the fly and I had to make the exchange.'

'You said it couldn't be copied. Like NFTs, or whatever.'

'We lied. Techno bullshit. We just made it look that way. We were bound to get found out eventually. But people didn't have to believe it forever. Just long enough to write the check. And with this report, exclusivity isn't such a big deal. Loads of countries out there want it. I have Vidic's contacts. You could sell it again. Multiple times, if you want.'

'So now I have the copy, why do I need you?'

'Because you can't open it. So you need to let me go. When I'm safe, I'll text you the password.'

'That could work, I guess. The file is the same as Vidic's? Exactly the same?'

'It is.'

'In every way?'

Paris nodded her head.

'Including the password?'

Paris frowned.

Kane smiled. He raised Ivan's phone and said, 'Oops.'

*

302

Reacher spotted the landscaping van the moment their Uber pulled up outside the hangar. He made it immediately as the FBI surveillance vehicle. But unlike Vidic, he made no effort to avoid being seen. The Bureau guys were going to get involved at some point. He saw no reason to stand in the way of the inevitable.

The reception area was deserted when Reacher stepped inside. Knight followed. She looped around and checked behind the desk. Reacher opened the door to the hangar and even before he went through he could smell the blood. He stepped inside. Saw the scales. The broken-down plane. The freight cages. And two bodies. Vidic's. And Paris's. He crossed to take a closer look and saw both of them had been shot in the head. Once each with a small-calibre weapon. Knight stayed in the doorway. She said, 'Reacher. That's a crime scene. Be careful. The agents from the van will be here any second.'

Reacher said, 'Watch the door,' then went to search the bodies. When he was done, Knight came to join him.

She said, 'Anything?'

Reacher nodded toward one of the storage cages. 'That one's been used recently. It's the only one that's not locked. There's an empty pallet. A few shreds of packing straw.'

'Someone cleaned it out.'

'I can't find Vidic's phone. Everything else is normal. Except for that.' He pointed at the hem of Paris's shirt.

'They didn't shoot each other. Not with matching head wounds like that.'

'No.'

'Kane.'

'Most likely.'

'Why is Paris's shirt unbuttoned? Do you think he molested her? Maybe that's how it got torn.'

'Doesn't look like the kind of tear you get in a sexual assault. Buttons torn off? Yes. Sleeves, too. But the stitching on a hem? It's more likely she had hidden something there. Something small. A handcuff key, maybe.'

'You think he cuffed her? There are no marks on her wrists.'

'Something else, then. Maybe the lab techs will pick up some kind of residual.'

Knight looked toward the door. 'What's taking the agents so long? Do you think they're calling for backup?'

'Maybe. I guess we should go and make contact. Make sure they know we're friendlies.'

Reacher closed the rear door and stepped away from the landscaping van. He borrowed Knight's phone and called Devine. He gave her the news. Two agents down. Two suspects down. Or three and one, given what they knew about Vidic. Plus one suspect unaccounted for and an unknown quantity of gold missing. Not the kind of news she was hoping for. Not with the PR issues she was dealing with. That was for damn sure.

Reacher hung up and handed the phone back to Knight.

She said, 'You didn't tell Devine you'd recovered the memory stick. Want to call her back?'

Reacher said, 'No.'

'Why not?'

'I don't know. Something in my gut told me not to. Maybe I will later. We'll see.'

'If you say so. What do you want to do now? It'll be better if we're not here when the circus arrives.'

What Reacher really wanted to do was head to the nearest Greyhound station or find a good spot to hitch a ride.

But a nagging doubt stopped him. It had to do with the scene inside the hangar. He was missing something. He was sure of it. He just couldn't put his finger on exactly what. He felt like he was looking at a print from an instant camera before it had time to develop all the way. The picture was blurry. The key objects were out of focus. That would change. He knew it. But it would take time, and it couldn't be rushed.

Reacher said, 'How about we head to that hotel you found.'

'The Courtyard? That works for me.' Knight opened her phone again and pulled up the Uber app.

The hotel was a big sprawling place and the room Reacher and Knight were given was all the way at the end of a corridor on the second floor. It turned out to be more like a mini suite. Aside from the bedroom and bathroom there was a kind of living room with a couch and a TV and a fridge and a microwave.

Reacher took a seat on the couch. The air was cranked all the way up. That was a welcome relief from the damp heat outside. Knight poked around the room and then began to pace up and down, unable to stay still.

Reacher said, 'You OK?'

Knight said, 'No. How could I be? Think of everything that's happened in the last couple of days. All the shit we've been through. And I'm still no closer to catching Kane. In fact, I'm further away. I'm just so frustrated, I want to smash something.'

'I get that. But Devine said your shield is waiting for you, back home. Kane is on the FBI's radar now. He's tied into a case involving a rogue agent. A dead rogue agent. They're not going to rest until they find him. You can count on that. Maybe it's time to pass the baton. Get back to your real life.'

'Would you do that, in my shoes?'

'Hell no.'

'Well then.'

Knight kept on moving. There was a coffee machine on a counter above the fridge. Reacher moved closer to see how it worked. There was a little plastic drawer that pulled out. It held perforated sachets. It looked like it took one per serving. There were two, not including the decaf options.

Reacher said, 'Want a cup?'

Knight said, 'Caffeine? Me? Right now? Yes, Reacher. Great idea.'

Reacher picked up on the sarcasm and just made one cup. He carried it back to the couch.

'Sorry,' Knight said. 'You hungry?'

'I could eat.'

'What do you feel like?'

'Anything.'

Knight took out her phone and looked for options. After a minute she said, 'Cuban?'

'Sure.'

'Want to see the menu?'

'Do they have a Cubano sandwich?'

'Looks like it.'

'I'll have one of those. And a pan con bistec. No lettuce.'

Knight added a mango Caesar shrimp salad and a selection of mariquitas, and placed the order. Then she started pacing again.

The food came in twenty minutes. It was delivered right to their hotel room door. Knight took a towel from the bathroom, spread it on the ottoman, and laid out the Styrofoam containers in a neat line. Neither of them spoke while they ate, but it wasn't a comfortable silence. Knight was on edge. She had nervous energy to burn. That was clear.

Knight took a last bite of her salad and said, 'I'm going for a walk. Want to come?'

Reacher shook his head. 'Have you got a computer with you?'

'What do you want a computer for?'

'I want to see what's on the memory stick.'

Knight pulled her laptop out of her bag and showed Reacher how to hook up the memory stick and select the document that was on it. A box appeared asking for a password. Reacher entered the string of characters he'd seen Vidic text to the guy's phone in the airport bathroom. He pecked away slowly with one finger, but he got the job done. The screen filled with words. Knight gave him a squeeze on the shoulder and made for the door.

The document was nothing like what Reacher had expected. He was anticipating all kinds of technical drawings and jargon he wouldn't understand and data he couldn't interpret. What he found was a long, scholarly discussion on the history of atomic weapons. It went all the way back to the early days of the first research programmes. It discussed reactor piles and heavy water manufacture and problems getting hold of sufficient uranium. Reacher found he was enjoying the material. He read fast and his mind soaked up all the detail and the associated trivia. Then, when he was three-quarters of the way through, he stopped in his tracks. He had found out why the price tag attached to the report was so high.

The section in question concerned the fissile material that was needed to create the enormous explosive power of the weapons. How it was made, and how it was formed to best facilitate the nuclear reaction. It turned out the United States favoured a cone shape for the material, hence the company's name. Cone Dynamics. It was the leading specialist in the field. The analysis went on to detail how if the material degraded, the bombs would lose efficiency. If the degradation reached a certain level, they wouldn't function at all. The design of the US architecture assumed a span of one hundred years before this level would be hit. But there was a problem. The material was new at the time. There was no history associated with it. No experience to base the calculations on. The scientists had been forced to rely on projections. And the Cone Dynamics guys had discovered that these projections were wrong. The degradation occurred more quickly. The cone shape that had been adopted exacerbated the decline. The effective life wasn't one hundred years. It was closer to seventy. The bulk of the warheads in the US missile systems had been built in the 1950s. Which meant that practically the whole of the nuclear arsenal was obsolete. If the weapons were fired, they would reach their targets. There was no problem with that. They might make a crater when they landed. But they would not explode. There would be no mushroom cloud. No heat. No windstorm. No radiation. And therefore no deterrent. The United States was vulnerable in a way it had never been in its entire history.

THIRTY-SIX

Reacher read to the end of the report then closed the computer and leaned against the back of the couch. He was trying to make sense of what he'd learned. The country's entire nuclear arsenal was inoperable, but did that matter? If an enemy nation discovered the secret, would they really launch an attack, safe in the knowledge that they wouldn't face any retaliation? It would be the end of mutual assured destruction. There was no doubt about that. Back in his army days, Reacher knew that people on the US side had flirted with the idea of preemptive strikes, even knowing there would be a response. Credible intelligence suggested Soviet generals had done the same. There was speculation about the Chinese. And all the non-state actors that kept popping up. That was all years ago, of course. But the world had only gotten crazier since then. And someone had just paid a prodigious amount of gold to get their hands on the report.

Reacher was driving himself crazy with the speculation.

He had no crystal ball. All he could say with certainty was the fewer people who knew the secret, the better. There was less chance of it leaking, that way. Which led him to another question. Who already knew? Vidic and Paris had, for sure. But they couldn't leak because they were dead. Bowery may have known the details, but he was also dead. Devine and the team that had analysed the memory stick from St Louis would – if the document on it was the same. And Kane most likely would. He would have demanded details when Vidic proposed the trade for his life.

The picture in Reacher's mind suddenly came into focus. The scene from the hangar. Two things now connected. Paris's torn shirt and Vidic's missing phone. The hole in the hem was the perfect size to conceal a memory stick. And the phone contained the password to open the report.

Kane not only knew, he had another copy. He could put the report back on the market anytime he wanted to.

Reacher picked up the room phone and called Devine. He gave his name and she came back with, 'I'm busy, Reacher. Make this quick.'

He said, 'You have another problem. There's one more memory stick. Kane has it.'

Devine didn't respond right away. Then she said, 'And you know this, how?'

Reacher explained about the shirt and the phone.

Devine said, 'That's it? It's pretty thin, Reacher.'

'Maybe. But if I'm right . . .'

Devine sighed. 'I'll look into it.'

Knight let herself back into the room half an hour after Reacher finished his call. She walked over to the couch, slumped down in the spot next to Reacher, and closed her eyes.

Reacher said, 'Feeling any better?'

She said, 'No. Did you read the report?'

'I did.'

'Was it worth all the song and dance?'

'And some.'

Knight opened her eyes. 'Really?'

'It's serious stuff. Want to take a look?'

'No. I have no bandwidth left for serious stuff.'

'OK then.' Reacher dropped the memory stick on the floor and crushed it with his heel.

'What did you do that for?'

'Like I said, it's serious. I'd trust you to read it, but no one else.'

Reacher and Knight slept in the same bed but nothing happened between them. They didn't even touch. They were both too restless. And they were both awake when Knight's phone rang the next morning. It was Devine. Reacher answered.

Devine said, 'I'm just checking in. Yesterday was quite a day. Are you OK? Is Knight?'

Reacher said, 'We're fine.'

'Specifically, I'm checking in about reporters. Bloggers. Conspiracy nuts. Has anyone been in touch with you?'

'Do they count as nuts if what they think is true?'

'Whatever. Has anyone been sniffing around, is the point.'

'No one. What about Kane?'

'We've located him. He's in the Bahamas. We can't do anything, unfortunately. He's in a sovereign nation and our case is just too weak.'

'It's weak? He killed two agents. Three, if you count Vidic.

311

A retired detective. And that's before you scratch the surface.'

'I was talking about our official position. Unofficially? People do all sorts of dangerous things in the Bahamas. Take scuba diving as an example. Equipment fails. Air tanks run dry. Who knows, maybe you'll read the paper on, say, next Thursday? Maybe there'll be a story about a fatal accident. Maybe you'll recognize the victim's name.'

Reacher hung up and handed the phone to Knight.

She said, 'What was that about Kane?'

'They're running a black bag op on him. They're going to drown him in the Bahamas, next Thursday.'

'Sweet. Fancy an island vacation? I'd love to be there when they bring the body in.'

Reacher didn't reply.

She said, 'Sorry. I know your passport has expired. I didn't mean to be insensitive.'

'It's not that. I'm thinking about the memory stick. Assuming Kane has it. If he's still breathing for another few days that gives him plenty of time to set up a sale. The report is in demand. Look at how fast Vidic off-loaded it. And Kane has Vidic's phone. He has access to his contacts. He could get in touch with the same folks that tried to buy it before. Offer them a second bite at the cherry. Or find a new buyer. Or hide it, then someone might find it after he's dead.'

'I see that. What do you want to do about it?'

'Go to the Bahamas. Find Kane. Get it back.'

'How? Your passport has expired.'

'Someone flew Kane there with a bunch of illicit gold. On short notice. Kane only got the address of the hangar an hour or so before we showed up. That person can fly us.

I just need your phone again. I need to ask Wallwork for two more favours.'

Andrew McLeod, the pilot, lived alone in a V-shaped single-level home. It was at the corner of a triangular street, which was called a circle, about five miles away from the executive airport where his hangar was located. Most days he could drive to work in under ten minutes but that morning there was no point. His premises were closed by order of the FBI. The building was swathed with crime scene tape and it was under 24/7 observation.

McLeod was still in his bathrobe when the doorbell rang. He'd slept late. He was exhausted. A combination of lots of hours in the air and the shock of finding two dead bodies in his workplace. When he heard the sound, his first thought was *Reporters*. He'd been warned not to speak to any. The FBI agent who had interviewed him had been clear on that point. But still, he was tempted. He wanted to see his name in the paper. More importantly, he wanted his ex-wife to see it. He crept toward his living room window. Peeked out at his front path. And saw two people. A huge guy, not unlike the man he'd been forced to transport the day before. And a woman, quite similar to the one he'd seen dead on his hangar floor. He pulled away, fast. And that was a mistake, because the movement caught the huge guy's eye.

Reacher abandoned the bell and hammered on the door. He got no response. He hammered again, harder. There was still no answer. So he called out, 'McLeod? We're coming in. There's nothing you can do to stop us. The only question is, are you going to open the door first?'

Five seconds ticked past then Reacher heard footsteps.

313

The door opened. McLeod stood at the threshold, trying to block the way.

Reacher said, 'Can you fly in that robe?'

McLeod said, 'No.'

'Then you better change.'

'Why?'

'You flew a guy to Andros yesterday. In the Bahamas. You're going to take us to the same place.'

'I don't know what you're talking about. I didn't fly anyone anywhere yesterday. I couldn't. Some lunatic broke into my place. There was a shootout. Bodies on the ground. Blood. The FBI.'

'The guy who did the shooting. He gave you gold to fly.'

McLeod didn't respond. Reacher's statement wasn't technically true. One of the dead guys had given him the gold. Kane just took the ride the stiff had paid for. But McLeod didn't think it was the time to dwell on the details.

Reacher said, 'Tell me about flying. Do you like it?'

McLeod nodded.

'Do you need legs that work, to fly? Arms?'

McLeod changed into jeans and a Hawaiian shirt with shoulder tags to hold his captain's epaulets, then drove Reacher and Knight to the executive airport in his BMW. He parked two hangars away from his own then led the way between a pair of buildings. They approached the apron where his planes were parked, on foot. There were three aircraft clustered together. All were different models. Reacher recognized one kind. It was an ancient de Havilland. Built in Canada for a few decades after World War II. The US Army had used them for search and rescue missions. Reacher had been involved in a few of those. Although in his experience they generally wound up as search and recovery.

McLeod crossed to the left-hand side of the de Havilland. He opened a small door and gestured for Knight to crawl through to the middle row of seats. Reacher looped around and got in at the front. McLeod circled the plane. He was serious about his pre-flight inspection, despite the illicit nature of the flight itself. He climbed in behind the yoke, next to Reacher. Inside the plane, everything felt flimsy and worn. The seats were thin and the springs poked through the scant padding. Exposed metal was everywhere. All the signs and warnings had been applied with red paint. Some freehand. Some stencilled. Several almost completely rubbed off. The same went for the calibration markings on some of the controls. Most of the instruments looked like they'd been stolen from a museum. Although Reacher was surprised to see some modern ones shoehorned in, with digital readouts and colour displays.

McLeod took a headset that had been hooked over his front sun visor and put it on. It had a microphone sticking out at the side. He pointed to a set of ear defenders in front of Reacher's position, and another on Knight's right-hand side. These were standard home improvement store items, hard and orange and plastic. Reacher and Knight pulled them on, anyway. McLeod started the engine. The propeller turned erratically for a moment, then fell into a steady rhythm. McLeod spoke to the tower, then eased a lever forward. The plane started to move.

The taxi out to the runway was bumpy, but not too loud. They trundled to the end, turned, and waited. Then McLeod opened the throttle. The plane shook and rattled and built up speed until it was able to claw its way into the air. McLeod held it straight, climbed, then pulled a tight 180-degree turn. Reacher could see a soccer stadium below them. A few wide, straight roads lined with businesses. Residential streets fringed with neat, square houses, many with pools. Strips of water. Taller buildings in the distance, including one that looked like the body of a giant guitar.

The plane was soon out over the water. It settled into a steady drone. The sun was to their left, halfway up in the sky. Land appeared after a shade under a half hour. Andros Island. Reacher could see a sandy coastline. Occasional clusters of cabins on the beach. Boats moored just offshore. Several piers jutting out into the water like pointing fingers. Many had structures at the end. They were mostly made of rough wood with roofs thatched with palm fronds, though a few were more substantial. A wide river cut through the island at one point. Trees covered most of the land, except for a handful of deep round holes that were filled with bright blue water.

Their destination had been determined before leaving McLeod's house. Reacher had initially been in favour of going to the same landing strip that McLeod had taken Kane to the day before, but a problem had emerged. They compared the strip's position on the map with the location of Vidic's phone, which Wallwork had provided. The two did not match. The phone, and therefore presumably Kane, was about ten miles from the strip. McLeod reported having seen no taxis or vehicles or facilities of any kind when he had deposited Kane and unloaded his crates of gold. The place sounded like a dead end, so they decided on the island's established airport, instead. Fresh Creek.

The landing was bumpy. The runway was rough. It was a series of concrete slabs, set close together, but with definite gaps between them. McLeod bounced his way to the only building that was in sight. *The Terminal.* A hand-painted sign announced its international status, but one of the screws holding it up had rusted through, leaving it hanging down at a drunken angle.

Knight climbed out and walked toward the door marked *Arrivals.* She had her passport in her hand and she moved slowly and calmly, like a regular tourist. McLeod swung the plane around. He guided it back along the runway, all the way to the far end. He swung the plane around again. When it was side-on to the terminal Reacher opened the door. He slid out, dropped onto the ground, and rolled to the side. Then he scrambled up and darted into the belt of trees and shrubs that lined the site. McLeod rumbled the plane back toward the terminal. Reacher pushed his way through the undergrowth. He was expecting to find a fence to climb, but soon arrived at the side of a road that ran parallel to the runway. No cars were passing. No vehicles of any kind. No one had seen him. He glanced around one more time then sat at the edge of the blacktop.

Knight appeared after ten minutes. She was in a taxi. An aged Nissan minivan. She was driving it. She had struck a deal with its owner to rent it for the day. She had offered a thousand dollars. The woman hadn't taken much persuading. Her only condition was that Knight gave her a ride home first, which was five minutes from the airport. When they pulled up outside her house, Knight struck another deal. A hundred dollars for the use of a pair of binoculars.

Reacher climbed into the passenger seat. Knight didn't speak for the first few minutes. She was busy adjusting to driving on the left. It was the first time she'd ever done that. She pulled up a map on her phone and entered Vidic's

317

location. It was fifteen miles away. The roads were wide and generally straight with a few tight turns and narrow bridges over rivers and streams. There was next to no other traffic. Very few houses. The ones they saw were small and low, set back from the road, and mostly disappearing into the trees. A handful of new ones were under construction, all concrete and rebar. The sites were all fenced off and no one seemed to be actively engaged in the process of building them. There were several churches, which looked to be in good condition, and numerous vehicles abandoned at the side of the road, which did not. There were trees everywhere, but not many flowers.

When the phone's map said they were a quarter mile from their destination it called for them to turn left, toward the ocean, along a straight, narrow road. In reality it was little more than a track, cutting through a mangrove swamp. Knight stopped the cab. Reacher got out. He had the binoculars. He used them to observe the one building that was visible. It was ahead and to the right. But not on the land. Not even on the beach. It was perched on the end of a pier, thirty yards from the shore. Three cars were parked at the water's edge. They were nondescript Japanese sedans. Probably all that was available to rent or buy on the island at short notice.

Reacher climbed onto the roof of the minivan to improve his vantage point. He lay flat and trained the binoculars on the building. It was the most substantial structure he'd seen on a pier, either from the plane or the taxi. It was an octagonal shape for optimal views of the island and the ocean. It was built of brick and stone, not wood. It had a tiled roof that was covered with solar panels. Glazed windows. And a solid-looking front door. A deck ran all the way around it, edged with a rustic wooden railing. A ladder ran down to the surface of the water and a boat was moored to one of the stone pillars that supported the house. A Zodiac, with twin outboard motors. It looked fast even when it wasn't moving. The pier led away from the centre of a gentle cove, and the nearest points of land were symmetrical promontories, each about a quarter of a mile from the house itself.

Reacher stayed on the roof for ten minutes, then slid down and told Knight what he'd seen.

She said, 'What about Kane?'

'He was there. And so were his four guys.'

THIRTY-SEVEN

Reacher and Knight climbed back into the minivan and took a moment to assess their situation. The outlook was not favourable. They were outnumbered five to two. Their opponents had a prime position. It had an unobstructed 360-degree view of its surroundings and the only dry approach was along an exposed pier that offered no cover whatsoever.

Reacher said, 'The best approach would be a siege, all things being equal.'

Knight said, 'We could do that. Keep watch. Stop anyone who tries to approach in case they're here to buy the memory stick. Then hand the gig over to the Feds on Thursday.'

'True. But all things aren't equal. What if Kane emails the report to a buyer? What if the buyer shows up on a boat? How would we stop them? Or a float plane. Or a helicopter. Or Kane leaves on his boat? No. The only option is a deliberate attack.'

'That's impossible.'

'No. Just difficult.'

'So what's the plan?'

'Two phases. First we reduce their numerical advantage. I want you to set a marker on this road. I'll hide in the mangroves at the side. There's plenty of room in their crazy roots. You continue. Drive all the way up to the parked cars. Then make a nuisance of yourself. Crash into one of the cars, maybe. Set its alarm going. Slash its tyres. Make it look like you're going to steal it, or light it on fire. Keep going till one of the guys comes running across the pier. More than one, if we're lucky. Then turn around and hightail it out of there. Don't stop till you reach the marker. The road's so narrow they'll have to stop, too. Get down in case they open fire. Then I'll hit them from the side.'

The least satisfactory part of the plan's execution from Reacher's point of view was the lack of visibility from his hiding place. He saw Knight drive away. Then he could only listen. The engine sound faded. A couple of minutes passed, then he heard glass smashing. A car alarm blaring. More glass smashing. Then nothing for another two minutes. Three. Then he heard a vehicle approaching. But slowly. Not trying to outrun anything. There was no doubt about that. Then the minivan trundled back into sight. Knight jumped out. She stood at the side of the road, hands on her hips, and said, 'Sorry, Reacher. I did what I could. The fish didn't bite.'

Reacher emerged from the tangle of mangrove roots and stood by Knight's side. He said, 'No problem. Time for a new plan. Can you look up what time the sun will set tonight?'

Knight prodded and swiped at her phone, then said, 'A whisker after 7:30.'

'OK. That means we'll have to stick around a little longer than I'd hoped, but so be it. Maybe we'll get lucky. Maybe they'll come out on their own. But because they probably won't, I want you to drive to the airport. Go back through passports. Find McLeod. And tell him to fly to this spot at exactly 7:20. Then it'll be time for him to channel his inner barnstormer. I want him to fly around like a maniac. Pretend he's trying to land on the beach but keeps having to pull up. Make it look like he's out of control. Like he's going to crash. Like he's drunk. He can do anything he wants as long as it's eye-catching. OK?'

'No problem.'

'He needs to keep it up, as wild as possible, till seven-thirty. Then return to the airport and wait for us at the far end of the runway, where I got out.'

There were six hours to kill before McLeod performed his tricks, and under different circumstances it would have been pleasant to spend the time together. The landscape was beautiful. They enjoyed each other's company. Reacher and Knight talked about it. They were tempted. But in the end, practicality won. Neither of them knew McLeod. All they had learned so far was that he was happy to break the law, given the right incentive. Not something that built confidence in his reliability. He had promised to wait, but if he got cold feet and baled on them, their plan would fall apart. There were no attractive alternatives. So Knight left right away. They figured that with her by his side, McLeod's backbone would grow a little thicker. And his appetite for taking the easy way out would become a great deal thinner.

Reacher found another spot in the mangroves with a view along the whole length of the road and settled in for the duration. He would have preferred to be with Knight but with that possibility off the table he didn't object to waiting alone. Stillness bordering on the comatose was one of the two natural states that suited him. The other was explosive action. If the plan worked the way he anticipated there would be time for that, as well, after the sun went down.

No vehicles drove toward the shore the whole time Reacher was watching the road. None drove away from it. Reacher heard no boats and no planes. So when the clock in his head hit 6:00 p.m., he was as sure as he could be that Kane and his guys were still holed up in the house at the end of the pier. He broke cover and made his way west, along the edge of the swamp. He saw fish sheltering behind the mangrove roots. Turtles going about their business. But no people. He covered the ground slowly and steadily and made it to the rocky outcrop overlooking the house with twenty minutes to spare.

By seven-fifteen the sun had sunk low in the sky behind him. Reacher took off his shoes and socks. He tucked his passport and ATM card and toothbrush safely inside and weighed the shoes down behind a root with the Glock. He moved into the cover of a large mangrove plant and stepped into the water. He lowered himself until he was submerged up to his neck, moving gently, causing no ripples.

Two minutes later Reacher heard a plane engine. It was coming closer. He scanned the sky. He caught sight of a dot against the inky background. It grew larger. He recognized the shape. It was McLeod's de Havilland. The airplane was coming in hot. For a moment Reacher thought it was going to crash into the ocean near the shore. McLeod turned at the last moment, banked hard, and began to climb. Reacher set out to swim. He cut through the water steadily. Smoothly. He made no jerky movements. No splashes. No sounds. The plane buzzed the beach, west to east. Reacher kept swimming, stroke after stroke. The plane rose, then wobbled in the air like it was losing its invisible support. It fell, then levelled out. Reacher swam on. He pulled a little closer to the house on the pier. He kept on going. The plane kept swooping and diving and banking. Reacher pulled to within a hundred yards of the house. Fifty. Twenty. The plane darted across the sky, heading west. But this time it didn't pull up. It didn't turn. It kept going on the same heading. It grew smaller, then disappeared. Reacher was still in open water. He was completely exposed. If he was spotted, that would be the end. The worst shot in the world would have all the time he needed to hit the target.

Reacher took a deep breath and ducked his head under the water. He let himself sink a couple of feet straight down, like a falling rock. Then he kicked with all his strength. He stretched and pulled and hauled himself through the water. The sudden increase in effort set off an abrupt throbbing in his head. He couldn't see anything through the darkness. His lungs began to hurt. Then burn. He forced himself to take one more stroke. Two. Then let himself float to the surface. He opened his eyes and looked around. He saw the underside of the pier. He was safe. For the moment.

Reacher swam to the ladder. He grabbed hold with his right hand. Pulled. And immediately let go. There was no strength in his wrist. Only pain. It couldn't take his weight. He couldn't climb with one hand. And he couldn't get his feet on the lowest rung. It didn't extend into the water, which left him marooned. There was no way forward, and no way back.

Reacher took a moment to bring his breathing under

control. The throbbing in his head had subsided a little, but it was still there. He ignored it and looked around. He focused on Kane's boat. The Zodiac. He pushed off from the ladder and swam across to its mooring line. He pulled himself up with his left arm. He slithered over the side and rolled onto the boat's slatted wooden floor. Then he moved to the stern. He stood up, stretched out, and closed his fingers around the vertical side of the ladder. He stepped onto the bottom rung and began to climb. He made it to the top. He paused. He listened. He heard a creaking sound. But not footsteps. He figured it was just the ladder binding against the stone column supporting the house. He risked a peek above the highest rung. He saw no one. He took another breath and scaled the last few feet until he was standing on the deck. He darted across and pressed his back against the blank wall between two windows.

Reacher chose the window to his left. He crouched down and took a quick look through the glass. He saw a bunch of living room furniture but no people. He looked again to be sure then tried to take hold of the window frame. He couldn't get a grip. The paint was too shiny. Too slippery. And his right hand was no help at all. The false start on the ladder had messed it up worse than it had been after the car wreck. So he stretched up to the top of the casement with his left. He heaved. He used all his strength but couldn't move it an inch. The frame was stuck solid.

There were three more windows on the ground floor. They were for the kitchen, a dining room, and a study. All the rooms were empty. All the windows were jammed. Reacher stepped back until he was leaning against the railing. He craned his neck to get a glimpse of the first floor. He could see another four windows. Three were dark. They had plain glass and they were closed. One had frosted glass. And it was open a crack. Reacher climbed onto the deck rail and leaned forward to use the wall for support. He studied the stones it was made from. One stuck out a little further than the others. It had a flat top. Reacher would have preferred a deeper ledge but there was nothing he could do. It was the best available. He planted his right foot on top and tried to grip its edge with his toes. The stone was rough against his bare skin. He shifted his weight toward the wall, pushed down with his foot and shot his left hand up, aiming for the windowsill. He grabbed hold of it. He spotted a tiny ledge for his left foot. Moved his foot from the rail. Gripped with his toes. Pushed down and at the same time shoved his hand through the open window. His fingers found the inside edge of the sill. He shifted his right foot up. Pushed. Levered the window up with his wrist to increase the gap. Slid his forearm through. Then his useless right arm. His head. His shoulders. His chest. With each move he walked his feet higher, shifting them from one joint or crack in the stone to another. Finally he wriggled his body far enough through the window frame for gravity to stop fighting him. He slithered across the top of a toilet cistern, took a moment to regain his balance, and lowered himself to the floor.

Reacher lay still. He listened. He heard nothing so he got to his feet. He took a towel from a rack on the wall. He needed to dry his hair to stop water from dripping into his eyes. Then the door opened. A guy stepped through. His hands were on his belt, already loosening the buckle. He saw Reacher standing in front of him. He stopped dead. Then he raised both his arms and lunged forward, clawing at Reacher's throat. Reacher threw the towel in the guy's face and batted his arms aside. Then he grabbed hold of the guy's

326

shirt. He pulled, adding to the guy's own momentum. He stepped to the side and pivoted, swinging his shoulders around to bring every ounce of centrifugal force to bear. Then he let go. The guy continued straight. He was out of control, like a falling-down drunk. His arms were flailing like windmills. He was desperate to find anything to brace himself against. The wall. The window frame. The toilet. But he missed every solid surface. His head disappeared out of the window. His body followed. His legs. His feet. Reacher heard a crash from below. He heard wood splintering. A long, drawn-out scream. Then silence.

Reacher rushed out of the bathroom. The corridor was empty. He turned left and dived through the first door he came to. It was a bedroom. Small, and sparsely furnished. He pressed back against the wall to the side of the doorframe. He heard footsteps on the stairs. Two sets, running. They continued straight, into the bathroom. Reacher looked around for anything he could use as a weapon. He saw a chair sitting in front of a vanity. It was made of wood. It was old. Rustic. It looked sturdy. And its legs narrowed markedly toward its feet.

Reacher grabbed the chair and made for the bathroom. The two guys had found out it was empty. They had turned around. They got to the doorway at the same moment as Reacher. They were rushing out. Reacher was charging in. He was holding the chair out in front, legs-first. One caught the leading guy in the gut. Reacher pushed forward. The second guy was slow to react. He slammed into his buddy's back, pinning him like the meat in a sandwich. The chair leg pierced the guy's shirt, then his skin. He howled. Reacher pushed harder, driving both the guys back through the door. The chair leg bit deeper into the first one's abdomen. He screamed. Blood soaked his shirt and streamed down, staining the front of his jeans. Reacher kept on shoving. The second guy slipped. He fell onto his back. The first guy tumbled on top of him. Reacher let go of the chair then stamped down onto its seat. Hard. Maybe harder than he should have. A shock wave ran all the way up from the sole of his foot to the top of his skull. He felt a jolt of pain, sharp and hot. His vision split into two identical images. They stayed separate for a moment, then reunited. Reacher saw that the chair leg had disappeared further into the guy's gut. He twitched, then stopped moving. The guy on the ground struggled and wriggled and managed to shove the corpse off to the side. He flattened his hands on the floor, ready to push himself up. He wasn't done fighting. That was clear. So Reacher stepped around and stomped on the guy's throat. His larynx collapsed. He wheezed and gurgled and clawed at his neck. His eyes bulged. No air was getting to his lungs. He rolled over onto his front. Some kind of primitive instinct was coming into play. It was driving him to protect his wound. To shield his weakness while he searched for a last-ditch manoeuvre. It was unlikely that he would find a way back, but Reacher was in no mood to take chances. He slammed his heel down against the base of the guy's skull. He heard a crunch. The guy stiffened. His shoulder blades pulled back, then he flopped down, face-first. He twitched. Then he was still.

Reacher heard a sound behind him. Another set of footsteps on the staircase. He spun around and rushed out of the bathroom. Kane's fourth guy was running up the stairs, heading right for him. He had a knife in his hand. Reacher hated knives at the best of times, and at that moment he was far from his best. The throbbing in his head had wound up a notch and his vision was blurred around the edges, so he picked his moment. He tracked the guy's trajectory. Stepped forward at the perfect time and kicked the guy under the chin like a lineman looking to make his name at the Super Bowl. The guy's head snapped back a full 90 degrees. Reacher heard a crack. It was crisp and loud. The guy's neck was broken. There was no doubt about that. His body spun around, landed on its back, and slid headfirst all the way down to the bottom of the stairs.

Reacher stopped and listened. The house was silent. The four guys were accounted for. The *secondary players*, as Knight had christened them. But there was no sign of Kane. And the front door was open. Reacher suddenly saw the potential flaw in his plan. He had done what he had described to Knight, the day before. He had projected his own attitude onto Kane. Reacher stood and fought when he was attacked, no matter the circumstances. No matter the odds. There was no guarantee that Kane would do the same. If he ran, and he didn't take Vidic's phone with him, it would take one hell of an effort to find him again. All he had to do was cover the length of the pier. The same stretch of walkway that had made the house so hard to assault was now Kane's cakewalk to freedom.

Reacher pushed the doubt aside, picked up a Ruger 9mm that the guy he'd impaled with the chair had dropped, and checked the rest of the first floor. There were two more bedrooms. Both were empty. There was no sign of Kane. No indication he'd ever set foot inside them. Reacher made his way downstairs. The treads creaked under his weight but otherwise the house was silent. There was nothing to give away any hiding places. No sounds or misplaced chinks of

329

light. Reacher stopped in the hallway. There were four doors. All of them were closed. That meant there were four chances to find Kane. And four chances to walk into a trap.

Reacher called out, 'Kane? You surprise me. Vidic said you were an asshole. A sociopath. A Neanderthal. I believed him. But when he said you were a coward? I thought he was wrong. I know better now. No wonder everyone laughs at you. You're a joke. You have a yellow streak that's fatter than your head. Which is pretty extraordinary, if you think about it.'

Reacher paused. There was no response. He wasn't entirely surprised but at least he'd tried. Now there was no alternative. He checked each ground-floor room in turn. The kitchen. The dining room. The living room. And finally the study.

There was no sign of Kane.

Reacher felt his stomach grow tight. He thought of the memory stick falling into the wrong hands. The consequences could be unimaginable. And then there was Knight. She had been so sad the night before when the reality of Kane's latest escape had come home to roost. Each time he slipped through their fingers it only hit her harder.

Reacher shook off the negative thoughts and forced himself to focus. The boat was still there. He would have heard the motor if Kane had sailed away in it. That meant his only route off the island was by air. There were two options. The official airport at Fresh Creek, or the private strip Kane had flown into the day before. Knight was at Fresh Creek. She would stop Kane if he tried to leave from there. Or she would die trying. Reacher was sure about that. Which left the new strip for him to cover. He checked the pockets of the guy who was lying at the bottom of the stairs. He ignored the guy's wallet and a spare magazine, then found what he was looking for. A car key. He slipped it into his pocket and took a step toward the front door. Then stopped. The door was standing open, like an invitation. Like someone wanted him to walk through.

Reacher went back to the living room, unlocked the window, and climbed out. He glanced at the body of the guy who'd walked in on him in the bathroom. The top of the railing was gone, presumably into the water, and two of the uprights had speared the guy's torso. Reacher looked away, checked the Ruger, and started to edge around the building. He was moving clockwise, expecting to find Kane lying in wait beside the front door. His sight was still grainy so he decided to take no chances. He would shoot Kane in the leg, the first chance he got. He made it halfway around. Heard a thumping sound, behind him. Then something slammed into him. It felt like he'd been hit by a truck. The impact knocked him down. He hit the deck. The gun slipped out of his grip, skittered across the deck, and fell into the water. The air was driven out of his lungs. His damp clothes were slippery and he slid into the railing. His head hit a post and his vision split in two. A wave of dizziness washed over him, just like it had done after the car wreck. Then he heard a voice. He realized it must be Kane's. It said, 'You're clever, Reacher. Just not clever enough.'

Reacher rolled to the side and Kane's boot smashed down onto the spot where his head had just been. He scrambled to his feet and dodged backward, struggling for balance. Kane was looming in front of him, arms wide, blocking his path. He took a step closer. There was no way past him. He was the same height as Reacher, but he was heavier. He didn't have a cast on his wrist. And he could see straight.

331

Reacher looked up and said, 'You're the one who's not clever enough if you're thinking about killing the guy who wants to make you rich.'

Kane took another step.

Reacher said, 'You don't know who I am. I work for . . . it doesn't matter. The name wouldn't mean anything to you. But the money will.'

Reacher moved his left foot slowly to the side. Kane would be in range very soon. He would only have one chance to spring forward and poleaxe the guy, even though he could currently see two of him, so he needed to get his foundation just right.

He said, 'The gold those Europeans gave Vidic? That's peanuts next to what I can get you.'

He felt something against the side of his foot. Something hard with a straight edge.

'Why do you think I'm here? Why do you think I went to the trouble of infiltrating your tedious little group?'

He glanced down. It was a strain to focus but he was able to make out that the deck plank had snapped where Kane had stamped on it when he tried to crush Reacher's head. The rows of screws showed it had been fixed down at its front end, its centre, and its rear end. Now it was broken between its centre and its rear edge.

'We knew all about Paris and Vidic and their little hacking sideline. Truth be told, we were impressed. They got some good stuff. Like the example you have. I hope you've got it somewhere safe.'

Kane's gaze dipped for a moment toward his right-hand pocket. Then he looked up and said, 'I like you, Reacher. It's a shame I'm going to have to kill you. But you're bullshitting me. Vidic was a Fed. You got wrapped up in this whole thing by mistake.'

Reacher said, 'Kill me? You'll have to catch me first. I hope you can swim.'

Reacher feinted to the side like he was going to jump over the railing. Kane lunged forward. Reacher stamped on the broken plank, just ahead of where it was cracked. His weight forced that section down. The joist in its centre acted like a pivot. The front end shot up, right as Kane reached it. He tripped and went down, face-first. He lay still for a moment, winded. Reacher didn't hesitate. He didn't waste time on taunts or insults. He just curled his toes up and smashed the ball of his foot into Kane's temple. He did it again, to be safe. Kane was completely inert. The back of his neck was exposed. Reacher raised his foot, high. He was ready to slam his heel down and mash the delicate vertebrae, just like he'd done to the guy in the bathroom. Then he heard a voice. It was female. It was loud and insistent. It said, 'Stop. Please.'

THIRTY-EIGHT

Reacher looked up. He saw two versions of Knight standing at the side of the house, next to the railing. He blinked one copy away and saw that her eyes were wide. She was breathing hard. She said, 'Don't kill him. He needs to stand trial. Everyone should know what he's done. He should pay the price, the legal way. That's what my father would have wanted. I know that now.'

Reacher lowered his foot, then crouched down and checked Kane's pockets. The first was empty. There was a bunch of coins in the second. And a memory stick. Reacher pulled it out. He set it down on the deck. Took the gun from Kane's waistband and used the butt like a hammer. He smashed the memory stick and swept the broken fragments into the water. Then he steadied himself, straightened up, and looked at Knight. He said, 'Go ahead. He's all yours.'

*

Agent Devine was waiting in the little customs and immigration area at the Fort Lauderdale executive airport when Reacher and Knight got there. She had sent two agents outside to arrest McLeod, and two more to accompany Kane to the hospital and secure him there. Knight stepped up to the desk when she was called by the officer. She showed her passport, answered a couple of questions, and was allowed to formally reenter the country. Devine waited for the glass doors to slide closed behind her, then turned to Reacher. She said, 'So, the Bahamas. Do you think Kane wanted to retire to the beach and count his gold? Or is there some other attraction to the place? I've never been.'

Reacher kept a neutral expression on his face. It could have been a genuine question. It could have been an attempt to kickstart some small talk. But he figured it was more likely that Devine was trying to find out if he had read the Cone Dynamics report. The information it contained could conceivably lead to a nuclear attack against the United States. If that happened, someplace upwind of the radioactive fallout would be the best location to hunker down. And if the world economy was decimated in the aftermath, there would be no better currency than gold.

Reacher said, 'I have no idea. I doubt Kane did, either. Vidic picked the location. He found the house. The landing strip. It was all Vidic's plan.'

'Vidic. Albatross. Whoever picked that cover name must have been able to see the future. I'm glad Vidic is out of the picture, but I'm not going to lie. Things would be a lot neater if you'd finished Kane, as well, when you had the chance.'

Reacher said, 'Knight wanted her father's killer to stand trial. I guess I'm just a romantic at heart.'

'This isn't romance. This is a mess. If Kane goes to trial

335

there's no doubt he'll play for a deal. He'll threaten to spill what he knows to the press. And once we start down that road, it's only a matter of time until something leaks.'

'You said, *if* he goes to trial.'

Devine didn't reply.

Reacher said, 'Jails are depressing places. People get suicidal thoughts. Sometimes they act on them. Maybe I'll be reading a paper one day soon. Maybe there'll be a story about how Kane hanged himself in his cell. In fact, I'm pretty sure I've read that story before. More than once. Just with different names.'

Devine said, 'I couldn't comment on that.' Then she lowered her voice. 'I think it's more likely that Kane will need surgery due to his head injury. He won't make it off the table. A tragedy, yes, but so commonplace it won't even make the papers.' Then she turned to the officer and flashed her badge. 'This man's passport was destroyed during an official Bureau operation. Any follow-up, send it to me.'

Reacher and Devine walked side by side toward the glass exit doors. They were frosted but Knight's silhouette was still easily recognizable. Devine stopped. She said, 'You go ahead. There's something else here I need to deal with. Goodbye, Reacher. And good luck, wherever the future takes you.'

Devine turned and made her way back to the immigration desk. Reacher stepped forward. The doors slid open and he walked outside. Knight moved over to stand in front of him. She pulled something out of her purse. A felt-tip pen. Then she took Reacher's right hand and lifted his arm until his wrist was horizontal. His fracture had been reset at a clinic in Andros Town before they left the island. It was encased in regular plaster of Paris, this time. Old school, plain white, and itchy as hell in the heat. Knight started to write on the rough surface. She set out a string of digits. Thirteen, altogether, followed by an 'x' and an 'o'.

She said, 'That's an ISBN number. You can use it to identify a specific book. I would have ordered a copy for you online, but I didn't know where to send it. Maybe you'll pass a bookstore on your travels. If you do, buy a copy. You'll need it.'

Reacher said, 'What for?'

Knight dropped the pen back in her purse and took out a piece of folded paper. She handed it to Reacher. He straightened it out. It was covered with more numbers, all grouped together in sets of three.

Reacher said, 'It's a book code?'

'I put it together last night, at the hotel, when it turned out it was too late for the plane to take off. I wanted to say a few things but I was having a hard time getting my words straight. It's about my father. About Kane. About you helping to catch him. And not killing him when I asked you not to. How I feel about all of that. The code seemed like a good way to do it. That way you can't read it right away. It's still a little raw for me, and it's not like I can email you later.'

'There's a great bookstore in New Orleans. I'll hit them up the minute I get to town.'

'Do that. And Reacher? There's one other thing in there. My phone number. If you're ever near Phoenix, use it. When we met I tried to bring you a fake breakfast, as a trick. One day I'd like to buy you one, for real.'

ABOUT THE AUTHORS

Lee Child is one of the world's leading thriller writers. He was born in Coventry, raised in Birmingham, and now lives in New York. It is said one of his novels featuring his hero Jack Reacher is sold somewhere in the world every nine seconds. His books consistently achieve the number one slot on bestseller lists around the world and have sold over one hundred million copies. Lee is the recipient of many awards, including Author of the Year at the 2019 British Book Awards. He was appointed CBE in the 2019 Queen's Birthday Honours.

Andrew Child is the author of nine thrillers written under the name Andrew Grant. He is the younger brother of Lee Child. Born in Birmingham, he lives in Wyoming with his wife, the novelist Tasha Alexander.

dead good

Looking for more gripping must-reads?

Head over to Dead Good –
the home of killer crime books,
TV and film.

Whether you're on the hunt for an intriguing
mystery, an action-packed thriller
or a creepy psychological drama,
we're here to keep you in the loop.

Get recommendations and reviews from
crime fans, grab discounted books at bargain
prices and enter exclusive giveaways
for the chance to read brand-new releases
before they hit the shelves.

Sign up for the free newsletter:
www.deadgoodbooks.co.uk/newsletter

Find out more about the Jack Reacher books at www.JackReacher.com

- Take the book selector quiz

- Enter competitions

- Read and listen to extracts

- Find out more about the authors

- Discover Reacher coffee, music and more . . .

PLUS sign up for the monthly Jack Reacher newsletter to get all the latest news delivered direct to your inbox.

For up-to-the-minute news about Lee & Andrew Child find us on Facebook

 /JackReacherOfficial

 /LeeChildOfficial

and discover Jack Reacher books on Twitter

 /LeeChildReacher

Excerpts from an interview with

Steph McGovern,

Lee Child and Andrew Child

Transcription of conversations printed here
from a live event held at the 2023 Theakston Old
Peculier Crime Writing Festival on
22 July 2023

With thanks to Steph McGovern and event hosts,
Harrogate International Festivals

Steph McGovern:

Oh, it's lovely to see you all here. Thank you so much for joining us tonight. What an honour and a treat it is to be on stage with these two legends. As Val said, Jack Reacher is a global phenomenon, and he mentioned there is a Jack Reacher book being sold every nine seconds somewhere in the world. That's over one hundred million books which have now been sold, and of course, there's the whole franchise operation off the back of it: the film starring Tom Cruise and the Amazon TV series created, of course, by Lee Child, and now enjoying a second phase of life in collaboration with his brother Andrew. Before this, Andrew had written nine thrillers under his given name, Andrew Grant. Before we get into the books, can I ask you a bit about your childhood? So there's fourteen years' difference, isn't there, between you? You grew up in Birmingham, Lee. Tell us a bit about what it was like.

Lee Child:

I was born in 1954, and my first reliable memories are about 1957. And then Andrew was born eleven years after that, during which a lot changed. And to be honest, for me, it was a miserable childhood. It was that post-war austerity, which was not really a big deal because if you hadn't ever had something, you didn't know you were missing it. And we were not poor, not in the sense of starving. We always had three meals a day and we always had leather shoes. But apart from that, we had nothing. And I felt like a fish out of water at that point because I had two other brothers. I'm the second of a batch of three. Number one and number three were very similar, very, very boring, and not at all like me. And I literally felt that I was a changeling. I'd been mixed up at the hospital, I did not belong there—

Steph McGovern:

Really?

Lee Child:

Yeah. Hated it. I remember being eight years old in the summer of 1963. I was about to turn nine and just thought, 'This is horrible. I've got to survive another ten before I can get out of here.' But then my life changed really happily. We were on some dreadful summer vacation in Wales, in a caravan with the rain lashing down, and this boring, repressed family all around me. I was utterly depressed. I had just had enough. I got out of the caravan, scurried through the rain and sat in a car just to be on my own. And I turned on the radio and it crackled to life, because it was an old tube radio in this old Rover that we had.

The first thing I heard was Brian Matthew on the *Saturday Club* saying, 'And here it is, the new one from The Beatles.' And it was 'She Loves You'. It was the 23rd of August 1963, twelve years to the day before I got married, as a matter of fact. I hadn't really been aware of The Beatles before that. I thought, 'Yes, this is fun. This is good. This is exciting. It's full of joy and energy. There is something for me.' And that completely changed my life.

From that point on, I had a pretty good time because I just ignored everything at home and enjoyed the sixties. And then, five years later, Andrew came along. Of course, he was just a newborn baby at that point, and I was quite fascinated with that, actually. My mother occasionally trusted me to babysit, which was a terrible mistake because by the time he was a year old, I was a huge pothead. It was April 1969 and I was fourteen.

As Andrew grew into a person, I could tell, 'Actually, yeah. Genetics is right. We are related.' This was a revelation to me. It was really strange that I was a middle teenager by this point and he was a tiny toddler, but I felt intensely connected. The family then started to have some value for me.

Steph McGovern:

Andrew, what was it like for you, then? On the other side of this?

Andrew Child:

Obviously, I didn't know a lot of this until I was much older. But as a little kid myself, certain things had changed. We were still living in the same place, but years had passed and the oldest brother had left home. But really, the experience was exactly the same, of feeling different. As I got older, I really loved reading spy fiction. I think it was because a spy is pretending to be someone else in order to fit into this environment that he shouldn't really be in, which is how I felt all my childhood. The only thing that was different for me, it wasn't listening to The Beatles in the car, it was the fact that Lee had escaped. And so it was this little chink of light on the horizon that made me think, 'Yeah. He got out, so I can get out.'

Steph McGovern:

Yeah. And I want to come to that escape. But can I just check something that I read about you, Lee? You were saying you weren't poor, but it was a pretty tough environment you grew up in. Am I right in thinking, in your school uniform, you had razor blades in the lapels of your blazer?

Lee Child:

I did. It was a long time ago. It was Birmingham and it was an emotionally inarticulate culture. Nothing could ever be talked about, good or bad, no problems could be resolved by conversation. And if you had a problem with another kid or anything like that, it was always violence. I mean, I was a smart kid and I loved to read. And so, in one pocket I would have a book, and in the other pocket I would have a knife. Then I saw or read somewhere about a guy who had those old-fashioned shaped safety razor blades. If you sew them in a line under your lapels, then the next bully that grabs you is in trouble. And that worked like a charm for quite a long time.

Steph McGovern:

Goodness.

Lee Child:

I still had a knife, but I didn't really use it. I didn't like knives, and that is reflected in Reacher. The only thing Reacher really doesn't like is knife-fighting. So I had a rule at primary school. If you pulled a knife on me, I would break your arm. I had to do it twice and then everybody left me alone.

Steph McGovern:

That's incredible. You worked in telly originally, didn't you?

Lee Child:

I did, yeah.

Steph McGovern:

And how was that for you? You said you read a lot. Were you always thinking, 'I'd quite like to write,' or—

Lee Child:

No, I never thought about being a writer. It's the weirdest thing. I never, ever thought about it. But what I wanted to be essentially was The Beatles. I wanted to be doing something that gave people joy and happiness, and in exchange for that, I would receive love and approval, which I was not getting anywhere else. And so it was an actual transaction. I wanted to make people happy. The school I went to was a very traditional old primary school that was all about reading, writing, arithmetic, and it was a great school from that point of view. I'm sure people of my age will agree that, in Birmingham, if you were born late in the year like I was, you did everything a year early. So I left primary school when I was ten, never stayed on for the eleven-plus. I figured that I knew enough at ten to get through the whole rest of my life without learning another thing. I could read, I could write, I could add things up. That's all you really need.

Steph McGovern:

Yeah.

Lee Child:

I first fell in love with the theatre. That was my thing because of a very strict, disciplinarian headmistress. All she wanted to do was give people a good, practical education, but she was insanely in love with American musical theatre. In fact, her niece was an actress called Carolyn Lyster, who starred in *Crossroads*. Twice a year, at Christmas and in the summer, she would put on a big show, which was basically all her favourite musical numbers strung together with a completely meaningless plot. I saw the first of them as a spectator in the audience, and I just loved it. I loved the whole vibe and the feel, these beaming children brightly lit on the stage, and these beaming parents in the audience just loving it. And I thought this was what I wanted to do.

So I wanted to be in the next show. It was very embarrassing actually because they gave me this sheet of lyrics and said I should sing. You know how it is if you can't do something, but you don't yet know that. I was standing there singing the song, wondering why everybody was going pale. I have no musical talent at all, really no onstage talent. I was always the third spear carrier from the right sort of thing. So I quickly migrated to backstage and I did that all the way through secondary school. I had what they would now call intern jobs at the Birmingham Rep and even the Royal Shakespeare Company. I loved the theatre. And I still do go to the theatre, absolutely love it, but it's insecure and nobody makes any money. It's difficult.

I was incredibly earnest. There was a British theatre director called Peter Brook who was very progressive and really the voice of the sixties. He did that *Midsummer Night's Dream* at Stratford. It was fabulous. He wrote a book called *The Empty Space* and argued very persuasively that all the theatre needs is some actors, a script and a space. And I agreed with him, which meant that backstage people like me were fundamentally unnecessary. I didn't want to be fundamentally unnecessary, so I thought, 'Well, I'll go to television,' where it's all about backstage people. I mean, nobody would see you apart from all these people like me who are enabling the transmission. It is completely germane. So, yeah. I ended up at Granada in Manchester. Back in the glory days, Granada was terrific. When I got there, they were making *Hard Times* by Charles Dickens, *Jewel in the Crown*, *Brideshead Revisited*, *Prime Suspect* and *Cracker*. Just one great thing after another, plus a fabulous documentary line too. It was a vibrant place and I loved it.

Steph McGovern:

Andrew, you dabbled a bit in the theatre world as well, didn't you? And then you went into the corporate life after that?

Andrew Child:

It's surprisingly similar, but we got there through different paths really. When I was at senior school, my favourite thing was English, English literature, and that was down to our teachers. They were fantastic.

Steph McGovern:

Makes such a difference, doesn't it?

Andrew Child:

It really does. They would introduce you to these amazing books, encourage you to read them, and then let you talk about them. You could come up with any theory you liked as long as you could justify it. And that's what I liked best, because then it almost became a challenge to come up with the most bizarre interpretation and then be able to back it up sufficiently. I wanted to do English literature at university, but all my teachers said, 'No, Andrew. You're not actually that good at it. What you should really do is economics.' A major problem that I have is that if ever someone tells me I can't do something, I've got to do it twice and show them the photographs.

So I insisted on doing English literature, and it was absolutely awful. I thought it would be the same, only bigger and better. But it wasn't because instead of teachers who wanted to encourage you, you had these professors who were published. They had their theories that they had built their reputations on. And if you questioned them or said, 'No, I think it's something different,' they took it as you were being insulting or you were being disrespectful. To the extent that I was actually thrown out of a class because I didn't agree with the professor. He got so mad at me and said, 'I am the world's leading authority on this subject. I'm telling you this is how it is. And unless you apologize, you can get out.' So I got out.

Steph McGovern:

You didn't apologize, then?

Andrew Child:

No, I did not. And that was 1986.

I hated it. I wanted to do something different. But in those days – I think it's better now – you couldn't really just change course. You had to drop out, and then come back the next year. And in our family, our father was this hard-nosed guy from Belfast who fought in the Second World War, so the idea that you might fail at something or give up, it was just not acceptable. The closest I could get to changing the course was to switch to doing half English literature and half drama.

And that was just unbelievably good fun because, all my life, I've been obsessed by stories. When people ask if I had always dreamt of being a writer, well, I hadn't. I knew there were books, but I never really connected that with somebody sitting down and writing them and so I hadn't thought about the mechanics of it. I just like telling stories and the theatre is the purest way of telling a story because you've got people standing in front of you, acting it out and speaking the lines. I absolutely loved it.

But when you do something for a course or an exam, you never really get to explore it all the way, do you? You get the exam passed, and then you have to move on. So at the end of it, six of us decided to set up our own company before we got bogged down with mortgages. We wanted to explore all of those things that we got a glimpse of but were never able to take all the way.

We ran that for about two years. We had a list of everything we wanted to achieve and thought we could do it in one year. It really took two. What sensible theatre companies typically do is they alternate a new play with a Shakespeare or something like that because that brings in the money. But we didn't do that. We weren't sensible. We only did our own stuff. So we were an unheard-of company performing unheard-of plays by unheard-of people. Unsurprisingly, at the end of two years, we were completely broke and I needed to get a regular job. This was before the internet.

This is when if you wanted to get a job, you had to buy the *Sunday Times* and look for the—

Steph McGovern:

Yes, the job ads.

Andrew Child:

So what I did was extremely scientific. I lined them up in order of which had the highest starting salary and applied for that, and by some miracle, managed to get my way into a job. It was good because it fixed the hole in my bank balance, but it was bad because it trapped me into the corporate world. And it took me another fifteen years to get out again.

Steph McGovern:

I want to come to the writing now then. Lee, you were working in telly and you then famously got made redundant, didn't you? Talk me through then what happened and what was going through your mind at that point.

Lee Child:

Well, there were two strands to that. One is that I had a colleague, Stephen Gallagher, who very early in 1983 quit to become a writer. He's really good, check him out. He wrote fantasy, science fiction. He wrote radio plays, television plays. He wrote *Doctor Who* for a while. I think he wrote *Spooks* for a while. He was all over the place when he should have focused on something and made that his channel. But he loved it, and so he did everything. That was influence number one – that you can get out and make your living creatively on your own.

Then in about 1988, I don't know if you remember the history of ITV, but we started overnight broadcasting, which was really valueless. We never did any worthwhile programming overnight. But it was mandated by the Thatcher government to bust the union who were against working overnight. This was because TV management was so inefficient that you had to guard yourself against excessive demand and so you had punitive overtime rates if you ran too long. So the government mandate necessitated a whole new agreement that was very satisfactory to management and not so satisfactory for us.

Granada did not want to hire a separate overnight crew because that would bring in more employees. They wanted us to reorganize our shift pattern so that we would do it. By this point, I was shop steward for ACTT, the Association of Cinema and Television Technicians. I remember the final meeting; it lasted until two o'clock in the morning. At about one thirty, they caved in and doubled our salaries so that we would work overnight. They thought they were done, but I said, 'No, not yet, because we're going to be asleep all day, so we need answering machines for our phone. And you've got to provide that. And we're going to miss *Neighbours* at five o'clock, so you've got to give us a VCR so that we don't miss life.'

We lived like kings for a couple of years. It was fantastic. But I knew at that point that they would get revenge. It was only a matter of time. They would run it as little as they could and they would get rid of us. In fact, it took seven years before they figured it out and got rid of us. But I knew it was coming. And by total coincidence, after the distress of that big deal, we went on vacation to Mexico with my parents-in-law. Flying back through Miami, I bought a book in the airport to read on the plane, and it was the *Lonely Silver Rain* by John D. Mac-Donald. I'd not come across him before and did not know it was the twenty-first of a 21-book series. I just bought it as a book, and I loved it, and I thought it was terrific. So I read all the other twenty and they were great stories.

Somehow at that time, at that place, they were also a blue-print. I could see what he was doing and I could see why he was doing it. And really for the very first time ever, I understood how to construct a book. It was a guide, a how-to. And I remember thinking, 'Yeah, I could do this. I would enjoy this.' But I had an incredibly busy job so there was no chance that I would actually do it at that point. So I filed it away and said to myself, 'When this comes to an end, which it will, I'm going to write a book.' And then, seven years later, it did, and it was time to put up or shut up.

Steph McGovern:

So where did Jack Reacher come from, then?

Lee Child:

Well, by that time, I'd been in entertainment for twenty years, and I'd learned that you cannot overdesign a thing. You cannot say, 'Okay, he's got to be this and that. And I want women aged thirty-one to fifty to be into it, but I also want young men aged nineteen to twenty-four to be into it.' You can't do that. Because as soon as you start thinking like that, then you beat the life out of the thing, and it just becomes a laundry list. It becomes cardboard and useless. So I knew enough to know that I couldn't overthink it. In fact, I couldn't think at all. I just had to do it. I literally sat down and wrote that first book, without any thought at all about satisfying anybody except myself, because I thought that is really the only way you can do it. If you're 100 per cent happy with it, maybe somebody else will be too.

Steph McGovern:

Andrew, you were the actual first person to read it.

Andrew Child:

I think I was, yeah. Because this was a perilous time. I had a decent job and he was out of work with a mortgage to pay and a family to feed. And so I've never been as nervous in my life reading a book as when he said, 'Would you read this manuscript?' written in pencil on paper that he bought at WHSmith. I had to read this book and tell him honestly whether it was any good or not, because I didn't want him to embarrass himself if it was terrible. I didn't want him to go down a path where it was going to fail and he wasn't going to be able to earn a living.

That was obviously *Killing Floor*, the first in the series. And if anyone's read that, it's written in the first person. So it's telling it from Reacher's point of view. But the one thing I really remember is the way the story unfolds. It takes ages before he has to say his name and I remember thinking, 'I don't know this character's name, but I know this character.' It just resonated instantly. And it was wonderful because I could call him up and say, 'You don't have to come and live in my spare bedroom.'

Steph McGovern:

And there's so many wonderful anecdotes to how even Jack Reacher got the name Reacher.

Lee Child:

Yeah. And it's significant that it was first person, and I was putting off him having to say his name because I hadn't thought of it yet.

Steph McGovern:

Oh, interesting.

Lee Child:

And I'm terrible with character names. It's actually the hardest thing for me, and I was aware of that. I kept thinking, 'Yeah, what name? What name?' But I had to get on with it because I was literally running out of money week by week. So I was just writing and finding reasons why he didn't have to say his name yet. Before the detective sat him down and said, 'Right. Name?' I was trying to put that off.

I must say that one of the hardest things about being unemployed was you're at home all the time. And when you're at home all the time, your partner expects you to be somehow available for doing things. There was one Friday night that proved two things for me. I had written part of a scene and was really looking forward to finishing it the next morning with exactly that same anticipation of reading a great book. But my wife, Jane, said to me, 'You've got to come with me to the supermarket tomorrow because we've got to get a lot of stuff.' And she's a tiny woman and can't lift anything so I have to do all the hauling around. I was disappointed because I couldn't write the next scene.

That was the moment I knew this was going to work for me because it was exactly like the feeling you get when you're stopped from reading. I remember one year my daughter was supposed to come over at about six o'clock for Christmas. She was a cinema manager by this point, and was working the daytime on Christmas Day because New York is very self-consciously multicultural. I was reading a great Val McDermid book and found myself hoping that her car would break down or there would be a snowstorm so that Christmas could be delayed till I'd finished the book. You know that feeling. And I felt just that and knew it was going to work. But I still had to go to the supermarket on Saturday morning.

Now, every single time I've been in a supermarket, there is always a little old lady who says, 'Oh, you're a nice tall gentleman. Would you reach me that can?' So that Saturday morning, we were in the supermarket and an old lady says, 'Would you reach me that can?' And Jane, who was being very brave about me being out of work, said to me, 'You know what? If this writing gig doesn't work out, you could be a reacher in a supermarket.' And I thought, 'Wow, that's a good name.'

So I carried all this crap home and threw it in the cupboards, and then, 'What's your name?' 'Reacher.' That's how it started.

Steph McGovern:

That is such a good story. We were talking backstage about how you're going to get a blue plaque somewhere. Could it be Alcester, that you were in when you—

Lee Child:

No, seriously. Alcester and Kendal were going to do that. 'Jack Reacher was invented here.'

Steph McGovern:

And what about the decision to have a pen name? Why did you decide to do that?

Lee Child:

Well, because I had worked for Granada, which was a staff position, and you were theoretically not allowed to work for anybody else. You were exclusively contracted to Granada.

But they turned a blind eye pretty much, if you wanted to go and do some moonlighting. I made a movie with Stephen Gallagher and did lots of other little side jobs that I was interested in. That was fine, as long as you didn't throw it in their face. And so you used a different name. By the time I left, I'd used probably six separate names and it just became second nature to me. New project, new name. I chose the pen name and, to be absolutely honest about it, and it's a disgraceful thing to admit, I was seriously misinformed about publishing. I had heard certain things. One of which is that if your debut novel fails, then you're gone. So my strategy was to do an infinite series of debut novels under different names until one of them worked.

Happily, the first one did. But I had a big supply of alternative names if necessary. Also, this was so important to me. It was life and death, because I'd been shop steward in a very militant fashion and was utterly blacklisted in television. There was no other job I could have got. And so writing had to work. I was taking it seriously in the commercial sense, because I've learned a lot about how to relate to an audience commercially. That's what ITV is. And one of the things was, even now, but especially back then, it's a total word-of-mouth business. If you have a name that is difficult to remember, difficult to say, it's a huge disadvantage. Because let's say I say to you, there's this great book by whoever, and if it's a complicated name, you'll forget it, and you won't go and buy the book tomorrow. If you do remember it, maybe you will. And so I thought, 'I'll use Lee Child because child, first of all, it's early in the alphabet, which is incredibly important—

Steph McGovern:

Yeah, between the Christies and the Chandlers—

Lee Child:

And Michael Connelly, and Harlan Coben, Robert Crais, Patricia Cornwell at the time, Tom Clancy. Huge number of people. In fact, I did the research, I was taking it seriously: 63 per cent of *New York Times* bestsellers were written by authors with the initial C.

Steph McGovern:

Oh, interesting.

Lee Child:

Because in the West, we browse from left to right, and we get bored very quickly. A is usually badly shelved, it's knee-high at the end of some other section. So you really start with B, C, D. And after that, you get fed up and you walk away. C was perfect, and that's why I did it. Partly habit and partly sheer commercial instinct.

Steph McGovern:

And it's a name that you've now taken on, Andrew, to be part of the collaboration, because, as I mentioned right at the beginning, you've written thrillers, haven't you?

Andrew Child:

Yeah. Although actually I was going to use a pen name originally. Because bizarrely enough, given where we've ended up, I wanted to make sure at the beginning of my career that I made it on my own. I didn't want to be associated with Lee in any way. I had a different agent, different publisher, and even though he was already one level of separation away from our real name, I wanted to have another level. So I invented a different pen name. And I had that pen name right up until my first book was finished and it was under offer from a publisher. I was about to sign the deal, and one piece of advice he gave me was tell the relevant people that it's a pen name early so that it's not some weird, awkward thing ten years later. So I told my agent and she said, 'Well, what on earth are you doing?' She said the pen name I'd picked was awful, and that my real name was more marketable.

Being a complete mercenary, I ditched the pen name. I felt like it had done its job because you're reinventing yourself. I walked away from my day job because this is what I wanted to do. I walked away from the pension, and the company car, and the private health scheme and all of that. And it felt like a really dangerous, dodgy thing to do, and I needed to summon as much self-confidence as I could. And I felt like if I was reinventing myself as this new person, having a new name helped. But by this point, I'd written the book and somebody wanted to buy it so I felt, 'Okay. Well, the pen name did its job. Now I can—'

Lee Child:

I've got to interrupt the story there because he was not made redundant, but he tried to be.

Steph McGovern:

Of course you did, for the money.

Lee Child:

They had a scheme at BT where you could be made redundant, but it was entirely at the discretion of management. We would speak to each other week after week and his strategy was to sit in these meetings and come up with the most ludicrous ideas so that they would think, 'Oh, well, this guy's no good, we'll put him on the list,' and then he would get money to leave. But you could have made a movie out of it because he would come up with the most ridiculous idea and the bosses would say, 'That's a great idea.' I laughed about this for weeks on the phone.

Andrew Child:

It's absolutely true. For about the first twelve years, I was trying to pay my mortgage, I was trying to do well, I was working as hard and as conscientiously as possible, and I got nowhere. It was only when I was trying to make them kick me out that I started doing these things, thinking what the most ridiculous thing is I could possibly suggest, and they loved it. By the time I left, I'm not joking, I had share options.

Steph McGovern:

Oh, that's so funny. Right. Let's talk about the books, then, and about you guys working together. So tell me – *No Plan B* is the third collaboration together. Why collaborate with your brother? Andrew, why did you want to be part of it? Because you said yourself there, you wanted to distance yourself from your brother when you were writing.

Lee Child:

You remember when I said I was a very earnest kid? I still am. I set myself ridiculous rules and one rule I felt – well, it wasn't really a rule, it was a feeling I had as a young person that I was sick and tired of old people sticking around and giving the rest of us no room. I wanted them to get out and let other people have a chance. So that was feeling number one. And then feeling number two, everything I did as a writer was based on how I felt as a reader. And I felt long-running series authors with many, many books had a fatal flaw in a lot of them. I think people work much better now, but in the past, you would start a series and the first few books would be fabulous, and then you would get the next one and sense that the author was getting lazy, running out of gas, getting drunk a lot. I often felt so betrayed as a reader because I placed so much trust in the anticipation and I was really let down by that. So I made myself a promise long before I was a writer. I said, 'I will never phone it in. If I feel myself running out of gas, I will do the honest thing and stop, rather than give people a substandard product.' I was totally hypervigilant about that.

The last one I did on my own, book number twenty-four, was called *Blue Moon*. It takes me about eighty or ninety days to write a book, but twice during that, I remember thinking, 'I really don't want to do this.' And I just took that as a sign that it was over. I had to live up to that rule that I'd promised myself: 'I will not give a substandard product.' But of course, twenty-four books in, Reacher had become hugely popular, not just commercially, but emotionally. People love the guy. I mean, I've met children named Reacher because of him. It happens at book signings and you can see it ahead of time because it's always the man carrying the baby, and they often have the birth certificate to prove it. The mother is embarrassed behind them.

I had this thing at book events where, in the questions, people would say, 'How many of these are you going to do?' And I would say, 'I'm going to do twenty-one because of John D. MacDonald. That's what he did. And I want to match that, but as a matter of respect, not exceed it. The last one is going to be difficult to plot because Reacher's a very smart guy, but he will be backed into a situation where he either has to give himself up or the person he's protecting. Obviously, Reacher will give himself up to save a life and so the book will be called *Die Lonely*. The final scene will be him bleeding out on a filthy motel bathroom floor.' And I would hear the groan in the audience, a groan of real emotion, and knew I couldn't do this to people. They want this guy. So I had to think about what I was going to do. Was I going to carry on past the sell-by date?

Then I started fantasizing. Suppose I could take a magic potion and wake up tomorrow fifteen years younger with all that stamina, and energy, and all those ideas that I had fifteen years ago, wouldn't that be great? Of course, there are no magic potions, but then I thought, 'Wait a minute. You know somebody who is you fifteen years ago who is already a writer. Maybe I should ask him if he wants to continue it.'

It was an experiment to me. Right from the very beginning, I wanted it to be about the character, not about the author. And seriously, we thought about persuading the publisher to leave any author name off the book. It's just a Jack Reacher book. It's about him. And so it was an experiment. How important is the actual author?

I was reluctant to ask Andrew because he was writing some really good stuff. There was the janitor series about a military intelligence guy who's working as a janitor in the courtroom, and the janitor is completely unseen and unregarded, so he could do all kinds of investigation and surveillance. And I really loved those books. They were great. I thought if I asked him to do Reacher, I won't get any more of those books. Plus Andrew is the most stubborn human being ever to exist, and I knew that he would rather starve to death writing his own books than do mine. It was very trepidatious.

One day, we were driving back to Wyoming from Denver after the launch of his latest book when this enormous blizzard blew up. In Wyoming, you get what is called a ground blizzard because the wind is so strong it's whipping the snow. It's sixty miles an hour horizontally in front of you, like driving across the ocean. You've got no idea where you are, and you're steering by the GPS screen essentially. Andrew was driving at this point, knuckles white on the steering wheel, trying very hard not to kill both of us. So I thought it was the perfect time to ask the question because he wouldn't react in the moment. He's so desperately trying to keep us alive. I said to him, 'I'm going to retire. Would you like to take over?' And the rest is history. I honestly expected him to say no.

Steph McGovern:

I'm going to open it out to the audience in a sec, but so from your perspective, Andrew, it's such a big thing to take on this character, and what was it like for you?

Andrew Child:

Well, looking back, I could almost feel a little ashamed because I'm driving the car and my brother says that he's thinking of retiring. If I was a nice brother, I would've said, 'Yes, you absolutely should retire. You've worked so hard for so long. You've helped so many people in the industry. You've brought so much pleasure to so many readers. You deserve a break. You deserve to enjoy the fruits of your labour.' That's what a nice person would've done. But instead, given that I was the first person to read a Reacher book, and I'd looked forward to a Reacher book every year for a quarter of a century, I said, 'Well, what do you mean, retire? What about Reacher?' Because I didn't want there to be no more Reacher.

A lot of it came down to what he was saying about the question at the events. I was at a lot of those events and I remember it wasn't just the groan or the outpouring of emotion. You could feel the temperature drop in the room. The first time somebody asked was in the third book, because the first one could be a standalone, second one could be a fluke. Third one, yeah, pretty much you are on track for a series. And so the first one, he said twenty-one, and you could see people, 'Oh, okay. Nothing to worry about just yet.' And as each year went by and the same question came up, you could feel the nervousness growing and the temperature dropping further. And I felt the same thing because I'm the oldest Reacher fan in the world. I didn't want there to be no more Reacher, and I certainly didn't want it to be my fault.

Steph McGovern:

You do the majority of the writing now, don't you? And so how does that feel for you? What's your plan for Reacher?

Andrew Child:

It's just been wonderful because we get to do all the fun stuff together. We used to do this before, but for fun. We would get together – I hope there's no psychiatrists here because Reacher was an invisible extra brother – and sit around and talk about it. We would say, 'What would Reacher do about this? What would Reacher think about that?' Now, we still do the same thing, only I've then got to go and write it down afterwards. But it's just doing what you love to do and getting to do it with your brother. Can't get better than that.

Steph McGovern:

I've got so much more to ask you, but I know it's really important we get questions from the audience. We'll get the house lights up, and if you've got a question, pop your hand up and we will get a microphone over to you. So, yes, we've got a gentleman over there.

Speaker 1:

Can I firstly say that I could listen to you two all night? I think your voices are terrific. I might be a little bit contentious here, but I look at the Reacher films starring Tom Cruise, and for me, he was the absolute opposite of the Reacher character, but I loved him in both films. I've never been able to develop the same love for the Amazon Prime Reacher. And I just wondered about who you prefer playing Reacher?

Lee Child:

First of all, you won me five dollars there because he said we're going to do some Q&A, and I said, 'I bet the first question is about Tom Cruise.'

I absolutely think you've got to separate the two movies. There was the one based on *One Shot*, and then the one based on *Never Go Back*. And I think as a movie, in and of itself, the first movie was excellent. And I thought the second movie was a bit standard. But I loved the first movie and I absolutely loved working with Cruise. He's the nicest man. Nothing that you hear about Tom Cruise is true. He's just a lovely guy. Completely natural, unpretentious, and a joy to hang around with, fun to do things with, and an excellent, fabulous theoretician about storytelling, with very little ego. At the beginning of every scene, we'd rehash it and check. And he was not thinking, 'How do I make myself look good here?' He was thinking, 'How do we tell a better story here?' And to the point where he often gave away his best lines, he thought, 'You know what? The co-star should have that line,' or whatever.

Steph McGovern

Generous.

Lee Child:

Yeah, totally generous, to the point where, especially with the second movie, we had to say, 'Tom, this is a Tom Cruise movie. Keep some lines.' But he was just delightful. I've got nothing negative to say about him other than he's five foot seven. And there's absolutely nothing wrong with that. I mean, I was five foot seven once, when I was about nine. Nothing wrong with it.

In 2005, when I did that Tom Cruise deal, streaming television was completely unknown. There is not a novelist alive who would choose a feature film over streaming television if the choice was available. Streaming is just wonderful, the hours that you've got. So I said no to more movies, because I knew Tom is purely a cinema actor. He will never act on television. I thought that solves that problem and it gives us more running time, and it means we can choose an actor. And the whole financial structure of streaming is different. The actor does not have to bring the money. Feature films are entirely funded based on the appeal of the lead actor; not true in television.

It was freedom in so many ways. And I actually thought Alan Ritchson for Amazon, first of all, looked a lot more like Reacher. And I thought he did an excellent job. I'm very happy with him. And I think the first season was great, and the second season is in the can. The third season, I can't talk about, because as it happens, I'm a member of both the Writers Guild of America and the Screen Actors Guild, and we're on strike. One of the strictures is to say that we can't promote our current projects, so I'm not going to say anything about season three other than we did three episodes and now it's paused. But season two is ready to go, and is excellent.

Steph McGovern:

And when's that coming out? Is that December?

Lee Child:

Yes. Given my readers, what happened with season one is that everybody signed up for Prime, binged the thing in two nights, and then cancelled Prime. And Amazon was not delighted with that. So they're doing a different strategy. They're going to drop two episodes, and then the next six are going to be weekly, which takes you outside of the cancellation period.

Steph McGovern:

Gosh. I think there was a question at the front. Should we take that?

Speaker 2:

Thank you. That was brilliant, Brothers Grimm—

Lee Child:

Brothers Karamazov, we prefer.

Speaker 2:

I was going to ask something about Tom Cruise, but I won't now. Five foot seven is fine. I'm five foot seven, and it's great. But what I'd like to ask is what happens when Andrew becomes the established writer and Lee wants to come back?

Andrew Child:

So what you're really asking is if Lee wants to do extra work? Yeah, don't really see that happening.

Steph McGovern:

Have you got a plan for when you'll just do it on your own, Andrew? Have you got in your head, Lee, a number of books? Or is it—

Lee Child:

Well, I'm done now. I did twenty-four, and then we did four as a collaboration, as a transition. Now it's Andrew's thing. But we were just talking today actually, that what I might do if I get bored, I might secretly write one and give it to him and see if anybody reacts differently.

Steph McGovern:

So you've got *No Plan B* out now, but then the next one coming out is *The Secret*, isn't it?

Andrew Child:

Yeah, it comes out in October.

Steph McGovern:

Oh, great. And in writing Reacher now, have you got plans to slightly change him in any way?

Andrew Child:

No. I mean, our father was Irish, and he used to talk about things being the same, only different. We want Reacher essentially to stay the same because we love him how he is. One thing I personally hate is if you really get invested in a series, you fall in love with a character, and then another instalment comes out and the character is completely different. I hate that. So I love to show Reacher in different sides of him, different aspects of him, and it's fine for him to learn things, it's fine for him to become more cynical. All of those things are fine, but we don't want to fundamentally change his character. The plan is to keep trying to find new adventures and new scenarios for Reacher, but to keep the same old Reacher that everybody knows and loves.

Steph McGovern:

Have you got them in your head, do you think?

Andrew Child:

Some of them. I was never a completely focused outliner. Some people write really, really detailed outlines of the entire book. I never did that. But I did like an idea of where I was going and where I was going to end up. And Lee doesn't do that. I wanted the books, the parts that I've done, to sound and feel as close and as similar as possible. So it made sense to write them in the same way. I adapted my methods by distributing that planning throughout the book so that at the end of every scene, you're saying, 'Okay, what is the next scene going to be?' and not referring to some master plan that says, 'Scene ninety-seven is going to happen in this way.' I've deliberately not tried to set some multi-year blueprint that I'm then forced into following.

Steph McGovern:

Any other questions before I wrap things up?

Speaker 7:

A very random question, but if you were to be fictionally murdered, would you want Reacher to solve your case? And if not, which fictional detective would you prefer?

Steph McGovern:

I like that question. Brilliant question.

Lee Child:

I think I'd like to be murdered by Reacher. That would work for me. And then maybe Harry Bosch could figure it out or something like that.

Steph McGovern:

What about yourself, Andrew?

Andrew Child:

Yeah, I think Bosch is an amazing detective. He has that expression, 'Everybody counts or nobody counts.' So I think I would go with Bosch as the investigator.

Steph McGovern:

Brilliant. We'll end on you both dying, then. It'll be a nice place to end this. Thank you so much. I could probably go on for another couple of hours, but I appreciate it's quite late and people want to get home. Please put your hands together for Andrew and Lee Child.

.